# TARGET: SUPERCARRIER
# *THOMAS JEFF*

Lieutenant Tahliani knew ... s
had been hit, a warhead ... e
sea while trying to evade ... to
him. And now Soviet MiG ... ier
from above . . .

But the American carrier was less than sixty kilometers away. He radioed the order to lock on primary target. He saw the telltale blips of enemy missiles sprinkled across his own VDI. There wasn't much time left now. He pressed the trigger and felt his Sea Harrier leap as the pair of Sea Eagle missiles dropped away, one following the other.

Within seconds, a spread of twenty cruise missiles was racing toward the *Jefferson*, now thirty-six miles away . . .

*  *  *

# SPECIAL PREVIEW!

*Turn to the back of this book for a sneak-peek excerpt from the all-new action series . . .*

## STORMRIDER

*. . . an explosive novel of motorcycle mayhem on the highways of post-nuke America.*

*Books in the CARRIER series from Jove*

CARRIER

CARRIER 2: VIPER STRIKE

CARRIER 3: ARMAGEDDON MODE

Book Three

# ARMAGEDDON MODE

Keith Douglass

JOVE BOOKS, NEW YORK

CARRIER 3: ARMAGEDDON MODE

A Jove Book / published by arrangement with
the author

PRINTING HISTORY
Jove edition / June 1992


For information address: The Berkley Publishing Group,
200 Madison Avenue, New York, New York 10016.

ISBN: 0-515-10864-2

Jove Books are published by The Berkley Publishing Group,
200 Madison Avenue, New York, New York 10016.


PRINTED IN THE UNITED STATES OF AMERICA

10 9 8 7 6 5 4 3 2 1

# PROLOGUE

**0735 hours, 23 March**
**IAF Fulcrum 401, nearing Hyderabad, Pakistan**

Lieutenant Colonel Munir Ramadutta peered through his canopy, watching tan desert sand and gravel blur past a hundred meters below. Power surged against his spine through his ejection seat, the muted thunder of twin Tumansky R-33D turbofans, and the morning sun flashed brilliant from his wingtips. He grinned behind his oxygen mask and helmet visor as a verse from the Ramayana came to mind: ". . . *golden in its shape and radiance, fleet as Indra's heavenly steed.*"

The ancient Hindu epic's description of Prince Ravanna's celestial car could easily have applied to his own aircraft. The MiG-29, code named "Fulcrum" by NATO, was almost identical in size, looks, and performance to the American F/A-18 Hornet and was considered by most observers to be more than a match for any fighter interceptor in the world. The Indian fighter was brand-new, fresh from the production lines at Nasik. Forty-five Fulcrums had been purchased directly from the Soviets, and another one hundred fifty were in licensed production now, sleek and deadly weapons certain to give the Indian air force crushing aerial superiority over India's old foes.

Pakistan. The barren, dun-colored desert was giving way to the patchwork green of the river-laced Indus Valley. There was still no sign that Wind Strike had been spotted by the Pakistani defenses. They were coming in hard and low on the deck, avoiding radar sites and villages. Even the date—Pakistan Day, anniversary of the 1940 decision to separate from India—had been chosen as a time when Pakistan's defenses would be at less than one hundred percent. Operation *Paschim Hawa*—West Wind—had been carefully planned, and the planning was paying off. They were now one hundred fifty kilometers inside the Radcliffe Line, the border between India and Pakistan. Hyderabad, second-largest city in the Sindh, lay one hundred twenty kilometers ahead.

"Green Wind One, this is Green Wind Three," a voice said in Ramadutta's headset. "Something on the threat indicator. Might be an APG-66."

Ramadutta's grin broadened. A signal from an APG-66 pulse-doppler radar almost certainly meant F-16s. Two of Pakistan's eleven air defense squadrons were outfitted with F-16 Falcons purchased from the Americans. The Fulcrum's abilities as an air superiority fighter were about to be put to the test.

"Roger Three," Ramadutta answered. "I have it." His HUD was showing targets now, two of them, fifty kilometers ahead and closing. They were probably part of an air patrol out of the military air base at Kotri. "Full power now!"

He pushed his throttles forward, and the Fulcrum's thunder escalated to an avalanche of noise and power. There was a moment's rattling vibration as he pressed toward Mach 1, then the sudden, silk-smooth transition to supersonic flight. At low altitude, the Fulcrum could manage Mach 1.2, faster by twenty percent than either the Hornet or the Falcon.

Three more Fulcrums paced Ramadutta's MiG, hurtling westward in tight formation. Behind them, another four Fulcrums escorted the squadron of ground-attack MiG-27 "Flogger-Ds." When Wind Strike completed its mission over Hyderabad, Pakistani air power in the Sindh would have all but ceased to exist.

"No reaction from the targets," Green Wind Three reported. "Is it possible they have still not seen us?"

"It is possible," Ramadutta said. "This close to the ground, our radar returns may be lost in ground clutter." The Indian air force planes had been operating under strict radar silence to avoid alerting Pakistani receivers. Radio silence was less critical, so near the Indian border and the vast armada of IAF planes preparing the way for West Wind.

"Range thirty kilometers."

"Pakistan air defense is going on alert," another voice warned. "I think they have us."

"It doesn't matter now," Ramadutta said. "They still won't be sure whether or not we're IAF or Pakistani. Active radar!" Information was more important now than stealth.

His Fulcrum's powerful pulse-doppler radar painted the sky ahead, pinpointing the two targets.

"Arm weapons!"

His Fulcrum carried R-23 and R-60 missiles, the AA-7 and AA-8 air-to-air killers designated "Apex" and "Aphid" by NATO. For this attack, they would stick to infrared targeting as long as possible, the better to keep the Pakistanis in the dark. He selected an Apex for his first launch. With a range of over thirty-three kilometers, it already had the targets within range. He kept his eyes on the paired blips on his radar screen. The range was down to twenty-four kilometers, still closing. A warbling tone sounded in his ear, his missile informing him that he had a solid IR lock.

"I have lock," Three reported. Wind Two and Four would hold back, in reserve. "Northern target."

"Targets breaking off," Ramadutta snapped. "Launch!"

His thumb caressed the trigger on the Fulcrum's stick, and he felt the bump as the AA-7 cleared the launch rail and arrowed toward the target on the end of a streaming plume of white smoke. The F-16s were veering sharply toward the south. Whether they'd identified the intruders somehow or were simply changing course for the next leg of their patrol was immaterial now. At better than Mach 1, the Apex homers would reach the targets in a little more than a minute.

The dazzling blue of a canal exploded beneath Ramadutta's MiG. He glimpsed blurred details on the ground that might have been grazing cattle. The thought struck him with unexpected force. *Such a peaceful scene . . . and the war has already begun.*

*War!* Somehow, Munir Ramadutta had given little thought to the reality of that word. He'd thought his training—and the long expectation of war's coming—would have braced him for this moment. They had not.

Since Pakistan had separated from India in 1947, there had been four major wars between the countries and almost continuous sniping and artillery duels in the barren and ruggedly mountainous districts of Jammu and Kashmir in the far north. The most serious clash had been in 1971, when a Pakistani attack led to the Indian conquest of East Pakistan and the subsequent creation of a new nation, Bangladesh.

The 1971 war had proved that India was now the preeminent military power of the region, with an air force, navy, and army that dwarfed anything Pakistan could bring against her. But still, Pakistan had continued the skirmishing and the border incidents, railing against India for her silence during the Soviet invasion of Afghanistan, steadfast in her refusal to allow the Moslem separatist movements of the Kashmir to settle their long-standing dispute with New Delhi. Lately, Pakistan's jingoistic tirades had taken on a new and ominous tone; of all the Islamic nations of the world, Pakistan was perhaps the most technically advanced . . . and the closest to the development of a working nuclear device.

India already had the bomb, of course, but that was scant comfort when facing a nation of ninety million Moslem fanatics. Kashmir was the flashpoint for this war . . . and the war's excuse, but the New Delhi government had already decided to settle things *now,* before India's troublesome western neighbor became too dangerous to deal with, before the anti-Indian rioting and violence in the Sindh, the Pakistani agitation and terrorism in the north went out of control.

Operation West Wind would end the Pakistani threat once and for all.

He picked out the tracings of the AA-7s on his radar screen. The gap between targets and missiles narrowed. . . .

Far ahead, through the transparency of his canopy, he glimpsed a telltale flash, and the northernmost blip on the screen seemed to expand, then broke into pieces. "Hit!" Green Wind Three exalted. "Kill!"

A moment later, Ramadutta's missile merged with the southern target. A second tiny flash announced the explosion of a forty-kilogram warhead. He lost the blip when it merged with the ground return.

"Two kills!" Wind Three called over the radio. "Our first two kills of the day!"

"There will be more, my friend," Ramadutta reminded him. "We have aircraft airborne now over Kotri. Range . . . fifty kilometers."

"This is Red Wind Leader," a new voice said. Red Wind was the MiG-27 squadron. Their first target was the air base at Kotri. Their second was a munitions factory north of Hyderabad. "Breaking off for target run."

"Roger," Ramadutta replied. He was surprised at how easily the words came. "Good hunting."

The Pakistanis were rising now like hornets from a nest prodded by a small boy's stick. It didn't matter. Their destroyers were upon them. *Fleet as Indra's heavenly steed . . .*

As the silver arrowhead shapes of Pakistani Falcons and IAF MiGs clashed, swirled, and loosed their deadly payloads, Ramadutta thought briefly of the Americans. They had been much in the news of late, with their aircraft carrier battle group in the Arabian Sea off the west coast of India. The Americans had been trying to interfere with Indian interests in Kashmir, or so the news reports had claimed, and there were rumors that the Americans had threatened to attack India if their Pakistani allies were invaded.

At close quarters now, Ramadutta pulled back on his stick, following a Pakistani Falcon in a steep-climbing roll into the cloudless skies above Hyderabad. An AA-8 leaped from his wing, curving to meet the enemy interceptor in a white flash and a shower of debris.

If the Americans decided to go to war in defense of their Islamic friends, so much the worse for them. Ramadutta had no illusions about American military might . . . but he had no illusions either about the problems of fighting a war halfway around the world. India could deploy over nine hundred combat aircraft. The Indian navy boasted two aircraft carriers, purchased from Great Britain along with a number of Sea Harriers. It seemed unlikely that the Americans would risk intervening in a war so far from their own borders.

And if they did, that carrier battle group now lying over the horizon to the south would be a tempting target. A nuclear supercarrier, the U.S.S. *Thomas Jefferson* . . . now *she* would be a worthy target for some eager Indian pilot!

Lieutenant Colonel Ramadutta watched the Pakistani Falcon burn as it tumbled toward the blue waters of the Indus River far below.

# CHAPTER 1

**0945 hours, 23 March**
**Tomcat 201**

Lieutenant Commander Matt Magruder, running name "Tombstone," eased the throttles back on his F-14D Tomcat and put the aircraft into a gentle, twelve-degree port turn. Sunlight glared off the surface of the water thirty thousand feet below, a dazzling blaze of white light mirroring the tropical sun above the vast emptiness of the Indian Ocean. The sky overhead was as huge and as empty as the sea, a piercing blue impossible to describe to anyone who'd not seen it from the vantage point of an interceptor's cockpit.

To starboard, a second F-14 hung suspended between sea and sky, its modex number 216 visible on its nose just ahead of the cockpit and the American star-and-bar insignia. Lieutenant Commander Edward Everett Wayne, "Batman" to his squadron mates, was Tombstone's wingman for this patrol.

"Viper Two, Viper Leader," Tombstone called over his radio, using the tactical frequency. "What do you say, Batman? Let's tank up."

"Roger that, Stoney," Batman's voice replied. "It's going to be a long, dry morning."

The two Tomcats had been catapulted from the deck of the U.S.S. *Jefferson* only minutes before. Their operational plan called for them to top off their tanks from a KA-6D, then assume BARCAP—BARrier Combat Air Patrol—between the ships of the carrier battle group and the unseen coastline a little more than five hundred miles to the north. They would be airborne for about four hours.

Bringing the stick back to center, Tombstone switched channels and spoke into the helmet mike once more. "Homeplate, Homeplate, this is Viper Leader," he said. "Do you copy, over?"

"Viper Leader, Homeplate," a voice replied in his helmet phones. "Go ahead."

"Homeplate, we're on station Bravo Sierra four-niner at angels three-oh. We could use a drink right about now. Whatcha got in the way of a Texaco, over?"

"Viper Leader, Homeplate. Come to heading two-seven-four at angels two-seven. We've got some guys up there with a six-pack waiting for you. Call sign Tango X-Ray One-one."

"Roger that, Homeplate." He dropped the Tomcat into a new turn, Batman's F-14 pacing him a hundred feet off his starboard wing. "Viper now coming to two-seven-four."

"Ah, Homeplate," Tombstone's Radar Intercept Officer added. "I have a single contact bearing two-seven-four at fifteen miles. Confirm that's our target, over."

"Roger. That's your Texaco, boys. No other traffic. Have a cool one on us." The voice from *Jefferson*'s Carrier Air Traffic Control Center sounded calm, almost bored. CATCC—the acronym was universally pronounced "cat-sea"—was tasked with keeping track of everything going on in the skies around the supercarrier beyond the radius commanded by Pri-Fly and the Air Boss.

The way things were going now, Tombstone thought, that job could quickly become more important than ever. That morning's situational briefing had not been encouraging.

"Affirmative, Homeplate. Viper out." Tombstone switched his mike to the Tomcat's intercom system. "Well, CAG? How's it feel to strap on an airplane again?"

"Pretty good, Tombstone," Commander Stephen Marusko replied over the ICS from the back seat. "I thought I was going to forget what it was like."

Marusko was the officer in charge of *Jefferson*'s air wing, CVW-20, over ninety aircraft and three thousand men. His title of CAG was a holdover from the days when it stood for Commander Air Group. Recent changes in the way the Navy ran things had emphasized the administrative part of the job at the expense of flying. Nowadays, a CAG started off as an aviator, like Tombstone, in command of a carrier fighter squadron, then was rotated stateside for a tour in Washington, becoming, as Marusko put it, a prime, Grade-A desk jockey. After that he went back to sea as a carrier's CAG.

Administrative duties or not, he was still expected to fly with his men, but the press of work—paperwork for the most part—always seemed to get in the way. Tombstone's usual RIO, a young j.g. named Jerry Dixon, had been given a medical downcheck the day before, and Tombstone had offered CAG a ride as backseater at morning briefing. Marusko had been almost embarrassingly eager for the chance. Contrary to popular belief, Navy RIOs were neither permanently assigned to a specific aviator, nor were they ''failed pilots.'' Experienced aviators took the back seat of Navy Tomcats from time to time to log out some flight time, or simply to keep their hand in running the F-14's complex radar and communications systems.

But it might not be much longer before airborne CAGs were a thing of the past. The Navy was experimenting with a new way of running things, introducing the ''SuperCAG'' concept that would make CAG a captain's billet and let him share responsibilities with the carrier's skipper.

And won't *that* be fun, Tombstone thought with an ironic grin beneath his oxygen mask. The poor bastard might never get to fly anything but his desk.

All of this had set Tombstone to thinking. He was the CO of the Tomcat squadron designated VF-95, socially known as the Vipers. Almost thirty years old, Tombstone had lived for carrier aviation since the day he'd shown up for flight training at Pensacola. Before long he'd be up for promotion to commander, and that Stateside billet on his way to a CAG slot of his own. All along, he'd been moving up the Navy career ladder, the goal of CAG clearly in sight. And after that . . . well, to be skipper of an aircraft carrier, you had to have served a stretch as CAG. There were only fifteen carrier command billets in the whole U.S. Navy and openings were rare, but Tombstone had never really entertained doubts that he would make it . . . some day.

But the doubts were with him now. Not whether he would make it, but whether he should even try. He had some tough decisions coming up.

"Viper Leader, Viper Two," Batman said over the tactical frequency. "Tally-ho! Tanker ahoy at twelve o'clock low."

"I see him," Marusko said.

Tombstone glanced up from his controls and caught the flash of sun glint off an aircraft canopy far ahead. "Got him, Batman. We'll take first crack. Breaking left."

"Copy, Leader."

Tombstone slid the F-14 into a left-hand barrel roll while CAG was still speaking, going inverted and following his starboard wing over in a long, sideways fall that bottomed out at 27,000 feet. Ahead, the KA-6D tanker plowed toward the horizon at a steady 250 knots.

"Tango X-ray One-one," he called. "Viper Two-oh-one. Coming in for some of your basic I&I."

"Affirmative, Two-oh-one. Come on in. We're sweet, hot, and willing."

I&I, intercourse and intoxication, was the Navy man's reworking of the more traditional R&R. Much of the slang and banter associated with air-to-air refueling carried a strongly sexual content, for obvious reasons. *Sweet* meant they had fuel.

The KA-6D was a conventional A-6 Intruder converted into a fuel tanker, a "Texaco" in Navy jargon. With 500-gallon drop tanks slung beneath wings and fuselage plus what was carried on board, it could transfer up to 21,000 pounds of fuel—over 3,200 gallons—to other aircraft. As Tombstone approached the tanker from the rear, the tanker extended a fifty-foot boom from its belly, a slender hose tipped by a basket that resembled an iron mesh shuttlecock.

Tombstone pulled a selector switch and the Tomcat's fuel probe swung out of the right side of the nose with a small whine of hydraulics. He eased the F-14 forward until the broomstick-thick snout of the probe stabilized about six feet behind the trailing basket. Turbulence buffeted the F-14 and its small target.

At this range, the tanker loomed overhead, an enormous gray whale precariously suspended just beyond the canopy. Tombstone needed every ounce of concentration to keep the F-14 steady, easing the aircraft gently forward, countering the rumbling vibration of the tanker's slipstream. Since he had to concentrate on the other aircraft only yards away, his RIO watched the relative positions of probe and basket and gave him the instructions to drive the plug home.

"Left a tad," Marusko said over the ICS. Tombstone corrected gently, still concentrating on the tanker. "And up. Three feet. Looking good . . ."

Tombstone was sweating beneath his oxygen mask and helmet, despite the cool, dry air in the cockpit. Air-to-air refueling was a routine part of any patrol, with the aircraft topping off their tanks after they'd catapulted from the deck and reached cruising altitude. The procedure was not nearly as nerve-racking as, say, landing on the deck of an aircraft carrier in a heavy sea at night . . . but there was a definite pucker factor involved in the maneuver that had very little leeway for error. Tombstone could feel his heart beating faster as he studied the relative positions of the two aircraft and the slowly closing gap between them. Both planes were traveling now at 375 knots, and the rate of closure was down to less than a foot per second. Sweat blurred his vision . . .

"Back out!" Marusko shouted. "Abort! Abort!"

Tombstone tried to correct . . . too late. One hundred pounds of iron basket smashed into the canopy like a sledgehammer. The noise was so loud, so sharp, that for a second Tombstone thought the cockpit had been blown. The Tomcat shuddered again as the basket rebounded, then snapped back into the aircraft's side with a jarring thump. The danger was as sharp as it was sudden. The loose basket could easily splinter the F-14's canopy or get sucked down an intake and shred turbofan blades, engine, and fuel lines.

"Damn it, Stoney," Marusko shouted again. "Back out!"

Tombstone's thumb was already nudging the thumbwheel on his stick to raise his lift-control spoilers, dumping some of his plane's lift. The Tomcat sank several feet, as the basket skittered above the canopy and threatened to rap the F-14 on the port side as well. Gently, Tombstone dropped the throttles back a notch, letting the tanker slip farther away. "Sorry about that, Tango X-ray," he said. "Bitch got away from me."

"No sweat, Two-oh-one. Have another go."

Carefully, he urged the Tomcat up and forward once more, positioning himself six feet behind the recalcitrant basket. He braced himself, took a deep breath, and willed his aircraft ahead.

"Looks good," Marusko said. "Four feet . . . two . . . no!" The Tomcat's refueling probe struck the rim of the basket, sending it dancing aside. "Abort!"

"Shit!" The basket swung back and hit the probe, then bumped and clattered across the canopy inches above his head. Tombstone eased back again.

"Let's clear out and let Batman have a shot," Marusko said.

"Rog." Tombstone let the Tomcat continue to slide astern of the tanker, until he had room to pull away to port. "Viper Two, Leader. You chase the damned thing for a while."

"Right, Tombstone." Tomcat 216 edged forward, taking 201's place astern of the Texaco. "Okay, Tango X-ray One-one, this is Tomcat Two-one-six. Let's show those old men how it's done. Spread 'em!"

"Come ahead, Two-one-six."

From a hundred feet astern and to the left, Tombstone watched as Batman's refueling probe slid smoothly into the basket. Automatic locks snapped home when the basket had been driven forward six feet. "That's contact," Batman said. "Gimme a thousand of high-test."

"Capture confirmed," the tanker pilot replied. "She's coming."

It was an odd sight. The Tomcat was seven feet longer than the KA-6D and had a much larger wing area, especially now with the variable-geometry wings swung forward to improve lift and handling at low speed. Size and the twin tail fins made the F-14 look far more massive than the tanker, though in fact the fully loaded takeoff weight of both aircraft was about the same, thirty tons. To Tombstone, the sight of a Tomcat refueling from a KA-6 always reminded him of a big dog nosing a smaller dog's tail.

He took the time to force relaxation into his arms, his hands. He felt weak, as though his hands were shaking, though when he held one gloved fist up it was rock steady. What was wrong with him?

"You okay, Stoney?" Marusko asked from the backseat.

"Yeah, CAG. No-problem."

But there *was* a problem, and Tombstone knew what it was . . . or rather, *who*. The thought of Pamela came unbidden, a flash of memory, an image of her the last time he'd seen her in Bangkok. That had been two months ago, just after the coup attempt that had nearly overthrown the government of Thailand and involved Carrier Battle Group 14 in a short, sharp air and ground action against rebel forces.

Pamela Drake was an ACN News reporter who had been covering the turmoil in Bangkok. Tombstone had gotten to know her pretty well during the crisis, well enough that they'd managed to fall in love with each other. She was back in Washington now, but her letters had been coming with each COD mail delivery to the *Jefferson,* and Tombstone, never much of a correspondent, had answered them all . . . all but the last two.

"Tango X-Ray One-one, this is Two-one-six." Batman's voice sounded steady over the radio. "Best lay we ever had. Slam, bam, and thank you, ma'am."

"Our pleasure, Batman," the tanker captain replied. His dry chuckle rasped in Tombstone's headset. "Two-oh-one, Tango X-ray One-one. How's it looking for you now, Stoney?"

Tombstone's eyes scanned his instrument panel one last time. He'd been concerned that the impact of the basket might have damaged his fuel probe, but there were no signs of fuel or hydraulic leaks, no warning telltales on his caution advisory board.

"Green all the way," he replied. He took a deep breath. "Two-oh-one, in for another take."

"You know what they say, Tombstone," Batman said over the headset. "Just try to imagine hair around it."

"Roger." The basket neared his canopy once more, closer . . . closer . . . Tombstone felt a tremor and glanced down. His hand was shaking now. *Damn,* he thought. Not now! Not now! Teeth grinding, he fought down the feeling of weakness, blinked through the sweat that pricked at his eyes. He focused his concentration on the belly of the KA-6, aware of the basket's jostling dance just beyond the canopy's right front side out of the corner of his eye.

"Three feet, Stoney," Marusko said, his voice emotionless. "Two feet. You're right in the groove, guy. Left . . . left a bit more . . . Keep it coming . . ."

The refueling probe speared the basket dead center, with a thump and a jolt as the catches snapped home. "Two-oh-one, contact," Tombstone said. He snapped up the switches that opened the F-14's tanks. "Ready to receive."

"Capture confirmed," the tanker pilot said. "Here it comes."

Fuel rushed down the narrow hose, greedily devoured by the Tomcat. Tombstone kept his mind on maintaining the interval between the two aircraft. Mercifully, both CAG and Batman kept their silence.

Shit, Tombstone thought. Sooner or later the odds are going to catch up to me. And when they do . . .

"We read you full, Two-oh-one."

"Roger, Tango X-ray." He snapped the switches closed. "Ready to disengage to port."

"We're clear."

Tombstone backed clear of the drogue, then broke left. The two Tomcats flew in formation with the KA-6D for a moment. Then the tanker began dropping away toward the sea, angling into a turn that would take him back toward the *Jefferson.* "It's been grand, guys. Look me up again when you feel the need."

"Thanks," Batman radioed. "Just put it on Tombstone's MasterCard, okay?"

Tombstone's hand was no longer shaking. He flexed it a couple of times, then grasped the stick firmly.

Pamela's last letters. What was he going to do about them? They'd arrived only three days earlier, both of them on the same COD flight in from Diego Garcia, and they were eating away at him. He'd not answered them because he didn't know how, didn't know the answer to what Pam was asking.

Pamela was as sharp as she was attractive. Was she right? Was it time for him to leave the Navy and find a saner job?

He wondered if he'd lost the edge.

It wasn't the problem spearing the basket. Hell, there was nothing wrong with his two-time failure to engage the tanker's drogue. That sort of thing happened all the time in the day-in, day-out routine of Navy aviation. Danger, as the aviators said, went with the territory, was as much a part of their issue gear as flight suit and helmet.

But that was just it. That sort of thing *did* happen routinely. There were so many ways to screw up in the cockpit . . . most of them deadly. Navy aviators needed an incredible blend of skill, training, reflexes, and luck to make tasks like snagging a fuel drogue in flight or making a night trap on a pitching carrier deck seem routine, to do them again and again and again as though there was nothing to them.

It wasn't that Tombstone was afraid, but he was tired. Every man on board the *Jefferson* was tired, with eight months of the CBG's nine-month deployment down.

And tired men make mistakes.

Tombstone said nothing as he took up the Tomcat's patrol zone and throttled back for a long orbit. Sooner or later, something had to give.

The question was whether or not to get out now, before it did.

**1206 hours, 23 March**
**Bridge, U.S.S. *Biddle***

Captain Edward Farrel turned in his high-backed chair to take the phone handset from one of the bridge watchstanders. "Captain speaking."

"CIC Officer, Captain," Lieutenant Commander Mason's voice replied. "We have a passive sonar contact, towed array, bearing zero-five-four to zero-five-six."

Farrel's eyes shifted toward the windscreens on the bridge's starboard wing. The U.S.S. *Biddle*, one of Carrier Battle Group 14's two Perry-class guided-missile frigates, was scouting far ahead of the *Jefferson*. Her primary duty was as part of the carrier's ASW screen, searching for submarines that could pose a threat to the CBG. The horizon was empty under a brassy, tropical sky. The impulse to keep looking, to try to see *something* out there against the featureless skyline, was irresistible. "Can you manage an ID yet?"

"Chase thinks it sounds like a Foxtrot, sir, but not one he's heard before. They're running it through the library now."

Antisubmarine ships and aircraft either carried or had access to a tape library of underwater sounds, everything from the grunts and squeaks of fish and other marine life to the characteristic noises made by various undersea vessels. It was often possible to match a particular set of sounds not only with a general class of submarine, but with the acoustical profile of a particular boat. Good Navy sonarmen could sometimes pick out old friends by ear alone, and Sonarman First Class Chase was one of the best.

Farrel came to a quick decision. ''Ping him. I want to know if we're on top of him.''

''We'll give it our best shot, sir. Conditions aren't very good below, though.''

''Understood. Call me when you have him nailed.'' He handed the phone back to the waiting sailor.

Passive sonar was listening only, using sensitive underwater listening devices to locate a submarine by the sounds of its engines, pumps, and the rush of water across its hull. *Biddle*'s SQR-19 was a towed array, hydrophones trailing behind the ship that could pick up underwater noises as much as thirty nautical miles from the ship.

*Biddle* also mounted sonar equipment in her keel. Designated SQS-56, it could either listen passively or broadcast sharp pings of sound, then pick up the echoes from any subsurface targets. Unfortunately, passive sonar could give direction—at least to within a few degrees—but not distance. Active sonar gave distance but was limited both in range and by conditions in the water. The SQS-56 could pick up a submarine if it was within perhaps six nautical miles of the ship . . . but the range could be sharply reduced by shallow, warm, or highly salty waters, and all three of those conditions applied to this part of the Indian Ocean.

Worse from a tactical point of view, active sonar would alert the submarine to the fact that it had been spotted.

Farrel would feel a lot better knowing just where that sub was and where it was going. Peacetime or not, international waters or not, tensions were running hot in the Arabian Sea just now. Since early that morning, war had engulfed the India-Pakistan border, and these waters could become a shit-hot war zone any time now. Every man in the CBG knew how easy it would be for an attack to be launched by accident—the missile strike against another Perry-class frigate, the U.S.S. *Stark* in the Persian Gulf during the Iran-Iraq War, was a case in point—and one hell of an expensive target was trailing *Biddle* a hundred miles astern.

Foxtrot was the NATO code name for a class of diesel-powered attack subs first produced by the Soviets in the 1960s. Three hundred feet long, with a complement of seventy-eight men, it was designed to hunt and intercept hostile task forces. The Russians had built sixty of them between 1958 and 1962, and most were still active, though some had been reported lost at sea. During the '70s, the Soviets had manufactured nineteen for export: three for Cuba, eight for Libya . . . and eight for India.

In these waters, the contact could be either Soviet or Indian. Either way, the battle group's new admiral was not going to care for potentially hostile subs getting too close to his command.

Minutes dragged by. Farrel was beginning to wonder what Mason was playing at when the CIC Officer called again.

"No joy on the pinging, Captain," Mason said. "He may be out of range."

Farrel scowled. "Understood. Alert the Air Officer. I want a LAMPS up ASAP. Maybe we can peg the contact with sonobuoys. And have the comm shack raise *Jefferson*. Admiral Vaughn's going to want to know about this."

"Aye, aye, sir."

Farrel replaced the telephone handset, then walked to the starboard wing. He raised his binoculars and scanned the horizon toward the northeast. There was nothing there, no periscope wake, no oil slick, only endless blue water under a cloudless sky.

Submarines these days could launch homing torpedos from ten miles away . . . or pop a sea-skimming cruise missile from three hundred miles out. A Foxtrot would not be carrying SSMs, thank God, but the threat was serious nonetheless.

"Now hear this, now hear this," the shipboard loudspeaker brayed from the afterdeck. "Stand by to launch helo. Stand by to launch helo."

Farrel heard the thutter of the LAMPS III helicopter as its engines revved to takeoff rpms. Then the SH-60 Seahawk lifted from *Biddle*'s fantail with a roar, its shadow momentarily flicking across the bridge. He turned his binoculars on the gray insect shape as it angled off toward the northwest, low above the water.

*Biddle*'s two Sikorsky SH-60B Seahawks were LAMPS III helos designed for ASW. The LAMPS designation stood for Light Airborne Multi-Purpose System, a computer and sensor array that integrated surface ships and helicopters to extend the reach and effectiveness of antisubmarine warfare. Each Seahawk was equipped with dipping sonar and air-dropped sonobuoys. Foxtrots were antiquated diesel-electric submarines, neither quiet nor nuclear-powered. Whoever this one belonged to, it should be easy enough to pinpoint by checking along the general direction of the contact.

Who *did* the Foxtrot belong to, India or Russia? With the outbreak of war between India and Pakistan, it was important that they know. The threat of war with the Soviet Union had receded for the past several years, as Russia's internal economic and political problems grew worse. But if that was an Indian sub out there . . .

Just how close was the battle group to becoming caught in the crossfire between two warring powers . . . the way *Stark* had been caught in 1986?

Farrel continued to study the ocean surface with a growing sense of unease.

# CHAPTER 2

**1318 hours, 23 March**
**Bridge, U.S.S. *Thomas Jefferson***

Captain James Fitzgerald shifted in the high-backed, leather-covered seat on the bridge. Golden light spilled through the broad, slanting windscreens, highlighting wiring conduits in the overhead and the gleaming brass handles of the engine-room telegraph. The enlisted men in whites, the chiefs and officers in khakis, went about their duties with the calm efficiency Fitzgerald had come to expect of them during these past, grueling eight months.

His gaze went outside the bridge and to the deck forward, where the jet-blast deflector was rising behind an F/A-18 Hornet of VFA-161. The deadly little multi-role fighter was squatting over the slot of Cat One as deck handlers in their color-coded jerseys moved about, poking, prodding, checking, readying the aircraft for launch. Steam from the last catapult launch still swirled about the handlers' legs. A second Hornet shuddered on one of the waist cats further aft as its engines blasted against the unyielding steel of its JBD.

The voices of the Air Boss and his assistants aft in Pri-Fly could be heard over a monitor.

"Cat Four, Four-oh-one, stand by!"

"Thirty seconds. Red. Green on fifteen."

"Deck clear. Stand by! Stand by!"

"Green!"

A throbbing roar sounded from the carrier's waist, and the F/A-18 on Cat Four vaulted forward, sweeping past the first Hornet still waiting on Cat One.

"Four-oh-one airborne."

"That's three to go."

The dance on the deck continued, ponderous, complex, and deadly. Aircraft carrier flight decks were the most dangerous workplaces on Earth. Everything was in motion: men, machines, the deck itself. There were no guardrails if a jet blast caught a man, or if he took a careless step backward. Engines shrieked continually, making speech possible only through the bulky Mickey Mouse ears the directors wore. Jet intakes could suck a man to his death in an instant . . . or thirty tons of aircraft could break free from an improper tie-down and crush him like a runaway truck.

Fitzgerald worried about his command, about his men. This cruise had strained all of them to the breaking point, and he feared that worse was on the way.

*Tired,* he thought. *They're all tired.* He reached up, cocked the ballcap with U.S.S. *Thomas Jefferson, CVN-74* emblazoned in gold above the bill to the back of his head, then removed his aviator's sunglasses so he could rub his eyes. *And I'm tired too.*

The international situation was worsening . . . fast. The cold war between Pakistan and India had just flashed hot.

Was this their fourth major war, or their fifth? It was easy to lose track, and it depended, Fitzgerald decided, on just how the skirmishes were counted. This current clash along the Indian-Pakistan border looked like it might blow up into something as nasty as the war of '71. There were reports of Indian armor gathering along the rim of the Thar Desert, and air strikes at Pakistani Air Force units as far west as Karachi. Tensions in the region had been mounting for weeks, the situation serious enough that the Joint Chiefs of Staff had ordered CBG-14 north from the tiny reprovisioning base on British-owned Diego Garcia to patrol the waters west of the subcontinent of India.

Such orders were typical enough for a U.S. carrier task force, charging the battle group with the protection of American lives and property. Similar orders had taken *Jefferson* into Sattahip Bay two months earlier during an attempted coup in Thailand. There were thousands of American citizens in both Pakistan and India, everything from diplomats and their staffs to businessmen to guru-chasing remnants of the '60s at Goa and Kovalum, the "heepies" as native Indians called them. *Jefferson*'s presence in international waters was a warning to both governments that the United States could consider military options in order to protect U.S. citizens.

The special orders received four days earlier had diverted *Jefferson* and the five other vessels of CBG-14 to an imaginary circle on the Indian Ocean three hundred miles south of Karachi, and about one hundred miles southwest of India's broad, fan-shaped Kathiawar Peninsula. *Jefferson* would reach that spot, informally labeled "Turban Station," in another twenty hours. After that . . . well, then things would be up to the Indians and the Pakistanis, and to the new CO of Carrier Battle Group 14.

Fitzgerald made a face as he replaced his sunglasses. He still didn't know what to make of Rear Admiral Charles Lee Vaughn.

On the forward deck, the Hornet was revving its engines to full afterburner, sending waves of heat shimmering above the deck. The white-jacketed Safety Officer was making his final check, signaling the Catapult Officer with an upraised hand.

"Amber light," the voice of Pri-Fly said over the speaker behind Fitzgerald's head. "Stand by. Stand by."

Admiral Vaughn seemed competent enough, but Fitzgerald had a suspicion that it was his political connections more than his seamanship that had brought him to the *Jefferson.* At the very thought of politics, Fitzgerald's stomach knotted. It was impossible to look at Vaughn and not remember the man he'd replaced.

Admiral Thomas J. Magruder had been the carrier group's commanding officer throughout the roughest deployment Fitzgerald could remember . . . and his memory included three tours off the coast of Vietnam. Nothing he'd seen then or since matched what the *Jefferson* had experienced in this one single tour.

In eight months, CBG-14 had twice seen combat. In September *Jefferson* had been deployed in support of a combined Navy-Marine operation to rescue the crew of the *Chimera,* a Navy intelligence ship captured on the high seas by the North Koreans. Three months later, *Jefferson*'s battle group had been deployed to the Gulf of Thailand to support the Bangkok government during a coup attempt.

Immediately after the Thailand crisis Admiral Magruder had

been hurriedly summoned to Washington, and Vaughn had come aboard to replace him.

There was a hint of scandal in that summons, and the threat of a Senate inquest. The operation in Thailand had not violated the War Powers Resolution—U.S. participation had been limited to two Marine actions ashore, air support, and two alpha strikes off the *Jefferson*—but it had a number of Congressmen operating in full Administration-bashing mode. Since it had come hard on the heels of *Jefferson*'s intervention in North Korea, some of the President's sharpest critics were accusing him of being trigger-happy, an accusation that had trickled down to the man in charge on the scene as well. Admiral Magruder had enjoyed a distinguished and rewarding career, but if Washington needed a scapegoat he would be elected. His advice to the White House had led directly to the Presidential order to send in the Marines and the air strikes.

Admiral Vaughn had been tapped in his Pentagon office to fly to the Far East before the last of the rebels had been rounded up, arriving only a few days after the formal awards ceremony in Bangkok. He remembered Magruder's face during the full-dress muster on *Jefferson*'s flight deck that muggy afternoon while the battle group was still anchored in Sattahip Bay. The man had looked drawn, worn, possibly a little subdued as his replacement stepped off the Sea Knight helo in his crisp and spotless dress whites. Only then had Fitzgerald realized how old Admiral Magruder looked, old and . . . *beaten.*

Fitzgerald had known then that Magruder was being sacrificed in the name of Washington politics.

Something was happening on Cat One. The Safety Officer was making sharp motions with his hands, and the orange glow of the Hornet's afterburners was fading. The captain turned in his seat to watch one of the big PLAT monitors suspended from the overhead for a better view. Someone down there had scrubbed the launch.

"Four-oh-seven is down," a voice called from the monitor speaker. "Pressure failure to Cat One."

"Break him down and get him the hell out of there," the Air Boss said. "Bridge, we have a downcheck on Cat One."

Fitzgerald had already picked up the handset of the direct-access telephone known universally as the batphone and punched in Pri-Fly's number. "Pri-Fly, Bridge. We see it. What happened?"

"Damfino," the Air Boss replied. "I'll let you know as soon as I know myself."

Fitzgerald replaced the handset and studied the organized confusion engulfing the Hornet on Cat One. Almost certainly, the problem was human error . . . and directly attributable to the strain the men had been under for months. Damn, but that had been close! If the steam failure had occurred as the Hornet was being shot off the deck, the F/A-18 would not have attained airspeed and would have gone off over the bow. Unless the aviator had been both very quick and very lucky and had managed to eject safely, *Jefferson* would have run him down in the water.

We'd have lost another aviator, Fitzgerald thought. With so many lost already.

The Captain sensed rather than heard a change in the atmosphere around him. Several of the ship's officers had been engaged in low conversation on the starboard wing of the bridge, but they were silent now, and the enlisted men at wheel and engine-room telegraph were standing a little straighter, a little more studiously correct. Fitzgerald turned further and saw Captain Henry Bersticer stepping across the knee-knocker onto the bridge deck.

Bersticer was Admiral Vaughn's chief of staff, a tall, swarthy man with a meticulously groomed black goatee that gave him a somewhat saturnine aspect. He walked over to where Fitzgerald was sitting. "Admiral's compliments, Captain, and would you join him, please, in CVIC?"

He spelled out the letters, which stood for Carrier (CV) Intelligence Center, instead of pronouncing them "civic" in the time-honored fashion. Bersticer was, Fitzgerald thought, new to carriers and didn't yet have the hang of bird-farm language.

He wondered if his CO had things down any better.

"Very well," Fitzgerald said. He slid off the stool. "On my way."

Admiral Vaughn was waiting alone in CVIC, a pale, heavyset man in his late fifties, with hair that might once have been red but was mostly silver now. Fitzgerald looked around as he walked toward the admiral. The room, used as a TV studio for the Chief of the Boat's morning broadcasts over one of *Jefferson*'s on-board TV stations, had a cluttered feel, and many of the lights and electrical cables had not been struck. Fitzgerald winced inwardly when he saw it. Vaughn had an oft-stated love for order and the proverbial taut ship.

"Jim," Vaughn said as Fitzgerald approached him. Bersticer shut the door, leaving them alone. The admiral reached into his shirt pocket and extracted a folded-up computer message flimsy. "This just came up from CIC. Have a look."

Fitzgerald's eyes held Vaughn's as he took the flimsy and unfolded it.

It was a decoded flash priority from the skipper of the U.S.S. *Biddle,* now steaming some one hundred fifty miles northwest of the carrier. Quickly, Fitzgerald read the details of the sub contact, now only minutes old. He looked up at the admiral and handed the message back. "Farrel says it sounds like a Foxtrot," he said. "Soviet or Indian?"

"God knows," Vaughn said. "No matter which, I don't want that damned thing closer than a hundred miles from this carrier, understand me?"

"Yes, sir," he replied slowly. "If we can't nail down that sub's position, though, we'll have to alter course pretty far west to maintain separation. It'll mean quite a detour, and a delay in reaching Turban Station."

"I know that. Frankly, I hope we can ID that sub as a Russkie. If it's Hindi . . . God, we don't know what the Indians are going to do."

Fitzgerald grinned. "I hardly think they'll mistake us for the Pakistani navy, sir." *Jane's Fighting Ships* gave the strength of Pakistan's navy as seventeen ships, not counting patrol craft. The largest was *Babur,* a former British destroyer of 5440 tons. He'd looked it up earlier that morning.

"Damn it, Captain, this is no joke!" Vaughn scowled, rubbing at his short and bristly mustache with a forefinger. "You saw the latest set of dispatches from Washington. The Indians don't want us out here. This whole situation could blow up in our faces at any moment."

"I realize that, sir." The word from Washington that morning was that a formal protest had been delivered to the White House by the Indian Embassy in Washington, objecting to U.S. warships in their waters during time of war. Accidental attacks were a possibility, the communiqué had pointed out, especially in the confusion of jamming and electronic countermeasures in the region once fighting started.

"Listen, Jim," Vaughn said. "I called you off the bridge because I wanted to talk with you about this command. I've been following the weekly reports. Performance is way down, you know. And morale."

Fitzgerald ran one hand through his thinning hair. "That's hardly surprising, Admiral. They've been through a hell of a lot this cruise."

"That's no excuse, hey?"

"It's not intended as one, sir." Fitzgerald's lips compressed into a hard, thin line. "This is a good ship, Admiral. And damned good men."

Vaughn studied him for a long moment. "I want to know I can depend on them, Captain. And on *you.*"

"That goes without saying. Sir." Fitzgerald knew his tone verged on the insubordinate, but he was angry now and working to keep the words formal and correct. It was Vaughn's responsibility to direct the entire battle group; it was Fitzgerald's responsibility to hand the admiral a ship he could work with, manned by a well-trained and highly motivated crew. When Vaughn criticized the men, he was criticizing *him.* That might be Vaughn's right as CO, but Fitzgerald had the feeling that the admiral didn't really care about *Jefferson*'s crew or how capable they really were.

And that worried him.

Vaughn did not seem to be aware of Fitzgerald's anger. "Good. I'll want you to bring the *Jefferson* to a new course at once to avoid that submarine."

"Of course, Admiral."

"And I want an ASW alert. Get some of your King Fishers up there in case they're needed." The King Fishers, VS-42, were *Jefferson*'s antisubmarine S-3A Viking squadron. "Intelligence briefing at 0800 tomorrow. I want to discuss our options."

"Aye, aye, sir."

"See to it." Vaughn turned abruptly and strode toward the door. "Oh, and you might speak to your Exec about the mess here in CVIC. I like a taut ship, Captain. Can't go into combat with gear adrift, hey?" Then he was gone.

Fitzgerald stared after him for a long moment before following. Vaughn, he decided, was still an unknown quantity. An *untested* quantity.

Well, odds were he would get his testing on *this* cruise.

**1423 hours, 23 March**
**Tomcat 201**

"Tomcat Two-oh-one, charlie now."

Tombstone heard the words and felt the tension ebb somewhat from his shoulders and back. "They're calling us in, CAG," he said. He nudged the stick to the left, putting the Tomcat into a shallow, sweeping curve that would roll it out of the holding pattern several miles astern of the carrier.

"Suits me," Marusko replied. "My safe little office back on the old bird farm is looking better and better."

"Viper Two, Viper Leader," he called, opening the tactical channel. "Batman! We're charlied. Going in."

"Roger that," Batman's voice replied a moment later. "Save us a cold one. We're right behind you." That was almost the literal truth. His wingman was now half a mile behind Tombstone's aircraft and three thousand feet higher, locked into the aerial racecourse of the carrier's traffic control holding pattern, called a Marshall stack. They'd been circling there twenty-one miles from the *Jefferson* while the Air Boss brought in some S-3A Vikings that had been out on a sub patrol.

Tombstone leveled off. He could just make out the *Jefferson*'s stern far ahead, a gray rectangle nearly lost on the ocean. The flight decks on Nimitz-class carriers covered four and a half acres, but they looked ridiculously tiny from the cockpit of a fighter plane positioning itself for a trap. As they got closer, his eyes shifted to the carrier's port side where a yellow speck of light, the "meatball," or Fresnel optical landing system, appeared centered like a bull's-eye above the LSO platform.

"Two-zero-one," the voice of the Landing Signals Officer said over Tombstone's headphones. "Call the ball."

"Two-zero-one," Tombstone replied, identifying his aircraft by number. "Tomcat ball, three point one." By "calling the ball," Tombstone was letting the LSO know he had the landing signal in sight, that the incoming plane was a Tomcat with 3,100 pounds of fuel left on board so *Jefferson*'s recovery crews would know how to set the tension on the arrestor cables stretched across the deck, and that he was properly aligned for a trap.

"Roger ball," the LSO confirmed. "Looking good."

Tombstone felt his heart begin to race. It was always like this during a carrier landing, day or night, fair weather or foul. Naval aviators without exception rated recovery on the deck of a carrier as having a higher pucker factor than air-to-air combat or an enemy SAM launch.

He lowered his arrestor hook, cut back on the throttles, and let the Tomcat sink toward the *Jefferson*'s deck. The carrier's stern appeared much larger now, swelling rapidly as he dropped from the sky.

**1425 hours, 23 March**
**Viking 704, flight deck, U.S.S. *Thomas Jefferson***

Lieutenant Commander Christopher Goodman had the throttles all the way back on his ungainly S-3A Viking as he spit out the arrestor cable and retracted his tail hook. Gently, he eased the throttles forward again, using the rudder pedals to steer the aircraft off the part of the flight deck delineated by broad white stripes and make way for the next incoming plane. A yellow-shirted handler backed away just ahead of the aircraft, arms extended forward, jacking them up and down, up and down as he signaled Goodman to come ahead.

He taxied slowly toward the line of planes along *Jefferson*'s starboard side, aft of the island. His crew—Lieutenant Hyman Gold, the co-pilot; Lieutenant j.g. Roger Kelso, the tactical coordinator; and AX/1 Bill Rocco, the systems operator—all were already relaxing now that the trap was successfully completed, unstrapping their seat harnesses and preparing to shut down the bird and log out.

There was very little swell this afternoon, and the *Jeff* was riding the sea almost rock-steady. That was always a blessing on the rare occasions when it happened. An airplane, *any* airplane, might be sheer poetry in motion in the sky, but on an aircraft carrier's deck it was transformed into a bulky, clumsy, and barely manageable beast. With a pitching deck made slippery by ice or rain, things were just that much worse.

The handler gave a two-handed pushing movement to the side, indicating a particular parking space with the aircraft lined up along the starboard side, aft of the island. Goodman swung the foot pedals farther, maneuvering toward the narrow slot. A long line of aircraft noses swept past the cockpit as he turned, all painted in dull pale grays: F-14D Tomcats, wings angled sharply back along their flanks; a pair of bulky E-2C Hawkeyes with their wings rotated sideways and back to avoid the flat, saucer shapes of their radomes mounted above their fuselages; A-6F Intruders with their wingtips nearly meeting above their backs. Space was always at a premium at sea, both on the flight deck and down below, on the carrier's cavernous hangar deck. Planes were parked side by side with folded wings nearly touching.

Easing the fifteen-ton aircraft toward the target, he gently applied pressure to the tops of the rudder pedals, engaging the wheel brakes.

Nothing happened. Goodman felt a sinking, mushy sensation through his flight boots, then nothing at all. The Viking's brakes were gone, and Goodman was rolling across the deck toward a narrow cul-de-sac lined with multi-million-dollar aircraft.

There was no time to speak, even to give warning. With one hand he cut the throttles all the way back, then flicked on the Viking's external lights and dropped the arrestor hook to signal the deck crew that he was in trouble. His momentum was too great to allow the plane to roll to a stop, and if he kept going he was going to roll with irresistible momentum squarely into the side of a Hawkeye. Working the foot pedals, he swung the Viking hard to the left, turning away from the flight line and back onto the one patch of clear flight deck within reach. . . .

**1426 hours, 23 March**
**Pri-Fly, U.S.S. *Thomas Jefferson***

Commander Dick Wheeler was *Jefferson*'s Air Boss, a bald, sour-faced man with a football player's physique and a voice to match. He was already in motion when he saw Viking 704's tail hook hit the steel deck in a shower of sparks. If his brakes were gone, the pilot would have no choice but to swing back onto the main flight deck . . . and squarely into the path of incoming Tomcat 201.

It was a disaster in the making. "Fouled deck!" Wheeler barked over the Pri-Fly frequency that connected him with the deck crew and the LSO. *"Fouled deck!"*

The Tomcat was already drifting toward the carrier's round-off, scant yards from touchdown. . . .

# CHAPTER 3

**1426 hours, 23 March**
**Tomcat 201**

"Wave off! Wave off!" The words shrilled in Tombstone's helmet just seconds from the deck. To port, the bull's-eye of the Fresnel lens lit up red as the LSO triggered the pickle switch he held in one hand.

The warning caught Tombstone completely by surprise. Until that moment he'd been squarely in the groove, with only the slightest of corrections necessary to keep the Tomcat floating gently toward the three wire stretched across the deck in front of him.

Tombstone's left hand was resting on the F-14's throttles, ready to provide small adjustments to power and set to engage the afterburners the instant his wheels touched the deck . . . a standard precaution in case his tail hook missed the arrestor cables and he needed to get airborne again in a hurry. Now he shoved the throttles to full power and brought the Tomcat's nose up. The wings were already extended to provide maximum lift at low speed. As the Tomcat's twin engines blazed into afterburner, the plane accelerated, passing over the carrier's roundoff and straight down the flight deck, twenty feet above the dark gray steel.

He caught a blurred image of motion below him, of men running, heads down, of a pale gray aircraft with engine pods slung beneath each wing lumbering into his path.

Tombstone thumbed off the spoilers and eased back on the stick, willing the Tomcat to miss the sharp, skyward thrust of the other plane's tail. Acting on instinct alone, he brought the

F-14's right wing up, narrowly missing the Viking's rudder. Afterburners thundering, he flashed past the island, across the waist catapults, and out over the open sea once more.

"Wheee-oh!" Marusko said from the back seat. CAG had not said a word during the final approach and near-collision, but his relief now was heartfelt and enthusiastic. "Goddamn it, Stoney! You didn't have to do that to impress me!"

Tombstone found he couldn't reply, didn't trust himself to speak. He brought the aircraft into a shallow port turn, circling back for another pass. The S-3A Viking's tail extended about twenty-two feet above the deck. He'd not seen the actual clearance but doubted that his wingtip had missed the sub-hunter by more than a foot or two.

In all the time that Tombstone had been flying Navy jets, he'd been shot at and shot up. He'd engaged in dogfights, ejected from an aircraft suddenly gone dead, and trapped aboard a carrier deck at night with heavy seas running. Never, he thought, had he been closer to buying the farm than that near-miss. If he'd connected with the Viking, at least six men would have died right there: himself, CAG, and the S-3's crew of four. God alone knew how many deck division people would have been caught in the fireball as plane after plane ignited, turning *Jefferson*'s waist into an inferno. Deck crashes were always bad. When they involved more than one plane . . .

He took a deep breath. "CAG?" he said. "I think that one just about did it for me."

There was a long silence. "Wait before you make any decisions, Stoney. We'll talk in my office."

"Sure." But Tombstone's mind was already made up.

**1630 hours, 23 March**
**Flag Plot**

Admiral Vaughn leaned over the chart table with other members of his flag staff, studying the grease-penciled markings and time notations that plotted the paths of each of the vessels of Carrier Battle Group 14. Currently, *Jefferson* was cruising eastward at thirty knots, the hub of a circle spanning two hundred miles. The destroyer *John A. Winslow* was one hundred twenty miles ahead, the DDG *Lawrence Kearny* following a hundred miles astern. The frigate *Gridley* patrolled the CBG's flank to the south, while *Biddle* continued searching for the lost sub contact to the north. The group's Aegis cruiser, U.S.S. *Vicksburg,* lay thirty miles off *Jefferson*'s port quarter.

One last member of the carrier group prowled far ahead of the *Winslow,* two hundred meters beneath the surface. The U.S.S. *Galveston* was one of the Navy's newest Los Angeles-class attack submarines. The nuclear-powered SSN had joined the task force only five weeks earlier. Attack subs often worked closely with carrier battle groups, but CBG-14 had been operating without close sub support so far on this cruise. The Sea of Japan had been too shallow for sub operations, while the Thailand crisis had been resolved before *Galveston* could rendezvous with the *Jefferson.* Her usefulness in the Gulf of Thailand would have been limited in any case, but the situation here in the Arabian Sea was different. Here they were surrounded by hundreds of miles of open ocean, and under a potential threat from the world's eighth largest navy.

It was, then, a far-flung empire that Admiral Vaughn surveyed as he studied the lines and cryptic codings on the chart, a battle group spread across an area of ocean the size of his home state of Missouri. But it was the silent and unresolved hunt of the *Biddle* that occupied his mind.

"Henry!" he demanded. "Still nothing from Farrel?" Damn the man, he should have had something by now.

"Nothing, sir," Captain Bersticer replied, joining the admiral at the plot table. "His last message stated that the contact might be lying low, hiding on the bottom."

Vaughn reached down and traced the line marking the limits of the continental shelf south of Kutch and Kathiawar. "What's the depth up there . . . about fifty fathoms?"

"Yes, sir. That's probably what's limiting their sonar."

"You'd think he could find something as big as a goddamned submarine in water three hundred feet deep," Vaughn muttered. "How about we send *Galveston* in to help *Biddle* with the search, hey?"

Bersticer rubbed his dark beard thoughtfully. "I don't know, Admiral. It'd take a day for the *Gal* to get there, and we don't know the contact is even still in the area."

"That's right." Vaughn looked up, alarmed. "God! It

could've given Farrel the slip. Hell, that thing could be heading straight for us at this minute, flank speed."

"Captain Fitzgerald has informed me that he has two Vikings flying in support of *Biddle* now. If that Foxtrot is up there, Admiral, I'm sure they'll run him down."

"He'd goddamned well better!"

A familiar, scratching pain rasped within Vaughn's stomach. Almost, he reached for the antacid tablets in his shirt pocket, but he held himself back. As he refused to tolerate weakness in his subordinates, he refused to reveal his own weakness to others. Gently, he massaged his stomach. "I want a full report for transmission to CINCPAC first thing in the morning," he said. "I don't like to say this, but I really don't think this ship is up to the, ah, challenge of this mission. Damn! Did you see the operations reports today? We nearly had a major smashup right on the flight deck!"

"I saw, sir."

"Brakes on a Viking failed. Probable cause, faulty maintenance. *Faulty goddamned maintenance!* Someone wasn't doing his job, that's sure. And we all came within an ace of getting fried when a Tomcat nearly hit the Viking on final approach!"

"The pilot, I gather, is one of the best, Admiral. We were lucky there."

"I dunno." Vaughn looked away. "That kid is Admiral Magruder's nephew. You know that?"

"No, sir! I thought the names were a coincidence!"

"Well, he is. Maybe he owes his billet as much to politics as to skill, hey?"

"It's possible, sir."

"Damned straight it's possible. I don't like brown-nosing. A man should get where he is on his own steam, right? Not by *politics!*" Vaughn caught himself. He'd been about to launch into a diatribe against Navy career politics. It was a sore point with him. Once a man made commander in this man's navy it was *all* politics, with careers made or broken by who you knew.

He'd almost been broken, once, but god-*damn* he'd had the last laugh! Here he was in command of a carrier battle group again after twelve bitter years.

The one thing that could screw things up for him was failure. Vaughn had a thorough fear of failure, and it seemed to him that whatever gods of the sea had granted him his wish of another CBG command were being capricious with him. Why did the new command have to be *Jefferson,* at the end of her deployment, her crew so worn down that disaster was an hour-to-hour possibility? It wasn't fair.

"I'm going to want to tighten up the group, Captain," he said, still studying the chart. "Bring those guys in closer. Hell, no one's going to nuke us, for God's sake. And the individual ships are goddamned sitting ducks scattered all over the ocean like that. Write up the orders. When we hit Turban Station tomorrow, we'll tighten up."

"Aye, sir."

"Next. We'd better start holding exercises. Sharpen up the men. I don't like being this close to a shooting war with men who could fall asleep at their stations, hey?"

"Yes, sir."

"And signal *Biddle*. I want that goddamned Foxtrot found, and fast. No excuses!"

"Aye, aye, sir."

"An aggressive posture, that's the ticket, hey?" He studied the mark that showed *Biddle*'s last position. Where the hell was the Foxtrot now?

**1650 hours, 23 March**
**INSS *Kalvari*, 100 miles west of Bombay**

"There has been nothing for almost two hours, Captain."

"It's possible they've left us." Captain Raju Khandelwal braced himself with one hand against an overhead conduit. "Blow forward ballast."

"Blow forward ballast, aye." There was a rumble, and the thin shriek of compressed air forcing water from the submarine's tanks. The deck shifted beneath Khandelwal's feet.

"Take us up, *Shri* Ramesh. Level at twenty meters."

"Twenty meters, yes, sir." His Exec took his place behind the planesmen, reading the depth gauge over their heads. An ominous creak sounded through the boat as hull metal flexed. The *Kalvari* was not the most modern of submarines, nor the most silent. As she stirred and lifted from the bottom and her hull took up the full strain of the vessel once more, her framework creaked protest.

The sounds seemed especially loud. *Kalvari* had been resting on the bottom for almost five hours, ever since the sharp sonar pinging had warned them that a ship was searching these shallow waters for them.

Now, though, the waters around the Indian sub were silent, had been silent for a long time. The intruder, whatever it was, had no doubt decided to move on.

If it had not, then it was certain to hear the submarine's underwater groanings, but that could not be helped. Khandelwal's orders had been to leave Bombay Harbor submerged and to avoid detection by other vessels until he reached his station fifty miles off the Pakistani port of Karachi. He was operating under a tight deadline and had to be in his assigned patrol area no later than noon tomorrow.

*Kalvari*'s mission was to interdict Pakistani shipping, including that of Pakistan's allies. That was why secrecy was so important. India's Moslem neighbor could not survive for long without help from the outside, but New Delhi feared that world opinion would shift toward Pakistan once it was known that international shipping had been targeted by Indian submarines.

Who had the intruder been? Soviet, possibly . . . though an American task force was approaching the area. It was unlikely to have been Pakistani, not this far from Pakistan's waters . . . but his orders had been explicit.

In any case, the exercise had been good for the men. He had a good crew, but none of them had combat experience. A taste of what awaited them under relatively safe conditions would help get them into the spirit of the patrol.

The deck, slanting somewhat as the sub rose, began to level off. He would take the sub up to periscope depth for a quick look around, to make sure they were really alone, and then proceed with the mission.

The hull creaked once again.

**1651 hours, 23 March**
**Bridge, U.S.S. *Biddle***

"Bridge," Mason's voice yelled. "CIC! We got the bastard!"

Captain Farrel picked up the handset. "Where? Whatcha got?"

"Solid passive contact, bearing zero-one-five. Hull noises . . . and Chase says he just blew ballast. He's close!"

"Go active." He turned to the helmsman. "Zero-one-five, son. Ahead two thirds."

"Zero-one-five, ahead two thirds, aye, sir."

*Biddle* heeled sharply to port as she went into a hard turn.

**1652 hours, 23 March**
**INSS *Kalvari*, 100 miles west of Bombay**

"Contact!" the sonar operator called. "Single screw to port! It sounds . . . it sounds like a *Perry,* sir!"

A Perry-class frigate. That *could* mean American, or . . .

"Go active! Range!" Khandelwal clung to the brass grip on the periscope well, his eyes on the depth gauge. Ninety meters. Too deep yet to see what was going on.

He heard the chirp as the sub's sonar operator began probing the water around them with sound. The ping of the echo followed close behind.

"Contact! Bearing one-nine-five, range two thousand meters! Closing at two-five knots!"

His boat's survival would be determined by the decisions he made within the next minute, Khandelwal knew. He picked up an intercom mike and held it to his mouth. "Torpedo room! Stand by!"

"Torpedoes standing by, sir. Tubes one and two loaded, wire-guided."

The Oliver Hazard Perry-class frigate was an American design, but in this modern age of arms sales and weapons package diplomacy, that meant nothing. Only the year before, two had been purchased by Pakistan.

He listened to the chirp of sonar, his experienced ear noting the decreasing intervals between ping and echo. If this was one of the Pakistani frigates, as its aggressive pursuit suggested . . .

"Captain, sonar! Splashes to port, *close*!"

Splashes! Depth charges or ASW torpedoes! He clicked the switch on the intercom mike. "Torpedo room! Fire one! Helm, evasive!"

**1653 hours, 23 March**
**Bridge, U.S.S. *Biddle***

"Bridge! Sonar! Torpedo launch at zero-one-five, range one-eight hundred!"

Farrel's fist came down on the console. "Left full rudder! Ahead flank!"

The guided-missile frigate leaped across the water, sea spray lashing across the bridge windscreen. It was possible to outrun a torpedo, but the range was damned tight for a stunt like that. *Biddle* could make thirty knots. A torpedo might do forty or more, depending on the type.

"Bridge, sonar. Torpedo is maneuvering. Looks like it might be wire-guided, sir."

That might be a break. "Where's our LAMPS, Bill?" he asked his Exec.

"Sonobuoy run. He's right over the bastard!"

Farrel faced a terrible choice: try to outrun that incoming torpedo—probably impossible when it was less than a mile away—or try to break the concentration of the men directing it. Wire-guided torps were homed on their targets by commands sent down a thin wire unreeling behind the weapon. Once the torpedo acquired its own sonar lock the wire was cast off . . . or the sub could steer the thing all the way to the target.

If he could force the sub to turn away he might break the wire, but he had only seconds before the torpedo locked on by itself.

"Pass the word to the LAMPS," Farrel said. "Fire on the target."

He'd taken the step, and it was a terrible one. But by loosing the torpedo, that sub skipper had just forced Captain Farrel to choose between his ship and the submarine.

**1653 hours, 23 March**
**Over the Arabian Sea**

The location of *Biddle*'s sonar target had already been relayed to the circling Seahawk, which was further pinpointing the contact by dropping a chain of sonobuoys around the sub's suspected position. Target data was fed into the two Mark 46 ASW torpedoes slung from the Seahawk's hull.

At the command to fire, one of the torpedoes dropped away, a drogue chute opening at its tail to position it at the correct angle for entering the water. Arming when it hit the surface, it picked up the submerged Foxtrot almost immediately, circled onto a new heading, and dove.

**1654 hours, 23 March**
**Control room, INSS *Kalvari***

"High speed propeller to port!" The hydrophone operator's voice was sharp with fear. "Very close!"

"Hard to port!" Khandelwal's knuckles whitened on the periscope railing. The maneuver might make them lose their own torpedo, but perhaps the launch alone might make *Kalvari*'s attackers back off. If they could just elude this new threat . . .

At forty-five knots, the lightweight Mark 46 torpedo slammed into *Kalvari*'s hull just forward of her conning tower. The detonation of ninety-five pounds of torpex ripped a gaping hole through both the inner and outer hulls.

Captain Khandelwal was hurled across the control room as an avalanche of water exploded through the port bulkhead. His exec, Lieutenant Joshi Ramesh, was smashed against the conning tower ladder by the waterfall. In seconds, watertight doors imperfectly seated in concussion-warped frames gave way, and the Indian submarine began its final dive into darkness.

**1654 hours, 23 March**
**Bridge, U.S.S. *Biddle***

White water fountained high into the sky a mile off *Biddle*'s starboard side, accompanied by a bass earthquake rumble felt through the ship's hull and decks.

"Bridge, sonar! Torpedo has gone ballistic. Passing two hundred yards astern."

Farrel's eyes stayed riveted to the plume of seawater, now cascading back across a troubled sea. "Make to the LAMPS helo," he said. "Lay more buoys and listen for the sub. Stand by to recover survivors."

But he already knew there would be no survivors. He'd saved the *Biddle* . . . but sent a submarine and seventy-eight men to their deaths.

The political repercussions would be spreading out already . . . and far more quickly than the base surge from the underwater explosion now rocking the *Biddle*.

**1710 hours, 23 March**
**Admiralty Offices, New Delhi, India**

The Indian rear admiral studied the teletype message in his hand and felt tears of loss and anger burn his eyes. There was precious little information there, but the statement needed no elaboration.

INSS KALVARI SUNK BY US FFG, PERRY CLASS. NO SURVIVORS.

The message, transmitted from an IAF MiG-25 reconnaissance aircraft overflying the area, included coordinates positioning the loss one hundred miles west of Bombay, in international waters but well within the usual Indian patrol zones.

*Kalvari* sunk by a U.S. frigate! Why had the American opened fire? *Why?*

The admiral crumpled the message in his fist, then stood at his desk. It seemed plain enough. The Americans were coming to the aid of their Moslem ally after all. The Indian Parliament might have something to say about that. The war fever gripping the entire nation was like nothing he had ever seen before.

And Rear Admiral Ajay Ramesh would win his vengeance for the death of Joshi, his son.

# CHAPTER 4

**1829 hours (1759 hours India time), 23 March**
**50 km southeast of Derawar Fort, Thar Desert, Pakistan**

The sun had set moments before, leaving the sky a glory of yellow, pink, and blue. General Abdul Ali Hakim was less interested in the sky than in a spindly tower silhouetted against the sunset some twenty kilometers west of the bunker.

The Great Thar Desert stretched from the swamps of the Rann of Kutch in the south clear to Haryana State and the Punjab, straddling more than eight hundred kilometers of Indian-Pakistani border. Until this day it had been a barren waste of sand and gravel with but one significance to Pakistani military strategy: more than once the Thar had proved to be a superb barrier against the Indian army. Now it was going to have a second significance, one arguably far more vital than the first.

"One minute, General," an aide said at his side.

Hakim grunted in reply. His mind was on the border, some fifty kilometers further to the southeast. A hostile border, now that the Indians had finally stopped rattling their sabers and actually drawn them.

Not that the New Delhi regime's army was anywhere that close. As always, the Tharparkar, as Hakim thought of it, was a natural barrier more formidable than endless fortifications, minefields, and interlocking fields of fire. While there were rumors of enemy armor massing near the Jodhpur-Hyderabad Road far to the south, the nearest Indian troops were probably at the Rajasthan Canal, fully a hundred kilometers from this lonely outpost on Pakistan's frontier.

It was a pity, Hakim thought with a rare flash of humor, that the pigs weren't closer. *Much* closer.

"It's been a long road, Abdul."

Hakim turned to face the speaker. General Mushahid ul-Shapur was a powerful man, a member of Pakistan's ruling military clique and Hakim's own patron at Islamabad.

"It has indeed, sir."

"But a worthwhile one. Today, the nations of Islam take their rightful place with the superpowers of this world. No longer will the *kafir* of India seek to dominate us by force of arms!"

*"Inshallah,"* Hakim said softly. "As God wills."

Shapur looked at him with hawk's eyes, then turned back to the viewing slit in the bunker wall without another word. Hakim himself was surprised at his response to the general's observation. Moslem by birth and upbringing, he nonetheless had always resisted the insidious Islamic lure of allowing Allah to take the blame for everything, good or ill. Surely, a man bore *some* responsibility for the deeds of his own hands.

"Twenty seconds," a technician behind him in the bunker said.

"Sir," the aide said. "Your goggles."

"Of course." He lowered the binoculars, then slid the dark-lensed goggles he wore under his high-peaked army cap down over his eyes. Around him in the bunker, aides, officers, and politicians likewise settled their goggles into place, shielding their eyes.

"Five," a young Pakistani technician intoned from his console farther back in the bunker. "Four . . . three . . . two . . . one . . . *detonate!*"

Daylight returned to the empty desert, first as a pinprick of unutterably brilliant blue-white radiance, then as an expanding ring of white flame burning through the protective layers of the goggles. The desert lit up with stroboscopic clarity, with each pebble, each chunk of gravel and depression in the lifeless ground throwing ink-black shadows across the sand.

Hakim was surprised at the complete absence of sound, even though he'd known what to expect. Every man within the bunker seemed to be holding his breath. The silence stretched on and on and on as that first blindingly intense light faded, replaced by the angry yellow-orange glare from the rising fireball. The shock wave became visible, a blurring against the growing pillar of light. Ground wave and sound reached the bunker at the same moment, almost a full minute after the first searing flash. Suddenly, Hakim was leaning into a windstorm, sand and grit burning the unprotected skin of his face. The thunder of the detonation was muted by the roar of the wind.

Pandemonium broke loose within the claustrophobic confines of the bunker. At his elbow, Shapur was dancing and clapping his hands, a look of triumph on his face, but Hakim could hear nothing but the shout of God Himself, rolling on and on and on . . .

And this, Hakim thought, this was only a five-kiloton *tactical* device, with an explosive force of a quarter of the weapon exploded by the Americans over Hiroshima!

The blinding light faded, and Hakim removed his goggles. In the desert, a roiling cloud of sand and debris boiled skyward, spreading near the top into the familiar, flattened mushroom shape, its upper reaches high enough now that it caught the rays of the sun from beyond the horizon and reflected them, blood-red and ominous.

Surely it was a sign from God, a holy sign . . . but was it blessing or curse for his country, his people? Hakim could not be sure.

He watched the cloud continue to crawl toward heaven in blood-lit splendor.

**1044 hours EST (2114 hours India time), 23 March**
**National Security Council Conference Room, Washington, D.C.**

The room was wood-paneled and richly furnished, dominated by a large conference table and an array of executive-style leather chairs. One wall could open at the touch of a button to reveal display screens or maps. That wall was closed now, however, flanked by the flag of the United States and the Presidential Seal. The room, one of many, was located some dozens of feet beneath the Executive Building within the network of underground corridors that connected with the White House basement.

The men waiting around the table stood as Phillip Buchalter entered the room. ''Good morning, gentlemen,'' he said in a brisk voice. "Thank you for coming on such short notice. We seem to have a situation here."

As National Security Advisor, Buchalter was responsible for the day-to-day operation of the National Security Council.

In 1989, President Bush had organized the NSC into three subgroups. Senior of these was the Principals Committee. It was currently chaired by Buchalter, and its members included Ronald Hemminger, the Secretary of Defense; James A. Schellenberg, the Secretary of State; General Amos C. Caldwell, Chairman of the Joint Chiefs; Victor Marlowe, Director of Central Intelligence and head of the NSA and the rest of the U.S. intelligence network; and George Hall, White House Chief of Staff.

There were others in the room, aides and secretaries for the most part. The ID card pinned to the breast pocket of one elderly man identified him as Dr. Walter Montrose of the Lawrence Livermore National Laboratory.

Buchalter stood at the end of the table, hands braced on the wooden surface. "Gentlemen, we are facing a NUCFLASH crisis."

There was an uneasy stir around the table, followed by an absolute and unnerving silence. NUCFLASH was the flagword on an OPREP-3 PINNACLE message which indicated that a serious risk of nuclear war existed. Normally, the coded alert was concerned with accidents, launchings, overflights, or malfunctions that could lead to war with the Soviet Union. A NUCFLASH alert could also apply, however, to any unauthorized or unexplained nuclear detonation.

"Just over two hours ago, several of our NDDS orbital packages detected a nuclear explosion in the Pakistan desert near Derawar Fort, about three hundred fifty miles northeast of Karachi. We calculate the yield at about five kilotons."

"Damn," General Caldwell said in the silence that followed. "They've finally gone and done it."

"They have indeed," Buchalter said. "We know Pakistan has been working to develop a nuclear capability since 1972. It was believed that their research reactor facility outside of Islamabad had the potential for assembling warheads for the past several years. 'Only a screwdriver away,' as they say." He gave a wan smile. "Their test this morning confirms it."

"Five kilotons," Schellenberg said. "That's not very big. Strictly tactical stuff."

"Nuclear artillery shells . . . atomic warheads on Frog 7 missiles?" Caldwell pointed out. "That's plenty bad enough, Mr. Secretary, believe me."

"It's worse than that, gentlemen," Dr. Montrose said. He carefully folded his hands on the table top before him. "The orbital sensors gave us quite precise data on the device, precise enough that we were able to make some educated guesses about its employment. The Derawar blast was almost certainly the field test of a nuclear trigger."

The reactions of the men around the table ran the gamut from surprise to outright shock. "A trigger!" Hemminger said. "You mean—"

"For a thermonuclear device." Montrose nodded. "Yes. The low-yield trigger is used to create the temperature and pressure necessary to induce nuclear fusion. They might well have the capability of manufacturing nuclear devices in the megaton range, a thousand times more powerful than the blast we detected this morning."

"That's ridiculous," George Hall said. "You're saying the Pakistanis are leaping straight to H-bombs and superpower status in one jump. That's just not possible!"

"I'm afraid it is," Marlowe said, shaking his head. "We've been expecting this for years, you know. Our old friend Qaddafi has poured millions of dollars into Pakistan's atomic research program since the seventies . . . and supplied them with uranium from his territorial acquisitions in Chad as well. The theory is simple enough. The hard part, as I understand it, is purely technical, separation and purification of the uranium and so on. They were bound to get it sooner or later."

Hemminger pursed his lips. "I find the timing of this . . . this test somewhat coincidental. Anyone else here concur on that?"

Marlowe nodded. "My people are looking into that, but I think I can tell you the result now. Pakistan has probably had the capability to assemble a thermonuclear bomb for at least the past five years. It is possible they have been hiding the fact even from the Libyans . . . who, of course, would expect some return on their investment in the form of several complete warheads."

George Hall shuddered. "The Libyans with nuclear weapons. God help us."

"God help the world," Buchalter said. A shiver ran down his spine. He remembered watching a televised interview with Qaddafi. Libya's dictator had been insisting that had he possessed nuclear weapons, he would have used them to retaliate for the 1986 bombing of Tripoli and Benghazi by Navy and Air Force jets. "Wait a sec, Victor. You say they were hiding their capabilities from the Libyans?"

"Yes, sir." He gave a dry chuckle. "Pakistan gets several billion dollars of aid from us every year. They know damn well they're not likely to stay on the gravy train if they turn nukes over to a flake like Qaddafi. But the Indian attack may have changed things over there. India is a thermonuclear power too, remember, has been since 1974. Pakistan has its back up against the wall. They could do something . . . extreme."

Hemminger's eyes widened. "Are you suggesting that we could be looking at a nuclear war over there?"

"Mr. Secretary, we think that the detonation this morning was a test . . . and a warning. They did nothing to try to hide it. They set it off on the surface instead of underground, where the shock could have been blamed on an earthquake, or out at sea, where they could have denied any knowledge of it. We think that it was meant as a clear signal to the Indians: 'Back off. We have nukes too.'"

"Will India press her attack?" Schellenberg asked. "Damn, they're not suicidal!"

Marlowe studied his hands, folded before him. "Maybe not. But these two countries have been at each other since Partition in 1947. Islamic extremists have slaughtered Hindus living in Pakistan and waged a terrorist war in Kashmir, which is still officially Indian but predominantly Moslem. Slaughter has been answered with slaughter by Hindi extremists in India. New Delhi has accused Pakistan of interfering with Indian affairs, aiding rebels, spreading unrest, and preaching open revolution.

"We're afraid that India might react to Pakistan's warning in an . . . unexpected way. They have a population of nine hundred million to Pakistan's ninety million . . . that's ten to one, gentlemen. They have the eighth largest navy, the fifth largest air force, and the third largest army in the world. They might decide that they could end the Pakistan threat once and for all by replacing the government in Islamabad with one of their own choosing, just like they did with Bangladesh in 1971."

"But, my God!" Hemminger said. "If they start tossing nukes at each other . . ."

"Pakistan's only delivery system would be by air," General Caldwell observed. "They bought thirty F-16 Falcons off of us a few years back. They'd do the trick."

"That'll look good in the press," Hall muttered aloud. "American-made planes nuke New Delhi!"

The DCI ignored the interruption. "Early indications are that the Indian air force is specifically hitting Pakistan's offensive air capabilities," Marlowe said. "Pakistan has suffered heavy losses already, possibly as high as forty percent. If India can knock out Pakistan's air, Pakistan won't have any way of delivering her bombs.

"Even if that doesn't work out, the present Indian leadership might decide that the loss of a city or two would be worth it. There's at least an even chance that the Indians will call the Pakistanis' bluff."

"God in heaven," someone breathed softly.

Schellenberg nodded slowly. "When the antagonists are as *unpredictable* as Pakistan and India, anything is possible."

"Nuclear war on the Indian subcontinent is unacceptable," Buchalter said. He marveled at the calm way he said it, as though discussing weekend plans for golf. "I've already conferred with the President on this." He shook his head slightly as he remembered the President's anger.

Or was it fear?

"Damned right it's unacceptable," Caldwell said. "It would be opening the genie's bottle. We'd never get the damned thing back in again."

"Not to mention tens of millions of folks dying," Hemminger said sarcastically.

Caldwell held up his hand. "Don't get me wrong, sir. I'm not forgetting the casualties. But think of this. In all of history, there have been two, and only two, nuclear weapons dropped in wartime. We've managed to keep the lid on things ever since. Now some damned Third World country nukes a Third World neighbor. Suddenly people start thinking about *using* those nukes in their stockpiles. And those who don't have them start looking for ways to join the club. Everything we've accomplished in holding back proliferation could be negated by a single attack."

"It would be a nightmare," Marlowe said. "A nightmare come to life."

"How can the United States fit into this?" Hall asked. "I mean, like you said, Pakistan depends on us for aid. Maybe we could pull some strings."

"Might work with Pakistan," Buchalter said. "But not India. Especially now."

"What do you mean, 'especially now'?" Schellenberg asked.

Buchalter opened a folder and removed a sheet of paper. "This just came in from CBG-14," he said. He glanced at Marlowe, who nodded. "Confirmed by NSA intercepts of Indian communications. Approximately four hours ago, one of our ships was fired on by an Indian sub. Our ship returned fire . . . and sank the submarine."

"Oh, God, no," the Secretary of Defense said. "Now India thinks we've already sided with Pakistan."

"So much for our getting them to arrange an armistice," Hall added.

"What about the Russians?" one of the Defense Secretary's aides asked. He held up two fingers, tightly crossed. "India and the former USSR have always been like that."

Schellenberg shook his head. "It's not that simple, son. India has pursued a policy of strict neutrality. What was the Soviet Union was India's largest trading partner, and India has been one of Russia's best sources of hard currency. India's armed forces are mostly outfitted with Russian equipment, yeah, but with a few exceptions, India managed to steer clear of East-West politics. I doubt that the Russians exert that much influence over them, not if knocking out Pakistan is really important to New Delhi."

"Then what can we do?" Hall asked. "What can the President do?"

"That, gentlemen, is why the President wanted us to meet here this morning," Buchalter said. "We are to examine our options, and I am to report to him with the consensus later this afternoon." He opened the folder in front of him and leafed through it to a marked page. "Gentlemen, if you would turn in your briefs to the National Security Decision Memorandum, NSDM-242. I direct your attention to Point Two." He cleared his throat and began reading. " 'In conjunction with other U.S. and allied forces, to deter attacks—conventional and nuclear—by nuclear powers against U.S. allies and those other nations whose security is deemed important to U.S. interests.' "

He looked up and faced the men around the table. "This memorandum was formulated by the Nixon-Ford Administrations and reaffirmed by NSDD-13 in 1981. In other words, if the President says that it is in the national interest to prevent a nuclear war on the Indian subcontinent—"

Schellenberg blinked. "Are you saying we should declare war on India?"

Buchalter smiled tightly. "I think, Mr. Secretary, that the President would appreciate an option less extreme than that. But he *does* want an option." He turned to Caldwell. "General, I'd like to hear more about this carrier battle group we already have in the area. Anything we do out there is going to rely on them."

"We could take this up with the United Nations," Hemminger said. The Secretary of Defense rubbed his chin thoughtfully. "A nuclear war in South Asia could have repercussions on lots of countries. Afghanistan, Burma, Thailand . . ."

"Not to mention the former Soviet Union, what is now the Commonwealth of Independent States," Marlowe said. "I imagine that they're burning the midnight oil right this moment in the Kremlin, trying to decide what to do about this. I assure you, the Soviet Union will not be pleased at the prospect of a nuclear confrontation so near her southern frontiers."

"The President has already informed our representative at the UN," Buchalter added. "I imagine Pakistan's nuke . . . and the incident with our frigate . . . will both be pretty high on the list of topics discussed on the East River today."

The discussion went on for three hours. In the end, it all came down to one thing.

CBG 14 was already in the area. Any other military forces short of ICBMs or long-range SAC bombers would require days or weeks to deploy. Every man there was remembering the long buildup in the Arabian desert during Operation Desert Shield.

Any short-term answer to the crisis was riding on the flight deck of the U.S.S. *Jefferson*.

# CHAPTER 5

**0730 hours, 24 March**
**Viper Ready Room, U.S.S. *Thomas Jefferson***

Tombstone walked into the Vipers' ready room, exchanging greetings with the other aviators already there. Most of VF-95's pilots and RIOs were there, standing about in small groups or already sitting in the rows of chairs facing a large TV screen mounted on the far bulkhead. Those scheduled for patrol within the next few hours wore their flight suits. The others were more comfortably attired in their khakis.

Looking around the room, he spotted Batman and his rear-seater, Lieutenant Ken "Malibu" Blake, standing in one corner underneath the PLAT monitor, deep in a heated debate. He hesitated a moment, then walked over to join them.

"Ho, Stoney!" Batman said. "Help me straighten out this guy."

"Hopeless," Tombstone said. "You should've known that when you married him."

"Yeah, I know, but where there's life, there's hope, even for the brain-dead. This guy's trying to tell me that the Russians aren't a threat anymore."

Malibu took a sip from a can of soda. He was, in his own words, a Coke-aholic who needed a can of the stuff to get jump-started in the morning. "Seems to me they're having enough trouble just holding this commonwealth together without trying to project their air- and seapower all over the world," he said.

"He's got a point there, Batman," Tombstone said. "When was the last time we got buzzed by a Bear?"

"Just before Korea, but that's beside the point. The Iron Curtain was lifted for a while, but it fell again with a thud when things started going sour inside their borders, and now who knows what will happen?"

"Which means they're too busy to bother with us or the Indian Ocean," Malibu insisted. "Look at the record, man! They gave Cam Ranh back to the Vietnamese. Yemen decided it didn't want Soviet ships at Socotra. They're not even on particularly good terms with the Indians anymore. If this keeps up, they're not going to have any overseas bases at all. I don't think they're going to be bothering us much from now on."

"Yeah? Wake up and take a look at this." Batman turned and slapped a map that was tacked up to a bulletin board on the nearby bulkhead. It was a full-color, 1:4,500,000-scale map showing most of the Indian Ocean from Malaysia to Somalia. The Indian subcontinent jabbed southward like a huge, blunt dagger. A black line started at Diego Garcia far south of the dagger's tip and extended north along the western coast of India before cutting sharply to the west. Dates written in along the way traced the battle group's progress over the past week. *Jefferson*'s current position was marked, two hundred miles south of the Indian-Pakistan border.

Six hundred miles southwest of Turban Station, off of Oman on the Arabian Peninsula, another line had been roughed in, this time in red. It showed the day-by-day recorded positions of the (former) Soviet Indian Ocean Squadron, SOVINDRON. A week before, those ships had been moving slowly south down the Red Sea. Now they had rounded the corner at the Gulf of Aden and were steaming all-out toward the Pakistan coast.

Batman tapped the squadron's last charted position. "Trouble projecting their seapower? You can say that when they have a fair-sized task force just six hundred miles over the horizon? Man, I'd call that some kind of major power projection!"

"Trying to assert Commonwealth power?" Malibu crumpled the empty aluminum can and dropped it in a wastebasket. "Or they're looking after their people here, like we are. Mark my words, guys. We'll be out looking for work if this keeps up!"

"What do you say to that, Stoney?" Batman asked. "Ready for a job with United?"

The joke stung. Tombstone managed to keep the easy smile

on his face. "Not just yet," he said. "Not if they won't let me pull an inverted dive in a 727."

They laughed as he slumped into a seat. For him, the question was dead serious.

His eyes went to the lieutenant j.g. working on the squadron's greenie board. Every ready room had one, a large chart with the names of all of the aviators in the squadron, and squares colored in with magic markers where his performance for the past month was recorded. A green square meant the LSO had graded his trap as "OK," the highest praise possible for an excellent pass or for timely corrections of minor deviations. Yellow was for "fair." No color meant "no grade," meaning the trap had been dangerous to people and planes on the deck. Red with a C stood for "Cut," a landing so unsafe it could have resulted in disaster. The squares were divided into two or three sections for multiple passes, with a "B" signifying a bolter, or missed trap, and a "W" a wave-off. A small black triangle up in one corner meant the trap had been made at night.

The VF-95 Vipers were a good squadron, green and yellow marks predominating, with a few white patches and no reds. Their overall record was not as good as that of either VFA-161 or VFA-173. The intense competitions between squadrons—recorded on a huge greenie board for the entire Air Wing in a passageway outside Pri-Fly—were nearly always taken by those squadrons, for the nimble F/A-18 Hornet was a lot easier to plant neatly on the number-three arrestor wire than the massive Tomcat.

But the Vipers were good, and Tombstone was fiercely proud to be one of them.

It would hurt to leave them.

He reached into the breast pocket of his khakis, pulled out the last letter from Pamela, and began rereading it.

*You'd think a TV news anchor would know everything that's going on,* she'd written. *It seems like I'm hearing just enough to know how hairy things are getting over there. Everything coming into the network here points to a major war breaking out between Pakistan and India before the end of the month.*

She'd certainly guessed right about that. Tombstone looked up, his eyes going to the PLAT monitor. An A-6 Intruder was descending toward the roof. He watched it touch steel, seeming to flatten itself to the deck, then rebounding slightly, nose down as the arrestor wire dragged it to a halt. Good trap.

He looked back at the letter, his eyes shifting down the page to what she'd written later on. *I worry so about you, my darling Matt. Maybe this isn't the best time to bring it up, but I have to admit that I've been thinking about us, about our future, an awful lot in the past weeks.*

*Have you thought much about what our life together will be like? ACN will be sending me out on special assignments every so often, and I'll be tied down in Washington the rest of the time. And you? Assignments at naval air stations all over the country, interspersed with nine-month deployments at sea.*

*We've talked about getting married quite a lot during our last few letters. I love you, Matt, but I think the time has come to take a hard and decidedly unromantic look at our careers, and our futures.*

Leave it to Pamela to be practical about all this, Tombstone thought. He turned the page to a smudged and oft-read paragraph just before the end.

*You wouldn't have to give up flying. A friend of mine at the FAA told me the other day that the airlines are crying for experienced pilots, and that Navy aviators are prime candidates. Scheduling our time together might still be a problem, but at least we would have schedules, and not be apart for so long at a time.*

*I love you more now than when I was with you last in Bangkok. I want to marry you. But we have to face reality. As long as you stay in the Navy, I don't see how we can have much of a life together. . . .*

"About time for the show, sir."

Startled, Tombstone looked up and found himself staring into the pudgy features of Master Chief Julius Fleming, the Avionics Technician assigned to the squadron. "Oh, right." Hastily he stuffed Pamela's letter back into his flight suit, then glanced around at the other men in the squadron taking their seats. "Put it on, Chief."

Each squadron ready room on the carrier had a television monitor tied into the closed-circuit network. Moments after Fleming turned it on, the Air Wing 20 logo was replaced by the face of CAG Steve Marusko. With a wry flash of humor,

Tombstone thought to himself that CAG looked none the worse for wear after the harrowing trap the day before. He remembered that he'd been supposed to go down to CAG's office and talk things over. Somehow, there'd been no time since yesterday afternoon.

Well, the talk wouldn't change his mind now. Tombstone's mind was made up.

"Good morning, men," Marusko said briskly. He was standing at the CVIC podium. By broadcasting his address over the CCTV system, he could speak to all of the aviators aboard *Jefferson* simultaneously. It saved time.

"I should start off by saying that there's been a big change in the green sheet." The "green sheet," named logically enough for its color, was the daily schedule of air operations put out by OX Division, Ops Admin. "As of 0800 this morning, this carrier battle group will go to full alert."

"Yesterday afternoon at 1655 hours, the U.S.S. *Biddle* was fired upon by a Foxtrot-class submarine of the Indian navy. *Biddle* evaded and returned fire. The Foxtrot is believed to have been lost with all hands."

The stir grew to a subdued murmur of voices. "Knock it off, people," Tombstone said, raising his voice. "Let's listen up."

"As a result of this incident," CAG continued on the screen, "diplomatic relations with India have become seriously strained. Yesterday evening, our time, their embassy in Washington delivered a formal protest to the President and threatened retaliation if we stay within what they describe as their military interdiction zone.

"That zone, incidentally, extends three hundred miles south from the mainland to latitude twenty degrees north. That describes a line from just above Bombay clear across the Arabian Sea to the island of Masirah, off Oman. Washington has responded by declaring that we do not recognize that zone, which includes the approaches to the Persian Gulf. The Navy's mission includes insuring free passage through those straits, something we can't give up without serious repercussion among our allies.

"*Jefferson* is now well inside the exclusion zone, and we're not leaving. A message to that effect has been delivered by our State Department to New Delhi.

"At 0435 hours our time this morning, *Jefferson* received an alert order from CINCPAC." CAG picked up a sheet of paper from the podium and began reading.

"'CBG-14 is hereby directed,'" he read, "'to assume a defensive stance commensurate with full combat readiness in order to safeguard the vessels of CBG-14 from possible attack by hostile forces. COCBG-14 is urged to take every precaution to avoid conflict with potential hostile forces in the area within the framework of his operating orders. Ships and aircraft of CBG-14 will fire only if fired upon. Aggressive operations which could be construed as hostile gestures are to be terminated.'"

CAG put the paper down and looked back up at the camera. "In keeping with these orders, Admiral Vaughn has directed the battle ground to close up once we reach our assigned patrol station. Fighter CAPs will go as scheduled, but the patrol radius will be reduced from three hundred to two hundred miles. The strike exercises scheduled for VA-84 and VA-89 are canceled. Catseyes and King Fishers will continue their patrols as briefed. Every effort is to be made to avoid further contact with Indian forces."

That made sense. Practice bomb runs by the Intruders of the carrier's attack squadrons could be dispensed with. The Hawkeye radar planes of the VAW-130 Catseyes and the sub-hunting Vikings of VS-42 would be needed more than ever to alert the battle group to an approach by hostile planes or subs. He wasn't sure he understood the order to shrink the CBG's perimeter, though. An aircraft carrier was an extremely large and tempting target. The best way to hide it was to spread the battle group over as much area as possible, making it harder for hostile patrols to pinpoint the carrier.

The televised briefing continued, covering other, more routine matters, but the big bomb had already been dropped. Strained diplomatic relations with India? Possible combat with Indian forces? It seemed impossible, but wars had begun over smaller things than the loss of a submarine. What made this situation deadly was the fact that the Indians were already at war with Pakistan. Any hostile U.S. move would make New Delhi think that the Americans had sided with their old ally, Pakistan.

It was even possible that the battle group could be attacked by accident.

*And what the hell am I doing here, anyway?* he thought. I'm *not mad at the Indians. I sure as hell don't want to get into a war with them.*

His thoughts strayed to Pamela's letter. Maybe she was right, and it was time for a change. Four more weeks and the *Jefferson* would be returning to San Diego. At that time, Tombstone's current commission period would be up and he would have the option of resigning from the Navy.

Resigning from the Navy. The words carried an eerie feel to them.

For the better part of ten years he'd thought he'd known precisely his career's future course. The Academy, flight school at Pensacola, each decision along the way had led naturally and inevitably to the next. Memories of his father—a carrier pilot killed over Hanoi in 1969—had been one strong factor in those decisions. His uncle, Admiral Thomas J. Magruder, had been another.

If he stayed in, promotion would come within a year, and with it confirmation of his rather tenuous position as skipper of VF-95. Usually the COs of air wing squadrons were full commanders; he'd been made skipper because of a shortage of qualified aviator commanders with the fleet and, he still strongly suspected, a word or two in the right quarters from his uncle. The title of squadron skipper had rested uneasily on his shoulders for eight months now. Once he got his promotion, it would ride there a bit more naturally.

And after that? A few more years and he'd have had his shot at a CAG slot . . . with the ultimate goal of skippering a carrier of his own.

Yeah, his whole future had been planned out in year-by-year, step-by-step detail. And now the whole thing had been wiped away. It left him feeling shaky.

But he couldn't keep going with it, not this way. He'd lost his edge. He was starting to hold on too tight, maybe because of Pamela . . . maybe because he'd come too close too many times. The air-to-air refueling incident yesterday and the near-crash on the deck afterward had convinced him that it was time to pack it in.

Usually when an aviator faced that kind of personal crisis, he had the option of turning in his wings. That meant accepting some other Navy flyer's billet—piloting COD aircraft or transports, for instance—but escaping the deadly day-in, day-out stress of combat flying. Such a move was usually looked upon as a kind of death by the aviator's former comrades. It excluded him from that special, inner circle that was so much a part of the mystique of carrier aviation. He knew all about that. He'd wrestled with the decision several months earlier, had nearly turned in his wings because he'd been having a rough time with the responsibility of running a fighter squadron . . . with giving the orders that could get other guys, his friends, killed.

He'd managed to resolve that one. This was something different, a problem that couldn't be solved by something as simple as asking for a different assignment. What it came down to was the realization that he could have his career . . . or Pamela.

What kind of money was United paying for experienced pilots? Better than Navy pay, that was for sure, even with flight pay, combat pay, and Navy perks thrown in.

In another month he would sure as hell find out.

If he survived whatever it was that the Indians were about to do with the U.S. battle group trespassing in their ocean.

**1435 hours, 24 March**
**Headquarters, Indian Defense Ministry, New Delhi, India**

Rear Admiral Ajay Ramesh took his seat at the conference table as other men, admirals and generals, filed into the room. He'd been summoned to Defense Ministry headquarters with unseemly haste. The haste was fully justified, of course. He'd made certain suggestions during his report to the Ministry the day before . . . and it appeared that those suggestions were to be acted upon.

He glanced at the map dominating one wall of the room, showing the Indian-Pakistan frontier from Kashmir to the Arabian Sea. Arrows and the cryptic symbols identifying various military units had been marked in, showing troop movements and deployments since the beginning of the war almost thirty-six hours earlier. So far, the front had remained more or less static, though the Pakistani towns of Gadra, Nagal Parkar, and Satidara—all in the south—had been taken. Units in the Punjab, opposite Lahore and Sahiwal, were still bogged down at the border.

But slow progress had been expected. Much of India's armor had been held back in anticipation of Operation Cobra.

The double doors at the other end of the room swung open, and a military aide strode in, calling "Attention!" He was closely followed by Rear Admiral Desai Karananidhi, commander of India's western naval forces, and by General Sanjeev Dhanaraj, First Corps commander.

Dhanaraj took his place at the head of the table. "First of all," he said as the other men took their seats once more, "let me say to you, Admiral Ramesh, that I'm sure I speak for all here when I offer my sincere condolences for the death of your son. He was a credit to his uniform, and his nation."

Ramesh inclined his head gratefully. The news of Joshi's death still burned.

"To business, then," Dhanaraj said. "You have all read the recommendations of the Prime Minister and the directive from the Ministry of Defense. Comments?"

General Chandra Bakaya spread his hands. "Comments? Yes, sir. Has our government taken leave of its collective senses? We sit here and serenely contemplate adding the United States of America to our list of enemies? Insanity!"

Admiral Karananidhi glanced at Dhanaraj. "The Americans have allied themselves with Pakistan time and time again. Can this time be any different?"

True enough, Ramesh thought. For years India had walked a diplomatic tightrope between East and West, with an avowed policy of nonalignment with any other world power. The Americans' inability to grasp this crucial essence of Indian foreign policy was baffling. This time, it seemed, they were openly supporting the Pakistanis, had actually fired upon and sunk an Indian warship. *Joshi . . . !*

Several officers were trying to talk at once. General Dhanaraj pounded the table with the flat of his hand, demanding order, and the noise subsided. "Admiral Ramesh has joined us today to elaborate on the plan he submitted to the Ministry yesterday," he said. "It has been designated Operation Krait." He paused. "Admiral Ramesh?"

The admiral stood. His knees felt weak, and he leaned forward, bracing himself on the tabletop with his hands.

"Thank you, General. Gentlemen, since Pakistan's, ah, demonstration yesterday, it is obvious that we must win this war quickly. Cobra, once launched, *must* succeed within a few days of the initial assault, or we face disaster. American support for our enemy threatens that quick victory, threatens *us*."

Drawing a deep breath, he crossed to the front of the room, where he pulled down a second map over the first, one with the Indian Military Exclusion Zone marked in red. Notations pinpointed American ships, and the spot where *Kalvari* had been sunk.

Fighting the rising lump in his throat, he reached out, his finger touching the main American battle group that had taken up positions at sea south of the India-Pakistan border. "Our target, gentlemen, for Operation Krait."

# CHAPTER 6

**0950 hours EST (2020 hours India time), 24 March**
**The Pentagon, Washington, D.C.**

An Army lieutenant colonel stood in the doorway, resplendent in his Class-A dress uniform, complete with gold aiguillettes. "Admiral Magruder?"

Rear Admiral Thomas J. Magruder looked up from his desk, wary. "Yes?"

"Lieutenant Colonel Haworth, sir," the man said. He advanced three steps and handed Magruder an envelope.

Magruder's eyebrows raised when he saw the seal on the envelope. His eyebrows crept even higher when he saw the letterhead on which the note was written.

"This says I'm to accompany you right now."

"Yes, sir. I have a car and driver downstairs."

Magruder wasn't entirely sure that this was not some kind of elaborate joke, but he stood and retrieved his uniform jacket and hat from the coat rack by the door. "Very well, Colonel. I'm at your disposal."

Magruder was glad for the chance to escape. He hated the Pentagon. Men and women who had worked there for years had a variety of names for the place. "Puzzle Palace," "Fudge Factory," and "Fort Fumble" were a few common ones. His favorite, though, was "the five-sided squirrel cage." He'd been stationed in Washington before during his career, and always he had detested the politics, the back-stabbing scramble for larger cuts of the appropriations, the bumbling inefficiency.

He was ushered into a typically black Cadillac limousine waiting in a staff parking area underneath the Pentagon. It came fully equipped: car phone, TV, stereo, CD, air-conditioning, an Army staff sergeant as chauffeur, and an anonymous-looking man in a conservative dark suit and sunglasses riding shotgun in the front seat. Magruder got into the back with Haworth. The driver guided the vehicle out into blazing sunshine, then neatly threaded the cloverleafs that led to the Shirley Memorial Parkway, heading toward the 14th Street Bridge.

"How do you like your new assignment, Admiral?" Haworth asked as they accelerated smoothly into the traffic flow. Perhaps he was simply trying to make conversation, but the question galled Magruder. "It sucks, Colonel. It goddamn sucks. I'd rather be conning a carrier than a desk any day."

That effectively ended the conversation. Magruder gazed out the window at the ultra-modern glass towers of Pentagon City flashing by to the right. It was late enough in the morning that traffic was mercifully light. In moments, the Potomac River opened beneath them as they sped across the Rochambeau Bridge. The dome of the Jefferson Memorial rose above trees to the left that were not yet showing any green.

His new assignment was a particular and special purgatory for the fifty-seven-year-old admiral. Assigned to the Office of the Secretary of Defense, he'd quickly found himself caught between the lines of the war currently raging in Washington over cuts in the U.S. military. Within the walls of the Pentagon, the OSD was considered to be the enemy by the Joint Staff and other departments that were primarily military in orientation and personnel; the majority of managers and directors within the OSD were political appointees, civilian bureaucrats who tended to look down on, ignore, or simply mistrust the military members of the department.

To make matters worse, Magruder had come to Fort Fumble straight from the command of a carrier battle group. Before that, he'd been captain of a supercarrier. Battle groups and supercarriers together were coming under especially heavy fire as Congress and budget-management people at the White House looked for big and expensive military programs to cut. With the Soviets no longer an immediate menace, procurement programs were being slashed right and left, bases were being closed everywhere, and men were actually being paid bonuses to leave the service early. The B-2 Stealth Bomber, Star Wars, new supercarriers already under construction, the Sea Wolf attack sub program, all had come under savage attack during the past five years.

What made the whole situation seem like an exercise in complete futility was the fact that every program or base or weapon system also had its defenders. There were congressmen determined to kill the V-22 Osprey, which was already in production after millions had been spent on its development . . . yet who were fighting tooth and nail to keep an Army post open that served no tactical or strategic point whatsoever, simply because that post was in their district.

It was frustrating, and frightening. No one in the entire city seemed to understand that political realities could change overnight, while weapons programs took years to implement. A coup in Moscow, and America could be back in a shoving match with the Russians who were still gun-for-gun, tank-for-tank, and plane-for-plane the most powerful military force in the world.

A nuclear carrier could not be turned on or off so quickly. The budget for the U.S.S. *Nimitz,* for instance, had been approved in fiscal year '67. Construction had begun in June of '68, she was launched in May of '72, and she was commissioned on 3 May, 1975. Eight years from start to finish. And there were loud cries in Congress now to retire *Nimitz* and the other *Nimitz*-class carriers, *Jefferson* among them, because they were big, expensive to operate, and no longer had a part to play in the world political arena.

Magruder snorted at the thought, as the limousine exited the freeway and headed north on 14th Street. The green openness of the Mall caught him, as always, by surprise. To his left, the white concrete spike of the Washington Monument stabbed into the blue March sky. One mile away to his right, the Capitol Building rose in white magnificence beyond the Mall and the museums lining it.

In the years since communism had begun visibly crumbling, the world had become far *more* dangerous and uncertain, not less. The brief horror of the Gulf War had proven that. Now Pakistan and India were at each other's throats again.

And the bureaucrats wanted to trash the very ships and aircraft and men that could make a difference. Magruder leaned back, fingers pressing against his eyes. It was a losing fight.

Months before, in the Sea of Japan, he had faced personal and national disaster as he replied to a North Korean challenge with a military response. But the day-in, day-out struggle for sanity in the Pentagon was infinitely harder to bear.

The limo turned left at E Street, then swung north again onto Executive Avenue. Parts of the street had been closed off to vehicular traffic, but a Marine sentry ushered the limo past a checkpoint to a stretch of road that had been turned into a parking lot. The sergeant stayed with the car, but Haworth and the civilian accompanied him. Ahead, the White House stretched across green grass between the Treasury and the Old Executive Office Building. Magruder found himself staring like a tourist and had to tear his eyes away to watch where he was going.

"Ever been in here before, Admiral?" Haworth asked.

"Never have," Magruder replied. He gestured toward a colorful line queuing up for the daily tours. "Never could stand to wait in line that long."

"Well, you get the special tour today." The colonel seemed amused.

Magruder felt his stomach knot. The President of the United States had asked for him by name, had sent a driver and car to pick him up. Why? As they showed their ID cards to Marine and Secret Service personnel and were signed in at the east door, the questions grew more urgent.

They passed several more checkpoints before a civilian dismissed Magruder's escort. "Admiral Magruder?" the man said. "I'm George Hall, White House Chief of Staff. If you'll come with me, sir?"

The Oval Office was much as Magruder had pictured it, though it was smaller than he expected. The windows overlooking the Rose Garden and the South Lawn were heavily tinted and so thick he could barely see through them. He remembered reading that they were designed to stop heavy-caliber rifle fire. A TV monitor set into a wall cabinet was tuned to a cable news channel. The President rose behind his desk.

"Admiral Magruder," he said, smiling and extending his hand. He was considerably shorter than Magruder had imagined. He had the warm smile of the practiced politician. "We meet at last. Welcome."

"Thank you, Mr. President."

Hall showed him to a chair and he sat down. He'd not felt this out of place since the first time he'd attended a formal military ball. He was an ensign at the time.

"Well, Admiral," the President said, seating himself behind the desk. "How do you like your new assignment?"

That was the second time in the last thirty minutes someone had asked him that question. His eyes shifted to George Hall, then back to the President. "It's not quite what I expected, sir."

The President chuckled. "I daresay it's not." The politician's smile faded. "Listen, Tom. I know what you must be going through over there, across the river. And I'm sorry things worked out this way for you. But something has come up . . . something new, and right now I'm damned glad you're here in Washington. I need you."

Magruder waited. He could hear the undertone of worry in the President's words.

The President nodded toward the TV screen. "I'm sure you've been following the news. You know where your battle group is right now."

"Last I heard, they were in the Indian Ocean. Gonzo Station, I imagine."

"Actually, it's east of Gonzo Station, a couple of hundred miles south of Karachi. We call it Turban Station.

"CBG-14 was ordered there a week ago. Purely routine, in light of the events over there lately. We wanted to send New Delhi and Islamabad both a strong message, that we would not tolerate any threat to American lives or interests in the region.

"Twenty-seven hours ago, the U.S.S. *Biddle* sank an Indian submarine."

"My God . . ."

"What's worse is, even though the Indians fired first, they seem to think we provoked the action. Their ambassador was here in my office not two hours ago. He point-blank accused me of taking Pakistan's side and said that India would tolerate no interference in her . . . ah . . . 'military exercises along the Pakistan border.'"

"Then there's a possibility that CBG-14 could come under attack. Is that what you're saying, Mr. President?"

"Partly. There's more bad news." He glanced at George

Hall. "What I'm about to tell you is classified. We're keeping a lid on this one, for rather obvious reasons."

"Well, Mr. President, I'm cleared for—"

"I know your classification, Tom. I'm just reminding you that this is hot. *Very* hot. Yesterday evening, Pakistan exploded a nuclear device."

"*What?*"

"It appears to have been a test . . . and a warning."

"And India already is a nuclear power. . . ."

"Exactly." The President leaned back in his leather chair and sighed. "My predecessors in this office have all wrestled with nuclear proliferation. I guess we all knew that things would get out of hand sooner or later. Now they have, big time. We could be looking at a nuclear war over there if we can't work something out between these two countries, and damned fast!"

"What's being done about it?"

"The matter went to the United Nations yesterday afternoon. The UN Security Council voted fifteen to nothing to censure India as an aggressor and called for her immediate withdrawal from Pakistani territory."

"I imagine India's feeling rather isolated right now."

The President's mouth quirked. "Try surrounded. Anyway, the wrangling on the East River is going to go on for a while. In the meantime, Indian troops are still advancing into Pakistan, Indian planes are still hitting targets from Karachi to Islamabad. The Indians know they're going to be branded the villains in this, but they're determined to end the Pakistani threat to their internal stability. CIA believes they intend to install their own government in Islamabad."

"Pretty drastic."

"Yes. But from India's point of view, this is just an extension of that they call the Indira Doctrine. They want a Pakistan that is strong enough to serve as a buffer between them and the Soviets . . . but that is too weak to challenge them directly. Maybe they think the only solution is to put their own people into power in Pakistan."

Magruder nodded. India had long presented the Indira Doctrine as an expression of national policy. New Delhi maintained the right to intervene in the internal affairs of any neighboring country if disorder threatened to cross India's national boundaries. With that sort of thinking, their invasion might seem justified. Both countries had been engaged in a sharp buildup of arms lately.

"But the Pakistanis have the bomb. What does that mean . . . that if India presses too hard, Pakistan incinerates New Delhi?"

"It's a possibility. If the Pakistanis get pushed hard enough, well, the CIA tells me they'll use it. Desperate people do desperate things. As soon as the Pakistanis start nuking Indian troops, of course, we can expect the Indians to retaliate. There's a very real danger that the Indians might even welcome a nuclear exchange—"

"Good God, Mr. President," Hall interrupted. "No one *wants* a nuclear war. . . ."

"Okay. Maybe 'welcome' is too strong a word," the President agreed. "But look at it this way. If Pakistan launches a nuclear first strike, the world is likely to forget that India was the aggressor, the one who started this war. Pakistan becomes the guy who nuked some Indian city. If it comes to an arms race, well, India can produce more warheads than the Pakistanis, and they can strike anything in the entire country, while Pakistan's reach is limited to the range of their F-16s, a few hundred miles or so."

"Three hundred forty miles," Magruder said, quoting automatically from memory. "Assuming round-trip, three-thousand-pound ordnance load, and no drop tanks." He hesitated. He still wasn't sure why the President had brought him here from the Pentagon to hear all of this . . . and the President's earlier words, about *needing* him, were still tugging at his curiosity. "So where does all of this leave us, Mr. President?"

"We're beefing up our military presence in the area, of course, for starters. I'm putting the 82nd Airborne and other rapid-deployment forces on immediate alert. Unfortunately, there's not a lot that ground-based forces can do in a situation like this, not until the UN can set up a multinational peacekeeping force. We're going to push for a UN resolution to force the two sides to back away. Disarm them if we have to."

"That could take time, Mr. President."

"Yes. And that's time we don't have. If things go nuclear over there . . ." The President shook his head. "It's going to be up to the Navy, at least at first. I'm redeploying fleet elements to the region, effective immediately. *Eisenhower* is in the Med and has just received orders to join them. So has *Nimitz*, off the coast of Spain."

"Too far, sir. They can't get there in two days."

The President closed his eyes. "Don't I know it. A week for the *Ike*. Maybe ten days for the *Nimitz*. In the meantime, well, *Jefferson* is the only one on the spot."

Magruder frowned. "Are you asking my advice, Mr. President? One carrier battle group . . . compared to what India has, that's not a very large force."

"It's damned thin, Tom," the President said. "But it's all I have right now."

"Where do I come into this, sir? I mean, I'm flattered that you called me, but—"

"Flattered, hell, Tom. That's not my style and you know it! For the next forty-eight to seventy-two hours, your old command is going to be the only goddamned thing I've got over there that might make the Indians and the Pakistanis back down or at least lose interest in each other! And you know the people in the CBG, know how they'll react, know how far I can push them." He looked at Magruder hard. "Tom, I need to ask something of you. It's the real reason I called you here today."

Magruder felt a surge of sudden excitement. He was getting his command back!

The President seemed to sense the question in Magruder's face and shook his head. "I'm sorry, Admiral," he said gently. "No. I can't put you back out there. If I start swapping my admirals around like chess pieces, it'll make a shambles out of our defense establishment."

"Bad for morale too," Magruder said, nodding. He understood, but . . .

"Exactly. No, what I need from you is your help. I'd like to appoint you as a special military advisor over here at the White House. You've commanded CBG-14's ships, their men. You know them. Know how they'll take the heat. I'll be dropping a lot of shit on them in the next couple of days, and I'd like your advice when I do it."

Magruder opened his mouth, but the words refused to come. How could he refuse such a request?

The President didn't seem to be phrasing it as a request in

any case. He was already reaching for a phone. "I'll give the word to have your things transferred over from the Fudge Factory," he said. "We're going to set you up with an office in the White House basement."

Magruder gave a slow, inward sigh. At least he was getting out of the Pentagon!

But he felt little in the way of joy or relief. His thoughts were already focused on ships and men ten thousand miles from the Oval Office.

They'd be facing long, long odds, and they'd be facing them alone.

# CHAPTER 7

**2010 hours, 24 March**
**Tomcat 201, over the Arabian Sea**

The message coming in over Tombstone's helmet radio was routine but carried with it an undertone of urgency.

"Blue Viper, Blue Viper, this is Victor Tango One-niner," the voice said, identifying itself as the tactical officer aboard an E-2C Hawkeye radar plane circling in the sky above Turban Station far to the west. "Identify intermittent bogie, bearing your position zero-six-niner, range one-five-zero."

"Copy, Victor Tango," Tombstone replied. Outside of his Tomcat's cockpit, the last traces of sunset had vanished. The only difference between up and down in the inky blackness was the dusting of stars overhead, brilliant at thirty thousand feet. The red, strobing pulse of Batman's anticollision lights was visible a quarter mile to starboard. "Coming to zero-six-niner."

"Got 'em, Tombstone," Dixie said over the Tomcat's intercom system. One of the ship's medical officers had rated the young RIO fit for flight status that morning. "God, they're on the deck and headed straight for the bird farm!"

Tombstone pictured the unfolding situation, like a complex and deadly game, the playing pieces scattered across a board hundreds of miles across. The bogies were coming out of Bombay, one hundred fifty miles to the northeast. A hundred miles southwest lay the *Jefferson.* Much closer, to the southeast, was the *Biddle,* still on ASW patrol at the northern fringes of the fleet.

And hanging in the night squarely between the approaching threat and the carrier were the two F-14s on BARCAP.

"Batman! You get all that?"

"Sure did, Boss. Lead the way."

"Okay, let's goose it," Tombstone said. "Going to buster." He pushed the throttle controls forward, letting the engines roar to full military power. His speed indicator climbed, passing five hundred knots . . . then six hundred. The fuselage shivered as the F-14 approached the speed of sound, the vibrations building and building until the Tomcat blasted past the sound barrier and into the smooth, silent sky beyond.

Batman paced him, the thunder of their passage trailing behind them.

**2014 hours, 24 March**
**IAF Jaguar 102, southwest of Bombay**

Colonel Jarnall Rajiv Singh studied the screen of his Ferranti Comed, a combined map and electronic display on the console before him. The screen was empty, the enemy target still hidden beyond the curve of the horizon.

But it would not be much longer now. The four aircraft of his command were in position to strike. They required only the final order from Bombay.

His plane was arguably the most modern and deadly attack aircraft in the inventory of the Indian air force, a SEPECAT Jaguar International. Originally a joint design by the British RAF and the French Armée de l'Air, the Jaguar International was license-built by HAL in India as a single-seat, all-weather attack aircraft. Slung beneath his wings were a pair of sleek, ship-killing AM.39 Exocet anti-ship missiles, with a range of almost fifty kilometers.

"Krait, this is Mountain," a voice in his headset informed him. "Mountain" was the mission HQ in Bombay. "Execute. Execute. Execute."

"Mountain, Krait," Singh replied. The excitement rose inside him, making the reply difficult. "Understood."

He shifted to the tactical channel. The other Jaguar pilots would have been listening in, but he had to make it official.

''Krait Attack, this is Krait Leader,'' he announced. ''Come to two-one-zero. The word is *execute*.''

The command thrilled in his blood, as the other pilots acknowledged. In unison, the four Indian Jaguars screamed toward the American targets at Mach 1.

**2015 hours, 24 March**
**Flag Plot, U.S.S. *Thomas Jefferson***

Admiral Vaughn looked up from the map. ''What is it?''

''This just in from VT Nineteen, sir.'' Captain Bersticer handed him a printout. ''Our BARCAP is closing on the bogies. CIC has ordered them to close and investigate.''

''What?'' Vaughn looked up, surprised. ''Why wasn't I consulted?''

Bersticer's eyebrows shifted upward. ''Standard procedure, Admiral. Those bogies are heading straight for—''

''Damn it, we have *explicit* orders from Washington not to take any action that could be interpreted as hostile!''

''Those bogies are closing at Mach 1, Admiral,'' Bersticer said quietly. ''How close do they have to get before—''

''Order the BARCAP to hold their position,'' Vaughn snapped. ''They are not, repeat, not to make any threatening moves toward those bogies.''

''Yes, sir.'' Bersticer looked worried.

Well, damn it, Vaughn thought, he was worried too. He clenched his fists in frustration. What would they say in Washington if an international incident was blamed on him? It was possible, even probable that the Indians were deploying as a direct response to the sinking of their submarine the day before. But was it an attack, or bluff? This was definitely a fuzzy gray area of conflict in the political arena that he wanted no part of.

*Politics* . . .

He thought again of Tom Magruder and suppressed another shudder.

**2016 hours, 24 March**
**Tomcat 201, over the Arabian Sea**

"The word is, 'hold position,'" Tombstone radioed over the tactical channel.

"Copy that," Batman replied. He sounded furious. "What in God's name are they playing at back there?"

"If I knew that, I'd be an admiral," Tombstone studied the bogies, repeated to his screen from Dixie's console. Four of them, fading in and out as they arrowed toward the BARCAP aircraft. They were pressing the very limits of the Tomcat's radar. "Tell you what, Batman. Break high and right. Let's see if we can clear up the picture some."

"Roger that. We're outta here."

Batman's aircraft stood on its wing for an instant, and then it was gone, vanished into the darkness. By separating the two aircraft they could get a clearer radar picture of the oncoming bogies.

Minutes passed. The four unidentified radar targets continued to close, a diamond-shaped cluster of four . . .

No, *eight* points of light. Four more aircraft had been trailing the first four, masked by their radar shadow!

"Victor Tango One-niner, this is Blue Viper Leader," he called. "Victor Tango One-niner, come in, please. Over."

After a static-filled moment, the voice of the distant Hawkeye's tactical officer came on the line. "This is Victor Tango One-niner. Go ahead, Viper Leader."

"Victor Tango, we have eight, repeat, *eight* bogies inbound, bearing zero-six-niner. Range nine-two, speed seven-nine-oh knots."

"Affirmative, Blue Viper. We copy two groups, designation Alpha and Bravo."

"Roger, Victor Tango. Request weapons free. Repeat, request weapons free."

"Blue Viper, Victor Tango One-niner. Wait one."

Tombstone lightly fingered the firing trigger on his stick. The combat load for each Tomcat on tonight's CAP consisted of two AIM-9M Sidewinders, two AIM-7M Sparrows, and four of the deadly, long-ranged AIM-54-C Phoenix air-to-air missiles. With the Phoenix they could hit a target up to one hundred twenty miles away.

His heart pounded in his chest. The current rules of engagement called for shooting back only if American planes or ships were fired upon, and only after confirmation from *Jefferson*'s CIC. But eight high-performance aircraft were on a beeline toward the fleet. No way could they ignore such a threat.

The gloved fingers of his left hand drummed against his thigh. What was the delay? More indecision? Surely the enemy's intentions were more than clear!

"Victor Tango, Blue Viper. How about that release, over?"

And still the wait dragged on.

**2017 hours, 24 March**
**CIC, U.S.S. *Thomas Jefferson***

Admiral Vaughn had hurried down to the carrier's Combat Information Center, the better to stay on top of events that were unfolding with bewildering speed.

"From our Hawkeye, Admiral," Commander Barnes, the CIC officer, said. He stood behind one of the radar consoles, the padded cup of a radio headset pressed over his right ear. "BARCAP requests weapons free."

"We don't know they're going to attack," Vaughn said. He regretted the words as soon as he said them. Barnes's mouth twisted in an unpleasant quirk, and several of the other officers in the room, including his own aides, exchanged dark glances.

"Begging the admiral's pardon," Captain Bersticer said. "But we sure as hell don't have any reason to think they're friendly!"

"Comm!" Vaughn snapped. "Can you contact those aircraft?"

"We can try, sir," an enlisted rating sitting at one of the consoles said.

"Damn it, Admiral," Barnes said. "There's no *time* . . . !"

"Warn them off." It was all happening too fast. The best guess was that the incoming bogies were reconnaissance aircraft. How would this be interpreted by Washington?

Maybe it would be better to close with the bogies. Eight of

them sounded like something more than a reconnaissance flight.

"Okay," he said, deciding. "Order the CAP to close for a visual ID. Do you have Washington on the satellite yet?"

"Not yet, sir."

"Well, get on it! Give them an update on our situation and request instructions."

"Aye, sir." Vaughn didn't like the edge in the enlisted man's voice.

CIC was air-conditioned, often to the point where it was too cool for the admiral's comfort. He was sweating now, though. He reached up to loosen the collar of his khaki shirt. What they needed most now was *time,* but it didn't look as though they would have that luxury.

Not with the bogies closing at Mach 1.2.

**2018 hours, 24 March**
**IAF Fulcrum 401**

Lieutenant Colonel Munir Ramadutta watched the two bogies that had just appeared on his radar screen, well beyond the tight knot of Jaguars his flight was escorting. American CAP aircraft, certainly, probably Tomcats.

He felt a shiver of anticipation. Only the day before, his Fulcrum squadron had been stationed at Jamnagar, escorting bombing strikes against Pakistan from the Kathiawar Peninsula. The transfer to Kurla had been completely unexpected. The orders to escort a strike against American ships off the coast had been more unexpected yet.

Long ago, Ramadutta had decided that it never paid to question the decisions of the politicians who set the country's course. America could prove to be a formidable foe in war, but New Delhi must have decided that it was necessary to take them on, even while full-scale war was unfolding along the Radcliffe Line.

There were rumors of an Indian sub sunk by the Americans. He wondered if they were true.

"Mountain, this is Krait Cover Leader. Two contacts, probably enemy fighters."

"Roger, Krait Cover. Proceed with intercept. Engage and destroy."

That was it, then. "Krait Cover, this is Leader," he said. "Come to two-five-eight and deploy, wing-and-wing. We're going in."

Breaking away from the Jaguars, the four Fulcrums thundered into the night.

**2019 hours, 24 March**
**Tomcat 201**

The aircraft, two Tomcats and four MiG-29 Fulcrums, closed with each other in the darkness. As Tombstone watched the blips drifting across his VDI, he felt again the eerie sense of unreality that came with engaging an enemy he could not see directly. The night outside the cockpit seemed deceptively clear and quiet.

"Okay, Batman," Tombstone said. "Just like a football play. Bravo's the offensive line, Alpha's their quarterback. We punch past Bravo and go for the guy with the ball."

"You think the fighters'll let us go through?"

"I guess that's what we're here to find out, isn't it?"

Was he reading the enemy formation right? Alpha had to be attack planes, probably Jaguars. Bravo would be MiGs, running interference for the ship hunters.

And somehow, he and Batman had to get to the Jaguars before they could launch their Exocets.

Still invisible to one another, save as glowing pinpoints of light, the two groups of fighters grew closer . . . merged . . .

"Stoney!" Dixie called over the ICS. "Alpha's changing course too! New heading one-seven-niner . . . it's the *Biddle*! They're lining up for an attack on the *Biddle*!"

Clever. Tombstone could trace the tactics in his mind. Four attack aircraft, four fighters, all dead on course for the carrier. The carrier's BARCAP puts itself between them and the carrier, and the fighters break off and crowd the Tomcats to keep them busy. Meanwhile, the attack flight changes course toward another target—less tempting but much closer—the Perry-class frigate U.S.S. *Biddle*.

"Dixie! What's the range of Alpha to the *Biddle*?"

"Coming down to . . . three-five miles, Stoney."

Almost within Exocet range. *Too close!* "That's it, Dixie! We're not going to screw around with these guys. Select Phoenix, target Alpha. Batman! You copy?"

"Copy, Tombstone. Weapons hot."

"Maintain combat spread. Dixie, inform Homeplate that we are engaging Alpha." He pressed the throttle controls forward to full military power, then clicked past the detents into Zone One afterburner.

**2019 hours, 24 March**
**IAF Fulcrum 401**

Lieutenant Colonel Ramadutta heard the warbling tone in his headset which meant the Americans had just activated their powerful AWG-9 radar. That could mean only one thing, that the Tomcats were preparing to fire on the Jaguars, now fifty kilometers behind his flight and preparing to launch on the American frigate.

His orders were concise and explicit, to protect the Jaguars at any cost. Swiftly he armed one of his deadly Apex radar homers, listening for the warning buzz of target acquisition. *There!*

"Mountain, this is Krait Cover Leader. *Engaging!*"

His finger closed on the trigger and the missile leaped away from his aircraft, trailing white flame. An instant later, his wingman fired a second Apex.

Battle was joined. . . .

**2019 hours, 24 March**
**Tomcat 201**

"Homeplate, Homeplate, we are under attack!" Tombstone fought the vibration in his Tomcat as he jinked high and left. "Repeat, BARCAP One under attack!"

"Two missiles, range four miles!" his RIO called. "Can't shake 'em!"

Tombstone saw the blips closing on his own VDI, saw the rapid pulse of the console missile-warning light. He rammed the throttles forward, sending the Tomcat's heavy engines into Zone Five as he turned to face the slightly nearer of the two threats.

"Three miles! Two . . . !"

"Hit the chaff!" He felt the chaff canisters firing, then hauled the Tomcat back until it was standing on its tail. Stars wheeled across the sky through Tombstone's HUD, unspeakably clear and close as the F-14 climbed past thirty thousand feet.

"We lost one!" Dixie yelled. His excitement was shrill, exuberant. "Number two climbing to meet us. Range three miles!"

Tombstone dragged the stick over and back, flipping the Tomcat onto its back, then righting it with a brutal half-twist. As the nose came up, his HUD targeting diamond tagged the oncoming enemy fighter that had fired the second Apex. He thumbed the switch on his stick. There was no time now for confirmation. Only *survival* . . .

"Going for Sidewinder!" The HUD display showed target lock.

"Gotcha!" He squeezed the trigger and the Sidewinder dropped from its rail, trailing flame into the darkness. "Fox two! Fox two!"

Tombstone pulled the Tomcat into a snap roll that twisted it toward the sea. At the last moment, he saw the exhaust of the oncoming missile, an evil-looking pinprick of yellow light arcing toward him through the night.

"He's breaking! Tombstone! He's breaking!" Dixie's cry brought a relief-driven gust of air from Tombstone's lungs. By firing a Sidewinder at the other pilot, he'd forced his opponent to turn, breaking the MiG's radar lock on the Tomcat. And when the approaching missile lost its semi-active guidance lock . . .

"Second missile missed!" Dixie called. "God *damn,* Tombstone! You know how to push it to the edge!"

A moment later, a flash of white light pulsed against the night. The Sidewinder had found its target.

"Grand slam!" Dixie called. "Victor Tango, splash one! Splash one!"

Only then did Tombstone realize that he'd technically violated the ROEs. He'd been fired at, but he'd not received confirmation from *Jefferson* for weapons release.

The hell with it, Tombstone thought. It's time to turn and burn. . . .

**2020 hours, 24 March**
**CIC, U.S.S. *Thomas Jefferson***

Vaughn felt cold . . . *cold* . . . with the icy knowledge that events were now totally beyond his control. When that Tomcat pilot fired without waiting for a weapons-free confirmation, he'd crossed a boundary for the whole damned battle group.

He swallowed, working to stay calm, working to control the gnawing rasp in his stomach. This mess wasn't his fault. But would Washington understand that?

"What's going on?" he demanded. "Damn it, who fired first?"

"Hard to make out, sir," an enlisted rating said. He was relaying radio messages and radar scans transmitted through the circling Hawkeye. The air battle was taking place at the very limit of the E-2C's range, and information was fragmentary, the picture fuzzy. Confused bursts of noise and bits of conversation came over the loudspeaker mounted high on CICs bulkhead, allowing the tense officers and men standing in the red-lit room to listen in on the unfolding fight.

*"Splash one! Splash one!"*

The men in CIC broke into a ragged cheer at that. Vaughn scowled. Despite all he'd been able to do, a dogfight had begun. Transfixed, he stared at the radar feed from the airborne Hawkeye. There was little to be seen, the smear of clouds associated with a weather front to the east, and a tangle of slow-moving blips where the dogfight was taking place between Bombay and the convoy.

"If I may suggest, Admiral," Barnes said. "We should get some more guns into the area, fast. Before the enemy gets any closer."

"We have two more F-14s on BARCAP east of the carrier," Marusko pointed out. "And two more on Alert Five. We've got an honest-to-God furball up there, and our boys are going to need some help."

So there it was. The decision that, either way, would be the mistake the buzzards in Washington would pounce on, once they caught the scent of blood. The order he was about to give might well be the crowning achievement of his career . . . or the end of it.

But the decision had to be made. ''Order the BARCAP to engage,'' he said. ''And launch the Alert Five. Confirm weapons release.''

If he'd made a wrong choice he'd end up like Tom Magruder, on the beach and under a cloud. He didn't like the feeling.

# CHAPTER 8

**2019 hours, 24 March**
**Tomcat 201**

"Tally-ho!" Tombstone yelled, using the age-old call that meant the quarry was in sight. He could see the other plane as a starlit shape approaching in the darkness, marked by twin pencils of flame as the other pilot kicked in his afterburners. "He's climbing for us."

"Hot damn!" Dixie replied. "We're goin' head-to-head!"

"AIM-9." At close range, a Sidewinder launch gave them their best shot.

"What's he flying anyway?"

"Can't tell," Tombstone said. "It's damned hot, though. Look at him jink!"

Tombstone watched the bandit's approach narrowly as he cut his engine back to eighty percent. Standard tactical doctrine for ACM—Air Combat Maneuvers—called for passing an opponent as closely as possible when meeting him head-on, not giving him room to turn and latch onto your tail.

The Indian pilot was good, he thought. Way *too* good for Tombstone's peace of mind. By jinking his aircraft up, down, and sideways during the approach, he was making it impossible for Tombstone to calculate how much leeway to give him. The darkness didn't help. The other plane was almost invisible . . . and there was no way to judge distance by eyeball alone.

"Two thousand," Dixie warned.

Tombstone felt himself tense as the other plane loomed close. . . .

**2020 hours, 24 March**
**IAF Fulcrum 401**

Munir Ramadutta watched the oncoming aircraft swell in his Fulcrum's HUD. This American was good . . . but he'd expected no less. U.S. Navy aviators had a worldwide reputation independent of the militant posturings of their government.

He thumbed the switch arming his short-range AA-8 Aphid missiles. He was at a sharp disadvantage for close-in combat. The Aphid was not an all-aspect missile, meaning it had to "see" the enemy's engine exhaust in order to achieve target lock.

In any case, he was too close to the American now, approaching too quickly to allow any time for thought or action. He would pass the Tomcat close on his left, then pull a half-loop-and-roll to get on the enemy's tail.

The American drew still closer . . .

**2020 hours, 24 March**
**Tomcat 201**

. . . and then the other plane was past, flashing close by the Tomcat at supersonic speed. Tombstone immediately pulled into a vertical climb and went to Zone Five burner, hoping to do a half-loop-and-roll that would drop him on the other pilot's six, squarely behind him and a mile to the rear.

"Damn it, Stoney! *Watch out!*"

Tombstone yanked his head back at the warning, looking through the top of his canopy. The other plane was *there,* also climbing, cockpit-to-cockpit with the Tomcat.

It happened so quickly that he didn't have time to react to the icy fear that struck him in that instant. The other plane was eerily illuminated by stars and the glow from Tombstone's own afterburners, and so close that he could make out the other pilot's helmeted shape in the light of his cockpit instrumentation, could see the bold numerals 401 on the other plane's nose.

The other aircraft was close enough he could clearly identify it as a MiG-29, a Fulcrum, though his first impression had been that the nimble, twin-tailed aircraft was an American F/A-18 Hornet. The Indian pilot's skill had saved them both. He'd been pulling the identical maneuver as Tombstone, but at the last moment had recognized the danger and avoided a midair collision. For perhaps two seconds, the fighters climbed, canopy to canopy, a scant ten meters apart, aimed at the stars . . . and then the Indian MiG rolled left and vanished into the darkness.

Tombstone reacted instantly, breaking right. He was now less interested in getting on the Indian MiG's tail than he was in disengaging. A wrong move in the darkness at such close quarters would end in fiery disaster. ACM was especially hard when you couldn't pick up visual clues about the other pilot's attitude, speed, angle of attack, or energy state.

"Blue Viper, Blue Viper, this is Victor Tango One-niner." The Hawkeye's call came over Tombstone's headset as he started angling back toward the Indian Jaguars.

"Victor Tango, this is Viper Leader. Go ahead."

"Blue Viper, you've got new targets entering your area. Be advised they are friendly, repeat, friendly. Over."

"Hot damn," Batman said. "Cavalry to the rescue!"

Tombstone glanced at his VDI. He saw the new blips . . . and apparently the MiGs had seen them as well. They were turning, making for the mainland at high speed.

Which left the Indian Jaguars, dead ahead and in the clear, range thirty miles.

**2021 hours, 24 March**
**IAF Jaguar 102**

Colonel Singh checked his radio frequency. "Mountain, this is Krait Attack, inbound. Estimate range now sixty-five kilometers. Beginning attack run."

He glanced left and right at the other Jaguars in his flight, faintly visible on either side of his aircraft as they skimmed the black ocean toward the southwest. The Exocet missiles they carried were just within range of the target now clearly painted on his radar screen, dead ahead.

"Krait Leader to all Kraits," he said over the tactical frequency. "Initiate targeting procedure. Gyros up now."

They would launch in thirty seconds.

**2020 hours, 24 March**
**Tomcat 201**

"Victor Tango, this is Blue Viper," Tombstone said. "We've got four Alpha bandits lined up in our sights. Commencing Phoenix run."

"We copy, Viper Leader," the Hawkeye tactical officer replied. "Message from Homeplate. Green light. You're go for missile release."

"About damned time," Tombstone muttered. He didn't even stop to think whether the missile-release order referred to the attack planes ahead or his earlier request to fire on the Indian MiGs.

Time enough to sort that out later. "Copy that, Victor Tango." Tombstone reached out and flipped a switch on his console. "Master arming switch on." He opened the ICS. "Dixie? How about a solution on those bogies."

"Got it, Tombstone. We've got four targets, range now three-oh nautical miles. On track-and-scan. Acquisition. AWG-9 locked in. We're hot."

"Phoenix armed and hot," he confirmed. He flipped the target-designate switch with his left hand, watching the computer-generated graphics on his Vertical Display Indicator. "Okay, Dixie. Punch it!"

"Fox three!" Dixie announced. The Tomcat bumped as the heavy missile cleared and ignited. "Missile away!"

"Line up another one, Dixie."

"Set! Acquisition! Locked and hot!"

"Punch it!"

"Fox three! Fox three!" The second Phoenix roared into the night.

**2120 hours, 24 March**
**IAF Jaguar 102**

"Krait Attack, Krait Attack, this is Mountain! Be advised we have small, high-speed targets, bearing two-seven-three your position on intercept course."

Singh searched the sky through his cockpit. He could see nothing around his aircraft but stars partly blocked by a line of clouds behind him and the acquisition lights of the other Jaguars of his flight.

"Mountain, Krait Attack Leader. I don't see—"

Suddenly, a warning tone sounded in his headset. "Mountain, this is Krait Leader! We have missile-lock warning! Repeat, missile-lock warning. Someone is tracking us!"

"Krait Attack, we read two long-range air-to-air missiles. Range one-zero! Evade! Evade!"

"Krait Flight!" Singh snapped. "Do not evade! Maintain course . . . *fire!*"

He thumbed the release switch. There was a two-second pause. Then his Jaguar leapt skyward. Exocet weighed 660 kilos—well over 1,400 pounds—and he had his hands full for a moment battling to control his aircraft as the weapon dropped clear.

The missile's engine kicked in as its autopilot brought it down to an altitude of fifteen meters above the wave tops. Cruise speed was just under Mach 1.

At that speed it would reach its target in a little less than three minutes.

**2120 hours, 24 March**
**Tomcat 201**

"Batman!" Tombstone called. "Get in the game!"

The VDI showed the other Tomcat five miles to the west. "We're in! Looks like the bad guy CAP decided to get out of Dodge!"

"Rog." Tombstone said. "Let's splash these attack planes before they—"

"Tombstone!" Dixie interrupted. "Targets scattering. I read six . . . no, ten bogies! *Ten bogies!*"

*"Shit!"* His VDI was set to repeat the tactical data from his RIO's screen. He could see the closed-grouped radar targets separating now, just beyond the computer graphic representations of the two Phoenix missiles already on the way. The bandits were launching on the *Biddle*.

Tombstone had two AIM-59s left, and Batman had four. The Indians were launching their Exocets, and there just weren't enough Phoenix missiles to go around.

**2023 hours, 24 March**
**IAF Jaguar 102**

The maddening tone of missile lock continued to sound in Singh's ears as he pulled the stick to the left. He looked again. Still nothing . . .

A pinpoint flare of light came out of nowhere, twisting in a sharp, left-hand corkscrew as it bore down on Lieutenant Colonel Nijhawan's Jaguar from the west.

"Himmat!" Singh shouted. "Watch—"

Orange flame fireballed against the night. For an instant, the glare illuminated the front half of his friend's aircraft and one shattered wing as the Jaguar crumpled, folding up on itself as though it were a balsa-wood model crushed by a child's hand.

The second explosion came a pair of heartbeats later, blasting the left wing from Krait Four before the flare of the first explosion had faded away. Singh glimpsed a secondary flash as the pilot rocketed into the night on his ejection seat.

Colonel Singh had first learned fighter combat while attending a special air combat training school for foreign pilots at Frunze, in the Soviet Union. Later, he'd flown with the RAF while learning to handle the SEPECAT Jaguar. He was one of the best pilots in the IAF, but this was beginning to feel more like target practice than combat . . . with his squadron as the targets.

"All aircraft, launch and return to base!"

The missile-threat warning was off. Perhaps there had been two, and only two missiles. If they had a few more seconds . . .

**2023 hours, 24 March**
**Tomcat 201**

"Victor Tango One-niner, this is Viper Leader," Tombstone radioed. "We have air-to-surface launch . . . probable Exocet. Six ASMs . . ." Two more blips appeared, moving quickly behind the others. The two surviving Indian planes had released at maximum range, then turned away. "Make it eight ASMs in the air, targeting *Biddle*."

"Confirmed, Viper Leader," the Hawkeye replied. "We have them. Protect *Biddle*. Target priority is Exocet launch."

Tombstone had already arrived at the same conclusion. Wings laid back along its flanks, Tombstone's F-14 howled along an intercept course. At his instructions, Dixie had already targeted the lead of two closely spaced missiles. The Tomcat's AWG-9 had what is known as "look-down/shoot-down" capability, meaning it could track objects below the F-14, moving only a few feet above the water. At a range of ten nautical miles, Dixie announced a target lock and stabbed the launch button. Their last Phoenix dropped clear, then ignited, rocketing into the darkness on a vivid comet tail of flame. Tombstone watched the graphics on his VDI, counting off the seconds as the AIM-54 closed the gap on the lead Exocet. Ten seconds after launch, the two blips merged. . . .

"Hit!" he called.

"Target destroyed!" Dixie confirmed. "Holy . . . Second target gone! We nailed 'em, two for one!"

The twin detonation of almost five hundred pounds of high explosives on the two missiles a few feet above the water had created a terrific shock wave. The second Exocet had flown into the blast and either been torn apart or driven into the sea.

"Two-one-six, fox three!" Batman's familiar voice sounded over Tombstone's headset. "Don't be greedy, Stoney. Save some for us! Fox three!"

Tombstone's VDI was becoming a confused tangle of targeting symbols and radar returns. He felt a sinking sensation as he watched the wave of missiles crawling across the screen. "Viper Leader is dry." With no more Phoenix missiles slung under his Tomcat's belly, there was little more he could do to halt the storm.

"Viper Two," Batman added. "Down two. Firing two. Fox three! Fox three!"

Batman's last two Phoenix missiles joined the clutter of radar blips. Four more incoming Exocets died.

Two Exocets remained, vaulting the last small gap to the American frigate at the speed of sound.

**2024 hours, 24 March**
**U.S.S. *Biddle***

The terrifying aspect of modern naval warfare is its sheer speed. In 1805, when Admiral Nelson faced the Franco-Spanish fleet at Trafalgar, the enemy had been in sight for hours by the time they finally opened fire; Nelson could have taken the better part of an afternoon deciding on tactics or changing his plans had he wanted to.

Modern warfare did not give the combatants that kind of luxury. Blows were exchanged, casualties taken, within a space of minutes, sometimes of seconds.

*Biddle*'s Close-in Weapons System, or CIWS for short, commonly pronounced "sea-whiz," housed its tracking radar, six-barreled Gatling gun, magazine, and control electronics inside a prominent, white-painted silo fifteen feet high; hence, its other popular nickname, "R2D2." The weapon, also called Phalanx, was mounted aft on Perry-class frigates, high atop their helicopter hangars and overlooking the helo pad on the fantail. As soon as the Indian Jaguars had launched, Captain Farrel had immediately ordered the ship turned away from the oncoming missiles in order to give the CIWS an unobstructed view of the targets.

The only problem was, Phalanx had been designed as a last-ditch, close-defense weapon, its effective range limited to about twenty-one hundred meters, less than a mile and a half.

An Exocet could cover that distance in something like seven seconds.

The missiles came in from *Biddle*'s stern, ten feet above the water. The heavy thump of her chaff launchers sounded like cannonfire as they attempted to divert the deadly Exocets. On the frigate's hangar, the Phalanx tower slewed about sharply on its axis, the six-barreled cannon swinging into line as the target came into range.

The barrels spun, rotating over one another like eggbeater blades, accompanied with a short, sharp, buzzsaw shriek. The flare of light from the muzzle flash lit up *Biddle*'s afterdeck like a stream of liquid fire.

"Firing phasers!" one sailor yelled, shouting above the screaming weapon, his hands pressed against his ears.

Phalanx fired depleted-uranium rounds, spin-stabilized slivers manufactured from the waste product of various nuclear programs. Neither explosive nor radioactive, each round was two and a half times heavier than steel, 12.75 millimeters thick, and was hurled from the gun at a velocity of 1000 feet per second. With a fire rate of fifty rounds per *second,* the CIWS was capable of dropping what was in effect a solid wall squarely in a missile's path. The Phalanx's J-band pulse-doppler radar simultaneously tracked target and projectiles, correcting the aim for each brief burst.

The CIWS fired again, corrected, then fired once more. A blossom of living light erupted in the darkness of the frigate's starboard side, illuminating the ink-black sea. The Phalanx Gatling slewed again, its computer tracking the second target. Again, the shriek like a living thing . . . and a second flash lit up the night.

Total engagement time: 5.2 seconds.

And *Biddle* would survive to fight again.

**2209 hours, 24 March**
**Tomcat 201**

"Tomcat Two-oh-one," the voice in Tombstone's headset intoned. "You're clear for approach. Wind fifteen to eighteen at zero-four-five. Charlie now."

"Roger, Homeplate," Tombstone said, acknowledging the call to come in for his trap. He was tired. The weight of his flight helmet seemed intolerable, and the inside of his pressure suit was clammy with old sweat and fatigue.

They'd been summoned back to the carrier almost as soon as it was clear that the IAF aircraft were on the run. The

Americans had been the clear victors in that nighttime dogfight, with at least four kills to their credit and no losses. It had been a close-run thing, however. One of the Indian MiG pilots had been a real pro, and only the rapid approach of more Tomcats had convinced the guy to break off and run for home.

Tombstone found himself wondering who that pilot he'd briefly seen was . . . where he lived, what he thought of the orders that had sent him against the U.S. battle group. That was never a particularly healthy thing to do, not when your life or the lives of others in your squadron might depend on your shooting that other pilot out of the sky, but Tombstone had always found it difficult to think of the enemy as unmanned drones, as lifeless targets to be racked up and taken down.

His thoughts complemented his mood. He'd become involved in a savage dogfight in pitch darkness, guided only by the impersonal flickers of light on his radar screen and the tersely coded guidance of his computer. With that one terrifying exception he'd not even *seen* the other aircraft in the battle, including the ones he'd chalked up as kills.

Well, such questions were pointless anyway. Tombstone kept his eyes on his instrument displays, especially his VDI where the ILS needles were guiding him through the night toward *Jefferson*'s deck. The carrier was completely invisible in the darkness, an unseen speck of life somewhere ahead in that black ocean. Of all maneuvers performed by Navy aviators, traps on a carrier's steel deck at night were unquestionably the most disliked, the most feared. According to the flight surgeons keeping records of such things, a night trap tended to elevate heartbeat, respiration, and blood pressure more than a dogfight.

Tombstone, though, was past caring. The dogfight had left him drained, his reactions as automatic as the navigational guidance information from his Instrument Landing System. They had rendezvoused with a tanker for air-to-air refueling after the battle, and he'd gone through the motions like a machine, had not even remembered the problems he'd had in a similar maneuver . . . had it only been yesterday?

"Two-oh-one," Lieutenant Commander Ted "Burner" Craig, Viper Squadron's LSO, called. "We have you at three miles out, altitude one-four-double-oh. Looking good."

"Rog."

"Hey, Skipper?" Dixie said over the ICS. "You see the bird farm yet? I can't see diddly in this soup."

"No sweat," Tombstone replied. "We're almost in."

But he couldn't see the ship either. During the past hour, a thick layer of clouds had moved in from the northeast, as though the Indian subcontinent itself were conspiring to drive the American ships and planes from her shores. The wind was picking up as well. He imagined that *Jefferson* would be a bit lively with a fresh breeze blowing across her flight deck.

And then the Tomcat dropped through the cloud deck and Tombstone saw the carrier's lights. Perspective during a night trap was always a curious and stomach-twisting thing. The flight deck's center line was lit up, and a vertical strip of lights hanging off *Jefferson*'s roundoff provided a clue to the vessel's three-dimensional orientation. From the sky, the lights seemed no brighter than the stars overhead.

"Two-oh-one," sounded in his ears. "Call the ball."

It was time to stop flying the needles and bring his ship in. Tombstone glanced at the meatball, saw that he was a little low, and corrected automatically. "Tomcat Two-oh-one, ball," he said. "Four point two."

The F-14 slid down out of the sky, the nearly black mass of the carrier deck expanding to meet it. At the last moment, Tombstone saw the green cut lights go on by the ball, the nighttime signal that he was clear to land. There was a momentary illusion that he was flying into a hole outlined by lights . . . that the deck was winging up into a vertical wall dead ahead. Then the Tomcat slammed into the deck at one hundred thirty knots, the arrestor hook snagging the number-three wire in a perfect night trap as Tombstone first rammed the throttles forward, then brought them back to idle.

"That's an OK," Tombstone heard the LSO say over the net. "Two-oh-one down."

Ahead of the Tomcat, deck crewmen moved in nearly total darkness, their hand signals revealed by colored light wands eerily visible suspended against the black. Carefully, Tombstone followed a pair of wagging yellow wands across the flight deck.

"Commander Magruder, this is the Boss," Dick Wheeler's voice said over the radio. "CAG wants a word with you as soon as you unstrap your turkey.'' *Turkey* was popular carrier slang for the Tomcat.

''Copy that,'' Tombstone replied. He glanced up toward the rounded, glassed-in protrusion from high up on the island, Pri-Fly, where the Air Boss reigned supreme.

There was no sense asking the man further questions, for he'd be concentrating already on Batman's 216 bird, due in forty seconds behind Tombstone's. He was expecting to be debriefed, certainly. Aviators were always grilled after a combat engagement. But this sounded like something more.

Perhaps, Tombstone thought, the real fight was still to come.

# CHAPTER 9

**2258 hours, 24 March**
**CAG's office, U.S.S. *Thomas Jefferson***

"Off the line!" The words struck Tombstone like a smash to the solar plexus. "God, CAG! You're putting me in hack! What did I do?"

CAG Marusko leaned forward in his swivel chair, hands spread helplessly on the desk in front of him. "I don't make 'em, Stoney. I just read 'em. The word I got was that you're off the flight line until they can pull a full investigation of the battle. There . . . may be some problem with your interpretation of the ROEs. *May* be, I said."

Tombstone knew that *they* meant Admiral Vaughn. "Court-martial?"

"I don't think it'll come to that, Stoney."

It was very quiet in the office. Despite the fact that each department in a supercarrier was manned and fully operational around the clock, it was always quieter in the admin and other office spaces during the late hours. Indeed, Tombstone knew that many men went back to their offices in the evening to read, to strum guitars, or just to be alone and escape the crowding and noise of their quarters. For a long moment, the only sounds Tombstone heard were the whir from the air vent high up on the bulkhead and the never-ceasing, usually forgotten throb of the ship's engines through the deck.

Court-martial. Tombstone thought back to the chain of decisions he'd made that night over the ocean and knew that there was nothing he would change now. But he'd also been in the Navy long enough to know that the wisdom of any decision or order can be picked apart by some higher authority.

"I'm assigning you to Air Ops, Stoney," Marusko said, breaking the silence. "We're getting some new aviators in tomorrow, and we'll need some experienced hands looking over their shoulders up in CATCC."

There were always several aviators assigned to the Carrier Air Traffic Control Center. Sometimes they could read impressions or emotions in a squadron mate's words as they came in over the speaker that the men manning the consoles would miss. More often than not, though, the Air Ops watch standers were Me Jo types, the ensigns and newer lieutenants jokingly referred to as marginally effective junior officers. By watching operations in CATCC and Ops, new flight officers could get the feel of the electronic network that would be backing them up once they were in the air.

"So I'm a Me Jo now, huh?" Tombstone felt the growing anger, tried to keep it out of his voice . . . and failed. "Do they trust me with that much responsibility?"

"Getting a damned attitude isn't going to help, Stoney," CAG said. "We're both stuck with this, and there's not a thing we can do about it. Not now anyway."

Tombstone looked around the tiny room. It was cluttered with bits and pieces of Steve Marusko's life: a photograph of his family, a plastic model from the ship's store of an F/A-18 Hornet, books from the ship's library. Tacked to a bulletin board was a crudely rendered crayon drawing of an aircraft carrier with huge stars scrawled on the wings of each misshapen airplane. As much as he wanted to lash out at someone, Tombstone found it impossible to be angry at CAG. The decision had not been his.

"Right, CAG." He tried to keep the bitterness from his voice. "I'll accept this as a paid vacation."

"That's the stuff. Now haul ass out of here."

As Tombstone stepped into the deserted passageway outside CAG's office, he wondered if his getting grounded might not actually be a twisted kind of blessing. It would give him a chance to think about his role as a career fighter pilot, about his decision to quit the Navy.

He glanced at his watch. He could still get a bite to eat at the Dirty Shirt Mess. He turned and started down the passageway, pacing his steps to the knee-knockers that interrupted its endlessly dwindling perspective.

How much did he *really* love carrier flying? These next few days might tell him.

**1315 hours EST (2345 hours India time), 24 March**
**Oval Office, the White House, Washington, D.C.**

"Thank you for coming, Admiral." The President gestured to the upholstered chair in front of the desk. "Please, have a seat." The Oval Office was brilliantly lit by the early afternoon light streaming through the Rose Garden window.

"Thank you, Mr. President." Admiral Magruder took the offered chair and watched the man behind the desk with a guarded expression. George Hall, who had brought him from his new basement office, had told him nothing about the reason for the summons. The White House Chief of Staff took a seat across the room but said nothing. Something was bothering Hall, but Magruder didn't know what.

"Things are hotting up over there," the President said. He looked drawn and tired, as though he'd been up the entire night before. Magruder noticed that a large map of western India had been mounted on an easel set up in front of the Oval Office's north wall. There were a number of new marks and notations off the coast near Bombay, and a heavy red line threading south through the Red Sea, then turning sharply toward the northeast, bearing on Turban Station. From where he sat, Magruder could not make out the cryptic notations next to the line.

The President cleared his throat. "Tom, as usual, this is all confidential."

"Of course, sir."

"Three hours ago, the *Jefferson* battle group was attacked off Bombay. It seems evident that the Indians were trying to punish us for sinking their sub by launching a strike at *Biddle,* the frigate involved in that incident. It was also intended as a clear warning. An ultimatum, if you will." The President swiveled his chair until he was facing the Rose Garden window. He was silent for a long moment. Magruder waited.

"The Indian ambassador was in here again this morning,"

the President said at last. "They're pushing their version of the IOZP, and they want us to comply. Now."

The tangle of international politics that laid conflicting claims to the various oceans, straits, and sea lanes of the world was a basic part of every admiral's formal education. The Indian Ocean Zone of Peace concept had been presented to the UN by Sri Lanka—at India's urging—in the early seventies. It called for the exclusion of all extra-regional powers from the Indian Ocean, a measure aimed principally at the United States, the Soviet Union, and Great Britain.

Most of the nations around the Indian Ocean basin supported the IOZP, though the usual interpretation called for a reduction of *all* naval forces in the region, including India's. But of all of the regional maritime powers, India had by far the most powerful navy and was the country best able to project her military power from Bombay to the Cape of Good Hope, from the Gulf of Oman to the west coast of Australia.

India was determined to become a truly global power by the twenty-first century. Her detonation of a nuclear device in 1974, her launch of communications and military satellites, her race to build up her air force, army, and navy had all been carried out with that single goal in mind.

By comparison, Great Britain had largely dismantled her presence in the Indian Ocean during the seventies, leaving her base at Diego Garcia to the Americans. Australia, once a significant naval power in the region, had largely turned her back on the sea. The Labor Party government elected in 1983 had stricken Australia's one carrier, the *Melbourne,* canceled the construction of another, and transferred all fixed-wing naval assets to the RAAF. By the early nineties, Australia's entire navy consisted of six submarines, three U.S.-built guided-missile destroyers launched in the early sixties, and ten frigates, plus a handful of coastal patrol boats, mine-warfare ships, and survey vessels.

If India succeeded in excluding outside forces from the region, she would be the logical nation to fill the power vacuum.

And that brought New Delhi squarely into conflict with the United States.

Freedom of the seas, free access to international waters.

Those principles had always been high among the missions tasked to the U.S. Navy. More than that, though, defense of the West's sea lanes from the Persian Gulf to the rest of the world lay almost entirely with the U.S. The tanker routes from the Gulf were vital to the U.S., to Europe, to Japan, and no Western policymaker was ready to concede their control—or the responsibility for their defense—to New Delhi.

Magruder understood what the President was saying. The missiles exchanged in the Arabian Sea so far had less to do with mistaken perceptions or tit-for-tat retaliation than with a clash of mutually opposed national policies. The *excuse* for the attack on CBG-14 might well be the sinking of an Indian submarine; the reality was less well defined but far more vast.

"They want us out of the Indian Ocean then," Magruder said simply.

"That's it. They're phrasing it oh-so-politely . . . but it amounts to an ultimatum. All foreign naval forces are to clear out of their War Exclusion Zone at once. Foreign national military vessels or squadrons still in the Arabian Sea, or not clearly on a course leading out of the WEZ, will be subject to attack after noon tomorrow, our time."

"God."

"Other military squadrons, those not within the Exclusion Zone, are, ah, 'strongly urged' to honor the IOZP declaration by leaving the Indian Ocean entirely. The question of Diego Garcia is to be settled at a future conference either here or in New Delhi within the next six weeks. The ambassador informed me that they will be presenting a motion to this effect before the United Nations this afternoon."

Magruder digested this. "What are you planning to do about it, Mr. President?"

The man behind the desk sighed, his shoulders slumping. "There's not a hell of a lot of choice, is there? Our whole national foreign policy is wedded to the Persian Gulf and the traffic there. Our entire history has been dedicated to freedom of the seas. I can't back down on this . . . and they damn well know it."

"Then they want a war with us?"

"I doubt it. My guess is they're hoping to broker some sort

of agreement where they become responsible for shipping in and out of the Gulf, maybe with us as junior partners. For the moment, though, they just want foreigners out of the Arabian Sea so they can prosecute their war with Pakistan.''

''The war.'' Magruder gave a grim smile. ''I'd just about forgotten about that.''

''Hell, the Pakistan war is what this is all about, Tom. India has always distrusted our relationship with Pakistan and probably thinks we'll back Islamabad against them. If they can get us out of the way, they can blockade Karachi and not have to watch their backs.''

Magruder tugged at his ear. ''They're not giving you many options.''

The President looked up at the map across the room. ''Well, there is *one* option.''

''What's that, sir?''

''I had another visitor in here this morning. Crack of dawn. Anatoly Druzhinin, the Commonwealth representative. He made an interesting . . . offer.''

''And a highly questionable one, sir,'' Hall said, breaking his silence.

The President gave his advisor a wan smile. ''I know how you feel about it, George. You've told me. There doesn't seem to be much choice, does there?''

''The Navy staff has been champing at the bit on this one, Mr. President. Maybe they're right. We don't need the Russkies.''

'''Don't need . . .''' Magruder's eyes widened. ''You mean the Russians are offering to help, sir?''

''They are indeed. Their Indian Ocean flotilla, SOVINDRON, is already en route for Turban Station. They'll be there late tomorrow afternoon, though their aircraft will be within range before that. The squadron is built around the *Kreml,* one of their two new nuclear-powered jobs.''

*Kreml* . . . Russian for *Kremlin.* Magruder blinked. He'd followed the available intelligence on what had been the Soviet nuclear carrier program for years, of course, but so far the Russian flattops had not ventured far from their own waters. He remembered the red line on the map at his back and realized that it must mark SOVINDRON's position.

"Accompanying *Kreml* are six other warships of various types. An Oscar-class nuclear attack sub. A Kresta II cruiser. We think it's the *Marshal Timoshenko,* but that hasn't been confirmed yet. Two destroyers. Two frigates. They're suggesting we form a combined task force with their squadron and CBG-14 for the express purpose of pressuring India and Pakistan to back off. It would effectively double our force in the area . . . and demonstrate to India and Pakistan that there is a united world consensus behind this, well before the UN could do anything about it. We hope this might shake the UN into speeding things up. God knows, they don't have much time."

"Russians!" Magruder exploded. "Son of a bitch!"

"Do you have a problem with that, Admiral?"

Magruder was embarrassed. "Uh, no, sir. No problem. I'm just . . . surprised."

The President grinned. "It surprised the hell out of me, I'll tell you." He glanced at Hall, who was frowning. "I've been told that the Russians are more interested in reestablishing their global reach than in stopping that war."

"It's possible, sir. They've lost a lot of prestige worldwide lately."

"You're right. And I agree. This is probably the best chance Moscow has had since the Persian Gulf War to let the world know that the Commonwealth can be a world-class superpower."

"I also happen to believe they'd like to avoid a nuclear war that close to home," the President continued. He leaned forward, his hands clasping in front of him. "You know, Tom, if this thing spreads, if it turns nuclear, South Asia could just fall apart. Never mind whether the war spreads to other countries or directly threatens our interests in the region. We'll have vast areas of devastation from Afghanistan to central India. We'll have people starving to death by the hundreds of millions! And hundreds of millions more will be on the move . . . looking for food, for clean water, for a place to escape the horror. Can you grasp numbers like that? I sure as hell can't!

"My feeling is that the Russians have enough trouble inside

their own borders right now without having to deal with starving refugees by the millions . . . or Islamic warlords stepping into the power vacuum and calling for some damned religious crusade . . . or clouds of fallout drifting north across the border. Did you know Uzbekistan grows most of the Commonwealth's cotton? That some of their best wheat and livestock-raising lands are in Kazakhstan? My God, a nuclear war just a few hundred miles from their border could be a catastrophe for the whole damned country! They're having enough economic problems without nuclear devastation to add to it.''

''And if things get worse in the Commonwealth . . .'' Magruder began.

''They'll get bad for us too. We're looking at a situation as dangerous as anything in the Cold War days. Maybe worse!''

Admiral Magruder leaned forward in his chair. ''I'm still not sure what a carrier task force could do out there, Mr. President. Even with two carriers on station . . .''

''That's why I called you in here, Tom. Maybe you can give us some thoughts on the situation. The one hard idea that's surfaced in the NSC meetings so far calls for air strikes against Indian supply routes. The Indians have got to be gambling on a fast end to their war. If we could delay them, maybe things would bog down and we could get them talking to each other instead of shooting. Certainly, if the Indian advance stalls, the Pakistanis will feel less inclined to start tossing nukes around.''

''Mr. President,'' Hall said. ''This is an incredibly dangerous move. It could also be a political disaster for—''

''*Fuck* politics, George!'' The President stood suddenly behind his desk. ''We're talking about trying to disarm two tough street kids before they burn down the block!''

Hall looked stunned. ''Yes, sir.''

''Wait outside. I'll buzz if I need you.''

''Yes, Mr. President.'' Hall left the room.

''At the risk of getting kicked out on my tail, Mr. President,'' Magruder said, ''Mr. Hall's right. If we step in, with or without the Russians, it could touch a match to the powder keg. And if the Indians already think we're allied with Pakistan, what are they going to think when we send a couple of A-6s in to bomb their troop convoys?''

''I know, Admiral. If you have a better idea, I'm certainly willing to listen.''

''Do you really think the Indians and the Pakistanis will back down if you threaten them with a couple of aircraft carriers, sir?''

''Pakistan will,'' the President said. ''I've been talking with their ambassador too. All they want is for the Indians to return to the borders. They insist they won't do anything, ah, irrevocable, not until they're up against the wall. After that . . .'' He shrugged. ''We have that long, anyway, to try. Right now, the big question mark is with our own people.'' The President paused, then looked Magruder in the eye. ''What do you think they'll say on the *Jefferson* if I order them to join forces with the Russkies?''

Magruder thought about it. ''Can't speak for Admiral Vaughn, Mr. President. I don't really know him. Captain Fitzgerald might have a fit. But he'll follow orders.''

''Will the battle group be able to work with the Russians?''

''Depends on a lot of things.'' He thought about the question for a moment. The real unknown was the Russians. Moscow, he remembered, had openly supported the Indian-Sri Lankan Peace Zone proposal in the Indian Ocean, probably because they assumed that the idea would never work and it made a convenient point of Third-World-pleasing diplomatic opposition against the United States. Of course, a lot had changed in the world since Brezhnev's day. ''I guess it's really up to the Russians,'' he added. ''Their willingness to exchange codes with us, stuff like that. But for our part . . . Yes, sir. Our people will *make* it work.''

''Good.'' The President nodded. ''Good, because I've already told Druzhinin to put the plan in the works for his people. And I'll have the Joint Chiefs draft orders for Admiral Vaughn this afternoon.''

Magruder nodded. He felt suddenly very small, knowing that the decisions being made in this office were those that could save or destroy thousands—or millions—of lives within the next few days. Would India feel differently about the situation if both the United States and Russians made a stand against their ultimatum? Somehow, he doubted it, but perhaps it would make a difference for the men, those from the Commonwealth and America, who were out there south of Karachi.

He studied the lines in the President's face and knew again the cost of command.

# CHAPTER 10

**0945 hours, 25 March**
**Flight deck, U.S.S. *Thomas Jefferson***

Tombstone walked out onto the flight deck, accepting a helmet—a "cranial" in Navy parlance—from a sailor outside the mangler's shack, where the deck handlers plotted each on-board movement of every aircraft in Air Wing 20. He was officially on duty in CATCC, but things were slow in Air Ops and he'd checked out for a stroll up on deck to get some fresh air.

The cloud cover had thickened during the night, bringing rain and gale-force gusts of wind, together with towering waves that had crashed over *Jefferson*'s bows in the darkness with the fury of an avalanche. That morning the wind had abated to a steady fifteen knots, but the sky was still a dirty gray overcast anchored only a few feet above *Jefferson*'s highest radar mast. The ocean swells were running seven feet.

The carrier had come about so that the wind was blowing down her angled deck from bow to stern. *Jefferson* was pitching enough in the heavy waves to make any trap a challenge, and the rolling seas had imparted an extra twist to her movements. Tombstone could feel the corkscrewing motion through his legs as he settled the helmet on his head and stepped onto the open deck.

An E-2C Hawkeye had just completed its trap and was taxiing toward the ship's starboard side, its wings already twisting sideways and folding back along its flanks in order to avoid the twenty-four foot, frisbee-shaped rotodome above its back. A yellow-jerseyed deck director led the way, signaling come-ahead with his hands.

Tombstone had been following the incoming air traffic down in CATCC and knew that the next aircraft due on board was a C-2A Greyhound. A long-range twin-engine prop plane used to deliver suppliers, personnel, and mail to the battle group at sea, the Greyhound was called a COD, for Carrier On-board Delivery. Outwardly similar to the Hawkeye from which it was derived, the Greyhound had a larger fuselage than the E-2C and a rear-loading cargo ramp, and of course, it lacked the radar frisbee.

Looking aft, he could make out the COD aircraft already in the slot a mile behind the carrier, a silvery speck swelling rapidly against the overcast as it dropped toward *Jefferson*'s roundoff. He watched as the pilot made a slight, last-second correction, adjusting for the changing pitch of the carrier's flight deck. Then the Greyhound swept across the ramp and its landing gear slammed onto the roof, the lowered tail hook snagging the number-two wire and yanking the boxy aircraft to a halt. The propellers continued to describe brilliant silver arcs as the COD plane spit out the wire, then began creeping after the deck director toward the middeck directly opposite the island.

Unlike the aircraft of CVW-20 that were based aboard the *Jefferson,* the COD Greyhound was not permanently a part of the carrier's complement. It would be shot off the Number One Catapult as soon as its cargo and personnel were offloaded, the bags of mail from *Jefferson*'s crew lugged aboard, and its tanks refueled.

Tombstone was waiting as the COD's rear ramp whined down and a line of men began climbing down onto the deck. All wore civilian clothes and life jackets, all were lean, hard, and young. One saw Tombstone and broke into a broad, lopsided grin.

"Tombstone, you son of a bitch!"

"Coyote!" Their hands clasped, then they embraced, pounding each other's backs. "God damn, Coyote, welcome aboard!"

Lieutenant Willis E. Grant, call sign "Coyote," had been Tombstone's very good friend since they'd first been stationed together at Miramar several years before. Both assigned to VF-95 out of CVW-20, they'd joined *Jefferson* before she left

San Diego almost nine months earlier. Coyote had been Tombstone's wingman until a MiG-21's missile had knocked him out of the sky over the Sea of Japan six months before. Coyote had been captured by the North Koreans, escaped with the help of a Navy SEAL team reconning the camp where he was being held, and been wounded. He'd been medevaced to Japan and finally wound up at the Naval Regional Medical Center, Camp Pendleton.

They walked toward the island. "So!" Tombstone said. "How's the leg and arm?"

"No problems." Coyote flexed his arm, demonstrating. "I was out of the hospital inside of six weeks, but they had me humping in the RAG at Miramar until last week. Then they decided you guys needed me."

Tombstone grinned. "RAG," for Reserve Air Group, was an obsolete term still used by Navy fliers for the Fleet Readiness Squadrons from which the carriers drew their replacements. "I don't know, Lieutenant. We've been managing okay without you."

"Ah! Ah!" Coyote held up an admonishing finger. "Can that 'Lieutenant' crap, mister. I pulled another half stripe. Came through while I was in the hospital."

"Well! Congratulations! It's about time. Lieutenant Commander, huh?"

"On the road to fame and glory, son. My future career looks rosy as one of our Navy's elite."

Coyote's banter raised a small sting in the back of Tombstone's mind. It was ironic. Here his friend had finally made it back to VF-95 . . . and Tombstone was going to be leaving for good in another few weeks.

Well, that was Navy life. Good friends and good-byes.

"Hell, what's this elite garbage?" Tombstone said roughly, covering his feelings. "You look like a damned civilian to me."

Coyote looked down at his civvies. "Yeah. Didn't have time to change. They routed that COD out of Masirah. We had a few hours in Dawwah, but they wouldn't let us wear our uniforms. The locals are sensitive about American servicemen on their turf."

They entered the island and removed their helmets. A seaman took Coyote's life jacket. "Well," Coyote said. "I'd better get checked in. Hey, I hear your uncle's not the Flag anymore. How's the new guy?''

Tombstone's lips compressed, then he shrugged. ''Still settling in. You hear about our dustup last night?''

''No. What went down?''

''I imagine they'll fill you in. We had a run-in with the Indian air force.''

''No shit?'' Coyote whistled.

''No shit. We knocked down three of theirs.''

''So it's gone to a shooting war!''

''Just this side of one anyway.''

''Were you in on it?'' Coyote grinned. ''You get yourself another kill?''

The question bothered Tombstone. ''Yeah. I got a kill.''

''Then you can tell me about it. How about lunch?''

''I've got the duty down in CATCC. I'll see you tonight at chow.''

''Roger that.'' Coyote flashed a broad grin and was gone.

Heading in a different direction, Tombstone clattered down a ship's ladder to the O-3 deck, then made his way past Combat toward CATCC once more. There was a lot more he'd wanted to tell Coyote. His being grounded, for one thing, and the doubts he'd felt the night before when he kept asking for clearance to fire, with no response. Fog of war was one thing, but Tombstone had the feeling that someone at a high level had not been snapping off the decisions in an efficient and military manner.

True, the tactical situation always looked a lot different on the amber radar screens of CIC than it did in the cockpit of an F-14 on BARCAP, but the orders had been coming too little and too late during the evening's engagement.

Well, that was no longer Tombstone's concern. He brushed past the curtains that excluded outside light and entered the red-lit semidarkness of CATCC.

**1000 hours, 25 March**
**CVIC, U.S.S. *Thomas Jefferson***

CVIC was more than *Jefferson*'s briefing-room-cum-TV-studio. The acronym was also applied to the carrier's entire intelligence department, which was the joint domain of the ship's OS and OZ divisions. OS was made up of the cryptology technicians who encoded and decoded *Jefferson*'s communications. OZ—the two-letter designation led to the department's inevitable nickname of "the Emerald City"—was responsible for providing intelligence data to *Jefferson*'s decision makers. Divided into five interlocking work centers, including Mission Planning and Briefing (MP&B) and Multi-Sensor Interpretation (MSI), OZ was regarded by the rest of *Jefferson*'s people as a truly magical kingdom that provided the battle group with a day-to-day picture of what was going on around them.

Of course, there was plenty of wry commentary when Intelligence was wrong, jokes about Naval Intelligence being a contradiction in terms, or how they used the Meteorological Division's blindfold and dart board to come up with their predictions.

The division head was the Carrier Group Intelligence Officer, Commander Richard Patrick Neil. Boston-born and educated, Neil had a slow manner of speech laced with the broad vowels of New England. He stood at the podium before row upon row of folding chairs, facing the senior battle group officers gathered in the room. A projection screen had been unfolded behind him, next to a map of India's west coast.

The morning's briefing had been called for all of *Jefferson*'s division heads, as well as all senior personnel in *Jefferson*'s Operations Department. CAG Marusko and two of his staff officers were present representing the air wing, though individual squadron skippers were not.

Also in attendance were a number of special guests, visitors from other ships of the battle group. Captain Cunningham of the *Vicksburg* and several officers from his CIC and tactical staffs were sitting near the front. If a major air or surface engagement with the Indians *was* in the offing, the squadron would be counting heavily on the Ticonderoga-class CG and her SPY-1B radar.

"Attention on deck," someone snapped from the back of the room. Admiral Vaughn entered, trailed by his senior staff. The officers in the room rose as a body.

"As you were, as you were," Vaughn said, making his way to the front-row seats reserved for his party. The others sat down as he did, with a loud rustle and squeaking of chairs. "Let's get on with it, Neil."

"Admiral," he said, nodding. "Gentlemen. Good morning.

"By now, all of you have been informed that CBG-14 is being augmented this afternoon by the arrival of a Commonwealth naval squadron. I've been asked to brief all of you on the types and capabilities of the Russian ships, and on the opposing lineup we are likely to face if we're forced to engage Indian naval forces. Lights, please."

The room lights dimmed, and a slide projector at the back of the room winked on. Ships appeared on the projection screen, photographed in crisp, colorful detail. The largest vessel was a carrier caught obliquely in early morning light. Her wake was a pale green-blue trail in the dark purple water.

"These came down from MSI this morning," Neil said, unfolding a telescoping pointer. "SOVINDRON consists of six surface ships and one submarine. We managed to catch these three in a TARPS run at zero-six-fifteen hours. The carrier you see here is the *Kreml.* Her escorts are a Kresta II-class guided-missile cruiser, the *Marshal Timoshenko,* and a Kotlin-class destroyer, the *Moskovskiy Komsomolets.*"

He signaled with his hand and the slide projector chunked. A magnified image of the carrier from a slightly different angle appeared. "*Kreml,* gentlemen. The *Kremlin.* Second of the Soviet supercarriers, he was laid down at the Nikolayev south shipyard in December of 1985 and completed in 1991. He is nuclear-powered, with four reactors and a speed of better than thirty knots."

"She," Admiral Vaughn interrupted.

"Sir?"

"You said 'he.' Ships are female."

"In our Navy, yes, sir. The Russians refer to ships as 'he.' I just thought—"

"You're briefing Americans, damn it. You can use American terminology."

"Yes, sir." Neil turned back to the screen. "*She* has a displacement of about seventy thousand tons and an overall length of one thousand feet, which puts her in *Jefferson*'s class.

"*Kreml* carries a wing of approximately sixty-five to seventy aircraft. You can see some of them lined up here, starboard side aft. These here, as you can see, are Yak-38MP

Forgers. Nothing new there. They appear to be identical to the V/STOL aircraft carried aboard the smaller Kiev-class carriers in both fighter and strike roles. Four wing pylons. The usual combat configuration is two external tanks and two Aphid missiles. Actually, the Forger has about a twenty-five percent payload advantage over the AV-8B Harrier, but it is generally considered to be an inferior aircraft.'' Neil cracked a rare smile. ''If it's any indication, the Indian navy turned down a chance to buy some of these babies a few years ago and bought the Harrier instead.''

The pointer moved to a cluster of aircraft lining the side of the flight deck, wings tightly folded. ''These are Russia's naval version of the Su-27 Flanker. It is highly maneuverable and is probably roughly comparable to the American F-15 Eagle. It has the same track-while-scan radar as the MiG-29, has look-down/shoot-down capability, and can handle all-weather operation. Armament for the fighter version is eight AA-10 Alamo missiles. The Russians are supposed to be working on a strike version, but we have no information on that at this time, and we don't know whether any might be aboard the *Kreml*. Originally, the Flanker appeared with a variable-geometry wing like our Tomcat. We have to assume they ran into some problems with it, though, because current production models have been strictly fixed-wing. Next.''

The slide projector chunked. The image on the screen captured an aircraft just off the Soviet carrier's ski-jump bow. The detail was sharp enough that the viewers could make out Russian crewmen frozen in various mid-action positions about the deck. There was an audible intake of breath from several corners of the room. The aircraft, its red stars sharp on wings and tail, looked remarkably like an American F/A-18 Hornet.

''This baby's their prize,'' Neil said. ''MiG-29, naval version. *Jane's* calls it the first completely new generation of Soviet fighters. For air-to-air it carries six missiles, AA-8 or AA-9. Look-down/shoot-down, all-weather capability. Track-while-scan. Improved HUD. This is the best Soviet plane in service. Maybe the best in the world.''

''Bullshit,'' someone said near the front of the room.

''Helicopter roles, rescue and ASW, are filled by the Ka-27 Helix, the successor to the Ka-25 Hormone. We think that *Kreml* carries four of them.''

"You know, Commander," Vaughn interrupted again. "I notice your briefing is filled with a hell of a lot of 'maybes' and 'we thinks.' Is there anything about the Russkies you're *sure* of?"

"Intelligence work is largely guesswork, Admiral," Neil said stiffly. "*Educated* guesswork, to be sure, but still guesswork. OZ Div has assembled the best picture they can from various—"

"Guesses, huh? Well I *guess* that tells us something about our intelligence department, eh, boys?"

There were subdued chuckles from the front row of chairs, but the rest of CVIC remained cold and silent. Neil ran a hand through his short red hair and decided to press ahead.

"We have tentatively identified the other ships of the Soviet squadron. An Oscar-class nuclear attack sub, no known name. A second Kotlin-class DD, the *Vliyatel'nyy.* Two Krivak I-class ASW frigates, *Letushiy* and *Svirepyy.* Washington's assessment of SOVINDRON is that it is a tight, well-run, highly disciplined squadron," he said. "The Soviet frigates do not have the range or sensitivity of our ASW ships, and they lack helicopter capability. However, they are probably the most heavily armed frigates afloat, with SA-N-4 Gecko missiles and large torpedo and gun batteries. They are highly versatile and could be deployed in an anti-air role as well as for ASW."

Vaughn snorted with open contempt. Neil paused, then plunged ahead, wondering if Vaughn was going to let him complete the briefing.

"The destroyers are old designs—mid-fifties—but have been partly converted to missile configurations. The cruiser will be a definite asset to the battle group. He, excuse me, *she* mounts a twin launcher for the SA-N-3 Goblet, and two quad launchers for SS-N-14 Silex antisub missiles. Both weapons can double in an antiship role. I . . . sir?"

Admiral Vaughn was standing. "Commander, this isn't getting us anywhere. I think we all know that the Russkies aren't going to pull their own weight out here, not if it comes to a stand-up fight. Let's hear what the Indians have."

Neil swallowed his anger. "Yes, sir. Phil? Let's go to number twelve." It took a moment for the projectionist to skip ahead several slides and find the first one dealing with Indian ships. As he waited, Neil summarized the Indian forces.

"As I'm sure you're all aware, India has designs on being the number-one power in the Indian Ocean littoral. They have the third largest standing army in the world, the fifth largest air force, and the eight largest navy. While we will be primarily concerned with their naval capability, we have to keep in mind that the Indians will be able to support their naval operations against us with a sizable fraction of their ground-based air force. All together, the IAF maintains some 960 combat aircraft. The Indian navy consists of at least sixty combat aircraft, including twenty-six attack helicopters. Of course, these one-thousand-plus aircraft are spread out over the whole Indian subcontinent, and the majority are already tied down in action against Pakistan. Our best guess . . ." He hesitated. "Our best *approximation* is that the Indians can deploy between one and two hundred aircraft of various types against us here at Turban Station."

Another aircraft carrier flashed on the screen behind him, an odd-looking ship with a long island and a massive, upswept hump at the bow end of her flight deck.

"Okay. Here we go. India currently has two aircraft carriers, gentlemen," Neil said. "This is their latest, the *Viraat.* The name means 'Mighty' in Hindi. Her displacement is almost 24,000 tons. She has an illustrious history. Originally, she was the British *Hermes,* one of the two Brit carriers that supported the Royal task force in the Falklands campaign. The British sold her to the Indians in '86.

"For a while, the Indians operated her as a commando carrier and later used her for ASW. That ski jump you see forward lets her handle Sea Harrier V/STOL aircraft. Until recently, she carried one six-plane Sea Harrier squadron, plus a number of helicopters, but Intelligence believes the Indians have been upgrading her capabilities. Last year they completed purchase of thirty additional Sea Harriers from the British, and many of those are probably destined for the *Viraat.* She also still has provisions for 750 troops and carries four landing barges to facilitate landing operations. Next." A new slide appeared on the screen.

"The other Indian carrier is the *Vikrant.* She started off as a World War II-era Glory-class carrier, the HMS *Hercules.* She was purchased by India in 1957. She's smaller than *Viraat*—only 15,700 tons—but she carries six Sea Harriers. *Vikrant* is scheduled to be replaced by a 40,000-ton, Indian-built carrier sometime later in the late nineties, but that one's not off the drawing board yet."

Neil went on with a rundown of the Indian navy, concentrating on the warships known to be operating out of Arabian Sea ports. There was one nuclear sub, the *Chakra*—a Charlie I-class vessel on loan from the Soviet Union, but it was unlikely that the Indians would be in the mood to trust the Soviet technicians aboard her during the current crisis. There was a new Soviet Kresta-II cruiser, the *Kalikata,* recently arrived at Bombay. All together, the Indian navy included over fifty capital ships, plus numerous missile and patrol boats, auxiliaries, and the like.

As he continued speaking, he was distracted by the sight of Admiral Vaughn leaning over to the captain at his side, apparently in deep conversation.

Just what the hell was going on with the flag staff today anyway? It was as though Vaughn simply didn't care . . . or at least felt that the information was superfluous. It was impossible not to make comparisons with Admiral Magruder. That man might not always have agreed with OZ assessments, but at least he listened. And his questions had always been good ones, sharp and to the point.

Vaughn's indifference sent an icy tingle down Neil's spine, and he could sense that it was affecting the other officers in CVIC as well. Did he simply distrust his own intelligence department? Or was this something more than that, something deeper?

Neil didn't know, but he knew that Vaughn's attitude was being marked by the others, and that it could be deadly to the mission, to the *men*.

Deadlier, perhaps, than a third Indian carrier.

# CHAPTER 11

**1400 hours, 25 March**
**Headquarters, Indian Defense Ministry**

Defense Minister Kuldip Sundarji was a small, mustached man with rimless glasses that caught the fluorescent light from overhead and flashed it back at the generals and admirals sitting at the table. Rear Admiral Ramesh watched as he took a sip of water, then smiled at the assembly of high-ranking military officers arrayed about the conference room table.

"Gentlemen," he said without other preamble. "I thank you for your invitation to meet with you today. I bring the compliments of the Prime Minister, who is proud and pleased with your prosecution of the war thus far. The Political Affairs Committee has asked me to express their complete confidence in you and your good efforts."

Ramesh stifled a twinge of impatience. He didn't like Sundarji, though he understood the man's obsequious manner and politician's smile.

The political situation within the Indian Federation was, as always, an extremely delicate one, as was the balance between the civilian government and the military. The Indian Constitution vested command of the armed forces with the President, but *de facto* control lay with the Prime Minister and his cabinet. The cabinet's Political Affairs Committee, chaired by the Prime Minister, was responsible for all high-level decisions on defense matters. The Minister of Defense was the only true liaison between the Indian government and its military, and there was a tendency for the armed forces to become isolated from government decision making.

By the same token, though, the government tended to leave military decisions to the military in a live-and-let-live arrangement that both sides found politically useful. As the public clamored for an end to Pakistani border aggressions, the government could truthfully say that the matter was in the army's hands. And the service chiefs could count on a certain amount of noninterference from New Delhi when they sat down to plan their strategies.

Of course, that put a terrific responsibility on Kuldip Sundarji. The Defense Minister had to juggle two agendas—the government's and the military's—and make them come out to the common advantage.

He was, therefore, a master politician. Ramesh distrusted such people.

''General Dhanaraj,'' the Defense Minister said grandly. ''Would you be so kind as to brief us on the First Corps situation?''

General Sanjeev Dhanaraj scraped his chair back, rose, and walked to the wall map at the head of the table. Unit positions, movements, and defense lines were marked onto a transparent overlay that showed the broad scope and thrust of the war's first three days.

''Overall, we have every reason to be pleased with the accomplishments of the past sixty hours,'' he said. ''Intelligence estimates that better than seventy percent of the Pakistani air force has been destroyed or grounded. We have reason to be concerned that a number of F-16 strike fighters, which are, of course, nuclear-capable, are still being held in reserve. Efforts are underway to locate and destroy them.''

He indicated a cluster of marks in the south, a few hundred miles from the sea. ''Operation Cobra commenced at 0300 hours this morning. Following massive artillery and air bombardments, a full division is attacking here, at Naya Chor, on the highway from the border to Hyderabad. Two more divisions are in reserve. Our diversionary attacks in the Punjab appear to have successfully pulled Pakistani attention to the Lahore-Islamabad region. Our armor has reported a major breakthrough and is now moving west at a rapid pace. Lead elements have reached the Nara River, and pioneer units are preparing to effect a crossing. Success there will bring us to Hyderabad.''

The general turned from the map. "Coupled with the planned naval blockade and commando landings along Karachi's waterfront itself, it is the Senior Staff's belief that we will control the Sindh within another three days. Pakistani resistance can be expected to crumble shortly after that."

Dhanaraj thanked the group for their attention and returned to his seat. The Defense Minister took his place. "Thank you, General." He paused, hands on hips. "Well, I needn't remind you, gentlemen, of the serious threat posed by Pakistan's detonation of a nuclear device. It is the government's opinion that only an extremely swift and decisive victory in the field can end this campaign before Islamabad resolves to use such weapons against us."

Ramesh nodded. This was certainly the real reason the Defense Minister was here. The government was worried about Pakistan's bomb.

"Based on our own experience with atomic weapons, Intelligence believes that the Pakistanis have not yet succeeded in assembling nuclear warheads small enough to deliver as bombs, but their technicians are certain to be working on the problem.

"In addition, the government wishes to emphasize that growing pressure in the world community is working against us. Sooner or later, the UN will move to force an end to hostilities in this region. We must achieve our territorial and political goals first. We therefore have two reasons to see this affair through to a swift conclusion.

"Everything, *everything* depends on a rapid and successful drive to Karachi. With the country's major port in our hands, the Pakistanis will be cut off from outside aid and forced to capitulate. While we are taking seriously their threats to use nuclear weapons as a last resort, it is our considered opinion that they will refrain from doing so, at least for the time being. Use of such weapons would create a bad image for them in the world at large and could jeopardize their trade relationship with the United States. Nor will they be eager to detonate nuclear weapons on their own soil. We must beat them before they decide that such consequences are less important than their own survival, that, in fact, their very survival is at stake. We cannot afford to have our attacks become stalled or slowed by unexpected resistance.

"And this, my friends, brings us to the principal subject of our meeting today. The Americans."

Ramesh leaned forward, suddenly intent. What was the government going to do about the American threat?

"I need not remind you, gentlemen," Sundarji continued, "of American interference in this region during our war with Pakistan in 1971. At that time they stationed another of their nuclear carriers, the *Enterprise,* in the Bay of Bengal. This was a constant threat we could not ignore throughout our operations in Bangladesh.

"Since that time, they have commissioned their installation at Diego Garcia, stationed carrier battle groups in the Arabian Sea, and organized their rapid-deployment force for intervention in our part of the world. Now they have positioned a nuclear carrier battle group only a hundred miles from our shores. With their in-flight refueling capabilities, they are within easy range of Operation Cobra's supply lines. They can interdict our activities anywhere from Bombay to Baluchistan.

"The government is concerned that the Americans might interfere with our naval blockade of Pakistan, sever our supply lines with the Persian Gulf, or both. In the event of hostilities, our supply lines across the Thar Desert would be especially vulnerable.

"If we are to have a free hand in our operation in Pakistan, the American threat in our waters must be eliminated."

Rear Admiral Ramesh stirred in his seat, then raised a hand. The Defense Minister looked down at him with owlish eyes. "Admiral?"

"Your pardon, sir . . . but does this mean we are declaring war against the Americans?" He felt a fierce, inner surge of emotion. The events of the past days seemed to have gone beyond any one government's control, an explosion of encounters, blunders, and headlong stumbles toward the abyss of war. Was the Prime Minister actually choosing to ride events toward what seemed to be their predestined end . . . to take control and *anticipate* that war?

The minister frowned. "There will be no formal declaration, Admiral, no. But India will take action to guarantee her own sovereignty."

Ramesh was confused. "Sir?"

"Success in Pakistan, and our own security, demand that we

force the United States . . . and all other extraterritorial powers . . . to recognize our claims to the Arabian Sea and abandon military control of the Indian Ocean basin to us. Our requests before the UN Security Council have been rebuffed. This, then, leaves us with but a single course of action.

"Yesterday, as you all know, a maritime attack squadron, supported by one of our MiG-29 fighter units, struck elements of the American carrier force off Bombay. Our intelligence indicates that at least three U.S. planes were shot down in the engagement."

Ramesh pursed his lips. He knew better than to accept such figures at face value. He wondered what the kill figures really were, and how many IAF planes had been lost.

"The action of last night is being hailed as a major triumph. However, our leaders fear that American resolve has only hardened at this point. Their government stresses the concept of 'freedom of the seas,' which can be interpreted as their perceived right to continue to operate in our waters.

"Furthermore, the Commonwealth of Independent States has now joined the Americans. A Russian nuclear carrier group is expected to rendezvous with the Americans by mid-afternoon."

Sundarji raised his hand and snapped his fingers, gesturing. A civilian aide began going around the table, passing out slender folders to each military man present. Ramesh accepted his and opened it, removing the sheaf of papers inside. Written in English, as were all such documents in India, and stamped TOP SECRET across each page, it appeared to be a general directive entitled Operation Python. Cobra, Krait, and Python, Ramesh thought. New Delhi seemed entranced by the ideas of using snakes for code words this week.

"The government has decided that only one response on our part can be direct enough, sharp enough to discourage foreign intentions in the Arabian Sea," the minister continued as the military men read the orders. "The Political Affairs Committee has asked me to submit these plans to you this afternoon. We believe that enough ships and planes can be diverted from current operations to deliver a single, crushing blow to the joint American-Soviet battle fleet. Ideally, this should be carried out before the Russians and the Americans have a chance to work together, in order to maximize confusion.

"Their aircraft carriers, of course, will be the primary

targets. Destroy them, or simply damage their flight decks enough to prevent air launches or recoveries, and both squadrons will be largely useless. The foreign fleets will be forced to withdraw.

"New Delhi anticipates a strong reaction, of course, but by that time our objectives in Pakistan should be achieved. We can negotiate with Moscow and Washington over reparations or whatever is necessary, but . . ." He raised a forefinger, stressing the word. "*But* . . . our goals will have been achieved. Victory in Pakistan, and an end to foreign intervention in our ocean."

A rising murmur filled the room as generals and admirals scanned through the orders. "Excellency," General Bakaya said. "These call for stripping the Pakistan front of many of our best aircraft squadrons!"

Sundarji nodded. "Temporarily, yes. It is the government's belief that for this operation we can muster between two and three hundred aircraft, approximately a third of our total IAF assets. The strike force will include long-range bombers, cruise missiles, and multi-wave strikes by attack planes armed with Exocets, as well as our maritime aircraft operating off of *Viraat* and *Vikrant*. Losses should not be higher than ten percent, which leaves adequate forces to return to the Pakistan front."

Admiral Karananidhi stood, shaking the papers in his fist. "This is insane! You are saying we must abandon our blockade of Karachi!"

The murmurs grew louder. "I must protest," another officer in the back shouted. "This could stall the entire offensive!"

Sundarji raised his voice. "I must emphasize . . . Gentlemen, if you please! I must emphasize that this redeployment is for the short term only! Admiral Karananidhi, you are correct. The fleet assembled for the blockade of Karachi is to be diverted to support the attack on the Soviet-American forces. But the strike is expected to take less than four hours altogether and can be accomplished while your ships are en route to the Pakistan coast. The aircraft deployed for this exercise are those already in place within range of the targets. The delay will be minimal! And in exchange . . ." He spread his hands. "One lightning blow to cripple foreign air operations in the Arabian Sea! A strong message to the world that India is the master of her own destiny, her own ocean! A demonstration to Islamabad that we *will* see this through, regardless of world opinion! It will be, gentlemen, the gateway to our own future as a global power!''

Ramesh returned the orders to the folder unread. He didn't need to see them to know their content . . . or to know that, after a few hours of argument, the military staff would give it their stamp of approval. The possible benefits were enormous, the risks relatively small. There was a stronger possibility of Pakistan deciding to employ nuclear weapons, but perhaps Intelligence was correct in assuming that Islamabad was not yet able to deploy such weapons in the field.

Those considerations did not really touch him closely in any case, because he had seen one section of those orders, the paragraphs dealing with Indian navy deployment. The Indian aircraft carrier *Viraat* had been designated the flagship of the naval operation against the Americans.

And Rear Admiral Ajay Ramesh was commander of *Viraat*'s task force, with the carrier as his flag. It would be he who led the attack against the foreigners, opening the way for the IAF bomber strikes.

It would be a suitable revenge for poor Joshi's death.

**1725 hours, 25 March**
**Dirty Shirt Mess, U.S.S. *Thomas Jefferson***

''Yeah, Coyote, it's true,'' Tombstone said. The clatter of dishes and silverware rose around them, mingled with the low conversations of several dozen of the ship's officers. Tombstone was clad in his khakis, but Coyote was still wearing his flight suit after an afternoon of patrol and practice touch-and-goes off *Jefferson*'s roof.

''God, man, I don't believe it! How can they can the goddamned squadron commander?''

Tombstone pushed his dinner tray back on the table. He'd not felt much like eating. ''By not making it an *official* canning. They'll just take their time getting around to the investigation and hope I go away in the meantime.''

''Kiss of death, man! They can't pull that shit! An aviator's got to get out there and strap on that airplane every day, or he loses the edge!''

"Hell, they're doing it. Can't fight city hall. You know that." He shrugged. "Anyway, it's not bad. Gives me a chance to catch up on my paperwork. The Vipers are down two aircraft, and getting IM-2 moving on our work orders is like shoveling mud." The IM-2 division of *Jefferson*'s Aircraft Intermediate Maintenance Department (AIMD) was responsible for all inspection, testing, calibration, and repair of the aircraft embarked aboard the carrier. He knew his offhand statement was not entirely fair; IM-2 consisted of eight officers, 420 men, and thirty civilian technical reps with an impossible backlog of orders and requests. "Officially, I guess I'm still in charge."

"So who's running the squadron, guy? Unofficially, I mean?"

"Army. Fred Garrison. Remember him? He's squadron XO now. Anyway, he bosses 'em in the air and I take care of the paperwork. Good trade."

Coyote leaned back in his chair, a mug of coffee in his hand. "You can't fool me, Stoney. This has got you pissed off royally."

"Maybe." He wondered whether to tell Coyote that he was planning on resigning. It wasn't the sort of thing you just blurted out. There was an unspoken attitude among Navy aviators. The guys who turned in their wings or resigned were failures, fallen gods no longer possessing the edge, the all-important right stuff.

Tombstone valued Coyote's friendship and didn't want to risk it.

Another thought occurred to him. "Listen, Coyote. I haven't had a chance to ask. How's Julie?"

"Find, fine. She told me to send her love."

Tombstone and Coyote both had dated a good-looking insurance claims rep named Julie Wilson years before, when they'd first been stationed at Coronado. The rivalry had been friendly. In the end, Tombstone had been best man at their wedding.

"So tell me," Tombstone said uncertainly. "What does Julie think of your coming back out here? I mean, you came pretty close to buying the farm last time around. How'd she take it?"

Coyote studied his coffee mug for a moment. "Hell, I'd be

lying if I said she wasn't worried. But she knows that Navy aviation is what I do. She knows I miss her like nobody's business when I'm gone, but that flying is the next best thing to sex there is.'' He hesitated. ''You want to tell me what's behind that, Stoney?''

''Oh, nothing important.'' He knew the lie was transparent. ''Just trying to figure where my own career is going, that's all. I met a girl. . . .''

''Yeah?''

''TV news-type person. Met her in Bangkok during all the excitement there. I . . . I'm in love with her. . . .''

''But there're the old questions about whether love and salt water mix, hey?''

''Something like that.'' Tombstone grinned suddenly. ''You know the old saying. 'If the Navy wanted you to have a wife, they'd have issued you one with your seabag.' '' He looked at his watch. ''Shit. I gotta go.''

''Hey, wait.''

But Tombstone didn't want to talk about it, not now. He stood, picking up the tray with his unfinished supper. ''Catch you later, Coyote.''

''Yeah. Later.''

Why was he telling Coyote his problems? He shook his head as he returned the tray to the galley window and shoved it through. The Coyote had it made, excited about his career, about flying . . . and a smart and pretty woman waiting for him back in the World.

He sure as hell wouldn't understand. Tombstone knew he was going to have to face his problems with Pamela alone.

# CHAPTER 12

**1810 hours, 25 March**
**Bridge, U.S.S. *Thomas Jefferson***

"Now hear this," the 1-MC speaker on the bulkhead intoned. "Now hear this. Commence fuel transfer operations. The smoking lamp is out throughout the ship."

Captain Fitzgerald scarcely heard the announcement. His attention was fixed on the activity to starboard. *Jefferson* rode the heavy seas at reduced speed, her massive bows rising and plunging with each wave. Sliding along in her shadow one hundred feet to starboard, dwarfed by the supercarrier's bulk, the U.S.S. *Amarillo* paced her larger consort, matching her plunge for plunge.

*Jefferson*'s three starboard flight deck elevators had been lowered to the hangar deck level, giving men of the deck division places to stand as fuel hoses from the AOE were snaked across along span wires stretched from *Amarillo*'s topping lifts to pelican hooks secured to *Jefferson*'s side. Red flags, warning of the fire hazard, snapped in the breeze on both ships as deckhands secured the hoses. Suspended from the span wires by sliding pulleys called trolleys, the hoses were draped in a series of deep loops between the vessels, allowing plenty of give and slack as the ships went their separate up-and-down ways.

The carrier's two Westinghouse A4W nuclear reactors could keep *Jefferson* steaming for thirteen years without refueling, but she still carried over two million gallons of JP-5 in her aviation fuel compartments. During typical peacetime operations, fifty or sixty planes were flown off a carrier twice daily, each mission consuming two to three thousand gallons of fuel, and at-sea replenishment was scheduled about every two weeks. During the Vietnam War when fuel expenditures were much higher, reprovisioning at sea had taken place as often as once every three or four days.

*Jefferson*'s last UNREP—Underway Replenishment—had been carried out ten days earlier, in the waters north of Diego Garcia. Captain Fitzgerald looked down on the *Amarillo* from his vantage point on the supercarrier's bridge and wondered how soon he could expect the next resupply. UNREP ships were limited, and they had a long way to steam to reach CBG-14 in the isolated vastness of the Arabian Sea.

The *Amarillo*'s 194,000 barrels of fuel translated as over seven and a half million gallons, most of it JP-5 destined for *Jefferson*'s air wing. Normally, that was enough for six weeks of air operations—ASW patrols and CAPs, as well as daily proficiency flights as the aviators logged in their hours aloft.

The AOR *Peoria,* a second UNREP vessel, carried petroleum for the rest of the battle group, 160,000 barrels of it, enough for over a month of cruising for the CBG's non-nuclear vessels.

But if the tense political situation turned into outright war, fuel use would go up dramatically as the carrier's aircraft tripled or quadrupled consumption, and the non-nuclear vessels were forced to travel farther and faster each day. A worst-case scenario could see the *Peoria* and the *Amarillo* both emptied by the battle group's maneuvers within the next week.

And if *either* reprovisioning ship was sunk or badly damaged during that time, CBG-14 could be crippled within a matter of days.

He turned and walked the width of the bridge back to his leather swivel chair, stenciled "CO" and set near the port wing where it overlooked the flight deck. To the west, the sun was setting in a glorious burst of golds and reds that spilled across the horizon. Despite the still-heavy seas, the dirty weather appeared to be breaking up. The meteorologists down in the OA division had scrutinized their satellite photos and promised clear weather for the next forty-eight hours.

There'd been no further threats from the Indians since the previous evening's attack. That didn't mean the danger was over, but the immediacy of the crisis seemed to have eased somewhat. An hour earlier, CINCPAC had reported over

*Jefferson*'s satellite comlink that the diplomatic exchanges were continuing in Washington. Perhaps they were going to find a negotiated way out of this confrontation.

In any case, it was out of his hands. He was on station and on full alert. There was nothing else to be done until someone else pushed the button.

To the west, Fitzgerald could make out the familiar, boxy mass of the *Vicksburg*'s superstructure. Somewhere beyond the Aegis cruiser, well over the horizon, the Commonwealth task force was steaming on a northerly course parallel with CBG-14. Fitzgerald still wasn't certain what he thought of the orders to join the two squadrons into a single, international task force. Even if he trusted the Russians—which he did not, as yet—there would still have been an endless list of details to be worked out before the two forces could act together. And Kontr-Admiral Dmitriev, Vaughn's opposite number aboard the *Kreml,* had so far shown little enthusiasm for integrating the two fleets. SOVINDRON was steaming north in a tight-packed bundle, seemingly oblivious to the American ships out around them across a hundred miles of ocean. Nor did the Russians seem willing to make the exchanges of codes, call signs, and radio frequencies necessary for allowing U.S. and Russian ships and planes to work together.

The IFF codes alone were already causing considerable confusion in the fleet. Each aircraft in *Jefferson*'s air wing possessed a transponder that transmitted a coded signal when it was touched by radar beams from an American ship or plane. The system, called IFF for "Identification Friend or Foe," caused American radar displays to show the flight number of each U.S. plane in the air. The Russians had the same system, but with different codes responding to different radar wavelengths. So far, Russian planes flying above the *Kreml* were tagged as unknowns when they were painted by U.S. radar . . . just the same as the Indian aircraft during the attack the night before. If the joint squadron was attacked now, before IFF codes and protocol could be exchanged, the battle would very quickly become an unmanageable free-for-all.

What would Moscow think if some of their Naval Aviation MiGs were downed by American Sea Sparrows? Fitzgerald didn't even want to think about the consequences.

"Admiral on the bridge."

Fitzgerald slid out of his seat and turned to face Vaughn. "Good evening, Admiral."

"Captain."

Vaughn looked terrible. There were circles under his eyes, and he looked pale. He was chewing on something—an antacid tablet, Fitzgerald decided—and his eyes were focused past the bridge windscreen on something in the distance.

The Russians. Of course.

"Any problem with the replenishment, Captain?"

"Not a thing, Admiral. Everything's going smoothly. First stage refueling should be complete before it's fully dark." Because of the late hour, it had been decided to transfer fuel in two batches, one this evening, the rest the next morning. The dry stores and refrigerated supplies ticketed for the *Jefferson,* less critical at the moment than the JP-5, would be swayed across with the second refueling.

The admiral grunted, still staring at the western horizon. "So. What about the Russkies?"

Fitzgerald shook his head. "They don't seem to be in much of a hurry, do they, sir? Captain Krylenko sent me personal greetings a while ago. And I gather we're due for a joint conference tomorrow morning."

"Yeah. More damned socializing and politicking. Useless crap. These vodka-swilling bozos aren't going to be any help to us at all."

Fitzgerald studied the admiral, controlling his own growing worry. There was something about Vaughn. He groped for the right word. Irrational? No . . . that wasn't right. There was nothing *wrong* with the man that *Jefferson*'s captain could put his finger on. But he did seem preoccupied, his attention unfocused, and his derisive and egotistical attitude during that morning's briefing had not helped matters.

Perhaps it was just Vaughn's fear. Fitzgerald could smell it, could see it in the nervous way his eyes flicked back and forth as he studied the horizon, could hear it in his terse words and harsh judgment of the Russians.

There was no irrationality in fear. All of them were afraid, every man in the squadron, and there was no shame in that, not when tomorrow could find them in a war unlike any that had been fought in history.

But Vaughn's manner worried Fitzgerald. It was almost as

though the man was trying to link up the excuses before his failure, find a way to divert the blame. "It wasn't my fault because the Russians were no good." "It wasn't my fault because I wasn't given the intel I needed."

Fitzgerald shook himself mentally and tore his gaze from Vaughn's face. He would get nowhere thinking thoughts like that.

He signaled to an enlisted watchstander nearby. "Have some coffee, sir?"

"Eh? Oh, thanks. Thanks. Everything else quiet?"

"Absolutely." He kept his tone light, confident, and unworried. "I'd say our Indian friends have decided to bug out. Maybe the skirmish yesterday made them think twice about all this. Or maybe it was the Russians joining us. Attacking us now would be sort of like taking on the whole world, wouldn't it?"

"No, Captain. No, it's not like that at all." Vaughn spoke softly, his eyes still on the horizon as though he were trying to reach out and touch the mind of Admiral Dmitriev, out there on the bridge of the *Kreml.* He accepted a mug of coffee the sailor handed him without looking away. "Those bastards *will* be back, and from where we're sitting, it's going to look like World War III."

"How do you know that, sir?"

"Logistics." He blinked, then turned away from the window. He seemed to really see Fitzgerald for the first time. "The laws of logistics, Captain. The guy with the longest supply line has his head in a noose."

"Oh, I think we're set all right. *Peoria* and *Amarillo* are with us now. They have enough bullets, beans, and black oil to keep us going for quite a while." But he knew the admiral's thoughts were traveling the same ruts his own mind had been circling a few minutes earlier. Lose the UNREP ships and the squadron was crippled, their mission . . .

The realization hit Fitzgerald like a blow. It was the mission Vaughn was worried about . . . and his image back in Washington. That fit with the little he'd heard about the man prior to his assignment to CBG-14. He was worried about what would happen to his career if the carrier group failed to carry out its mission.

"A drop in the bucket," Vaughn said, responding to Fitzgerald's comment about the UNREP ships' provisions. He raised the mug and sipped noisily. "You know as well as I do how quickly we'll run through that stuff once the shooting starts, hey? Hell, we're twelve thousand miles from home. *Twelve thousand miles!* The Russians are five thousand from their nearest port, and they don't have our experience in long-range blue-water ops. The Indians' supply bases are right over the horizon. We're dangling on a limb out here, Fitzgerald. And the Indians are going to whack it off."

"Hell, I thought that dangling was what we're here for, Admiral." He laughed, trying to make it sound like a joke. "We're what the President calls for when he needs to reach out and touch someone."

Vaughn's mouth quirked in what might have been a smile. "Well, we'd better hope the President decides in favor of talking instead of touching. You know damn well we can't match the Indians plane for plane. Count their planes ashore and they outnumber us ten to one at least."

"No," Fitzgerald agreed, serious now. Vaughn's mood was gnawing at him, and he didn't know how to reply. "No, we can't match their planes. But we can match their pilots. I'm willing to bet we could match them ten for one in *that* department any day!"

"Maybe." Vaughn sighed. "But it's not the men who count. Not anymore."

The words chilled Fitzgerald. He glanced at the enlisted watchstander who was still standing a few feet away, face expressionless and his eyes fixed on the horizon forward. "How can you say that, sir?"

"God. You heard how the fight went last night. Out of control . . . Most of that battle was fought by computers, Captain. Do you understand that?"

"I think so, sir. But men were directing the battle, controlling the computers."

"No, Captain. Things happen too fast for humans to manage a modern battle. All humans can do is screw things up. Remember the *Stark*? And the *Vincennes*?"

"Of course." *Stark* was the Perry-class frigate that had been hit by an Iraqi Exocet in '87 because her combat crew had failed to take certain defensive preparations at the time. *Vincennes* was the Aegis cruiser that had misidentified an

Indian airliner and shot it down by mistake. "But I think we learned some things from those episodes."

"What's to learn? That your ship can be under attack before you even realize it. That any human decisions are going to be made too late to help when you only have seconds to react. No, Captain. If we fight, we're going to find that it's our mistakes that shape the battle more than our decisions. And we . . . we're at a disadvantage."

"How is that, sir?"

"Because we have the more complicated electronics, the faster computers, the more sophisticated gadgetry. That's more stuff to break down. And because we have to haul those . . . what'd you say? Beans, bullets, and black oil halfway around the world, while the Indians have everything they need right here." He shook his head. "Damn it. Washington expects the impossible. The *impossible* . . ."

The sun slipped beneath the horizon at that moment, the fire fading from the sky. The admiral drained the coffee mug and set it on a console. "Good night, Captain."

Fitzgerald watched him go with black misgivings.

**2135 hours, 24 March**
**Crew's Lounge, U.S.S. *Thomas Jefferson***

Seaman David Howard sat at the round table with three friends, accepting the face-down cards as RD/2 Benedict dealt them out. Once he glanced up at the paneled bulkheads and their neatly framed prints of various scenes out of the Navy's history and repressed a slight shudder. He remembered sitting in this same lounge two months earlier, with three other friends who now were all dead.

"Whatsa matter, Tiger?" the second-class radarman asked. "Lose somethin'?"

"Nah." Howard scooped up the cards and fanned them. "Just thinking."

*Tiger*. He still wasn't used to the handle they'd dropped on him. Short in stature, still three weeks shy of his nineteenth birthday, he didn't look much like a hero. His part during the Bangkok affair had won him a Silver Star; he still couldn't remember much of what had happened, still didn't *feel* heroic.

In fact, he didn't feel any different now than he had then. Perhaps the only real change beyond his raise in rank and pay was the new nickname. He liked "Tiger" a lot better than "Howie."

"Ah, leave the thinking to the fuckin' brass," Air Traffic Controlman Third Francis Gilkey said. "Gimme two."

"Make it three," YN/3 Reid said. "Thinking too much don't pay. Not on *this* boat." Unlike Howard, Benedict, and Gilkey, all of whom were assigned to Air Ops as part of *Jefferson*'s OC Division, Reid served on the CAG staff and, therefore, was technically part of CVW-20 rather than the ship's crew. As such, the third-class yeoman referred to the carrier as "boat" rather than "ship," to the good-natured derision of the others.

"That's 'ship,' airhead," Benedict said. He chewed a moment on his cigar. "Whatcha want, Tiger?"

"One." Howard glanced at Reid. "What about this ship?"

"I got a friend."

"Yeah." Gilkey chuckled. "It's called your right hand."

"Up yours. He's a quartermaster third. Had the duty up on the bridge tonight."

"Yeah? They let him drive? Shit. What a crappy hand. Gimme three."

"Raise you ten." Benedict studied his cards. "So what's the gouge?" "Gouge" was Navyese for straight information, shipboard scuttlebutt that carried the ring of authenticity.

"Ah, he was standin' by when Admiral Gone let slip what he *really* thinks of us."

Gilkey laughed. "Going, going, gone." The rhyming play on Vaughn's name was a popular one with the enlisted men aboard. "So? What'd he say?"

"Only that we don't count for shit. Raise you a quarter."

"See you and another two bits too. Shit. That's officers for you."

"In."

"All officers aren't bad," Howard said. "See you and raise you four bits."

"Hey, the hero's gettin' serious."

"Heavy bettin', yeah. Just remember, Tiger. Officers don't care a rat's ass about you or anybody else with thirteen buttons on their blues."

"What about Commander Magruder?"

"Who?" Benedict squinted over his cigar. "Oh, the other hero. Our ace of aces. What about him?"

"He seems like a good guy."

"Yeah, an' you notice he got canned," Reid said. "Scuttlebutt is he shot before he got permission. Bad move for the upwardly mobile career-minded, y'know?"

"The good 'uns always get the short end." Gilkey sighed. "Crap. What kind of fuckin' cards you handin' out over there, Ben?"

"My own special brand. So what do the airedales say, Reid? We gonna fight the Indians or not?"

"Shit, I'm not mad at anybody," Gilkey said. "Aw, fuck. I'm out. Anyhow, what the Indies ever do to me?"

"Shot at us, is what," Reid replied. "Raise you a quarter, Ben. Word is, they're gonna hit us again. Soon."

"Ah, bull crap," Howard said. He'd become more adept during the past months at separating fact from fancy during interminable enlisted discussions that ranged from sex to Navy life to liberty ports to sex again. "No one knows that. Not even the officers. Raise a quarter."

"What I heard was the Russkies have it all planned." Gilkey leaned forward, lowering his voice to a conspiratorial whisper. "They've been working undercover-like, to get close to us. Then . . . bam!"

"Shit," Benedict said. "What for?"

"I hear they'd like a close look at one of our Aegis ships," Reid said. "And there's ol' *Vicksburg,* just sittin' over there."

Howard shook his head. "You guys are full of shit. They might like a good look at how she works in action, sure, but it's the Indies who are out to get us, not the Russkies!"

"Aw, just jerkin' your chain, kid. Call it. What you got?"

"Two pair," Benedict said. "A pair of queens . . . and another pair of queens."

"Son of a bitch." Reid dropped the cards. "Fuckin' conspiracy, man."

"Nah." Benedict raked in the change. "Just teachin' Tiger there how to make his way in the world. Watcha say. Again?"

"Do it." Reid started shuffling. "My deal this time. Maybe it should be my cards."

"All I can say is that this deployment is royally fucked,"

Gilkey observed. "I don't think one gold stripe on this ship knows what the hell he's doing."

"Too long at sea," Benedict agreed. "You can feel it, man. Every guy aboard is stretched out like a piano wire."

"Shit," Howard said as Reid began thumbing cards off the deck. "So what do you care? We don't count, remember?"

Gilkey's observation about the ship's officers, though, was unnerving. Despite the company of the others, it left Howard feeling very much alone.

# CHAPTER 13

**1500 hours EST, 25 March (0130 hours, 26 March, India time)**
**White House Press Room**

Admiral Magruder stood backstage with a number of other presidential aides and advisors, as well as the ever-present Secret Service men with their wire microphones and searching, emotionless expressions. From the off-stage wings behind the curtains, he listened and watched as the President conducted his press conference. He'd already delivered his speech, announcing to the world the Indian attack on U.S. Navy ships, and now he was fielding questions from the reporters who packed the press room. Batteries of lights flooded the President and the banks of microphones on the stage lectern before him with their glare. Steadicams, each bearing a different logo of a TV networks or news service, were trained on him, and there was a steady whirr and click in the background as camera shutters were triggered.

"Mr. President," a reporter from ABC was asking. "Does the attack on our ships mean war with India?"

"As I said before," the President replied. "The United States of America will not tolerate any abridgement of our freedom of the seas, anywhere in the world. We will not tolerate attacks on our vessels or against our people. I think we amply demonstrated that resolve, that *commitment* in the military action against North Korea last year. It doesn't matter who the aggressor is; an attack upon the military forces of the United States will be met by an appropriate response.

"Now, this certainly does not mean that a state of war exists between the United States and the Indian Federation. It also does not mean that we are unwilling to talk . . . in fact, we are more than willing to open negotiations that could lead to a clarification of this problem and, I might add, a reduction of tensions throughout the region over there. The United States is capable of defending its interests without resorting to outright war." He pointed at an upraised hand. "Yes? Here in front?"

"Bob Rutherford, NBC. Mr. President, you said in your speech that a Russian naval force has joined our carrier group off the Indian coast. Does this mean that Russia and the United States are considering unilateral military action against India, without waiting for the final UN Security Council vote? And if you are considering a military response, what form might that action take?"

The President gave his best self-deprecating smile. "Well, Bob, you know I can't give you any specifics on a question like that. All I can say is that this Administration will not rule out *any* action at this time, and that includes a military response. The leadership of the Commonwealth of Independent States has gone on record as saying that they support our declaration of the rights of shipping in international waters. The UN vote supports that declaration, and both of our countries stand ready to enforce those rights in whatever way seems appropriate. Yes? Over there, the lady in blue. Yes?"

"Linda Bellows, Associated Press. Mr. President, what about Pakistan's threat to use atomic weapons against India, and India's declaration that they will meet nuclear weapons with nuclear weapons of their own? Is there any danger in our military forces becoming involved in a nuclear war in the Indian Ocean?"

"I'm glad you asked that question, Linda. It is our position, and, I might add, the position of every other nation engaged in the debate in the UN, that the use of nuclear weapons in this conflict is unthinkable and must be discouraged by every means at the world's disposal. Now, I don't think I need to add that a nuclear escalation at this stage of the game is extremely unlikely. While both India and Pakistan have a nuclear *capability,* being able to build a bomb and being able to assemble one small enough to deliver by plane or missile are two very different things. . . ."

Magruder listened as the President continued to answer the questions. We will defend our rights, the world is with us, and the situation is under control: those were the three dominant themes running through each statement he made.

Abruptly, the President said, "Thank you very much," and strode from the stage.

"Mr. President! Mr. President!" A chorus of calls followed him, as a forest of waving arms tried to signal for his attention. "Mr. President! What about . . ."

The President brushed past Magruder as he stepped off the stage, and the admiral heard his low-voiced mutter to an aide. "Thank God that's over with."

Magruder watched the man vanish around a corner with his entourage and smiled to himself. There'd been considerable worry among the President's advisors about how the press conference might go, but it seemed to have come off well. By now, the Washington correspondents of each of the networks would be recapping the speech before the camera, repeating the President's message. We will defend our rights. The world is with us. The situation is under control.

He turned to follow the Presidential party. "Admiral!" a woman's voice called from behind him. "Admiral Magruder!"

Magruder looked around, already choosing his words for a firm refusal to add anything to the President's statements. He believed in a free press but was less than enthusiastic about the persistence with which that press sometimes pursued their duties.

Then his eyes widened. He *knew* the woman.

She was tall and attractive, with shoulder-length blond hair and dark eyes that seemed to mirror some inner worry. A portable tape recorder was clutched in one hand, and she wore her press badge and White House admission ID pinned to the lapel of a smartly tailored beige business suit. "Admiral Magruder? Do you remember me?"

"Certainly, Miss Drake," he said, smiling. "It's a small world, isn't it?"

She flashed a smile, though her eyes still held a dark and haunted look. Pamela Drake, a reporter for ACN News, had been a guest aboard the *Jefferson* two months before, while she was covering the political unrest in Thailand. Magruder's nephew had become involved with her there. Admiral Magruder had known Pamela was in Washington. He'd seen her often enough on the ACN Evening News.

But Washington was a big city. He'd not expected to run into her in person.

Matt had written once since Magruder had been transferred to Washington. In the letter, he'd mentioned the possibility of marrying the woman. Looking at her now, Magruder could certainly understand Matt's feelings.

For a moment, Magruder thought that Pamela was following her reporter's instincts and was about to ask him something relating to the press conference. The question she did ask caught him by surprise. "Admiral, have you heard anything from Matt? Do you know if he's all right?"

Magruder managed a grin. "I'm afraid I haven't heard a thing, but that's no cause for alarm. He's not much of a letter writer. At least, not to old SOBs like me."

She smiled back. "He won't tell me a thing either. Did you know we might be getting married?"

Magruder nodded. "He said something about it."

"Then you can understand why I want to know. Is . . . is the crisis over there as bad as everyone's making out? Will there be a war?"

He wondered if, after all, she was questioning him as a reporter rather than as his nephew's fiancée. No, he decided, looking into her eyes. The worry, the *pain* there had nothing to do with her career.

"Pamela, there's really nothing more I can tell you. There's danger, certainly. Matt's in a dangerous profession. You know that. As to any extra danger . . . I guess we all just have to wait and see."

"I . . . know, Admiral. I'll tell you the truth, I've been worried sick about Matt ever since Bangkok. I'm afraid I've been pushing him to leave the service."

Magruder's mouth tightened as he thought how best to reply. "Well, that'll have to be his decision, won't it?"

"*Our* decision, Admiral."

"Hmm." He hesitated, trapped by an abrupt and unaccountable anger. He suddenly found himself comparing the Drake woman to his sister-in-law Kathy, Matt's mother. His brother Sam had not come back from a Navy raid over a Hanoi bridge in 1968. He remembered the look on Kathy's face when she learned that her son had been accepted as a Navy aviator candidate. There'd been pain and fear, yes . . . but also a burning and enormous pride.

He forced the anger back. The girl had no way of putting things in perspective . . . and maybe that was to be expected. "Miss Drake, I don't want to dampen the flames of true love, but you ought to remember that there are over six thousand other men on the *Jefferson* besides Matt. Counting our supply ships and the attack sub assigned to CBG-14, there's another twenty-eight hundred men in the rest of the carrier group, every one of them with a wife or a girlfriend or a fiancée or a mother . . . someone who cares for them and is scared to death that they're not coming back. What makes you so special?"

She stiffened. "As I said, Admiral, it's *our* decision. Our life. I . . . I'm sorry I troubled you."

A twinge of conscience twisted in him. He opened his mouth to say something soothing, but Pamela Drake had already gone.

Tom Magruder watched her slim back and blond hair receding with the crowd of reporters. Then he shrugged, turned, and followed after the President.

**0625 hours, 26 March**
**Flight deck, U.S.S. *Thomas Jefferson***

Rear Admiral Vaughn stood with Captain Bersticer and other members of his staff just inside the open door leading from the island onto the flight deck, a scowl creasing his face. All of the officers wore their dress whites instead of khakis to mark the formality of the occasion, but Vaughn chaffed at the ceremonial trappings. The stupidity, the *wrongness* of his orders still stung, and he wasn't sure he was going to be able to pull off the coming meeting without getting angry.

Correction, he thought. He was already angry. What was going to be difficult was not letting that anger show.

A staff officer standing at Vaughn's elbow was wearing one of the ubiquitous Mickey Mouse headsets worn by deck personnel who needed to stay in touch with the ship's radio network. "They're inbound, Admiral," the officer said. "Five minutes."

He nodded, his scowl deepening. Admiral Vaughn did not like this at all.

*"It is imperative that a close working relationship with your counterparts in SOVINDRON be established as quickly as possible,"* his orders, received at 0300 that morning, had read. *"To facilitate the exchange of necessary battle codes and communications protocols, you are directed to receive Rear Admiral Nicolai Sergeivich Dmitriev aboard your command at the earliest practical opportunity."*

Fine. He would welcome the admiral, shake the bastard's hand even. What had followed in the orders was worse.

*"Effective 26 March, you are further directed to shift your flag to CG-66, U.S.S.*Vicksburg, *the better to monitor ship deployments and possible air threats to your command. Commonwealth naval liaison officers will be assigned by Admiral Dmitriev as observers aboard CG-66, to facilitate joint tactical and strategic operations between vessels of CBG-14 and SOVINDRON. . . ."*

Micromanagement. It had doomed military operations before this one. Somehow, the Washington bureaucracies, both military and civilian, always thought that they knew how to fight the war from the safety and comfort of the Potomac better than the men who were actually in the field. How many times had narrow-minded, fuzzy-headed, point-by-point direction from the rear screwed up an operation better left to the man in charge on the spot?

Vaughn had hoped to deal with the Russian presence at Turban Station by ignoring it. It wasn't as though the battle group *needed* the Russians. If anything, the Russians would be a definite hindrance in any upcoming conflict. Their ASW was more primitive, their ships noisier than their American counterparts. They had no weapon system at all like Phoenix and nothing like *Vicksburg*'s Aegis or SPY-1 radar. The entire history of Soviet big-carrier operations was only a few years old, and Vaughn had no confidence in their abilities to handle blue-water air operations with so-called "navalized" Frontal Aviation aircraft and inexperienced pilots.

But he was being *forced* to work closely with the sons of bitches, and he didn't like it, didn't like it at all. His orders were specific and to the point, signed by Admiral Fletcher T. Grimes, Chief of Naval Operations, and originating with the National Command Authority. That meant the President himself, and the National Security Council, and you couldn't get any more high-powered than that.

It also meant that the decision was as much a political one as something born of military necessity. In this case, the politics far outweighed the military practicalities. Mixing the two naval squadrons, Vaughn thought, was a recipe for certain disaster.

But Charles Lee Vaughn was a flag officer of the United States Navy, and questioning the orders did not even occur to him. Grumbling about orders, however, was the Navy man's ancient and inalienable right. "What do you want to bet the Soviets worked all this out just to get a good look at Aegis?" he asked.

Captain Bersticer was standing between him and the open door leading out to the flight deck. "Could be, sir. The Russians have been wanting to look inside a Ticonderoga-class cruiser for a long time now."

"Well, they won't get a look now. Not at my expense. Did you pass my message to Cunningham?"

"Yes, sir. His intelligence officer has things well in hand, sir."

"He'd damn well better. I don't want these Russian bastards using this as an excuse to get their prying claws on Aegis."

"They're coming, sir," the officer with the Mickey Mouse helmet called. There was a stir among the officers and men waiting in the lee of *Jefferson*'s island. Vaughn could hear a distant, thuttering sound in the air that rose rapidly above the calls and last-minute shufflings of the greeting party.

Vaughn moved to where he could see past Bersticer and looked through the open door. The morning sun was still low, and the carrier's island cast a deep and moody shadow across the middeck where the Russian helo was supposed to land. A mackerel sky still tinged with the reds and oranges of a fiery dawn glowed above the horizon. The thuttering grew louder, more insistent.

The helicopter was one of the new Ka-27s, a boxy-looking machine with the NATO code name Helix. Like other Russian naval helos, it used two counter-rotating main rotors, one set directly above the other, eliminating the need for a tail rotor or boom. Instead, it had a stubby tail with two massive stabilizer fins that, to American eyes, gave it an oddly unbalanced, incomplete look.

Vaughn watched as it drifted out of the early morning light and was eclipsed by the island's shadow. The machine hovered for a moment, then settled to the deck with a bounce on four landing wheels, following the guidance of a yellow shirt who brought it in with crisp movements of a pair of bright-colored wands. The red star painted on the stabilizer looked very much out of place on an American carrier deck. Curiously, the machine also had the Aeroflot logo picked out in Cyrillic lettering on its hull. Vaughn remembered that the national airline of the former USSR had close connections with the Russian military services.

"Wait, boys," Vaughn said as his aides made last-moment adjustments to their uniforms and began to move toward the door. "We'll let them show themselves first. It's *our* carrier, after all."

As the rotors whined to a halt, U.S. sailors in dress whites were already unrolling a red carpet across the steel deck. The Helix's cargo compartment door slid open with a bang, as a chief boatswain's mate raised a bosun's pipe to his mouth and sounded a piercing, welcoming shrill. Behind him, the ranks of *Jefferson*'s Marines, resplendent in their red-and-blue Class As, snapped to present arms, and as the pipe's notes died away, *Jefferson*'s band crashed into an unrecognizable clashing that the tone-deaf Vaughn could only assume held some meaning for the Russians.

A Russian crewman appeared in the open cargo door, unfolding a metal ladder that extended to the *Jefferson*'s deck. The helo looked fairly roomy inside. The Helix normally served in the ASW role and would have had little space aboard for passengers. This one, evidently, had been refitted for use as a personnel carrier.

A heavyset man with steel-gray hair and a scowl to match Vaughn's own stepped down the ladder and onto the carpet, planting his feet on *Jefferson*'s deck as though defying anyone present to move him. He wore a blue uniform with one large and one slender gold bar on his sleeves and the insignia of a Russian naval *kontr-admiral*. Three other officers with less gold on their uniforms and caps, with fewer medals on their breasts, emerged from the helo and took their places behind their admiral.

"Show time, Admiral," Bersticer said.

"Right. Let's get on with it." Settling a facsimile of a smile in place, Vaughn followed his chief of staff out through the door and onto the flight deck.

Flight operations had been suspended for the time being, of course, and *Jefferson*'s roof was strangely quiet and still as Vaughn marched those long twenty yards to where the Helix was parked. He was conscious of the eyes on him. Vulture's Row, the railed open area high atop *Jefferson*'s island below the billboard tangle of radar antennae and masts, was crowded with those sailors who'd managed to jockey a ringside seat for themselves. Others watched silently from the walkways around the flight deck's borders, from the catwalks set along the island's sides, from vantage points on and under the A-6 Intruders and F-14 Tomcats parked wing by folded wing along the edge of the roof.

Vaughn stopped six feet from Kontr-Admiral Dmitriev and stood there stiffly, uncertain of what to do next. The Russian admiral gave him a wintry smile and raised one hand to the gold-heavy bill of his peaked cap. "Permission to come aboard, Admiral," he said.

The Russian's English was quite good, Vaughn thought as he returned the salute, though the man rolled the word "admiral" about his mouth in a rather odd way. "Permission granted. Welcome aboard the *Thomas Jefferson,* Admiral Dmitriev."

"I think, Admiral Vaughn, that this must be historic day." Dmitriev extended his hand. "Closest I have been to American nuclear carrier before today was reconnaissance photos taken by one of our Tupolev bombers."

Damn right it's a historic day, you gold-braid son of a bitch, Vaughn thought as he reluctantly took Dmitriev's hand and shook it. The phrase "a day that shall live in infamy" ran through his mind. "If you would care to come with me, please?" he said. "You can sample the hospitality of our wardroom."

"*Spasebah,*" the Russian replied. "Thank you. However, it is my wish that we spend no time on ceremony procedures. Our reconnaissance satellites have detected evidence of massive activity at Indian coastal bases. Is possible Indians are planning air strike against our forces."

"Our satellites are watching those bases as well, Admiral."

He'd seen the latest TENCAP images of Jamnagar and Uttarlai only a few minutes earlier. He wondered how recent the Russians' military intelligence was. TENCAP—Tactical Exploitation of National CAPabilities—was a new military communications system that allowed U.S. commanders in the field to tap photo intelligence data directly off American reconnaissance satellites, and Vaughn doubted that the Russians, with their historic emphasis on centralized command and control, had anything similar.

The photos Vaughn had seen that morning had been worrisome. Jamnagar, an Indian military air base on the Gulf of Kutch, was a hive of activity as military aircraft of every size and description assembled there from other airfields deeper in the Indian subcontinent. Satellite photos from Jaisalmer and Uttarlai, bases three hundred miles to the north, showed similar buildups of IAF forces. Surveillance of the Soviet-American task force had been intensifying over the past ten hours, mostly from Indian Bear-F and Illyushin-38 "May" naval aircraft, and the Indian navy appeared to be assembling a major task force at Bombay, centered on both of their carriers, plus a Kresta-II cruiser and numerous smaller vessels. That air and sea armada *might* be assembling to support further Indian operations against Pakistan, but the possibility that they had American targets in mind could not be dismissed.

"Then you are aware of seriousness of our position," Dmitriev said, responding to Vaughn's blunt statement. The Russian turned and gestured toward the three high-ranking officers who stood stiffly at parade rest behind him. "I have brought men who will serve as Soviet liaisons aboard your Aegis command ship. Admiral Vaughn, may I present Kapitan Pervogo Ranga Sharov, my Chief of Staff. Kapitan Vtorogo Ranga Besedin, my Tactical Officer. Kapitan Tretyego Ranga Pokrovsky, of *Kreml* Air Department. All are excellent officers and have my complete confidence and respect. All speak English good as me."

Each Russian officer saluted as he was introduced. Vaughn merely nodded to each in turn. Surely the dictates of formal military courtesy did not require him to return the salutes of these . . . these *spies*.

Vaughn had no doubt at all that the three men had had ties with the former Soviet military intelligence, the infamous GRU.

"Preparations are not yet complete aboard the *Vicksburg,*" Vaughn replied. It would help, he thought, if he could stall the Russians here for a time, while the Aegis cruiser's people prepared for these unwelcome visitors. "I assure you that we are carefully monitoring Indian air and sea activities, and that we will have ample time to board *Vicksburg* if they make a hostile move. We might as well wait here until they are ready for us over there."

The Russians did not seem pleased and grumbled among themselves in Russian. Vaughn had given them no choice, however. They could only scowl, shrug, and nod. "Very well, Admiral," Dmitriev said. "Lead way, if you please."

Vaughn turned and strode back toward the island, the thump of each footstep muffled by the red carpet on the deck. What had the President been thinking when he dreamed this one up? The world might be a different place, the Russians might no longer be the threat they once had been . . . but so far as Vaughn was concerned, they still presented a greater threat to America and her interests than any ten Indias. Hell, Moscow had provided the Indians with their MiGs and Kresta IIs, their Bear reconnaissance aircraft and Foxtrot submarines in the first place.

They were the *enemy.*

# CHAPTER 14

**0709 hours, 26 March**
**Strike Ops, U.S.S. *Thomas Jefferson***

Tombstone sat in the folding metal chair with arms crossed, listening as Commander Neil gave the latest rundown on Indian forces along the coast. Using a large-scale map of the area, with crisp colored symbols marked onto a transparent overlay, he'd already covered the Indian naval squadron now gathering some three hundred miles to the southeast. Now he was using a slide projector to present TENCAP photos showing SAM sites and mobile antiaircraft batteries along the beaches and inland between Karachi and the Gulf of Cambay. The lighting was set midway between fully light and completely dark, so that the speaker could refer back and forth between the maps and the slides projected on the screen.

The personnel in attendance included all of CVW-20's squadron skippers and XOs, though the briefing was obviously tailored primarily for the Hornet and Intruder COs. While all of *Jefferson*'s aircraft would have parts to play in the upcoming operation, it would be the strike aircraft, two squadrons of A-6 Intruders and two squadrons of F/A-18 Hornets, that would deliver the bombs and missiles to targets on the ground in Pakistan and India. Tombstone was sitting in even though he would not be flying. As a squadron liaison officer in CIC, he would need to know the overall tactical plan, call signs, and code designations to be used during the operation. He felt out of place, though, knowing that these men would be flying their missions while he remained safe on board the carrier.

It was strange having the Russian admiral and his three

officers in the Strike Ops briefing room with them. Past sessions in the compartment had discussed hypothetical strikes on Russian targets, both at shore and at sea. Tombstone could remember one practice run directed at a hypothetical target: the newest Soviet aircraft carrier, *Kreml,* and her escort.

Looking at the faces of the other Americans in the room, Tombstone knew they were thinking the same thing. It would have been amusing if it had not been so serious.

That seriousness was underscored by the fact that the Russians were being permitted to see TENCAP intelligence material. He was sure that the OZ people had screened it all before the briefing, but he knew that Intelligence was always leery of letting the Soviets see just how good American spysat capabilities were.

"So, here's the situation as of 0430 this morning," Neil said, concluding his report with a summary. "Indian penetrations have reached as far as the Nara River throughout the southern Thar. Bridging and amphib tank operations last night at Mirpur Khas, here, and Khewari, up here, appear to have been completely successful in establishing bridgeheads across the river and canal barriers along the edge of the desert. Indian armor will most likely move against Hyderabad within the next six to twelve hours, though whether the Indians plan to capture or bypass the city is still anyone's guess." He glanced sharply at Admiral Vaughn, then snapped his pointer shut.

"Pakistani forces in the region are digging in and preparing to defend the city, but satellite reconnaissance shows that they are badly outmatched. Pakistan has lost at least eighty percent of its air. They had one armor division here at Naya Chor, but that was overrun and largely destroyed in the fighting yesterday. With the other Pakistan forces tied down fighting Indian advances in the north and the threat to their capital, there isn't much standing between the Indians and Hyderabad.

"Beyond that, well . . . Karachi is the next logical target, and that port is absolutely vital to Pakistan's whole effort. If Pakistan loses Karachi, they will probably lose the war. Certainly they'll have lost most of their capability for bringing in supplies and arms from outside. It's a fair bet that the Indian task force now putting to sea is headed for Karachi. They will blockade the port, and there is a good chance that they will launch an amphibious assault on Karachi itself.

"So far, the Indians have been careful to maintain good, in-depth air defense as far as three hundred miles behind the Pakistani border. You can expect primarily SA-2 and SA-3 SAM batteries, as well as ZSUs and conventional triple-A." He paused and surveyed his audience. "Are there questions?" There were none. "If not," Neil added, "I'll relinquish my pointer now to Commander Aubrey."

Daniel Aubrey was a slight, rumpled-looking man with a brushy, unkempt mustache and a quick wit. He was the senior officer of *Jefferson*'s Strike Ops, a separate component of the carrier's OX Division. Strike Ops published the ship's pink and green sheets that listed upcoming operational events, prepared the daily flight schedule, and planned and coordinated underway replenishments.

And as their name suggested, Strike Ops was responsible for targeting and planning all tactical air strikes.

Aubrey accepted the telescoping pointer from Neil. "Thank you, Commander Spook," he said with a grin. He gestured at the TENCAP photos of SAM sites in the Indian state of Gujarat. "Now that we all know where not to go, maybe I can shed some light on where the party's going to be at.

"As our spook friend told us," Aubrey said, "the Indians have been heavy into snakes this week. Assuming, of course, that the crypto boys in OS Division have their ears screwed on tight, our radio intercepts suggest that New Delhi is calling their big push into Pakistan 'Cobra.'

"Naturally, that suggested the code designation for our counterstrike. Operation Mongoose will be directed at the principal logistical routes that are supplying Indian forces at the front." He used the pointer on the map. "The Indians have one pretty blatant Achilles' heel, and that's their logistical network into southern Pakistan. In this whole area, between Punjab and the salt marshes down here by the sea, they have exactly one decent road and rail line: Jaipur to Jodhpur, then across the border and through Naya Chor, Mirpur Khas, and . . . " He smacked the pointer tip against the map with a loud crack. "Hyderabad. We're calling that road Highway 101. Hit that supply line, hit it hard, and we could stall the entire Indian advance." He paused and looked at Admiral Vaughn. "And that, of course, is exactly what we want to do."

He gestured to the slide projector operator. A photograph

appeared on the screen, replacing an earlier shot of a SAM site in Gujarat. It showed a line of vehicles shot from overhead, canvas-covered trucks mostly, but there were a pair of ZSU-23s escorting them. The colors were the odd blend of greens, whites, and yellows that marked the slide as an infrared photo. The truck and tank chassis engines showed as hot smears of white against the cooler greens of the background. "This came through from a KH-12 early this morning," Aubrey continued. "It shows one portion of a supply convoy on Highway 101 east of Naya Chor that numbered over two hundred vehicles.

"Now, I don't want any of you to get the idea that cutting the Indian supply lines is as simple as just bombing the crap out of this road. The Great Thar Desert is largely hardpan gravel and is perfectly able to support tanks, trucks, or whatever. There are some sandy places. In the '72 war, a Pakistan armor advance bogged down in soft dunes near Ramgarh and got picked off. Most places, though, the Indians can choose their own route across the desert.

"But we have to keep in mind that the convoys themselves need supplies. Food. Water. Fuel. It's two hundred miles from Jodhpur across the desert to Naya Chor, three hundred to Hyderabad. The road not only helps the supply vehicles cross the desert faster, it serves as access for the supplies that keep those vehicles moving. If we knock out the roads, the Indians will be able to reroute their convoys to the north or south, but it is going to cripple their logistical efficiency. We could expect lots more vehicle breakdowns in off-road travel, especially in rocky or gravel-covered areas.

"The real high-priority targets, of course, will be the bridges. Every time Indian pioneers have to build or repair a bridge in this region, it's a major engineering operation, with the equipment and material being ferried all the way up from Jodhpur. The Indians are especially vulnerable here, with eight major streams or canals to bridge or ford between Naya Chor and Hyderabad. Some of these aren't more than a trickle in the sand, but the Nara Canal is a major obstacle. And, of course, once they get to Hyderabad, there's the Indus River itself. The Indians are probably planning massive bridging operations coupled with paratroop or commando landings to get across the Indus. If we can delay them here, we could cripple their whole operation."

Tombstone listened carefully as Aubrey laid out the essentials of Operation Mongoose. The Hornets would perform double duty, as usual. VFA-161 would be the first ones to go feet dry, striking at Indian radar facilities, airfields, and SAM sites along the coast. VFA-173 would fly TARCAP for the main strike force, protecting the bombers to and from the target. TARget Combat Air Patrol was intended to discourage enemy aircraft from attacking rather than actually shooting them down.

The A-6 Intruders, with their heavy bomb loads and laser designators, would be assigned the bridges and road convoys between Hyderabad and Naya Chor, with a priority on trucks carrying fuel, water, and ammunition, the essentials for desert warfare. Cratering munitions would be used to ruin sections of the road, most of which was dirt and gravel anyway. Low-level precision attacks would knock out the railway.

And the Tomcats would fly CAP for the CBG.

Each element of Operation Mongoose was designed to minimize casualties, both American and Indian, as much as possible. No one dared to think that the operation could be pulled off with no casualties at all. The weapons of modern warfare were too fast, too hard-hitting, too deadly for that to be a possibility.

Code names for each element of the plan were assigned. The two Intruder squadrons, eight planes each in the VA-84 Blue Rangers and VA-89 Death Dealers, were tagged Blue Strike and Gold Strike. The ten Hornets from the VFA-161 Javelins, tasked with hitting ground targets, were designated Lucky Strike, while eight Hornets from VFA-173, the Fighting Hornets, were split into two flights code-named Blue and Red Camel. EA-6B Prowlers from VAQ-143, the Sharks, would accompany each strike group, providing ECM jamming to mask Mongoose's deployments. Hawkeyes from VAW-130, the Catseyes, would circle above the carrier and just off the Indian coast, providing early warning for both the fleet and the strike missions. The two Tomcat squadrons would retain their squadron code names, Vipers and Eagles.

It was a gigantic enterprise, as large and as complex as Operation Righteous Thunder, when *Jefferson* had covered the Marine landings in North Korea. One problem stood out sharply, though. The Russian forces were not listed in the operational lineup.

Perhaps, Tombstone thought, it had been decided that it would take too long to get Russian and American aviators to work with one another. Certainly, with no time for practice or training runs, joint air operations could be more dangerous to the allies than to the enemy. Even so, Russian participation was conspicuous by its absence.

"The ordies began arming operations yesterday, and as of 0600 this morning they were ahead of schedule. Our current scenario calls for launch operations to commence at 1200 hours today. Hawkeye and tanker assets will be put up first, of course, followed by Red Camel and Blue Camel. At 1240 hours, launch operations will begin for the strike elements, beginning with Lucky Strike.

"Mongoose will be coordinated so that the various strike elements will arrive over their separate targets at approximately the same time. By maintaining an element of surprise, this will maximize both their chances of achieving successful runs and for avoiding enemy ground fire and fighters.

"We expect that the entire strike phase of Mongoose will take no more than thirty minutes over the target, with separate elements coming in at low altitude from different directions, to keep the enemy off balance, and to divide and scatter his triple-A defenses." His pointer slid down the map from the Sindh to an oval drawn near the Indian coast. "All aircraft will rendezvous here, at Point Juliet just off the Kori Creek inlet. Tankers will be waiting there to refuel them for the final leg back to the *Jefferson.* Are there any questions?"

Tombstone raised his hand. "What about the Russians?"

Aubrey looked from Tombstone to Vaughn, then back again. Tombstone was aware of the hard silence in the room as each man waited for the answer.

"Ah . . . it's been decided," Aubrey said slowly, "that a joint ground attack mission would present us with unacceptable risk. Russian interceptors will be available on a standby basis to help deal with threats to the fleet. However, Russian strike aircraft will be readied in case a second strike on Indian targets is necessary."

Of course, there would be no second strike. If the first strike failed to slow the Indian advance, there would be little more that the Russians—with fewer aircraft, more primitive targeting and delivery systems, and shorter-ranged strike aircraft—

could hope to accomplish. Tombstone heard a low-voiced, angry murmur spreading around the room. He imagined most of the aviators had expected the Russians to share some of the risks of what was already a very high-threat mission. At the very least, more targets in the air would cause more confusion on the ground and better each individual pilot's chances of coming through intact.

Another hand raised and Aubrey nodded. ''Captain Fitzgerald. Yes, sir?''

*Jefferson*'s captain stood. ''Yes, Dan. Is there an assessment yet on the possibility that the Indian fleet might sortie against this battle group? I mean no disrespect to our Russian guests, but two Tomcat squadrons and the interceptors off the *Kreml* are all we'll have for outer zone fleet defense. The Indians could conceivably put a great many ASMs in the sky and saturate our defenses.''

''That would be better directed at Commander Neil,'' Aubrey said. ''Our understanding in OX is that the threat from surface elements is low. Commander Neil, do you have anything to add to that?''

''Only that the principal threat to the CBG will be from ground-based aircraft. The fleet assembling at Bombay is almost certainly targeted against Karachi. And the MiGs . . .'' He looked at the Russians. ''Your MiG-29s have look-down/shoot-down capability, do they not, sir?''

Captain Pokrovsky—his full rank translated as ''Captain Third Rank,'' lower than a U.S. Navy captain but higher than a commander—consulted briefly with Admiral Dmitriev, then stood, his hands clasped behind his back. ''If I have meaning correct, *da. Sahv'yehrshennah,* MiG have capability kill cruise missile.'' *Kreml*'s Air Officer appeared completely self-assured on the point. Tombstone wondered if he didn't seem a bit *too* self-assured. His difficulties with English were obvious.

Aubrey spread his hands. ''There you have it, sir. The Russians will be able to help cover our fleet while the Hornets are out.''

''God help us,'' Vaughn said, his low-voiced comment unexpectedly loud in the near-silence of the room. There was no mistaking the disdain in the admiral's words.

''Admiral Vaughn,'' Dmitriev said with steady, icily correct control in the words. "Perhaps you disagree with your President's order to operate together as a fleet?"

Vaughn's mouth hung open for a moment until, with an effort, he closed it. "My apologies, Admiral," he said. "No insult intended. But I have grave concerns about our squadrons operating together in an environment where identification and control are going to be serious problems. You have still not provided us with the IFF codes for your aircraft, and misidentification could lead to . . . unfortunate incidents."

True enough, Tombstone thought. He remembered the Indian MiG he'd seen the night before. If the Russians didn't give the Americans their IFF frequencies and codes, how were the U.S. ships going to distinguish between Indian and Russian aircraft? There were going to be problems enough telling Indian MiGs from Navy Hornets. . . .

"Clearance to exchange codes is out of my hands, Admiral," Dmitriev said, and Tombstone could hear the heaviness in his voice. No doubt he'd had to buck the question back to Moscow, where the bureaucracy there was still debating the question.

Suddenly, Tombstone felt sorry for the Russians, professional men forced to operate with their former opponents, with neither understanding nor support from their own people further up the chain of command.

This, he reflected, was going to be one hell of a way to run a war.

**0715 hours, 26 March**
**Guided Missile Patrol Boat K91, INS *Pralaya***

The missile boat wallowed forward in heavy seas. Senior Lieutenant Javed Chaudry clung to the safety railing on the small craft's weather bridge and wondered how they could possibly survive.

The storm front had moved out of the area the night before, taking with it the overcast skies and dirty weather that had trailed the storm. All that was left was this swell, vast waves that lifted the four small patrol boats like wood chips, then sent them rolling into the trench between spindrift-capped crests in a blast of spray and wind.

The patrol boats were Osa IIs, purchased from the Soviet Union in 1976. Their primary armament consisted of four Russian-built SS-N-2b antiship missiles that carried the NATO designation "Styx." The Osas could spring ahead at thirty-five knots, but for the time being they were barely making way, riding with the heavy, following seas at just eight knots. It would have been far better, the lieutenant thought, if they could have blasted ahead at full speed, taking the waves, *riding* them, instead of this incessant up-and-down wallowing.

The *Pralaya* crested another wave, angled forward, then began the long slide into the trench. Chaudry clung tighter to the railing as his stomach suddenly twisted with a gut-wrenching pang that brought him to the very edge of being explosively sick.

For one desperate moment, he thought he was going to suffer the humiliation of vomiting in front of his men. Then, as *Pralaya* halted her plunge, he managed to look around at the other men on deck or on the bridge. Judging from the expressions on some of their faces, he wasn't the only one suffering. The thought steadied him.

The heavy seas were a blessing, Chaudry told himself. The tiny squadron was only the advance element of the Indian navy, which was trailing eighty miles astern. The Indians were under no illusions as to the sensitivity of American radar. Sneaking up on a Yankee carrier would be next to impossible.

But it might—*just* might—be possible to mislead the Americans by a critical few minutes. The American radar would not immediately be able to pick the Osas from the clutter of the surrounding waves. They would continue their stealthy approach, their own radars off but their receivers tuned to warn them at the first touch by a hostile beam. Soon, very soon now, they would be close enough to loose their missiles.

And then it would be a fast turn and a run for home, safety, and solid, unmoving ground.

The thought cheered Lieutenant Chaudry immensely.

# CHAPTER 15

**0727 hours, 26 March**
**Flight deck, U.S.S. *Thomas Jefferson***

Admiral Vaughn held his cap to his head as the Russian Helix gunned its rotors and lifted from the American carrier's flight deck. His free hand clenched into a fist at his side. *Damn* Washington for ordering him to transfer to the *Vicksburg*. And damn the Russians! Rather than fly across in their Aeroflot Helix, he'd snagged one of *Jefferson*'s HH-60 Seahawks to transfer himself and several aides to the *Vicksburg*.

As if an American admiral could consent to be flown aboard an American command ship by the *Russians,* for God's sake! But the use of two helos would mean a delay. The Russian helo would drop off the three liaison officers on the *Vicksburg* first, then return to the *Kreml* with Rear Admiral Dmitriev. Vaughn's helo would hang back until the Helix cleared *Vicksburg*'s fantail.

Every time he turned around, it seemed, the Russians were in his way. It was almost as if Moscow was carrying on some monstrous, clandestine plan to personally frustrate the plans and career of Rear Admiral Charles Lee Vaughn.

It was early in 1980 when he'd first run afoul of the bastards. Oh, he'd crossed swords with the Russians plenty of times during his rise up the Navy's command pyramid. It was impossible to command any American ship anywhere in the world during the '60s and '70s without meeting Russian Bear bombers and Soviet trawlers, aggressive sub contacts and games of chicken . . . "chicken of the sea," as the encounters were called. It was all part of the global muscle-flexing of the Cold War, a way for each side to test the other's defenses, and to polish its own.

But in 1980, Vaughn had just made rear admiral, and his first deployed command had been a Navy carrier group operating in the Pacific. The temper of the U.S. Navy had been dismal then. It was not a good time for men, like Vaughn, with strong military aspirations. The Carter Administration had been hell-bent on slashing defense spending, and some members of a short-sighted Congress had been pushing for virtual disarmament. The American public, still wallowing in the post-Vietnam mire, had cared little about the need to maintain a strong guard against the communists.

Against that political backdrop, Vaughn had seen his being given command of a carrier squadron as a truly important step. He'd been certain that he could make a real difference in the way America's battered military was perceived, both by the government and by the people.

One of the carrier's ASW heroes had picked up a sub contact during routine patrol operations. The carrier's antisub destroyers and frigates had converged on the area, searching, but had found nothing. Somehow, the contact had made its escape.

It had been a time of increased tension throughout the world. Only a few months earlier, in December of 1979, the Russians had invaded Afghanistan, and nothing, not diplomatic efforts, not threats of an Olympic Games boycott or a grain embargo, *nothing* had convinced them to back down. There'd been several incidents at sea and in the air, and the threat of a war starting, by plan or by accident, had been very real. Standing orders from Washington held that no squadron commander could let Russian subs get close to one of the Navy's precious carriers, and the vanished contact had already been well inside the squadron's defensive perimeter. Vaughn had ordered the squadron to zigzag out of the area, while intensifying the search for the missing sub with his ASW assets.

Then the sub had broached dead ahead, rising out of nowhere in spray and foam like some huge, glistening whale. With all the grace and maneuverability of an eighty-story skyscraper floating on its side, Vaughn's carrier had smashed into the Russian sub.

The full story might never be known, but later hearings and debriefings concluded that the Russian skipper had made a mistake. The sub, an Echo II nuclear-powered craft designed primarily for anti-carrier operations, had evidently been trying to probe the American squadron's defenses, another chicken-of-the-sea incident like hundreds of others. The Russian captain had probably eluded the earlier search by hiding his boat on the bottom, which, in those waters, was not very deep. When the American carrier had accidentally come bearing down on his location, sonar pinging away, he'd assumed that he'd been discovered and tried to get away. At the same time, the shallow water and the noise made by the other ships in the squadron had confused the American sonar. No one had heard the Echo II until it was already surfacing.

Why the sub had surfaced in the first place was another unknown. Possibly the Russian skipper had thought he was under attack and decided that a fast surface was the only way to defuse a situation suddenly gone out of hand. Or perhaps there'd been a mechanical failure or a confusion in orders. Whatever the reason, before the American carrier could slow or change course, it had hit the Echo II just forward of the conning tower. Both vessels had suffered extensive damage, though obviously the sub had gotten the worst in the exchange. The sub had refused offers of assistance and had last been seen limping west on the surface. The carrier had suffered minor damage to her keel, and her forward sonar dome had been knocked out, requiring repairs in the States.

And that was when Admiral Vaughn's troubles had *really* begun. An anti-military Congress had insisted on hearings to determine culpability in the matter. He'd been grilled mercilessly about his part in the affair, with most of the committee's attention focusing on whether or not he'd been patrolling too aggressively.

*Too aggressively!* The Navy had held its own inquest, of course, and Vaughn had been cleared. He'd done nothing questionable, had operated within the letter of his orders, and had done nothing to bring discredit upon his service or his command.

So why had he lost his command and wound up at a damned Pentagon desk?

His transport to the *Vicksburg* was ready on the spot just vacated by the Helix, an HH-60 Seahawk with rotors unfolded and engine turning over. Nodding to Bersticer and the others of his staff who were going across with him, he started across the flight deck.

It was inevitable, he thought, as he hurried across the steel deck, that the reason for his exile had been political. Once a Navy officer reached the rank of captain, hell, once he was a full commander bucking for captain, most of the forces that shaped his career were political in one way or another. But Vaughn's problem had been part of the very focus of the Cold War, as well as the ongoing political bloodbaths in Washington.

Incidents between U.S. and Soviet vessels had been particularly numerous back in the sixties, when the Russian navy was vigorously expanding under the guidance of its number-one sponsor, Soviet CNO Admiral Gorshkov. Harassment by both sides had been commonplace, with ships crossing one another's paths, penetrating each other's formations, even deliberately trying to ram. The number of incidents had grown until, at one point, collisions at sea were averaging an incredible one a month. One of the worst of those had occurred in May of 1967, when the U.S. destroyer *Walker* cut in front of a Soviet vessel and sheered off, then sideswiped the destroyer *Besslednyi,* tearing loose a whaleboat and punching a hole in her side. The next day, unbelievably, the *Walker* had rammed a *second* Russian ship, holing her twice.

In 1972, in a little-publicized agreement signed during Nixon's visit to Moscow, the U.S. and the USSR had agreed to hold yearly meetings, to exchange information and review charges arising from such incidents. Called the Incidents at Sea Agreement, or IncSeA, it was designed to stop harassment on and over the high seas.

It had worked well for eight years. Unfortunately, by 1980 the political balance in Washington had become extremely precarious. Russian aggression in Afghanistan, communist support for the Sandanistas, the collapse of détente all had suggested a final breakdown of *any* dialogue with the Soviets. Certain factions in Congress, with political careers riding on SALT II and good relations with the Soviets, had hoped to reverse what seemed to be increasing intransigence on the part of Moscow. The ramming incident had appeared to be the Americans' fault . . . or at least the fault of the admiral who had been aggressively hounding the Russian sub. By playing up the incident and doing some aggressive hounding of their own, they had hoped to prove the benevolence of U.S. intentions toward the Russians.

*Too aggressive,* the bastards had claimed. Even after being vindicated by the Navy board, there'd been little his supporters could do to shield him at the time. The Navy could not afford to antagonize the source of its yearly appropriations, and Vaughn, by fighting back, had made enemies on Capitol Hill.

So he'd been quietly shunted aside, out of sight, out of mind. In a crippling turn of irony, another U.S. carrier, the *Kitty Hawk,* had collided with a Soviet Victor I in 1984. The Russian had been running with no lights in the hours just before dawn, and the collision had left pieces of the sub's propeller embedded in the *Kitty Hawk*'s hull. By that time, though, America's military reawakening in the Reagan years had been well under way, and the men involved had suffered none of the probings or ostracism that Vaughn had suffered.

Vaughn understood the Navy's reasoning—at least he tried to convince himself that he understood—but that didn't change the bitter *unfairness* of it all. For twelve years he'd sat it out on the beach, his career at dead slow. His wife had left him four years earlier, a scandal in the tight circles of high-ranking Washington Navy society that had only added to his image as a has-been who'd never quite made the grade. He'd been ready to quit, to formally retire from the Navy, when the intervention of powerful friends in the Pentagon had opened up this new opportunity.

Command of CBG-14.

If he could carry out his orders . . . if Washington or the Russians didn't screw him once again, he could still salvage his career, salvage his *life*. But the sinking of the Indian sub had raised the old specters once more. *Biddle*'s aggressive patrolling had triggered the incident . . . or at least, that was how Washington would interpret it.

And as COCBG, *he* was responsible for *Biddle*.

He climbed up the ladder into the Seahawk, accepting a cranial and life vest from the crew chief. "We'll be a few minutes taking off, Admiral," the enlisted man said as Bersticer scrambled up the ladder and took his seat at the admiral's side. "That Russkie helo's on its approach to the *Vickie* now. We want to give them plenty of room."

Vaughn nodded as he strapped on the helmet. It figured. The Russians were always getting in his way!

Well, God help the bastards if they ever got in his way again!

**0738 hours, 26 March**
**CIC, U.S.S. *Vicksburg***

In Greek mythology the mirror-brilliant shield of Athena was Aegis. The hero Perseus used it in his battle with the gorgon Medusa, fighting her by watching her reflection in the shield.

It was a potent name for a potent modern air defense system. Linked by fifteen on-board computers and sophisticated electronics to the SPY-1 radar system, Aegis could track hundreds of targets simultaneously, could guide upgraded Navy Standard missiles, and could even coordinate fleet defense with other ships in the squadron. In the so-called ''Armageddon mode,'' Aegis could track and fire automatically, without any input at all from the crew beyond turning it on. Any target meeting certain criteria of speed, course, and altitude within ten miles of the ship would be fired on.

The vessel chosen to house Aegis was the end product of a long line of compromises. Originally designed as destroyers, the Ticonderoga-class cruisers had been intended as anti-air warfare complements to a new type of ship, the nuclear strike cruisers (CSGN) that were to have been fitted with Tomahawk cruise missiles. Aegis was to have been fitted to both of them, creating an electronically interlocked AAW system. Then Congress refused to fund the CSGN program, and cost overruns threatened to torpedo the Ticonderogas and their high-tech Aegis system as well.

At the beginning of 1980, the Navy changed the Ticonderogas' classification from destroyer to cruiser, a move that made the cost overruns look better on the Pentagon's books and better reflected the vessels' abilities. As Aegis cruisers, the Ticonderogas became a vital part of the Navy's global strategy. A total of twenty-seven were planned, providing missile and air defense coordination for each Navy carrier battle group as well as the four battleship combat groups.

America's Ticonderoga-class guided-missile cruisers were

widely regarded as the most capable antiair warships ever developed. U.S.S. *Vicksburg,* CG-66, was a recent addition to the class, having been laid down by Litton/Ingalls Shipbuilding, launched from the Ingalls floating dock in 1990, and formally commissioned early in 1991. Just over 532 feet long at the waterline, displacing 9,500 tons with a full load, *Vicksburg*'s hull was low and sleek with a sharply angled bow. Her superstructure was notoriously boxy, sandwiched between two massive gray cubes that faced fore and aft like gigantic bookends. Those cubes housed *Vicksburg*'s SPY-1B phased-array radars, which were visible on the slightly angled upper surfaces as flat hexagons, one aiming in each direction. The bridge was a flat line of windows planted atop the forward cube, dwarfed by the blunt steel mountain on which it rested.

*Vickburg*'s complement was twenty-four officers and three hundred forty men. Through the tangle of antenna arrays, data links, and satcom dishes, she was a high-tech spider at the center of a vast, electronic web, able to receive and process data from any of the other ships or aircraft in the squadron or, by satellite, to communicate with CINCPAC in Hawaii or the Joint Chiefs in Washington.

And the heart of the entire system was *Vickburg*'s CIC, where the ship's battle staff watched the electronic signatures moving within the reach of the ship's senses and worked to piece together a strategy to deal with them. A seaborne analogue of the E-2C Hawkeye, *Vicksburg* could serve as a battle management system to coordinate the movements and responses of the entire fleet. Her SPY-1 was a marvel of computer-directed electronics, constantly searching for small, pop-up targets such as aircraft or missiles within forty-five nautical miles of the ship, while simultaneously scanning a much vaster area out to a range of two hundred miles for larger targets.

Captain Randolph Cunningham of the U.S.S. *Vicksburg* had just entered the CIC. The Combat Information Center was part of an operational complex called the Command and Control Suite. The room was large, larger than the fact that the ship was built on a Spruance-class destroyer's hull would have suggested, and it was dominated by four Large Screen Displays, or LSDs, set side by side above a bank of computer consoles.

Elsewhere around the room were twelve smaller automated status boards, ASTABs in Navy jargon.

The array of screens was designed to present *Vicksburg*'s Tactical Department with every piece of information they might conceivably need during battle. Each screen was individually programmable. One LSD might be set to display surface shipping, a second close-in air contacts, a third distant targets, a fourth intelligence data or updates. ASTABs could show the status of ships or aircraft in the squadron, data on tanker loading, ship cargoes, engagement tracks, sub sightings, anything the tactical people needed to help them comprehend the incredible complexity and movement of the participants in modern combat. Seat after seat at console after console was manned by sailors monitoring the electronic world beyond the cruiser's bulkheads.

Cunningham studied the displays showing the *Vicksburg*'s helo status for a moment. The Russian Helix had landed safely, dropped off her passengers, and was now headed for the *Kreml* with Admiral Dmitriev. The three Russian staff officers were now being escorted forward to *Vicksburg*'s wardroom. The second helo, the Seahawk carrying Admiral Vaughn and his staff, was inbound with an ETA of four more minutes. He should have met the Russians, he knew, but Vaughn's instructions about no formal ceremony had been explicit. That was just as well. Seas were rough, and the Soviet officers would probably prefer to be greeted in the dry security of *Vicksburg*'s wardroom, rather than the spray-drenched openness of the CG's fantail.

He would have to go aft to greet Admiral Vaughn, of course. CBG-14's admiral would expect that.

He was just about to turn and leave the CIC when the Tactical Officer called to him. "Captain?" The officer was standing behind an ET chief seated at one of the consoles, puzzling at the display on one of the LSDs. "Something funny here."

"What do you have, Hark?"

Commander Gregory Harkowicz pointed. The screen displayed numerous white blips against a dark blue background. Letters and numerals tagged most of the contacts, identifying them as ships and aircraft belonging to the battle group.

But there were four close-spaced blips to the northeast, still unidentified.

Cunningham squinted at the screen. "Aircraft?"

"No, sir. Surface vessels. Range thirty miles. Contact is intermittent. They come and go. That suggests very small targets, maybe fishing smacks. Speed eight knots."

That made sense. Seas were running at three to five feet. A small boat could easily be lost in the radar reflection from the ocean, registering only as it rose to the crest of each wave.

"How long have they been there?"

"We picked up something maybe an hour ago, Captain," the ETC said. "But it disappeared and didn't show again. This has just been within the last ten minutes."

Cunningham stared at the display, trying to milk additional information from the uninformative screen.

"Five gets you ten it's a dhow fleet," he said softly. "But . . ."

Harkowicz looked at him. "You're thinking patrol boat?"

"Could be. Cruise Druze."

The TO chuckled. During the carrier operations off Lebanon during the early eighties, there'd been some concern that one of the warring Lebanese factions might attempt a suicide attack on a Navy ship with a light plane or speedboat packed with explosives . . . or even with a single fanatic on a hang glider. The hypothetical lone commando on a hang glider had been dubbed "Cruise Druze," and the word had stuck.

"Give me a *Jane*'s readout for India, Hark," Cunningham said. "List only."

An ASTAB nearby flickered, and a column of ship names, numbers, and types replaced a readout on fleet fuel consumption. Cunningham scanned the list as it scrolled. His eyes widened. "Stop. Oh . . . shit."

"Sir?" Then Harkowicz saw what the Captain had noticed. "Oh . . ."

"Thought I remembered Osas," Cunningham said. "Eight Osa IIs, each carrying four Styx SSMs. We'd better—"

"Captain!" the ET chief called. "Unknowns accelerating! Radar makes it twenty knots! Twenty-five . . . thirty knots!"

No native dhow could manage thirty knots. "Battle stations!" Cunningham snapped. The Tactical Officer's hand was already slapping down on a large, red button on a nearby console. "Sound fleet alert!"

But he wondered if it was not already too late. On the screen, new bogies were appearing, separating as if by magic from the larger blips marking the unknowns.

"It's goin' down!" Harkowicz shouted. *"Missile launch! Missile launch!"*

# CHAPTER 16

**0739 hours, 26 March**
**Patrol Boat K91, INS *Pralaya***

Senior Lieutenant Javed Chaudry was a fatalistic man, but that didn't stop him from slamming his fist against the bridge console and biting off a savage curse as the two Styx missiles roared off into the northwest, dazzling pinpoints of light drawing white contrails across the sky. INS *Pratap*, Patrol Boat K93, wallowed in the heavy seas to starboard, her two forward SS-N-2 canisters open and empty, the cloud of smoke from the double launch still boiling across the water's surface.

He'd hoped to get closer before launching, much closer. The American carrier was barely in range of the giant missiles now, and the launch would alert the U.S. squadron that it was under attack.

Control reasserted itself. Whatever *Pratap*'s problem—equipment failure or accident in the rough seas, overeagerness on the part of her weapons officer—what was done was done. He would have to make the best of it.

"Captain!" he barked. "Stand by to launch!"

"*Sir!*" Lieutenant Shahani, *Pralaya*'s commanding officer, snapped out in his best academy officer-on-parade voice. Afraid of crossing the tiny flotilla's CO, Chaudry decided. The thought made him grin.

"We might as well hit them with everything we've got!"

"Sir!" Shahani began giving the orders to his weapons officer. The missiles' inertial programming was already complete—it could have been a fault in *Pratap*'s inertial circuitry that had caused the premature launch, Chaudry thought—and all that remained was to release the safeties and fire. The SS-N-2s self-armed after launch.

Chaudry was aware that the Osa squadron's part in Operation Python was a small one, a means of dividing the Americans' defensive forces and forcing them to use up valuable anti-missiles, time, and fuel. Still, the thought that one of those sleek monsters now warming in their slatted tubes to port and starboard might be the one to strike the U.S. carrier and end the Yankees' dreams of dominating India's seas . . .

"Pass the word to all boats," he ordered. "Full launch, all craft. Stand by!"

"Missiles one, two, three, and four ready," Shahani replied.

"Very well." He looked about the bridge, realizing that every eye was on him. "Signal the squadron. Fire." He locked eyes with Shahani. "Captain, you may launch."

He'd been waiting for the order. "Missile one, *fire*!"

The narrow gray confines of *Pralaya*'s bridge were blasted by a deafening white sound, a waterfall of raw noise as flame and smoke engulfed the starboard bridge windows. Chaudry covered his ears with his hands. While he'd been through training exercises often enough, this was the first time he'd ever fired an SS-N-2 for real. The sound was like nothing he'd ever imagined.

"Missile two . . . *fire*!" The weapons officer was shouting to be heard above the roar. "Missile three . . . *fire*!"

*Pralaya* rocked wildly as the blunt-nosed, two-and-a-half-ton missiles blasted away, first from one side, then the other. Chaudry realized with some surprise that his high-peaked cap had been knocked from his head and was lying on the deck by his feet.

"Missile four . . . *fire*!"

Other missiles were rising on flaming contrails from the other vessels in the squadron. The sky to the northwest was aflame with pinpoints of dazzling brilliance.

The Battle of the Arabian Sea had just begun in earnest.

**0739 hours, 26 March**
**CATCC, U.S.S. *Thomas Jefferson***

Tombstone was in the 904 deck corridor just outside *Jefferson*'s CATCC when the GQ alarm sounded, the harsh clangor of the gong mingling with the metallic rattle of hundreds of feet hitting passageways and deck ladders.

"Now hear this, now hear this," the 1-MC on the bulkhead brayed. "General quarters, general quarters. All hands man your battle stations. Set Condition Alpha throughout the ship."

He stepped through the door into the red-lit CATCC, brushing past the heavy curtains that kept light from the passageway from leaking through and ruining the night vision of the sailors manning the ranks of radar displays in the room. CAG was sitting on the leather-backed throne that gave him an unobstructed view of the principal displays and status boards.

Tombstone walked over to where several other squadron officers were looking on. He stood next to Lieutenant j.g. Pete Costello, another Navy aviator who was serving a stretch as VF-97's CATCC liaison.

"Hey, Hitman," Tombstone whispered, addressing the j.g. by his running name. "What's the gouge?"

"Flash just came in from the *Vickie,*" Hitman replied. He nodded toward the forward bulkhead. Forty feet beyond it was the ship's CIC, where white blips freckled a huge amber radar display. "Surface targets. Word is they're Osa IIs and they've just popped their missiles!"

*Osas*. Tombstone knew what those were. The name was the NATO designation, *osa* being the Russian word for "wasp." Over 128 feet long and displacing 215 tons, the Osa was a larger version of the American patrol torpedo boats of WW II. Instead of torpedos, however, they mounted four large, ribbed canisters, two to port, two to starboard. A twin 30-mm rapid-fire cannon was mounted forward, and another astern.

Light, handy, and powerful, an Osa II could make thirty-five knots and had a range of 750 miles at a cruising speed of twenty-five knots. The Indians were known to have eight of the machines, purchased in 1976.

A substantial body of opinion and debate had been hung from the threat of small, powerful missile boats like the Osas. Critics of the modern Navy, *especially* critics of the big nuclear carriers, repeatedly and vociferously insisted that the large surface vessel had gone the way of the dinosaur. Why, after all, spend billions of dollars on an enormous and relatively slow target that could be destroyed by a million-dollar missile fired from a boat small enough and cheap enough to be built by the hundreds?

The missile carried by Osas was a proven ship-killer. With a warhead weighing over half a ton and packed with 880 pounds of high explosive, it could do grievous damage to any modern warship. Three SS-N-2 missiles fired from Egyptian patrol boats in Alexandria Harbor had sunk the Israeli destroyer *Elath* in 1967. Others had sunk a number of Pakistani ships during the 1971 war, including the destroyer *Khaiber*.

It would take a large number of SS-N-2s to sink a carrier as large as *Jefferson*, or great luck, or both . . . but there were sixteen of the ship-killers out there now. And a hit by only one in the right place could cripple the aircraft carrier and make further launch and recovery operations impossible.

''Range twenty-six miles,'' a voice said from a bulkhead speaker. Someone had set the CATCC intercom to pick up the voices from CIC. The only aircraft *Jefferson* had up at the moment were four Tomcats on BARCAP, a Prowler on ECM, and one of the ever-circling Hawkeyes. ''Twelve missiles . . . correction. Fourteen missiles in the air, closing at six hundred knots.''

Mach .9, Tombstone thought, calculating in his head. At that speed, the missiles would cover twenty-six miles in two and a half minutes. He glanced at a clock on the wall, a twenty-four-hour clock with a bright red sweep second hand. It was now 0740.

''Who's got CAP?'' CAG asked suddenly.

Tombstone glanced across at the flight status board and read the names grease-penciled onto the clear acrylic. ''Garrison and Wayne are BARCAP One, CAG,'' he said. ''Marinaro and Kingsly are BARCAP Two. Grant and Rostenkowski are on Alert Five.''

He felt a bitter, growing frustration. His place was with his friends, with Batman and Coyote, not down here in the 04 deck caverns of CATCC.

''Prowlers?''

Tombstone checked the board again. ''Sarnelli in 603.''

''Right. Let's get the Alert Five up there,'' CAG said. ''Notify CIC.''

''Aye, sir,'' a j.g. said.

''And inform the Captain and the admiral that we've got a

situation here. We're going to need to get the rest of our Tomcats airborne, ASAP."

"The admiral is in transit, CAG," another officer reminded Marusko.

"Damn. What a time to be caught out of the office."

"Shit, Tombstone," Costello whispered. One of the displays had been set to show surface targets, a feed from CIC. The blips representing the missiles were edging closer with each sweep of the beam. "We won't have time to launch any more aircraft!"

"Batman and Army will get them," Tombstone whispered in reply. But he did not feel the confidence he put into the words. "The Indies goofed."

"How, Stoney?"

"They launched from maximum range. Styx missiles only have a range of about twenty-seven, twenty-eight miles. Soviet doctrine is to close to ten or twelve nautical miles before launching. They just gave us longer to shoot them down." He nodded toward another repeater display, this one with much of the west coast of India outlined in white light and showing those positions of India's surface navy units that were known. "I'm more worried about their heavier ships. Their destroyers carry an improved Styx. They'll be able to hit us from out to about forty, maybe forty-five miles. But it'll be a while before they can get in position."

The intent of the Indians had been fuzzy until now. Because of the location of Turban Station, two hundred miles south of the Indian-Pakistan border, there'd been considerable question about whether the ships deploying out of Bombay and India's west coast were preparing to attack the Soviet-American squadron, or to bypass *Kreml* and *Jefferson* in order to hit Karachi or blockade the Pakistani coast.

Tombstone watched the approaching missiles. Their plans had just grown considerably less fuzzy. The Indians were out for blood.

Even so, New Delhi's opening gambit was puzzling. The main body of their fleet—two carriers, a large cruiser, and at least eight destroyers—was still a hundred miles away. Tombstone had assumed that the first Indian strike, if it came, would be by air.

"CAG!" a radarman chief called. "CIC reports new

contacts . . . multiple contacts over Jamnagar. Bearing zero-four-oh, range one-six-five.''

''Multiple contacts over Rajkot,'' another sailor announced. ''Bearing zero-four-five, range two-double-oh.''

''Homeplate, Homeplate, this is Victor Tango One-one,'' a radio voice announced over CATCC's 1-MC. ''We have evidence of massive air activity all along the coast.''

''Roger, Victor Tango One-one. We have them.''

''Ah, Homeplate, Victor Tango. We're also running into considerable jamming activity. This looks like it could be a major attack.''

Stunned silence reigned in CATCC as the impact of what was happening sank in.

''Now hear this,'' the Captain's voice said over the speaker. ''This is Captain Fitzgerald in CIC. Listen up, people. On my authority, weapons are free. Ready VF-97 and the rest of VF-95 for immediate launch. And I want more Prowlers up there *now*!''

The new contacts began appearing on the large display, positioned by the computers that recorded the radar contacts as they were relayed to the carrier by circling Hawkeyes or the other American ships. Aircraft were clustering over the main Indian fleet, and the coastline from the Pakistan border to Bombay was alive with moving lights, a ragged semicircle of contacts that all seemed to have the same focus.

The ships at Turban Station.

**0740 hours, 26 March**
**Tomcat 216, on CAP**

Batman angled his F-14 onto a southwesterly course, his eyes on his cockpit VDI rather than on the view of clouds and ocean wheeling past outside. The coast of India was a gray shadow behind him. ''We've got bogies,'' he said. ''Range eight-eight miles. Looks like ten or twelve of them, SSMs, spreading out and on a course for Homeplate.''

''Roger that, Batman.'' The voice of Lieutenant Commander Fred Garrison, Army to the others in VF-95, sounded flat and hard. VF-95's XO was a mile off Batman's left wing. He could see the other F-14, its canopy flashing in the sun. ''We have clearance from Homeplate. Weapons release. I say again, weapons release.''

Batman felt a surge of warm relief. At least there'd be no fumbling, half-measures delay in securing the ROEs *this* time.

''Hey, Batman,'' his RIO called from the backseat. ''I think we got trouble.''

''Whatcha got, Malibu?'' The Tomcat shuddered as Batman pushed the throttles forward, pressing the aircraft toward Mach 1.

''*More* bogies, Batman. About a million of 'em.''

''Let me see.''

The RIO hit the control that fed his radar plot to the pilot's VDI, an expanded plot that showed targets as far away as the Indian coastline, sixty miles to the north. ''Three guesses where they're headed, Batman.''

Batman studied the crawling confusion of radar targets. Half the Indian air force must be out there, all taking off at once. ''Shit,'' he said, almost to himself. '' 'Air raid, Pearl Harbor. This is no drill.' ''

''Air raid *Jefferson* is more like it,'' Malibu replied. ''These guys are like deeply serious, man!''

''You're getting this from the *Jeff*?''

''Tactical feed through Victor Tango One-one. On the fleet net.''

''Well, at least they know they're coming.''

''Yeah, but what are we gonna do, Batman?''

Batman was surprised at his own steadiness. He worked the target designator, setting the pipper on one of the closer blips. First priority was to stop the missiles south heading for the carrier. After that, they might have time to worry about the planes to the north. ''Target Alpha,'' he said simply. ''Track and lock. Go for Phoenix kill.''

''Affirm,'' his RIO said, flipping the switches that activated the Tomcat's AWG-9 radar. Now the F-14 was seeing with its own eyes, instead of the eyes of the fleet. ''Range seven-oh miles. We have lock.''

''Light 'er off.''

''Rog.'' Malibu called. The Tomcat bumped slightly as the heavy missile fell away, then ignited. ''Fox three!''

The Phoenix streaked toward the horizon, trailing flame.

**0740 hours, 26 March**
**INS *Viraat*, 160 miles west northwest of Bombay**

Rear Admiral Ramesh stood on the walkway at the peak of *Viraat*'s island, his hands clutching the damp railing like a talisman. The Indian aircraft carrier was plowing steadily into the heavy seas, taking spray across her forepeak with each lunge of the vessel against the waves. The wind was from the northeast, an unseasonably raw and gusty breath from the distant Himalayas that set the pennants above Ramesh's head snapping and cracking like gunfire. Captain Soni had swung *Viraat*'s oddly humped bow into the wind in order to assist the launching of the Sea Harriers.

The Sea Harriers. Ramesh watched as they continued to roll down *Viraat*'s flight deck, gathering speed as they hit the upthrust of the carrier's ski jump, then vaulted clear of the ship's bows, engines shrieking as they forced their way into the air. The ex-British carrier was designed to handle the odd-looking V/STOL fighters with their four vectoring engine nozzles set into the hull beneath the high, sharply angled wings.

Contrary to popular belief, the Sea Harriers did not simply lift vertically off the carrier deck like a helicopter, though they certainly had that capability. They used far less fuel and could carry a larger combat load if they used a rolling takeoff. Since the carrier lacked a steam catapult, the twelve-degree ''ski jump'' bow ramp was designed to give the Harriers the extra lift they needed to fly off *Viraat*'s 226-meter flight deck.

With her newest refit, *Viraat* carried four Sea Harrier squadrons, twenty-four aircraft armed with Magic air-to-air missiles. When India first took possession of the carrier from the British in 1986, she'd only carried six of the V/STOL jump jet fighters, but the Indian navy had been acquiring more as quickly as possible. Ultimately, it was planned to carry thirty jump jets aboard *Viraat* and six more on the smaller *Vikrant*.

Another Sea Harrier taxied into position below his vantage point on the island. The bright national roundels, green-in-white-in-orange, stood out in sharp contrast to the plane's overall blue-gray-over-white color scheme. ''Indian Navy'' was written in large English letters across the tail under a painted national flag, and the plane's number, 101, was distinct on its nose. That was the force leader, Ramesh remembered, a young man of good family named Tahliani.

He felt a momentary sadness. Many young men of good families would die this day, and he could not forget that the combined navy-air force strike against the American fleet had been *his* idea.

Ramesh watched as the pilot slid his visor down over his face, saluted the deck officer, and grasped the throttle controls. The Harrier began moving forward, slowly at first, then gathering speed as the pilot vectored the engine nozzles aft. He hit the ramp with a swoop timed to the rising surge of the ship cresting the next wave. As the ship's bow fell, the Sea Harrier was left hanging, fighting for altitude in the spray-misted sky.

By now, Ramesh thought, the Americans would know they were coming. The Osas had already launched . . . a deliberate thrust to force them to commit their fighters.

Today's action, Ramesh was confident, would be a slaughter. Years before, the Soviets had developed tactics for just this sort of war. Attack . . . attack . . . and continue to attack, with wave after wave, until the enemy's defenses were battered down by sheer weight of numbers. *Viraat*'s Sea Harriers would overwhelm the American defensive fighters, opening the way for Indian air force strike planes. There would be losses, to be sure, from the American AA defenses, but the Indians could afford to lose three planes to one and still come out of the engagement victorious.

Sooner or later, the American defenses would start leaking. Then the missiles would begin striking home. Young men would die on both sides, so that national honor, national policies could be upheld. And there was more to it than that. . . .

He found himself thinking of lost Joshi. He gripped the railing tighter, tighter, and still tighter . . . squeezing until the pain steadied him.

We will *win,* Joshi, he thought. Win or die! I promise you that!

# CHAPTER 17

**0741 hours, 26 March**
**Seahawk 912, approaching U.S.S. *Vicksburg***

"What do you mean, 'an alert'?" Admiral Vaughn had to shout to make himself heard above the racket of the helo's rotors. "Who called it?"

The Seahawk's crew chief shrugged and tapped his helmet's earphone. "Sorry, Admiral," he shouted. "It just came down from the pilot!"

Angrily, Vaughn thrust himself past the crew chief and made his way forward toward the cockpit. The HH-60 Seahawk was relatively new in the Navy's inventory, having been acquired to replace the older HH-3A Sea Kings in both the ASW roles and for combat search and rescue. The machine he was on was a SAR helo with two pilots, two crewmen, and room for eight passengers.

The ship's pilot turned as he stepped onto the cramped flight deck. "Word just came through, Admiral," the man said. "The Indians have launched missiles at the fleet from about twenty-five or thirty miles out. They don't know the target yet."

"Well, find out! No, belay that! Find someone I can talk to!"

"Aye, sir." As the copilot began speaking on the radio, Vaughn fumed. What should he do? He'd left the *Jefferson* five minutes before. It would be minutes yet before they landed on the *Vicksburg*. Should they return to the *Jefferson,* or press on?

He could see the Aegis cruiser through the windscreen ahead, long and gray with a knife's-edge prow, the twin fortress towers fore and aft giving her an ungainly, top-heavy look. The seas were a lot heavier than he'd been aware of back on the stolid and unyielding bulk of the *Jefferson.* As he watched, a wave broke over the bow in an explosion of white, engulfing her forward five-inch mount and smashing itself against the forward deckhouse. It looked like they'd be in for a rough ride.

*Vicksburg*'s fantail was clear. It made no sense to turn around. He would be in the cruiser's command suite in another few minutes.

"Admiral?" the copilot yelled, one hand pressed to his headset. "*Jefferson* CIC!"

"Patch me in!"

A radio jack was plugged into his helmet, tying him into the comnet. "*Jefferson! Jefferson!* This is Admiral Vaughn!"

"Commander Barnes, CIC, Admiral. Go ahead."

"What the hell's going on, Commander?"

"We have a full battle group alert, sir. We are tracking between twelve and sixteen missiles inbound."

"From where?"

"Probable launch platforms were four OSA IIs, Admiral. That means SS-N-2s."

"Target?"

"Safe money would be on the *Jefferson,* sir."

"Yes . . ."

"We've launched the Alert Five," Barnes said. "Captain Fitzgerald has authorized weapons free."

"Yes," Vaughn said. "Yes, quite right." He felt sick. The carrier . . . *his* carrier . . . was under a mass attack.

**0741 hours, 26 March**
**Over the Arabian Sea**

The SS-N-2 Styx flew more like an aircraft than a missile. Once it was launched from its storage pod with an assist from a solid-fuel booster, cruise propulsion was maintained by a conventional air-gulping turbojet slung under the missile's belly. The Styx was a direct descendant of the V-1 buzz bombs employed by the Germans in WW II.

As it traveled a few meters above the wave crests, its inertial programming carried it into a specific target area. Once it was within five nautical miles of its projected impact point, two separate on-board terminal guidance systems—an active radar-homing device and an infrared sensor—switched on, identifying and locking onto the largest target within the missile's electronic field of view.

Sophisticated as it was, the Styx had no defense of its own. The Phoenix missile hurtled in from the north at Mach 5 and exploded as it passed low above the missile's back. A fraction of a second later, the SS-N-2's warhead detonated.

The thunderous shock wave raised a geyser of water against the sky. Before the geyser had collapsed, the sky was alive with the contrails of more missiles, still bearing on the carrier. Phoenix missiles sweeping in from the north connected with the ship-killers, one by one. There were more explosions, and missiles died.

But they weren't dying fast enough.

**0741 hours, 26 March**
**CATCC, U.S.S. *Thomas Jefferson***

"That's a grand slam! Splash another one!"

Tombstone looked up as Batman's voice rasped over the CATCC speaker. He could imagine the tension in the cockpit of the F-14 now, as the RIO monitored the horde of airborne targets.

"Tomcat, Two-one-six, roger your kill," a CATCC controller said. But more missiles were coming in fast.

"Two-oh-one," Army Garrison's voice added. "Phoenix away."

Hurt twisted at Tombstone's gut. Although carrier aviators did not always fly the same aircraft, one plane in the squadron was generally thought of as "theirs." Further, there were no hard and fast rules to the practice, but tradition reserved the "01" aircraft to the squadron's leader. As skipper of VF-95, Tombstone generally flew Tomcat 201. Today, with his XO standing in for him, Army was flying the 201 bird.

He looked across the room at CAG. Marusko had just replaced a telephone handset and was now holding a microphone to his mouth. "Now hear this," he said, his voice sounding over the bulkhead speakers. "I've just had word from

Commander Barnes. The admiral is about to touch down on the *Vicksburg* and will be assuming control of the battle from there momentarily. Meanwhile, he has confirmed weapons free. As of now, the squadron is on full Battle Alert Status. Current ROEs are suspended and weapons are free. That is all.''

''BARCAP Two is ready to fire,'' a sailor reported. ''They're at extreme range.''

''How long before they get into position?''

''A few minutes, sir.''

''We don't *have* a few minutes. How long before the Alert Five gets up?''

Tombstone glanced up at the PLAT camera suspended from the CATCC overhead. The view was forward from the island, toward Cats One and Two on the bow. Deck crewmen were prepping a pair of Tomcats for launch, ''Shooter'' Rostenkowski in his 248 bird, Coyote in the Tomcat Army usually flew, number 204. The squat, boxy, yellow-painted tractors called mules were hauling the F-14s up to the catapult shuttles.

''Another two-three minutes on the Alert Five,'' Tombstone called.

''Closest missile now at twelve miles,'' a technician at one of the consoles said. ''We now have four positive Phoenix locks, closing. . . .''

''They're suckering us,'' CAG said suddenly, as though the thought had just struck him. ''Damn them, they're suckering us into eating up our outer line!''

Tombstone had already arrived at the same conclusion. Each of the four Tomcats aloft on CAP had been armed with six long-range Phoenix missiles. Two of the F-14s—the planes of Barcap Two—were far to the north, badly positioned to defend against the Osa-launched attack from the southeast.

The Osas carried four Styx ship-killers apiece. *Jefferson*'s CAP could knock out those first sixteen missiles easily enough, but they would then have just eight AIM-54-Cs left between them if the Indian aircraft launched a major assault. Besides the Alert Five, the carrier was preparing for an emergency launch, hoping to get every Tomcat it could into the air before the attackers could get close enough to fire more ship-killers, but the first wave of Styx missiles would arrive long before all of the carrier's defenders could get aloft.

And even for missiles not yet launched, it would be a deadly race, and with the numbers arrayed against the CBG, it was a race that the Americans were certain to lose.

Modern naval strategy placed the all-important aircraft carrier at the center of the task force inside a series of concentric rings. Each ring defined a volume of airspace, called a task force air defense zone, extending from sea level to 90,000 feet. The outer ring, reaching out to one hundred nautical miles from the carrier, was designated the aircraft defense zone. The middle ring covered an area out to forty miles from the carrier and was called the missile defense zone. The inner ring, a speck of sea only two miles high and reaching five nautical miles from the carrier, was the point defense zone.

The Tomcat CAP was responsible for the air defense zone. The missile defense zone was covered by missile fire from the ships. Point defense was handled by short-range missile fire and by the Phalanx Gatling guns mounted on each vessel. Protecting a task force like CBG-14 was envisioned as a layered battle, with the Tomcats knocking down everything they could, concentrating on eliminating aircraft and surface vessels before they could launch their deadly ordnance loads. Missiles that got past the Tomcats would be taken on by the fleet's Sea Sparrows. And any surviving missiles, the "leakers," would be downed by the computer-controlled Gatlings.

At least, that was the way it was supposed to work. Things were feeling crowded already, since *Jefferson*'s hundred-mile air defense zone extended all the way to the Indian coast to the northeast, while Indian surface ships were entering the zone from the southeast. And those Osas were much closer, well inside the missile defense zone.

The British had used a similar system at the Falklands, but determined Argentinian attacks and some mistakes on the part of the Brits had resulted in the loss of several ships. More than once, it had not been just missiles but bomb-carrying aircraft that had made it into the British task force's inner defensive perimeter . . . especially when the strike aircraft were able to get in close beforehand by utilizing the radar cover provided by the rugged mountains of the Falklands themselves.

There were no mountains to block radar here . . . but there was the heavy ocean swell, and radar jamming had already begun. Tombstone knew with a sure, sick certainty that those Indian aircraft would be moving south in waves any moment now. The Tomcats would never be able to stem that tide. How many Styx and Exocet missiles could the Indians throw at the American CBG? Would there be so many leakers that *Jefferson*'s three on-board Phalanx systems would be overwhelmed?

How many hits would it take to render *Jefferson* useless in the coming fight?

"Mr. Magruder?" Costello murmured at his side. "It's not looking good, is it?"

"We've been in tough spots before, Hitman."

But he knew *Jefferson* and her people had never faced anything like this.

**0741 hours, 26 March**
**Tomcat 201, on CAP**

Army Garrison studied the growing armada arrayed against them and wished Tombstone were here. The tall, quiet skipper of VF-95 had an uncanny tactical sense that had stood the squadron through some tough fights already, above Wonsan in Korea, and later over the Thai jungles.

*What would Stoney do?* he asked himself.

"Hey, Dixie," he called. "Can you do anything about this fuzz on the radar?"

"Negative. Commander Garrison. I think they're finding our windows and plugging them as fast as we open them."

For the moment, it was a high-tech war of computers and radio. Right now, *Jefferson*'s EA-6B Prowlers would be doing their best to jam Indian radars while leaving clear windows for the Tomcats' use. The Indians would be trying to locate those windows and fill them with snow. Finding the right combinations of clear frequencies for both radar and communications was part of the continuing Electronic Warfare battle between the two sides. The Indians, Army thought, probably had an EW aircraft patrolling somewhere near the coast. Where was it? he wondered.

And what were the Russians doing about EW right now? Army shook his head. This mess was becoming more confused by the second.

"Viper Two-one-six," he called. "This is Viper-Two-oh-one."

"Copy, Army," Batman's voice replied. "Go ahead."

"We're going to have to split up and take the missiles at knife-fighting distance."

"Roger that."

"See if you can run interference for Homeplate. I'll try an end run and catch them from the flank."

"Rog. We'll take 'em down on the deck."

"Victor Tango One-one," Army said, switching to the Hawkeye air controller's frequency. "This is BARCAP one-One. Did you copy my last?"

"Affirmative, BARCAP One. We concur with your plan."

The two Tomcats spilt apart as Batman pulled a wing-over and plummeted toward the sea. Army lined up with another target and started his descent.

With Phoenix missiles they could knock the Styx down six at a time, but that would leave them unarmed to face the Indian hordes. Perhaps the two Tomcats could take out their share of the ship-killers with gunfire.

**0742 hours, 26 March**
**Tomcat 216**

Batman brought his Tomcat down to within two hundred feet of the ocean's surface, skimming west at Mach 1.5. The F-14's wings, folded all the way back along the hull, transformed the Tomcat into a giant, pale gray arrowhead. Somewhere ahead, one of the enemy missiles was already between him and the carrier, now some twelve miles ahead. "Gimme a vector, Malibu!"

"You're fine on this heading," his RIO replied. "Range three-one-double-oh."

"I'm goosing it." He pushed the throttles all the way forward into Zone Five, watching the F-14's speed build past Mach 2. The air this close to the water was heavy with moisture. White clouds boiled off the Tomcat's wings as water droplets were shocked into visibility by the fighter's passage. They were well within the area covered by the CBG's missile defenses now and rapidly approaching the innermost point defense zone. *Jefferson* was only nine miles ahead.

"Range two triple-oh!"

Batman eased back on the throttle. It wouldn't do to skim past the target so quickly he couldn't even see it. Malibu continued to read off the decreasing range as the same numbers flickered past on his HUD. "Twelve hundred . . . one triple-oh . . . eight hundred . . . Still closing!"

Damn! He should *see* the thing by now. The Tomcat's radar lock was projecting a small square on the HUD, defining the bit of sky where the target was located. The square jittered just below the horizon, but he couldn't see anything inside it but water.

He cut the throttle some more, then opened his spoilers, letting the F-14 sink closer to the surface. If he could see the target against sky rather than sea . . .

There it was! A flicker of motion, no more, just above the horizon line. Now that he saw the thing, it rapidly took on greater definition and detail, expanding as the Tomcat bore down on it from astern.

"Tally-ho!" Batman called. "I'm going to guns!"

Styx missiles were nearly as large as a small aircraft: twenty-one feet long, with a nine-foot wingspan. Traveling steadily at Mach .9, they offered a marksman's dream, a target that was slow, steady, and completely predictable. He should have a chance of knocking the thing down with his M61 cannon.

The Styx was still little more than a black speck inside the targeting reticle on Batman's HUD. Coming in hard on the target's six, he didn't need to draw much lead or try to anticipate its next move. He switched his gun-speed selector to its lowest setting, 4,000 rounds per minute. At less than five hundred yards, he pressed the fire button.

The Tomcat's M61 six-barreled Gatling shrieked in a brief, precisely controlled burst. And again. And again . . .

Black smoke puffed from the missile's tail. The target was close enough now that Batman could see its blunt-nosed, dirigible shape, the three evenly spaced tail fins and the stubby wings amidships, the sustaining motor beneath the fuselage. Suddenly the Styx swerved up, nosed over, and plunged silently into the sea.

"That's a kill!" Malibu said.

"Splash another Styx," Batman reported over his radio.

''Roger that,'' their Hawkeye air controller replied. ''Nice shooting, guys.''

The gray mass of the U.S.S. *Jefferson* appeared on the horizon, swelling rapidly as Batman and Malibu hurtled toward it. He eased back on the stick, pulling the F-14 into a climb.

That missile had come far too close to the *Jeff* for comfort.

**0742 hours, 26 March**
**CATCC, U.S.S. *Thomas Jefferson***

''Hit!'' a technician announced. One of Army's missiles had just tagged another Styx. ''Splash five . . .''

''Ninety-nine aircraft, this is Homeplate,'' CAG said, using the code meaning all planes in the air. ''Break off attack on incoming missiles. Repeat, break off! CIC says to leave something for the boys at home.''

Tombstone watched the radar blips identified as *Jefferson*'s Tomcats. The missile wave had pulled them all in tight, clustering around the *Jefferson* as they tried to deal with the Styx missiles one-on-one. That kind of clumping would play havoc with the carrier's ability to defend herself. It was better for Tomcats to veer off and leave the *Jefferson* room to swing.

''Roger, Homeplate,'' Army's voice said. ''BARCAP One copies.''

''Affirmative, Homeplate,'' the leader of the second BARCAP element, Lieutenant ''Nightmare'' Marinaro, echoed. ''BARCAP Two copies.''

The electronic quality of the communications gear added to the timbre of the various voices, giving them an oddly detached character. Some voices sounded calm and professional, others flat or expressionless. As the aviators became caught up in the heat of battle or the chase, they tended to lose the prowords and the measured cadences of their training, to shout as though trying to make themselves heard, to become profane or vulgar. The tensions in the sky east of the carrier were raw, Tombstone could tell, and he found the waiting more and more intolerable as the minutes dragged by.

He glanced at the clock on the bulkhead. Zero seven forty-two. The missiles were seconds away now.

"Right," Fitzgerald's voice announced from CIC. "Point defense on automatic. Fire control ready?"

"Fire control tracking," Barnes's voice replied. "Nearest target now at six miles and closing . . ."

"Pass the word," Fitzgerald said. "To all ships that can bear. *Commence fire!*"

**0742 hours, 26 March**
**The Arabian Sea**

The Styx missiles had begun their flight close together, but their launch programming and slight differences of altitude and speed had caused them to drift apart, a deliberate strategy to scatter the defenders' attention and to hit the target from as many directions as possible. Several of the attacking missiles were being directed toward target points well past the *Jefferson*, so that when their terminal guidance systems engaged, they would begin searching for their target from the ship's far side.

By the time the first Sea Sparrow shrieked away from the launcher on *Jefferson*'s starboard side forward of the island, seven Styx missiles out of the original sixteen were approaching the American carrier from as many different directions, at distances ranging from six miles to twelve.

Guided by the carrier's fire-control radar, a second missile launched seconds later . . . then a third. Contrails drew white traceries into the western sky as missile sought missile in a fast-paced electronic game of hide-and-seek, a game that unfolded far too rapidly for humans to follow it.

Then the sky exploded into flame.

A Sea Sparrow launched from the *Jefferson* rocketed into an oncoming Styx, detonating in a fireball that sent pellet-sized fragments slamming into the water for a hundred yards around. The proximity fuze on a second Sea Sparrow warhead touched off when the missile was several yards behind the Styx. The explosion sprayed the SSM with shrapnel, punching holes in wings and fuselage, but the sturdily built SS-N-2 continued to fly, smoke trailing now from the exhaust bell of its turbojet.

Another Sea Sparrow scored a hit, the explosion visible from

*Jefferson*'s deck as a brief, sharp flash on the horizon. There were five leakers still closing . . . then four . . .

*Jefferson* mounted three CIWS Mark 15 Phalanxes. Their cartoon-character names had been inspired by the robotic heroes of a '70s SF movie: Huey, Dewey, and Louie.

Huey was mounted alongside *Jefferson*'s island, set outboard and facing to starboard. Dewey was aft, set on the port side of the fantail gallery beneath the flight deck ramp. Louie was on the port side forward, mounted on a faring flush with *Jefferson*'s hull midway between flight deck and waterline.

All three Phalanx weapons came to life as the Styx missiles entered the carrier's point defense zone. On the *Jefferson*'s stern, Dewey's erect white silo spun under totally automatic control, swiveling to face the nearest of the approaching threats. The six barrels extending from the gray metal box beneath the silo whirled furiously, the discharge sounding like the whine of a high-speed motor. Within two seconds of a target entering its electronic domain, it had tracked, fired, tracked, and fired again.

Painted by J-band pulse-doppler radar, the Styx plunged headlong into a cloud of depleted uranium projectiles. Metal shredded, the missile's alloy hull punctured in a dozen places. The turbojet engine tore free from its mountings, the stubby portside wing was ripped away like paper.

Before the shattered missile hit the waves, Dewey had already swung left to engage another target . . . and then another.

The last Styx missile, its radar guidance equipment smashed, smoke streaming from its propellant tanks, hurried past *Jefferson*'s island fifty feet above the flight deck. Sailors scattered or ducked as the projectile shrieked overhead. "Jesus!" one AE/2 shouted to the man lying beside him on the steel. "It's fuckin' World War Two!"

"More like War Number Three, man," his friend yelled back. The rest of the reply was lost in the thunder of the warhead detonating in the sea a hundred yards off *Jefferson*'s port quarter.

# CHAPTER 18

**0744 hours, 26 March**
**CATCC, U.S.S. *Thomas Jefferson***

Tombstone's eyes were on the PLAT monitor in CATCC. From his camera eye's vantage point, he could watch as the final preparations were made to kick the two Alert Five aircraft into the sky.

He checked the bulkhead clock with mild surprise. Less than five minutes had passed since battle stations had been sounded. The first Indian missile strike had smashed into *Jefferson*'s defenses and been broken.

Now, though, the stakes were rising. Once Coyote and Shooter were airborne, the launch procedure for the rest of the carrier's Tomcat defenders would begin. Tombstone could see more F-14s moving up into line behind Coyote's and Shooter's planes, and other aircraft were already being lined up on Cats Three and Four.

The Air Boss and his crew would be working flat-out to get the remaining Tomcats up as fast as possible. On the battle board, the Indian aircraft were moving southwest from Kathiawar, an unstoppable wave of machines. Against them were eighteen Tomcats, eight from VF-95, ten from VF-97. Four Vipers were already aloft; the rest would be joining them soon.

They looked slow-moving and clumsy on the deck. *Turkeys.* Once in the sky, though, it was a different story.

Tombstone studied Coyote's plane as though trying to memorize each detail, every line and marking. The numerals 204 on the nose were faint, hard to make out against the glare of the morning sun to starboard. Since the early 1980s, the Navy had been using a low-contrast gray-and-gray scheme called low-viz, eliminating the garish paint schemes and squadron markings favored by aviators during the Vietnam era.

Gone were the grinning shark mouths, the stripes and badges and crests. Even the numbers and nationality emblem were muted to near-invisibility. It had been discovered during air trials in the late seventies that these bright markings not only made a big difference in sighting an opponent, they actually helped provide the heat contrast necessary for all-aspect heat-seekers to achieve a lock.

The wings on the two ready birds were swung forward into launch position. Green shirts completed the final check of the shuttle links. White shirts went around the aircraft's bellies one last time, then signaled the launch director with thumbs up.

The jet-blast deflectors rose on hydraulic pistons from the deck behind the ready aircraft, protecting planes parked to the rear from the exhaust. Both pilots were throttling up now, as the launch officer rapidly spun his upraised fist.

"Deck clear," the Air Boss's voice said over the CATCC speaker. "Launch ready aircraft. Now launch ready aircraft."

The engine nozzles on the two F-14s glowed orange as Shooter and Coyote went to Zone One burner. Tomcat could not hear the shriek of the jets in the noise-muffling soundproofing of CATCC, but he'd been in the cockpit or on the deck through enough launches to imagine the pulsing throb of raw power.

The Safety Officers gave their final all-clear signals. At each cat, the Catapult Officer returned the pilot's salutes, raised one hand, and looked toward the shooter, the man with his finger on the button. Silently, Tombstone counted down the seconds. *Go, Coyote,* he thought fiercely. *Go* . . .

The officer at Cat One spun his hand and dropped to one knee, his thumb touching the deck. There was a hesitation . . . and then Coyote's Tomcat hurtled down the deck, trailing steam from the shuttle slot beneath its belly. A pair of heartbeats later, the Cat Two officer touched the deck, and Shooter's aircraft followed, leaping toward the carrier's bows ahead of twin spears of flame.

"Two-oh-four airborne," the Air Boss's voice announced. "Two-four-eight airborne. Let's get it the hell moving down there, people! We've got aircraft to launch!"

Tombstone shifted uneasily. He wanted to be *out* there! In the cockpit of 201, vectoring toward those hostiles!

With burning eyes, Tombstone watched the pair of Tomcats banking starboard off *Jefferson*'s bow in choreographed unison, his squadron mates, his friends. *Damn,* he wished he was going with them.

Silently, he cursed Admiral Vaughn, the Navy, and himself.

**0746, 26 March**
**Tomcat 216**

Batman glanced at his VDI. The radar screen was becoming increasingly fuzzy, and it was difficult to tell the true targets from random smears of light. Somewhere out there, Batman concluded, an enemy electronic countermeasures aircraft was doing its thing.

"Hey, Malibu. You see Army anywhere?"

The two Tomcats of BARCAP One had separated to launch their attacks on the incoming Styx missiles. Now the jamming was so bad it was difficult to see anything beyond a range of a few miles.

"Negative, Batman," the RIO replied. "I'm getting a lot of fuzz on the scope. Someone's doing some serious jamming."

"Yeah," Batman replied. His VDI showed broken patches of glare that partly obscured the oncoming bogies. "It's the ECM boys' war now."

"Viper Two-one-six, this is Victor Tango One-one," the Hawkeye called at last. "We have a target for you."

"Copy, Victor Tango." *A* target? The sky was *filled* with targets, or at least it had been when he could still see!

The Hawkeye air controller began passing on new information. "Come to new heading zero-four-one at angels base plus one-niner."

"Roger that, Victor Tango. Zero-four-one at base plus one-nine thousand."

He stood the Tomcat on its tail, grabbing for the sky. The "base" of the controller's orders had been set during Batman's preflight briefing that morning: eleven thousand feet. By saying angels base plus nineteen, the Hawkeye was telling Batman to go to thirty thousand feet without giving potentially useful information to an enemy who was almost certainly listening in.

The simple code was used only on combat missions, and then only when there was a real threat to ships or aircraft from what the enemy might learn.

Its use reminded Batman of how serious their situation was.

"Tomcat Two-one six, Victor Tango One-one," the Hawkeye controller called. "New target now at your zero-four-two. Range six-eight miles. Do you have him, over?"

"Nothing, Batman," Malibu said. "That's the center of the worst of the ECM."

"Zap him, Mal." By pouring more power into the beam, the AWG-9 radar might burn through the enemy radar interference, at least across a narrow area. The disadvantage, of course, was that the added power made their aircraft light up like a Christmas tree on the scope of any watching enemy plane. "Fry the son of a bitch with a goddamn microwave oven if you have to!"

"Okay!" Malibu said. "Pegged him, I think. Hard to read through the clutter."

"Roger that bogie at zero-four-two," Batman called, reading the display duplicated off Malibu's screen. "Range six-eight at angels three-five." Using the base code this time could have given it away to the Indians.

"That's the one. Two-one-six," the Hawkeye controller replied. "Target is probably Eye-el Thirty-eight, suspected hostile ECM aircraft. Engage with Phoenix and destroy. Over."

"Copy, Victor Tango." Well, I'm not going to ask him to dance, he thought. "Commencing run."

An Illyushin. The Indians used the Il-38, code named "May" by NATO, for reconnaissance. This one must have been outfitted as an ECM and EW aircraft.

He could hear Malibu in the backseat, muttering range and bearing to himself as he readied the Phoenix for launch. The RIO had forgotten to switch off the ICS.

"Take it down nice and cool," Batman said. "We have time."

"Rog," Malibu said. "Okay, we have AWG lock and are tracking."

"Let 'er rip!"

"Fox Three!" The radar-homer ignited beneath the Tomcat's belly and streaked into the sky, climbing to reach the target's altitude.

Batman checked his VDI. It was difficult to make out anything through the hash on his screen, but he could see that a number of antiship missiles were still on their way northwest, closing on *Jefferson*. To the north and west, unidentified aircraft were gathering, apparently still milling about at marshaling points as more and more aircraft joined them.

"All I can say, Mal," he told his RIO. "The goddamned cavalry better hustle. We got a shitload of company that's fixing to come step on us!"

**0747 hours, 26 March**
**CIC, U.S.S. *Vicksburg***

"Admiral on deck!"

Marine sentries snapped to attention and presented arms, but the rest of the officers and sailors in the Aegis cruiser's CIC suite remained motionless at their stations as Admiral Vaughn stepped across the knee-knocker and into the room. Captain Cunningham looked up, then waved him over. "Welcome aboard, Admiral," he said. There was a twinkle in his eye. "I trust you had a pleasant flight."

"Never mind that. What the hell's going on?"

*Vicksburg*'s captain began outlining the situation. Vaughn was uncomfortably aware of the surge and roll of the ship in the heavy seas and reached out to steady himself on a nearby console top.

"Aye, sir. The Indies fired sixteen missiles from an estimated four patrol craft. Range twenty-seven miles. *Jefferson* stopped them all. No damage."

"Thank God!"

"At the same time, they appear to have begun launching large number of land-based aircraft." He pointed toward one of the LSDs, which now displayed a portion of the Indian mainland in lines of white light.

Bhuj, south of the salt marshes of the Rann of Kutch. Okha, an Indian air force base on the very western tip of the peninsula called Kathiawar. The airfields outside the major Kathiawar cities of Jamnagar, Rajkot, and Bhanagar. Bombay to the east. At each location, aircraft were still rising into the skies, circling, gathering for the storm.

"Some of them are already skirting the edge of our air defense zone," Cunningham said "*Jefferson* reports she is now launching her remaining F-14s."

"How . . . how many enemy planes?" Vaughn asked, his eyes on the scramble of blips on the LSD.

"Unknown," Cunningham replied. "We estimate fifty to one hundred aircraft aloft so far. Jamming is very heavy."

"Anything out of the Indian fleet?"

"Nothing yet, Admiral. They could have launched their Sea Harriers, but our Hawkeyes haven't picked up anything yet. Like I said, the jamming—"

"Has Washington been apprised of the situation yet?"

Cunningham looked surprised. "Uh . . . no, sir. Unless *Jefferson* . . ."

Vaughn slumped. "There hasn't been time. Okay. My responsibility. Get me a satellite patch. Now."

"Aye, aye, sir."

"And bring the goddamned Russians down here. We might as well start working with the bastards."

Vaughn wasn't certain where or when the turning point had been, but he was surprised to realize that he was less concerned now about what the Joint Chiefs might say than with the handful of ships and men under his command. Not that he *should* have been surprised by that, he realized . . . but for so long his world had revolved around the tight little perimeter of the Washington Beltway. He'd been aware of the outside world, certainly, but his personal world had been that of career and peers, of position and politics.

All of that was lost now, under the hot rising sun of the Arabian Sea, and against the rising swarms of aircraft bent on destroying his command.

So far from home, against such odds, he would take any allies he could find . . . even if they spoke Russian.

If only there was time.

**0748 hours, 26 March**
**Sea Harrier 101, Blue King Leader**

Lieutenant Commander Ravi Tahliani held his aircraft steady at an altitude of less than fifty meters. Traveling at eleven miles a minute, just below the speed of sound, the Sea Harrier bucked and jumped, the vibrations transmitted to the young Indian pilot through his ejection seat and the control stick between his knees. At so low an altitude, the horizon seemed to be above him on all sides, and sea spray blasted across his windscreen like a stiff rain. He reached out and flicked on a device that he, trained on simpler aircraft like MiGs, still found strange in a fighter. Its utility was undeniable, however. The windshield wiper cleared the spray with several quick swipes.

He checked his console clock. He'd been airborne now for six minutes and had already crossed nearly half the distance between the Indian fleet and the American carrier. By now, he was deep inside the enemy's air defense zone. It was remarkable that they'd come so far without being detected.

Or perhaps not. The Indian Sea Harriers were flying at an extremely low altitude and beneath a solid blanket of friendly jamming. The Americans' attention would be focused in a different direction, toward the northeast and the Indian mainland. If they were watching the Indian fleet at all, it was with the assumption that *Viraat* and her consorts were bound for Karachi and the blockade of Pakistan.

The Americans would be in the midst now of launching their carrier-based aircraft. There would be a certain amount of confusion, both on the carrier's deck and among the pilots in the air as they formed up against the oncoming Indian aircraft. The Sea Harriers would have a good chance to strike a telling—and unexpected—blow.

He glanced again at the clock. Only a few more minutes . . .

**0750 hours, 26 March**
**Tomcat 216**

"Missile closing with target," Malibu said. "Closing . . . *got* him!"

On Batman's VDI, the blip marking the Indian EW aircraft, circling over the Gir Hills of southern Kathiawar, flared and fragmented as the marker for the Phoenix missile connected across nearly sixty miles.

"Victor Tango One-one!" Batman called. "Splash that bandit!"

The radar screen was clear! As though wiped by a cloth, the smears of light and static were gone, leaving the crisp images of moving bogies.

"Copy, Two-one-six," the Hawkeye controller replied. "Good shooting."

"I'm not sure I wanted to see the big picture, Batman," Malibu said. "I think those guys are mad now."

"Roger that." He put the Tomcat into a starboard turn, angling back toward the southwest. "Where's Army? I think we lost him back there."

"Got him," Malibu replied. "Range twelve miles, at two-seven-five. Got his IFF."

"I see him." He opened the tactical frequency. "Viper Two-oh-one," he called. "This is Batman. Do you copy? Over."

"Copy, Batman."

"What's the score?" It had been several minutes since he'd last heard from the *Jefferson*. He was wondering about her fate with so many missiles bearing down on her.

"Homeplate is in the clear," Army replied. "Alert Five is up and on the way. All . . . hold it. Wait one."

"Rog."

"Shit. Batman, can you get a reading on possible targets, bearing one-nine-zero to one-seven-five? Range . . . about ten miles."

"Got 'em," Malibu said. "Damn, Batman! Where'd *they* come from?"

"Roger, Army," Batman said, replying to Garrison's question. "We see them. I make it . . . eight . . . maybe ten bogies, heading west to west-northwest at five-five-oh."

"That's them. Too big to be missiles."

"My guess would be Sea Harriers, Army."

"Roger that. Victor Tango One-one, did you copy that, over?"

"Roger, BARCAP One-one. We are monitoring. Come to new heading one-nine-zero and intercept. Over."

"Roger, Victor Tango. We're in."

"BARCAP One-two, come to one-nine-five and intercept. Over."

"Copy, Victor Tango. The Batman's in."

He rammed his throttles to Zone Five burner and thundered toward the south.

**0751 hours, 26 March**
**Tomcat 204**

Army held his Tomcat level at ten thousand feet, racing south as Dixie plotted the bogies ahead. They seemed to be strung out across the sky. If they were Sea Harriers off an Indian carrier, they must have simply launched and flown, without waiting to assemble into a larger formation.

"Victor Tango One-one," he called. "Army Dixie Two-oh-four. We are tracking estimated twelve to sixteen bogies, now at three-five miles. They're low, wave-hopping. Two birds on board. Over."

"Roger that, Two-oh-four. You are clear to fire."

"Army Dixie Two-oh-four is engaging."

Two Phoenix missiles against sixteen targets. After that, they'd have nothing going for them but their guns.

"Locking onto Target Alpha," Dixie informed him. "Solid AWG track. For three!"

The Phoenix dropped clear of the Tomcat and ignited. The contrail etched a dazzling white scratch across the blue sky to the south.

"We have lock number two," Dixie said.

"Launch."

"Fox three!" The F-14 shuddered. "Okay, Army. We're empty."

"Right. Victor Tango, this is Two-oh-four. We've popped the last of our six-pack."

"Copy, Two-oh-four. Come right to two-eight-five and hold, angels base plus five."

"Rog."

Army was known as a fastidious dogfighter, preferring to make a kill from long distance, with air-to-air missiles, rather than getting "up close and personal" as the more flamboyant kids in his squadron liked to say.

Most Navy aviators preferred—or at least *claimed* to prefer—the John Wayne approach. "Would John Wayne shoot someone from a hundred miles away?" Coyote Grant had asked him once during a party in the Me Jo quarters. "Would John Wayne use a goddamn *missile*?"

That attitude had grown out of the Navy's Top Gun program. Tombstone, one of *Jefferson*'s resident Top Gun aces, gave regular training sessions and exercises for the other pilots. He liked to point out that Navy aviators had been getting into deep trouble early in the Vietnam fighting because they relied too heavily on missiles . . . and had forgotten how to dogfight. That piece of lore was basic to every lecture on ACM and was now drilled into Navy aviators from their first day in the air.

Army didn't disagree with the concept, but he was a technical pilot, flying by the book and making his decisions by the book. No hotdogging or seat-of-the-pants flying for him! If an aviator had a million-dollar high-tech missile with which to blow an enemy out of the sky before that enemy even knew he was being tracked, so much the better. As Patton had once put it, "The idea is not to die for your country, but to make some other poor bastard die for *his*." Combat, whatever the kids with their aviator's sunglasses and fighter jock jackets said or thought, was not a game, not a courtly joust between gentlemen, not a test of chivalry.

It was fire, pain, and sudden death. "Chivalry," he'd said during more than one Ready Room bull session, "gets you *dead*."

"Grand slam!" Dixie called. "Splash one bogie!"

On his VDI, his second Phoenix closed relentlessly on another target. On the radar screen, he could see the bogie twisting away toward the south, trying to outrun its Mach 5 nemesis. . . .

**0752 hours, 26 March**
**Sea Harrier 101, Blue King Leader**

Lieutenant Commander Ravi Tahliani pulled back on his stick, urging the Sea Harrier to climb above the waves. Smoke still boiled into the sky a mile ahead where Lieutenant Venkateraman's Harrier had vanished in orange flame and fragments.

''*Viraat! Viraat!*'' he called. ''Blue King Leader! We are under attack! Blue King Three is hit!''

''Roger, Blue King Leader. Overwatch reports several enemy fighters north of your position, range thirty to forty miles.''

''Blue King Leader, Blue Five!'' another voice interrupted. ''They've got a lock on me!''

Tahliani twisted his head, trying to see. Blue Five had been nearly four miles behind him and to the right. ''Break left, Blue Five!'' *Gods!* How could the Americans kill over such a distance?

He snapped his Harrier into a hard right turn, his eyes still scanning the eastern sky, looking for Blue Five. The pilot was Lieutenant Rani Gupta, son of an old family friend, and one of Tahliani's protégés.

There! He could just make out Rani's Harrier, a speck just above the water, streaking south. In the sky to the north, a white contrail was plunging toward the fleeing plane.

''Chaff, Rani!'' he yelled into his helmet mike. ''Chaff!''

There was no answer, but the speck was rising now, fighting for altitude, a standard maneuver for trying to disengage from a radar-homing missile after strewing clouds of chaff in its path.

It didn't seem to make any difference. The contrail continued to plunge from the sky. Faster than Tahliani's eye could follow, it stopped, merging with Rani's plane. . . .

A puff of flame and black smoke smeared the sky, followed by a much brighter flash as Rani's fuel and weapons detonated. Flaming wreckage continued to climb straight into the sky, paused a moment, then fell back toward the sea. If the young Indian flyer had managed to eject, there was no sign.

''*Viraat,* this is Blue Leader. Blue Five has been destroyed.''

"Roger, Blue King Leader. Continue the mission."

*Continue the mission.* Tahliani's face settled into a hard scowl behind his dark visor. His primary mission had been to engage the American fighter cover protecting their carrier, opening the way for ground-based strike aircraft. Only after the ground-based aircraft were engaged were the Sea Harriers to turn their attention to the American and Soviet ships. For that purpose, Blue King's aircraft each carried two Sea King missiles slung beneath their down-canted wings.

But for air-to-air combat, all they had were four R.550 Magic air-to-air missiles and their cannons. Magic was comparable to the American Sidewinder, IR-seekers with a range of perhaps two miles. He had nothing, *nothing* with which to counter an enemy still thirty-five miles away!

How was he supposed to carry out his mission when he could not even get close enough to the enemy to fire?

But possibly there was a chance. He had his Sea Harrier in a steady climb now, gaining altitude to extend the range of his Ferranti Blue Fox radar. Maximum range for an aircraft-sized target was about thirty-five miles for the system. Perhaps . . .

There it was, a lone aircraft at the very limit of his radar's range, traveling toward the northwest. If it was an American Tomcat, it had a top speed of better than Mach 2 and could easily outpace his Harrier.

But perhaps there was another way. . . .

# CHAPTER 19

**1925 hours EST, 25 March (0755 hours, 26 March, India time)**
**Oval Office, the White House**

"You sent for me, Mr. President."

"Yes, Admiral. Come in."

Admiral Magruder approached the enormous desk. He'd never seen the President looking this worn. The crisis of the past two days had drained the man.

As it had drained him, he admitted to himself. Magruder had not slept well—or long—these past few nights. He didn't expect to sleep this night either, not with the latest reports coming out of the Arabian Sea.

"I thought you should know, Tom," the President said. "The battle group is now under full attack."

Magruder felt his stomach knot. *Matt* . . .

"No hits, no casualties that we know of yet," the President continued. "But once the storm breaks, it's going to be bad. I've . . . I've *requested* the presence of the Indian ambassador. He'll be here in another fifteen minutes. Maybe we can still work something out . . . a disengagement, a cease-fire. But . . ."

He left the rest unsaid, and Magruder nodded his understanding. If Indian warplanes were already airborne, the chances of recalling them were slight.

The President leaned forward, his hands clasped on his desk. "Matt, this is the crunch. The reason I brought you here. I need your help."

Magruder couldn't tell if the President was referring to his summons to the office now, or the whole purpose of his transfer from the Pentagon. Perhaps he meant both. "I'll help anyway I can, Mr. President."

"We still have one chance, you know."

"Yes, sir?"

"Disengage. Break off and run for it." The President held up one hand as Magruder's face showed his surprise. "No, don't say it, Tom. Wait until I'm through. The whole question is whether our claim to those waters ten thousand miles from this desk is worth the lives of several thousand of our boys."

Magruder tried to smile, and failed. "Mr. President, it's a little late to reconsider *now,* isn't it?"

"Admiral, the man who sits at this desk thinks of carrier battle groups as a tool. A way to reach out and influence other parts of the world, other leaders. Okay, *threaten,* if you prefer. But in international politics, a threat is generally a lot more effective than a plea. It's the way the damned system works."

"Granted. You used us a time or two, remember? At Wonsan? In Thailand?"

"That's why I called you, Tom. Your battle group is really up against it this time. When I sent you into Korea, we both knew you'd be outnumbered, but it was a quick, sharp action. Get the Marines in, get our people, get them out. And the Koreans didn't have much to threaten your ships with beyond some outdated strike aircraft armed with free-fall bombs."

"Those were dangerous enough, sir."

"It was also a controlled response. If the North Koreans pushed too hard, well, we still had the U.S. air units stationed in South Korea and in Japan. We could keep things at a relatively low level, without escalating."

It certainly hadn't seemed that way at the time, Magruder remembered. They'd been worried about the Soviets, worried about Korean reinforcements. And at the end, the KorComs had launched a desperate attack on the invasion fleet with a number of low-level bombers. Sometimes, he thought, politicians could have remarkably selective memories. "Yes, sir."

"This time, it's totally different. *Jefferson* and the other ships with her, they're all we have in the region. *All.* And the Indians have just called our bluff. *My* bluff."

"*Nimitz* and the *Ike* will be in the region within another few days."

"By which time it will all be over. No, I'm beginning to

wonder if our best bet might not be to pull back. I feel sure that if I told Ambassador Nadkarni that we were disengaging, breaking off and heading back for Diego Garcia, well . . . I doubt that New Delhi wants to be perceived as aggressors. It'd be in their best interests to turn back and let us sail away, a bloodless, diplomatic victory."

"Not quite bloodless, Mr. President," Magruder reminded him. "There's the crew of that Indian sub that went down a couple of days ago."

"True. But if an Indian air strike hits our ships, that will be just the beginning. Maybe *now* is the time to stop the killing." The President rose suddenly from his chair. He turned and faced the tinted window, looking out past the Rose Garden toward the upthrust spike of the Washington Monument. "The point is, I *could* stop it. Now."

"But at what cost, Mr. President?"

He chuckled. "It would be political suicide, that's for damn sure." The President reached up and pressed his hands over his eyes. "After Grenada . . . Panama . . . the Persian Gulf . . . Wonsan? If I back down in front of the world and some nut starts tossing nukes over there . . . But I think I'm beyond caring about that anymore."

"I wasn't talking about the next election, sir. I think you know that." Magruder considered for a moment. "What's happening with the Russians right now? The ones at Turban Station."

"Some of their officers are aboard our Aegis cruiser now. There . . . there's no word from the Russian carrier. *Kremlin* is southwest of the *Jefferson,* farther from the Indian mainland and not in the direct line of fire. I've been talking with the Commonwealth representative today. Reading between the lines, I'd guess they're still trying to guess which way to jump on this one." He returned to his chair and slumped back into it.

"What do you think they'd do if we packed up and left? If we left the Indian Ocean to the Indians?"

"Lovely thought. My other military advisors don't think they could handle the Indians alone. The *Kremlin* isn't in the *Jefferson*'s league."

"My guess, sir, is that they'd follow through with what they're there to do. Continue the mission."

"Which is . . . ?"

"Two-fold, Mr. President. Extend Commonwealth power into the Indian Ocean, if for no better reason than to convince the world that they are still a world power. And, maybe more important, to try somehow to stop a nuclear holocaust near their borders."

"Holocaust. Such a heavy word. Such an *evocative* word."

"That's still our mission, isn't it, sir? To stop that holocaust?"

"Doesn't make much sense if we don't have a prayer of pulling it off in the first place, does it? I'm running the risk of plunging the United States of America into that same holocaust . . . beginning with nine thousand boys in CBG-14."

"There's another reason we're there, Mr. President."

"What's that?"

"Freedom of the seas. Our commitment to our allies in the region, to open sea lanes and right of free passage."

"I wonder how valuable that really is."

"It's *principle,* Mr. President. How important is a principle? Like freedom?" He took a deep breath. "You know, sir, the Navy has faced this same sort of thing before. The Gulf of Sidra, 1986."

"That was hardly the same as this."

"I don't see how it was that much different, Mr. President. Qaddafi decided the Gulf of Sidra was exclusively his, and he set out to prove it at the point of a gun . . . or at the point of some Su-27s and Nanuchka corvettes, if you prefer. The Navy challenged him on that, at the orders of one of your predecessors."

"The point was, it's foolish to lay claim to waters that you can't control. There was never any question that we could smash the Libyans. They gave us the provocation by threatening our ships and aircraft. We responded. The Gulf of Sidra is considered to be international waters, case closed." The President gave a grim smile. "This is different. We could *lose*!"

"Could be. We could take the history lesson back farther if you like. The *Mayaguez.* World War I and unrestricted U-boat attacks. The War of 1812. The Barbary Wars when Moorish pirates captured our ships and people and held them for ransom."

"We won those too."

"Yeah, but they weren't foregone conclusions at the time. Hell, the odds against us in 1812 weren't that much better than we're facing now, and in the case of the *Mayaguez,* we lost more Marines killed than the number of merchant seamen we rescued. In each case, the only thing that pulled us through was the willpower to *finish* what we'd set out to do . . . or what others forced on us in the first place."

"This thing goes beyond principle, Admiral. Or finishing what we started. A lot of reputations in this town are riding on the big carriers. You know that, don't you?" When Magruder nodded cautiously, the President went on. "Critics of the nuclear carriers have been saying for years that a single missile could sink one, that they're big, slow, vulnerable . . . and expensive. Can you imagine the uproar if *Jefferson* is sunk or disabled by an Indian attack?"

"And is that why you'd have them pull out, Mr. President?"

The President sighed. "No. Once, maybe. Not any longer." He appeared to be studying his hands, clasped before him on the desktop blotter, very carefully. "Things could have gone very wrong for us at Wonsan. Or at Bangkok too, for that matter. We could have lost ships there. We *did* lose men."

"Maybe the question is whether the men die for nothing. Or if it *means* something."

The President looked up at Magruder. "I should hire you to do my speeches. You have my speech writer beat all hollow."

"I only get passionate when I'm telling the truth, Mr. President. All I know, sir, is that if those big carriers of yours are to have any credibility in the future, you have to use them. Seems to me if you don't, you risk losing the whole damn fleet, simply because they're no longer a threat."

Magruder paused and swallowed hard. He was thinking of Matt. What he was saying now was going to have a very direct bearing on Matt's future, maybe even on whether he lived or died, and the knowledge was a searing pain in his breast. The irrepressible Tombstone would be in the forefront of the fight, no matter what. Winner of the Navy Cross at Wonsan, of the *Ramathepbodi*—the Thai equivalent of the Medal of Honor—at Bangkok, the *hero* . . .

But he had to say what he believed.

"Mr. President, you know as well as I do how important the

credibility of our fleet is in the world. You also know as well as I do how much we lose when the world sees us sacrifice principle for . . . for convenience. If the Indians attack, we fight. We have to. And if there's any way on God's Earth to get in there and separate those two before they start throwing their nuclear toys at each other, well . . . I think we should. We *have* to."

The President studied Magruder for a moment that dragged on and on. Then he nodded. "I know, Tom. And I agree."

"Testing me, Mr. President?"

"No, Tom. Testing myself." He reached out and pressed a button on his desk. A Secret Service man appeared in the door seconds later.

"Yes, Mr. President?"

"Ed, would you take the Admiral down to the Situation Room? Log him through on my say-so."

"Yes, Mr. President." Magruder looked at the President, who grinned.

"Go on down. I'll see you there after my meeting with His Excellency, Mr. Nadkarni, who'd better not be late. Then we'll see how the battle goes."

Magruder frowned. "Are you . . . *managing* the battle from there?" He remembered past attempts by Washington-based politicians and generals to manage fights halfway around the world. Carter had been in that same room while the helicopters were refueling at Desert One in Iran.

"Hell, no," the President said. "I'm no tactician. That's Vaughn's job. But we'll sure as hell be the first to know if he screws up."

**0756 hours, 26 March**
**CATCC, U.S.S. *Thomas Jefferson***

On the PLAT monitor, a pair of VF-95 Tomcats squatted side by side on the forward catapults. Tombstone did a fast calculation. All six of the current CAP aircraft, including the Alert Five, were from Viper Squadron: Army Garrison and Batman Wayne, Nightmare Marinaro and Ramrod Kingsly, Shooter Rostenkowski and Coyote Grant. Only two more Vipers remained to be launched in the dance on the deck,

Tomcat 220 piloted by Lieutenant Hardesty—"Trapper" to his squadron mates—and number 208, Lieutenant "Maverick" Bowman.

Trapper and Maverick were both replacement pilots, kids on their first blue-water deployment with a squadron. They'd flown in with Coyote on the COD aircraft, and Tombstone had not yet had an opportunity to get to know them well.

He grimaced. How many "Trappers" and "Mavericks" were there in the Navy? Or "Slicks" and "Ramrods" and "Shooters." The men—the *boys*—came and went. The running names never seemed to change . . . or the grinning faces and cocksure attitudes.

He watched as red-shirted ordies completed their checks of each Tomcat's weapons load, pulling the safing wires from the missiles' fuzes, then holding them up so that the pilot could count the red tags affixed to the wires and verify that his ordnance was ready to arm and launch. Unlike the BARCAP, which had been armed strictly for long-range interdiction, Trapper and Maverick were carrying standard interception warloads: a mix of four Phoenix, two Sparrow, and two Sidewinder missiles. The Tomcat had originally been designed as a stand-off interceptor, little more than a weapons platform for the Phoenix, but recognition that modern air combat demanded close-in weapons for down-and-dirty dogfighting had quickly led to the adoption of mixed loads.

They would need that range of distance and adaptability when the Indian horde closed with them. There simply were not enough Phoenix AIM-54-Cs for every Indian target . . . or enough planes to launch them. Unless the Indians got cold feet and backed off at the last moment, this was going to be one nasty, toe-to-toe fight.

The JBDs rose ponderously from the deck, and the Cat Officer stepped back from the Tomcats, vigorously cycling his hands above his head. The F-14's tailpipes glowed orange as their afterburners engaged.

Safe behind the shelter of the raised jet-blast deflectors, the Tomcats of VF-97, the War Eagles, were lining up to take their place at the catapults. First in line, he saw, was number 101, Lieutenant Commander Chuck Connelly's bird. "Slick" Connelly had been given the vacant squadron CO slot after the death of the War Eagles' previous skipper in Thailand. Tombstone heard Costello mutter something under his breath.

"What was that, Hitman?"

"Just wishing the skipper luck," Costello replied. "*Damn,* I wish I was going with them."

Tombstone knew the young, black-haired j.g. wasn't in hack the way he was. Someone had to draw CATCC duty, and today it was Costello's turn. But Tombstone could sense the kid's eagerness, his impatience.

"So do I, Hitman," he said. "So do I."

**0758 hours, 26 March**
**Sea Harrier 101, Blue King Leader**

Tahliani was in position. With his eyes on the radar returns indicating both the American Tomcat and the more distant U.S. carrier, he moved the targeting pipper on the screen, locked on, then pressed the launch button. With a whoosh of smoke and flame, one of the two bulky, black-and-red-painted missiles dropped from the Sea Harrier's underwing ordnance pad and ignited.

The Sea Eagle was a product of British Aerospace. Four meters long, four tenths of a meter thick, it had a range of well over a hundred kilometers. Far superior in every way to the small French Exocet, it had a 227-kilogram warhead that was believed capable of disabling even the largest warship.

But Tahliani was less interested in the Sea Eagle's target than he was in that target's guardian. As the missile dropped to its programmed flight altitude and reached its cruising speed of Mach .85, the Indian pilot could see in the movements of his opponents the consternation the launch had caused.

Sensing the right moment, he pulled back on his throttles, letting the missile skim ahead.

**0758 hours, 26 March**
**Tomcat 201**

"Victor Tango One-one, this is Viper Two-oh-one! We have a launch, repeat, launch. Probably ASM, bearing one-seven-one, range thirty miles."

"Copy, Army Dixie. We are tracking."

"Victor Tango, Viper Two-oh-one is engaging."

Batman had managed to knock down a ship-killer earlier using guns alone. Perhaps Army could do the same. As Dixie fed him speed and course updates from the backseat, he became convinced that the missile he was tracking was not another Exocet. This one was larger and slower . . . possibly a Brit-made Sea Eagle.

That fit with the notion that the air targets to the south and southeast were Sea Harriers off the Indian carrier. Well, there'd be time enough later to take them on.

First things first. His course and speed were all wrong for a guns-only approach on the ship-killer. Working for maximum economy of time, he swung the Tomcat into a broad turn to starboard, one that allowed the missile to cruise past at six hundred fifty miles per hour. He checked his course and position. *Jefferson* was fifty miles ahead . . . four and a half minutes at the missile's present speed.

He cut back on the throttles and settled into the slot squarely behind the missile.

"Army!" Malibu called. "I'm getting a radar signature from our six. Looks like Blue Fox multi-mode."

That meant a Sea Harrier on their tail. "Range!"

"Twelve miles. Closing."

No problem. A Sea Harrier could barely manage Mach 1, if that. There was lots of time. "Ah . . . Batman, this is Army," he radioed. "Where are you?"

"Your two o'clock and high," Batman replied. "Range five miles."

"Batman, I'm after this missile, but I've got a problem closing on my six. Can you brush him off, over?"

"Roger, Army. The Batman's on the way."

Army searched the horizon ahead for the enemy's missile. The range was down to two miles now. He'd have to be a bit closer before he could spot it with the naked eye. For now, the radar-directed target box drifted from side to side on his HUD, marking an empty patch of blue just below the horizon.

Gently, he eased his throttle forward, straining to catch up.

**0758 hours, 26 March**
**Sea Harrier 101, Blue King Leader**

Lieutenant Commander Tahliani watched the small, drifting box on his HUD that marked the position of the enemy plane. Another computer-generated graphic marked the second American plane, now approaching nearly head-on from the northwest.

He continued to concentrate on the first target, pushing his throttles full forward, picking up speed.

His plan had worked well, but now he had to take advantage of the setup he'd created. By launching the missile at the American carrier, he'd drawn the enemy F-14 into a chase, forcing his opponent to slow and turn in order to position himself behind the speeding ship-killer. As long as the American stayed behind the slower missile, trying to line up his shot, Tahliani had a chance—a small and very brief chance—to get close enough for a Magic Kill.

Unfortunately, the second American Tomcat was vectoring in to cut him off. It was going to be close, either way. . . .

# CHAPTER 20

**0758 hours, 26 March**
**Tomcat 216**

Batman adjusted his course, eyes glued to the graphic symbol marking the enemy Sea Harrier.

He still had one Phoenix . . . but the AIM-54 was not a dogfighting missile. With no Sidewinders left, he would have to make a head-on pass, guns blazing. He might get lucky on the flyby, and if he didn't, he should be able to swing around and take the bandit on his six. "Tomcat Two-one-six," he radioed. "I'm in. Going for guns." He flicked the guns control on his stick and saw the target reticle appear on his HUD.

He closed with the enemy head-to-head at better than Mach 2.

**0759 hours, 26 March**
**Sea Harrier 101**

The range to his target was eight miles, and slowly decreasing. With part of his mind Tahliani concentrated on the target, and with part he focused on the enemy F-14, coming in almost head-on. The Tomcat pilot was trying for a pass with his guns.

Grimly, Tahliani gripped the throttle with his right hand, the controls that vectored his four engine nozzles with the other. He waited, watching. . . .

The Tomcat exploded into view, a blur of motion felt more than seen. Tahliani's glimpse of the muzzle flash stuttering on the left side of the nose beneath the cockpit was so brief it was almost subliminal.

He yanked the vectoring throttles back. . . .

**0759 hours, 26 March**
**Tomcat 216**

Batman squeezed the trigger and felt the shudder of 20-mm Vulcan cannon shells spewing toward the target. . . .

Only the target wasn't there! With a curse, Batman yanked back on the stick. The enemy plane had just performed a maneuver Batman had never encountered before in training or in combat. A maneuver that was *impossible* . . .

**0759 hours, 26 March**
**Sea Harrier 101**

The maneuver was called viffing, a word derived by the Sea Harrier's British designers from the acronym for Vectoring In Forward Flight. By swinging the engine nozzles around, he had abruptly chopped his forward speed. The Sea Harrier hovered, then skittishly drifted backwards, rising. From the American pilot's perspective it must have appeared that he'd stopped in midair and started to fly backward and *up*.

Cannon shells slashed into the wave tops a hundred feet in front of him, where the Sea Harrier was supposed to be if it had been an ordinary aircraft. The F-14 pulled up and thundered overhead, its shadow momentarily blotting the morning sun astern.

Then Tahliani rammed the vectoring controls forward again, returning to forward flight. He'd lost a few seconds in his pursuit but gained many seconds more on his target's wingman. It would take a long time, long by the standards of modern aerial combat, for the wingman to swing around and come at him from behind.

**0800 hours, 26 March**
**Tomcat 201**

Army squeezed the trigger and his M61A1 Vulcan Gatling gun stuttered, sending a stream of 20-mm shells toward the target. He could see the missile now, a tiny black speck less than half a mile ahead.

"Batman, where are you?" he called. "This guy's still on my six!"

"Damn, Army! I missed him! Airplanes can't do that!"

Army shook his head, not sure what Batman was talking about. Gently, he squeezed the trigger for another burst. Gouts of water exploded on the ocean beneath the hurtling missile.

"Tomcat Two-oh-one, this is Victor Tango One-one. Break off pursuit! You are entering Homeplate's point defense zone!"

"Copy, Victor Tango! I'm out of there!"

He pulled up. *Jefferson*'s point Phalanx cannons would be on automatic, and any aircraft that came within two miles of the carrier would be shot down.

"We almost had the bastard, Dixie," he said. The Tomcat clawed for altitude. He could see the carrier in the distance, huge and isolated on a vast, gray-blue sea.

"Army!" Dixie yelled over the ICS. "That bandit's making his move! He's right on our tail! Range six miles!"

"Shit!" Army pulled the Tomcat into a hard left roll.

"He's still with us, man! Still with us! Five miles! No . . . four! He's lining us up for the shot!"

**0801 hours, 26 March**
**Sea Harrier 101**

Tahliani had them in his sights. He let the aiming pipper meet the graphic symbol representing an American Tomcat as it twisted across his HUD less than four miles ahead, and heard the satisfying electronic warble in his headphones as one of his Magic AAMs "saw" the target. His finger closed on the trigger.

The R.550 Matra Magic was a French weapon, one deliberately designed to compete on the world's market with the notorious American Sidewinder. It had an extremely flexible range for an all-aspect heat-seeker and was capable of engaging targets as close as two tenths of a mile, or as distant as six miles. It could even be slaved to controls in the launching aircraft's cockpit, allowing the pilot to guide it to the target. Its one quirk was the extremely large amount of smoke it released during firing.

The exhaust cloud enveloped the Sea Harrier's starboard wing, momentarily blinding Tahliani as it slid from the launching rail. Then he pulled out of the smoke in time to see the missile climbing rapidly on a billowing contrail, arcing up into the sky. The target was still too distant to be seen with the naked eye. Aware that the second Tomcat would be returning any moment, the Indian pilot pulled the Sea Harrier into a harsh turn to the left and struggled for more altitude fast.

Seconds after launch, the Magic air-to-air missile hit Mach 3.

**0801 hours, 26 March**
**Tomcat 201**

"Launch! Launch!" Dixie cried. "On our six, Army! Comin' fast!"

"Flares!" He heard no tone from a radar lock-on and assumed the missile must be IR-guided. He rolled hard to port, hearing the thump-thump-thump from astern as Dixie deployed flares in an attempt to confuse the missile. Trading altitude for speed, he let the Tomcat plummet toward the sea from sixteen thousand feet. . . .

**0801 hours, 26 March**
**Over the Arabian Sea**

The nitrogen-cooled PbS seeker head was not fooled. At Mach 3, the Magic AAM slid past the Tomcat's tail pipes. With less than a meter's separation, the twenty-seven-pound warhead was detonated by an IR proximity fuze.

There was a flash, and chunks of nut- and bolt-sized metal sprayed across the F-14's engine housings. One piece slashed through the starboard engine compressor assembly, smashing the fan mechanism and sending pieces of turbine blade whirling through the engine's guts like shrapnel. A fuel line from the wing tank was severed. JP-5 sprayed across hot engine surfaces. . . .

The explosion was a searing flash that scattered chunks of burning debris across the sky. Trailing flame, what was left of Tomcat 201's fuselage tumbled end for end in a long and spectacular funeral pyre toward the blue-gray sea.

**0802 hours, 26 March**
**CIC, U.S.S. *Thomas Jefferson***

''Missile incoming!'' Barnes yelled, rising in his seat. ''God-damn it, *where's point defense* . . . !''

The Sea Eagle launched minutes before had entered *Jefferson*'s innermost defensive zone. Computers, radars, and high-tech electronics were supposed to bring the carrier's Phalanx guns to bear automatically . . . but they did not.

It took an agonizing twenty seconds for the Sea Eagle to cross that final two-mile stretch to the *Jefferson.*

Someone had switched *Jefferson*'s point defense system off so that the carrier could launch aircraft without shooting down its own planes as they cleared the flight deck. By mistake, both the Sea Sparrow and Phalanx systems had been shut down rather than being put into hold. It took long, wasted seconds to realize what the problem was and correct it.

By that time the Sea Eagle was half a mile from the carrier's starboard bow, five seconds away.

Switches were thrown, the system brought back on line. On the starboard side of the island, the Phalanx gun dubbed Huey come to life, its J-band radar reaching out and acquiring a target within its range. Two seconds to acquire and track . . .

The target was almost too close to reach by the time Huey's silo slewed around and the Vulcan cannon fired its first shot, sharp burst. The stream of ultra-dense slugs reached past the speeding missile, missing. Huey's computer, following radar returns from both missile and rounds, corrected, shifted aim. . . .

Too late! The Sea Eagle struck *Jefferson* in the hull on her starboard side forward, halfway between her waterline and the flight deck, well forward of her Number One elevator.

The five-hundred-pound warhead punched through the outer hull and several bulkheads before exploding.

The ship lurched hard, knocking men on the flight deck to their knees, sending several men on the catwalk just above where the missile struck hurtling out and down into the sea. The clanging of an alarm bell cut above the yells and confusion. "Now hear this, now hear this! Damage control parties lay forward to the chain locker."

There was a gaping hole in the ship's side, and smoke was beginning to boil from the carrier and across the surface of the sea.

**0802 hours, 26 March**
**CATCC, U.S.S. *Thomas Jefferson***

In CATCC on the 04 deck, Tombstone had felt the deck shudder through his feet, but the impact was no more than a gentle rumble, like a far-off boom of thunder more felt than heard.

But he knew at once that something was wrong. It takes a fairly powerful kick to make something the size of an aircraft carrier shudder. The call over the 1-MC a moment later for damage control parties to lay forward confirmed it.

"We've lost one," CAG said.

That brought his attention back to CATCC's domain. He could hear a chief at a nearby console calling a rescue helo.

"Aircraft down, aircraft down," the chief was saying, "Angel One, this is CATCC. We have an aircraft down at bearing one-zero-four, range three miles from the boat."

"Angel One copies," a voice responded over the speaker. The heavy *thup-thup-thup* of helicopter rotors could be heard in the background. "On our way. Do you have reports of chutes?"

"Negative chutes, Angel One. No witnesses."

"Roger, *Jefferson.* We'll let you know."

Tombstone looked at the PLAT camera. Several sailors were still lying on the forward deck where they'd been knocked down by the impact. Black smoke was wafting across the deck between the camera and *Jefferson*'s bows. A pair of VF-97

Tomcats still sat on the catapult slots, steam boiling around them from the deck.

With a fascinated horror, Tombstone watched as the F-14 on Cat Two began to move, to slide forward toward the bow.

He couldn't tell if a cat shooter had accidentally pressed the button, or whether a malfunction had triggered the catapult without a signal from the deck. Whatever the cause, the F-14 was moving forward, but slow . . . slow . . . far too slowly to get airborne.

"Negative launch! Negative launch!" the Air Boss's voice sounded over the speaker. Another voice in the background was screaming. "*Eject! Eject! Eject!*"

The Tomcat reached the forward edge of the deck like a canoe reaching the precipice of a waterfall. There was a flash and a swirl of smoke. Two figures could be seen jetting into the sky on rocket trails as the Tomcat balanced precariously for a moment, then swung tail-high and vanished over the bow.

Two parachutes broke in the sky above the flight deck, drifting back toward the ship. One man dropped safely onto the deck a few feet from where he'd launched seconds before. The other drifted aft, landing among the A-6 strike aircraft being readied for Operation Mongoose along the carrier's port side. Deck crewmen rushed up to him as he struggled with his harness, collapsing his chute before it could drag him over the side.

Tombstone turned away from the PLAT monitor in time to see a sailor marking new information onto the transparent acrylic flight status board. He'd not caught the number of the F-14 that had been shot down.

Tomcat 201, Army and Dixie. The sailor was writing "MIA: 0801" in bold letters across the row reserved for them.

His Tomcat . . . and his place.

*I should have been there. . . .*

He dismissed the thought immediately. The fates that determined each twist of life and death in combat were too capricious to be analyzed in so simplistic a fashion.

But it would have been him in that aircraft, *should* have been . . . had Admiral Vaughn not pulled him off the flight line.

Suppressing a shudder, he walked toward CAG, who was leaning against a console, studying the radar returns of approaching aircraft.

"Tombstone!" Hitman said. "Where ya goin'?"
"To get me an airplane!"
"Well, hey! Wait for me!"

**0803 hours, 26 March**
**CIC, U.S.S. *Vicksburg***

"Goddamn it to hell." Vaughn rubbed his chin with one hand. His own skin felt clammy and cold. "God-*damn* it to hell . . .

"Damage isn't too bad," the radio voice continued. "Minor fires in some stored paint abaft the chain locker, but fire parties have those in hand. Casualties so far are light, but a muster's probably going to turn up some missing men blown off the deck.

"Our worst operational damage is to the catapults. One and Two are both down, and the cat crews are not real optimistic about getting them up again any time soon. There was some minor buckling to the deck, and the steam lines to the forward catapults are out."

"Shit," Vaughn snapped. "Are they still up at the waist?"

The radio operator passed on the admiral's question.

"Three and Four are still operational," was the reply. "Good pressure, and no apparent damage. We have DC parties checking them now."

"Well, that's something, anyway," Vaughn said.

"It's going to restrict operations, Admiral," Captain Bersticer said, frowning. "They'll have to shift aircraft aft to the waist to continue launching . . . and they won't be able to simultaneously launch and recover aircraft. Operation Mongoose is supposed to go down in four hours. We'll never make it without four working cats."

Vaughn stared at Bersticer for a moment as the words sunk in. If they couldn't launch the strike against the Indian supply columns . . .

They had failed. *He* had failed, and before they'd even had a proper chance.

His fists clenched at his side, the frustration, the rage of the past twelve years surging up inside like a black, unstoppable tide.

*It's not fair!* he thought. *It's not fucking fair!*

**0803 hours, 26 March**
**CATCC, U.S.S. *Thomas Jefferson***

"I want that airplane, CAG," Tombstone said, cold steel behind each word. "It's criminal idiocy to keep me here when we need aviators out there!"

CAG looked at Tombstone with level eyes. "What are you going to fly?" he said. "Two-oh-one just augered in."

"Two double-nuts," Tombstone replied immediately. "It'll fly."

He'd been spending his time since being put in hack catching up with his squadron's paperwork. Tomcat 200, the aircraft in Viper squadron traditionally reserved for the CAG when he flew, had not been operational since before Wonsan. Stored in the aft hangar bay for repairs at the time, the F-14 had been damaged during the battle at Sattahip Bay in Thailand when a rebel attack sent a rocket through an open elevator door and into the parked airplanes on the hangar deck. It was one of the two aircraft in VF-95 with a maintenance downcheck.

Maintenance personnel had only finished installing a new engine a week earlier. The job had been inspected, but not tested. No one knew for sure yet if Two-double-nuts would run.

Or fly.

"Stoney, I know how you feel," CAG said gently. "But I can't authorize a damn-fool stunt like—"

Tombstone jerked a thumb at the bulkhead speaker. The voices of several aviators could be heard calling to one another. "My God, look at that!" a voice was saying. "One-oh-three, we have bogies inbound! Bogies inbound at fifty miles!"

"Those are my people out there, damn you," Tombstone said, his voice carrying a deadly edge to it. *"My people!"*

"The plane's not armed."

"It'll take twenty minutes to slip some Sidewinders on her. It'll take that long just to get the rest of VF-97 aloft with only two cats working." Tombstone's voice raised suddenly to a shout, and every head in CATCC turned in their direction. "Damn it, CAG! I'm going with or without your say-so, but I'm going!"

"You're an asshole, Stoney," CAG said. He shook his head.

"And if you don't watch your mouth the brig is where you're going!"

The two men stopped, staring eye to eye. Then CAG looked away. "So you'd better go before you say something that makes me put you there. Who's your RIO?"

"Me, sir!" Hitman said. Tombstone turned, surprised. He'd forgotten Costello was behind him. "Hell, Stoney," Hitman continued with a shrug. "I'd rather be your RIO than stay here and get shot at!"

"Get into your flight gear, gentlemen," CAG said. "And get the hell out to your ship. I'll inform the Boss you're coming."

"Thank you, sir."

"Shut up and git. Before I shoot you for desertion."

Tombstone got.

"Commander?"

Tombstone stopped and turned. Three sailors were sitting at one of the consoles, watching him. By the light of a nearby radar screen he recognized the one who had spoken: Seaman David Howard, the sailor who'd become a hero at Bangkok.

"Good luck, sir," Howard said.

"That's right, Commander," one of Howard's companions said. The name stenciled over the pocket of his dungaree shirt read. "Gilkey, F." The man gave him a sharp thumbs-up. "Beat the shit out of the bastards."

"We're right behind you, sir," the third man, a second-class radarman, said. His shirt carried the name Benedict. "Kick some ass for us!"

It was strange. Tombstone did not know Gilkey or Benedict. A supercarrier was large enough that it was possible to live and work aboard her for months on end and never meet all the people aboard.

But these men certainly seemed to know *him.* Young Howard must have been shooting off his mouth, he decided. Still, it was a good feeling to know that he had men like these in his corner.

It would make the sky a lot less lonely.

Tombstone grinned and tossed them a casual salute. "Watch my back, guys."

Then he was through the door and pounding down the passageway toward the VF-95 Ready Room.

# CHAPTER 21

**0805 hours, 26 March**
**Tomcat 216**

Batman took the Tomcat up to twenty thousand feet, giving Malibu a clear view on the radar for sixty miles in every direction as they searched for the Indian fighter that had given them the slip. There were plenty of targets in the area, but the unidentified bogies seemed to be drawing off toward the east and Batman wasn't about to follow them, not when there were at least ten of them and only one of him.

"Any sign of the bastard, Mal?" He was still feeling stupid for having forgotten about the Sea Harrier's incredible maneuvering capability.

"He could be one of those guys on the run," Malibu said. "Or he could be wave-hopping to hide in the surface clutter. What you wanna do?"

"I don't know," Batman said. He was still feeling shaken by the encounter, and more shaken still by the sudden loss of Army and Dixie. That Sea Harrier must have put a heat-seeker into Army just as he was breaking off from his pursuit of the enemy missile. Two-oh-one had dropped from the screen like a stone. Then, nothing.

Batman had already made one quick pass over the area looking for chutes, but had seen nothing before *Jefferson*'s CATCC chased them away. A helo, they'd been tersely informed, was on its way to look for the downed aviators. The carrier's automated point defense was on and random overflights of the area would be dangerous.

"We're picking up a ninety-nine-aircraft alert," Malibu

informed him. ''Those Indie planes up north. They're moving.''

''Great,'' Batman replied. ''And us with one rock left to throw.''

He put the Tomcat into a hard turn, heading north.

**0805 hours, 26 March**
**IAF Jaguar 102, Okha**

Colonel Jarnall Rajiv Singh felt himself pressed back into his ejection seat as his SEPECAT Jaguar hurtled down the runway, then lifted into a morning sky of blue and gold. The runway vanished beneath the belly of his aircraft replaced immediately by the murky blue-green waters of the Gulf of Kutch.

''Okha tower, Jaguar One-zero-two airborne,'' he said over the radio. ''Coming right to one-seven five.''

''Roger, One-zero-two,'' the control tower replied. ''Switch to tactical command, three-five-five point three. Over.''

He put the aircraft into a gentle right-hand turn. Water gave way to gravel, scrub brush, and palm trees as he circled back over the Kathiawar Peninsula. Looking up through his canopy, he could see other elements of the massive Indian air armada gathering above him.

''Switching to three-five-five point three, roger.'' He adjusted the frequency on his radio. ''Rama Command, Rama Command,'' he called. ''This is Python Strike Leader, Jaguar One-zero-two. Do you read, over?''

''Python Strike Leader, this is Rama Command. We read you. You are clear to proceed.'' The new voice sounded tense, even harsh.

*What do you have to be worried about?* Singh thought, silently questioning the voice. ''Very well, Rama. We're on our way.''

Below, the dun-colored wastes of the western tip of Kathiawar blurred past, then gave way once more to the sea, the deep, cobalt blue of the Arabian Sea this time instead of the muddy shallows of Kutch. Around him, the other Jaguars of his flight group closed up, settling into the tight formation that they would hold for most of the trip to the target.

Singh was uncomfortably aware that this mission would

have little in common with his strike against the American supply ships two days before. That attack had been against relatively undefended targets and in the confusion of night. This time, the enemy was fully warned and prepared, aircraft in the sky and ready, ships on full alert. It was going to be a bloodbath.

He was afraid.

**0808 hours, 26 March**
**IAF Fulcrum 401, Jamnagar**

Sixty miles to the east of Okha, a pair of sleek Indian Air Force MiG-29 Fulcrums lifted into the sky above the airfield at Jamnagar, their landing gear folding into their bellies while they were still a few meters above the tarmac.

Lieutenant Colonel Ramadutta cleared his flight with Jamnagar Tower and set his fighter on a south-southwesterly course.

For Ramadutta, the coming battle would be a chance at recovering some measure of his pride. The near-encounter with the American Tomcat in the dark night sky thirty-five hours before had left him shaken, questioning his own abilities as one of India's elite pilot corps. In his last encounter, he'd run. Nothing had been said officially, but the knowledge that his failure could have led to the destruction of several Indian Jaguars during their successful strike against the American supply ships had left him with a burning shame . . . and a need to clear his honor, before his family, his comrades, and himself.

When his squadron, what was left of it, had been transferred back to Jamnagar the evening before, he'd wondered if he was going to be able to fly again.

As fighters and strike planes scrambled, he knew the answer. He would face his fear . . . and the American enemy in the skies above India.

His mission this time, the mission of his squadron, was to protect the Indian naval and air force strike aircraft that were deploying to attack the American and Soviet squadrons. But it would be more than that. He knew, beyond any doubt, that within minutes he would again be engaged in single combat.

He was having difficulty sorting out his own fiercely intertwined emotions–determination, fear, shame. . . .

But more than anything else, Lieutenant Colonel Munir Ramadutta was *angry.*

**0812 hours, 26 March**
**CIC, U.S.S. *Vicksburg***

Admiral Vaughn was angry, and he didn't know how much longer he could control it. He raised his fist, shaking it under the nose of a startled Soviet Chief of Staff.

"You Commie son of a bitch!" he shouted. Heads turned throughout the Aegis cruiser's command center. "If this damned *alliance* is going to amount to anything, Captain, then you people had better get off your asses and into the air, don't you think?"

"Please, Admiral," Captain First Rank Sharov said. "I have no authority."

"Then *get* some authority, damn it! You're in touch with your carrier now?"

"*Da,* Admiral. But the necessary permission from Moskva . . ." He shrugged helplessly. "We have received no orders."

Vaughn stopped himself, took a deep breath, then swallowed. He allowed his voice to drop, to become dangerous. "Son, if you don't clear things so that *Kremlin* can start launching planes and help defend this so-called joint task force . . ." He paused once more and licked his lips. When he spoke again, it was with a blast of raw fury that forced the Russian back a step. *"I'm going to open fire on your fucking fleet myself!"*

"I . . . will see what is to be done, Admiral."

"Do it! Get out of my sight and don't show yourself until you have some aircraft in the sky doing their part!" He whirled as an American lieutenant cleared his throat at his back. "What the hell do *you* want?"

"Sir! The Indian aircraft seem to be making their move."

Until now, the armada that had been rising from airfields from Okha to Bombay had simply been gathering, waiting and circling beyond *Jefferson*'s air defense zone like a flock of buzzards.

"You're sure?"

"Yes, sir. We have an estimated twelve strike aircraft—probably Jaguars—crossing into our outer defense zone south of Okha. We have ten more out of Jamnagar, big ones, possibly old Canberras. Range is now eighty miles."

"What about the Sea Harriers?"

"They've engaged with our BARCAP thirty to fifty miles southeast of the *Jefferson*. No news yet."

"Okay," Vaughn said. He wiped his face with his hand and was surprised at how cold it felt. "Okay. How's the *Jeff* doing?"

"Ten Tomcats are aloft now, sir, and they're continuing launch operations from their waist cats. That's in addition to two Hawkeyes, four Prowlers, two tankers, and a couple of ASW Vikings."

"Good, good." But it wasn't good. He hoped the people in *Jefferson*'s CATCC knew what the hell they were doing. With that many planes in the sky, keeping them all fueled was going to be a bitch with only two working catapults.

And there were no bingo fields ashore if someone miscalculated and planes started running out of gas.

"Things sound pretty confused over there, Admiral," the lieutenant continued. "But CATCC reports that they'll have sixteen Tomcats up within the next ten minutes."

Sixteen? He tallied them in his mind. Right. Ten from VF-97 and eight from VF-95. Minus one shot down a few minutes ago, and another tipped into the drink by a catapult malfunction.

Against an aerial armada of well over a hundred Indian aircraft. Most of those would be strike planes, clumsy with bombs and rockets for the fleet. But still . . .

"Very well," Vaughn said. "Keep me posted."

"Aye, aye, sir."

Vaughn watched the lieutenant hurry away and found himself, unaccountably, thinking of the Battle of Midway.

It was strange comparing that battle with what would probably go down in the history books as the Battle of the Arabian Sea. Midway, remembered now as the turning point in the Pacific campaign of World War II, was the subject of intensive study by every Naval cadet at Annapolis, and its lessons were part of the training and background of every U.S. Naval command and staff officer.

Beyond the obvious—the facts that this battle, like Midway, would probably be fought with the two fleets never coming within sight of one another, and that air power would be the dominant arm in the clash—there were few similarities. The Indians would be relying primarily on their airfields ashore to smash the American force. At Midway, American land-based aircraft had been largely ineffectual.

There was one important comparison, however, Vaughn realized. The lieutenant had said it: confusion. The Naval Academy's teachings on Midway emphasized the fact that *both* sides had made plenty of mistakes, usually because of poor intelligence.

Victory had gone to the side that made the fewer mistakes.

"Admiral?" Captain Bersticer said, approaching. He handed a message-transmittal sheet to Vaughn. "This just in from the *Jefferson*. They want to know if they should stand down from the preflighting for Mongoose."

Vaughn scowled, reading the message. *Jefferson*'s crew had been working straight through the night readying the carrier's Hornets and Intruders for the air strike against the Indian supply lines. With the carrier's flight operations sharply curtailed by the damage to her forward catapults, space and equipment would be at a premium. To continue with the strike might cripple their ability to get all of the Tomcats aloft and keep them up.

Yes, it might be best to abort Mongoose completely. No one would blame him, least of all his peers in Washington. The defense of the carrier and her consorts came first . . . and by breaking down the bomb-laden F/A-18 Hornets and loading them with Sidewinders and Sparrows, he could increase the battle group's air defense strength by two more squadrons.

The idea was tempting. . . .

Something made him hold back. "Negative," he said, handing the message back to Bersticer. "They can concentrate on getting the Tomcats up, but let's keep moving with Mongoose. I don't want to give up on that yet."

"Aye, aye, sir."

He continued toying with the idea. What was familiar about rearming the F/A-18s? Why shouldn't he . . . ?

Then he remembered. Only moments earlier, he'd been thinking about Midway, and the part confusion had played in the battle that reversed the trend of Japanese victory in the Pacific.

*Confusion.* Orders to unload the bombs and ground-strike missiles from the Hornets and replace them with air-to-air missiles would create incredible confusion among flight crews already exhausted by working some twenty-four hours straight. By giving those orders, he would be begging for a catastrophic accident, like the one that crippled the *Forrestal* off the coast of Vietnam in 1977.

But there was more.

At the Battle of Midway, the commander-in-chief of the Imperial Japanese carrier force, Admiral Chuichi Nagumo, had opened the battle by launching a bombing raid against the American naval base and airstrip on Midway Island. A second strike force of ninety-three aircraft was ready on the decks of his carriers, armed with torpedoes in case the American fleet appeared.

But the returning planes of the first strike force reported that damage to the island's facilities was not as extensive as had been hoped. Nagumo, unaware that the Americans were in the area, had ordered the second strike force to unload its torpedoes and rearm with incendiary and fragmentation bombs for another attack on the island.

Within the next thirty minutes, reports had come in locating the American fleet. Nagumo then issued new orders: rearm the strike force yet *again* with torpedoes to sink the American ships.

The flurry of orders and counterorders, reasonable at the time, had proved to be an appalling blunder. The Japanese strike was delayed long enough to be delayed again by the recovery and refueling of the first attack wave.

The American dive bombers that struck just after 1000 hours that morning could not have asked for better targets: four Japanese carriers loaded with refueling planes, with strike aircraft waiting to launch, with bombs and torpedoes carelessly staked on the decks by ordnance crews too hurried to observe proper safety procedures. Nagumo lost three aircraft carriers within the next few hours, and a fourth the following day. It was a disaster from which the Imperial Japanese Navy never recovered and could easily be identified as the defeat that doomed Japan's war in the Pacific.

There were lessons to be learned from history, Vaughn reflected. Not that history ever repeated itself exactly, but to try now, in the middle of an air assault, to rearm the Hornets with air-to-air weapons was inviting a disaster as great at that suffered by Nagumo at Midway.

Perhaps later there would be time to reassess the plan. *Later*, if the carrier battle group survived . . .

For now, though, they would follow though with what they'd begun.

**0824 hours, 26 March**
**Tomcat 200, Cat Four, U.S.S. Thomas Jefferson**

Tombstone watched as the mule driver herded his flat yellow vehicle clear of the catapult. Green-shirted hook-and-cat men completed attaching the catapult shuttle to the aircraft's nosegear as Tombstone and Hitman ran down the checklist.

"I've got a fault warning on the electrical system," Tombstone said. The red light on his right side advisory display was an ominous warning that this particular aircraft had not flown in many months.

"Wait a sec," Hitman said over the ICS. Tombstone could feel the slight shifting of the aircraft as Hitman moved around in the backseat. The fuzes for the plane's electrical system were located on a board behind the RIO's seat. Part of his preflight routine was to reach behind him and check each fuze by hand.

"Got it," Hitman said.

Tombstone watched the advisory panel light go out, then worked the electrical main switch several times. If popping the fuze back did not correct the problem, they would have to signal to the deck crew to break down the aircraft.

The light remained off.

On the deck outside, the hook runner, satisfied with the setup, pumped his fist up and down, signaling to the Cat Officer to bring the aircraft under tension. Tombstone heard a metallic creak as the Tomcat took the strain. A green shirt held up the chalkboard with number 200's launch weight: 62,000. That checked with the figure on Tombstone's thigh board and he acknowledged with a thumbs-up signal. Somewhere below decks the catapult crew would be adjusting their controls to deliver the proper amount of steam pressure to Cat Four in order to launch thirty-one tons of aircraft.

An ordie walked up alongside the cockpit, holding aloft a bundle of wires, each with a red tag. Tombstone counted eight tags and nodded. The F-14 was loaded with four Sparrow and four Sidewinder missiles.

Everything was ready. The light on the island had gone from red to amber. The jet-blast deflector came up astern, and Tombstone eased the throttle forward, feeling his high-tech steed tremble beneath him, aching to touch the sky. He took another look at the bridge. He could see men at the Pri-Fly windows, watching . . . and other figures, less distinct, forward at the carrier's bridge.

"All set back there?" he called to Hitman.

"Set, Tombstone. All green."

And the light on the island was green as well.

Tombstone saluted the Cat Officer, the signal that they were ready for launch. The Cat Officer took another look up and down the deck, checking his men, checking with the white-shirted Safety Officers who were in turn signaling readiness. The intimate dance of the carrier's team of professionals continued. The Cat Officer dropped to his knee and touched the deck.

The 5-G acceleration slammed Tombstone into his seat as it always did, his Tomcat speeding down the deck, hitting 150 knots in less than three seconds. The island flashed past on his right, then the expanse of deck where damage control teams were working on the warped deck and broken cats.

"Two double-oh airborne," the Air Boss said. There was a pause. "Luck, Stoney."

And Tombstone clawed for blue sky.

# CHAPTER 22

**0830 hours, 26 March**
**IAF Fulcrum 401**

Lieutenant Colonel Ramadutta could see the enemy's defensive line forming on his radar display screen. It was unlikely that the Americans had yet seen him.

The Fulcrum was a marvel of modern technology, with electronics that even surpassed much of what was available to American pilots. Unlike any Western fighter, the MiG-29 gave its pilot a variety of long-range tracking options, including an excellent pulse-doppler radar, an extremely sensitive IR imager, a helmet-mounted computer display—though this was absent from the MiGs sold to India—and a laser ranger. By flying close to the surface, Ramadutta was hoping to mask himself from American radar. At the same time, his own radar was off to avoid giving away his position directly. Instead, he was using the MiG's infrared search/track mode, or IRST. Meanwhile, enemy aircraft using their own radar were quite visible to him, plotted on his display screen by the Fulcrum's electronics.

Over his headset, he could hear the Indian strike aircraft calling to one another, reassuring and bolstering each other as they formed up their attack waves. Ramadutta had deliberately left the Jamnagar area in company with a flight of large, slow BAC Canberra bombers. Those relics of the fifties, Ramadutta thought, would not stand a chance against the American fleet. But their takeoff had given him the cover he needed to leave the airfield unnoticed by the watchful radar eyes of the American Hawkeyes.

He glanced left and right, making certain that the other three aircraft of his flight were tucked in close. Together, they could hit the American air defenses without warning. That would give the Indian strike planes their chance to get through.

He signaled his comrades with a waggle of his wings, then pushed the throttle forward. The Fulcrum thundered, shuddering as it approached the speed of sound.

Then he was through and still accelerating, pushing faster and faster as he hurtled south, skimming the crests of the waves.

**0831 hours, 26 March**
**Sea Harrier 101**

Lieutenant Commander Tahliani was worried about his Sea Harrier's fuel reserves. Harriers gulped enormous quantities of jet fuel, especially when they performed such unorthodox maneuvers as hovering or viffing.

After shooting down the American Tomcat, he'd expected the other U.S. fighters to follow him and had circled back toward the east in an attempt to draw them out.

The F-14s had not taken the bait, circling instead toward the north.

Tahliani could see the battle unfolding on his radar screen and understood the Americans' caution. They were heavily outnumbered in the air, and the ground-based aircraft from Kathiawar were beginning their move.

This, he decided, might present an opportunity to *Viraat*'s Sea Harriers. It seemed that they'd been momentarily forgotten, lost in the surface clutter of the sea, or simply overlooked in the enormous scope of the rapidly escalating battle. There were several targets within easy reach, targets that would let the Harriers prove their special place in the Indian fleet's aviation arm.

He was leery of launching another Sea Eagle missile at the American carrier. Tahliani was fairly sure his one shot, released solely to decoy the American Tomcat, had hit the ship, but there'd been no indication that he could see of damage, no reduction of power, no pillar of smoke on the horizon. Possibly the antiship missile had been shot down by the carrier's point defenses at the last second.

Or possibly the U.S.S. *Jefferson* was simply too large to be badly hurt by ASMs.

But there was another target within the Sea Harriers' reach, one much smaller than the nuclear carrier, but one that was vitally important to the American naval squadron. Kill it, and the battle might be won for India there and then.

"Blue King Leader to all Blue Kings," he called. "Close on my position."

From across the sea the scattered Indian Harriers came, joining Tahliani's aircraft and circling with him, their numbers growing.

**0835 hours, 26 March**
**Flag bridge, Soviet aircraft carrier Kreml**

Kontr-Admiral Dmitriev stood on his bridge, looking down through narrow windows at the aircraft arrayed on *Kreml*'s flight deck. MiGs and Sukhois crowded one another, competing for every square meter of deck space, strike planes and fighters, men and munitions. The ship's Captain, Captain First Rank Soni, stood beside him.

"My Operations Department informs me that we will be ready to launch the strike force within the hour, Admiral," Soni said. He was a small man, with sandy hair and pale, Nordic eyes. "MiG-29s and Su-25s. Their combat load will include cluster bombs and incendiaries, rockets, and both free-fall and laser-guided bombs."

"Excellent. You have done well, Captain."

"Admiral, we continue to get rather urgent requests from Captain Sharov aboard the American Aegis cruiser. Their Admiral Vaughn is pressing for us to add to their air defense posture."

Dmitriev shook his head. "We must get our strike force airborne first. What kind of CAP do you have up now?"

"Four Yak-38s."

Dimitriev made a face. He thought little of the V/STOL naval aircraft. "We need real fighters in the air. How soon can we launch the Forty-third Squadron?"

Soni looked surprised. "They are ready for immediate launch, Admiral. But they are reserved to fly protection for the strike—"

"Forget that. We need a strong CAP now. A *flexible* CAP, in case our American friends cannot handle the load. How long will it take?"

"Twelve Mig-29s? Less than thirty minutes, Admiral."

"Who is commander?"

"Captain Third Rank Kurasov."

He remembered Ivan Andreivich Kurasov, a young, intense man with eyes of blue ice. He nodded. "Very well. Have Captain Kurasov launch at once. He will be our contribution to this battle until we can get our strike planes in the air."

"Yes, sir."

"Kurasov is a good man. His primary responsibility should be the safety of the Russian squadron, of course, but he may use his discretion in aiding the Americans. And after the launch of our strike force, perhaps we can contribute something more."

"Very well, Admiral. I should mention, sir, that the Tactical Operations Department feels that it is unlikely that the Indians will attack our vessels. The American carrier is their primary target. We are both farther away and less, shall we say, politically expedient."

Dmitriev grinned. The Indians had balanced on their fence rail of neutrality for years. Today, perhaps, they would fall off once and for all. From New Delhi's point of view, it would be much wiser to anger the Americans rather than the Russians, who, after all, were much closer to their part of the world. "We will teach them a thing or two about political expediency, Comrade Captain! Give the orders."

As Soni turned away, Dimitriev's gaze returned to the Russian warplanes on the flight deck. His orders from Moscow had been as clear as they had been distressing. Pressed on every side by unrest and ethnic violence, by a chaotic economy, and—most significantly—by rising disaffection with the Russian military, the Kremlin desperately needed a stunning coup that would demonstrate to the world, as well as their own generals, that the Commonwealth of Independent States could be a world power.

Russian admirals such as Dmitriev had long admired the Americans' supercarriers to the point of envy. It had taken the drive, conviction, and the political connections of the immortal Admiral Gorshkov, however, to finally make the Russian carrier program a reality.

The thing was far harder to do than anyone had expected. The Americans, the British, even the French all had naval aviation traditions that extended back to the earliest days of military aircraft. They'd had a core of highly trained, highly experienced pilots to draw on throughout the thirties and forties, as carriers grew larger and more complex, their aircraft faster, heavier, and deadlier.

In the early fifties, when the rise of jets had forced the adoption of such British innovations as catapults and angled flight decks on aircraft carriers, Russia had continued to show scant interest in developing a carrier arm of its own. Back during the Great Patriotic War, of course, the navy had been visualized as an arm primarily geared for coastal defense and the support of amphibious operations. Stalin's sole interest in naval warfare had extended to submarines, with the result that the technology for undersea warfare had for years been pursued to the virtual exclusion of all else.

Later, as American superiority in naval air had become more and more apparent, the Soviet Union had begun experimenting with the *taktiches kye avianostny kreysera,* the tactical aircraft-carrying cruisers like the *Kiev.* These were odd combinations of capital ship and carrier, with an angled flight deck attached to a cruiser's hull alongside and aft of the superstructure. The design was good only for the various Yak V/STOL aircraft, imitations of the British and American Harrier jump jets that even the Kremlin admitted were not as good as their Western counterparts.

It wasn't until the eighties that the first true Soviet aircraft carriers had been conceived, designed, and constructed. Even then, there had been critics who'd insisted that the project would never work. An artificial carrier deck had been constructed on the Black Sea coast, and naval pilots had trained for carrier landings.

How many had lost their lives attempting something for which there was no tradition and no experience anywhere within the Soviet military? And dozens more had died when the first landings were actually tried at sea, when the flight deck was moving in three different directions at once.

But it had been worth it in the end. *Kreml* and his brothers represented an entirely new era for the Soviet Navy. Billions of rubles, hundreds of lives had been sacrificed to achieve this sleek and ultra-modern weapon.

And now, the world would see what that weapon could do.

It was necessary, a *vital* gamble. Russia's military leaders feared that the Commonwealth would become a third-rate, Third World nation unable to affect the course of world events beyond her own, strife-torn borders.

The word had come through from Moscow a week before. *Use* this gigantic symbol of naval might to end the crisis between India and Pakistan. The Commonwealth could not tolerate the use of nuclear weapons on the very stoop of her back door.

And the orders had stressed that, if possible, *Kreml* was to beat the United States to the punch, to deliver the telling blow without the help of the American carrier group.

Dmitriev had not been certain how he was going to manage that part of the orders, though they did give him leeway in situations that allowed no alternatives. Vaughn's short-sighted insistence on keeping control of the operation had played into Dmitriev's hands. The Russian admiral now knew the Americans' plan, the targets for their strike, the time the strike would be launched. By launching three hours ahead of time, the Russians would, as the Americans themselves might say, steal the show. Washington would be forced either to admit that they themselves had sabotaged any chance of the two squadrons working together . . . or adopt a face-saving stance which suggested that the Russian carrier had carried out the mission, *supported* by an American task force.

Yes, his superiors in Moscow would like that. The President could shore up his battered public image by presenting himself as a strong man fully capable of taking charge in an international crisis for the good of his people and the world.

And for Dmitriev, this command would be a magnificent first step toward bigger and better things. The Commonwealth was still changing so quickly. There were opportunities, *fantastic* opportunities, for a man with the courage to grab them.

Thunder rent the air, and Dmitriev pressed against the flag bridge window, looking forward. Two navalized MiG-29s shrieked against the catapult shuttles that bound them to *Kreml*'s forward deck, eager to leap into the clean blue sky. Their thunder spoke of the raw power of the Russian naval air arm, of its reach beyond the borders of the Motherland.

The admiral smiled. In one morning, Russian carrier aviation was at last going to catch up with the Americans, ending the superiority they'd enjoyed for forty years!

America and the Commonwealth were no longer face-to-face at the brink of war. The world had changed so much from the old days of confrontation and incident. But the old rivalry, Dmitriev knew, was still there. New world or not, new politics or not, he found he was looking forward to this particular confrontation.

**0845 hours, 26 March**
**Tomcat 200**

Tombstone was flying close to the water, ten miles behind the main American Tomcat formation.

"The bad guys are all over the place, Tombstone," Hitman reported. The Tomcat was vibrating heavily in the dense and bumpy air close to the water. Thick plumes of condensation sprayed off the wings, describing graceful spirals in Tombstone's jet stream. "Eagle Leader is lining up a shot. He's called it! That's fox one!"

"How's it look in our neck of the woods, Hitman?"

"All clear. There's nothin' . . . holy *shit*! Bogies! Four bogies at zero-five-niner and coming fast! Range fifteen miles!"

Tombstone shifted the control stick right to meet the threat. He'd expected something like this, an attempt to slip some planes past the main body at extreme low altitude. With the confusion higher up, it was possible they could slip through unseen, lost in the radar clutter of waves and thickly packed airplanes. From behind the American formation, they could strike at the fleet . . . or circle to take the defenders from the rear.

"Bogies are turning. Tombstone! Range now . . . twelve miles. Looks like they're going to swing onto the Eagles' tail."

Tombstone reviewed his options. With Sparrow he could

take all four bogies now . . . but he'd have to maintain course, illuminating them with his Tomcat's AWG-9 all the way. No. Better to save the Sparrows and take these guys up close. He pushed the throttles forward to Zone Five.

"Eagle, Eagle, this is Tombstone," he called. "Watch your six. You have four bogies, repeat, four bogies on your six."

On the radar, the American planes were turning, aware of the new threat behind them. Tombstone's F-14 thundered across the water, fifty feet between the waves and the missiles slung from the aircraft's belly. At Mach 2, the passage of the F-14 raised a wall of spray behind him, a sonic boom made visible in geysering water.

"We got 'em, Stoney!" Hitman cried, excitement charging his voice. "We're sliding right on to their six!"

"We'll go for Sidewinder," he said. No sense in warning them that he was coming. The enemy pilots' attention appeared to be focused on the Eagles in their sights.

"Range . . . nine miles."

"Targeting."

Computer graphic symbols danced on his HUD. Four small shapes marked the enemy aircraft. Using his controller, Tombstone dragged the targeting pipper across one and locked in. The square changed to a circle, with the word "LOCK" beside it. A warble sounded in his headphones as the first Sidewinder saw its target.

"Tone," Tombstone said. "Fox two!"

He squeezed the trigger and the Sidewinder slid off the launch rail with a whoosh. The instant the heat-seeker was away he was moving the pipper to a new target.

**0845 hours, 26 March**
**Tomcat 216**

Batman heard Tombstone's warning over the tactical channel. The Vipers were east of the Eagles and not threatened by the bogies coming in from the south, but it was a reminder that the American defensive formation was as porous as a sieve. The American response was going to have to be flexible and in-depth, or the individual aircraft was going to be overwhelmed by sheer weight of numbers.

"Find us a target and let's dump this last bird," he told Malibu. The F-14 handled better "clean," without the added weight and drag of the half-ton missile on its belly.

"Got one. Range two-zero miles, bearing three-five-one. AWG-9 locked in. Tracking."

"Punch it."

"Fox three!"

Their last radar-homer streaked into the northern sky. Batman brought the Tomcat hard left, turning into the approaching main body of enemy aircraft.

"Ninety-nine aircraft," the voice of the Hawkeye controller sounded in his headset. "We are tracking three primary groups of bogies, designated Alpha, Bravo, Charlie. . . ."

More long-ranged missiles lanced out from the American squadrons as the BARCAP planes shot off the last of their AIM-54-Cs and the newcomers began unloading their Sparrows.

The AIM-7 Sparrow was a design that, in various incarnations, went back to the early fifties. Naval aviators tended to distrust it, for the missile had more than once shown a nasty tendency to lock onto the water instead of the target. Just as bad, from the pilot's point of view, Sparrow had SARH guidance, which meant that once it was fired, the aircraft could not maneuver without breaking the radar beam that illuminated the target for the missile's sensors.

The latest F- and M-versions had ranges of up to sixty miles. Aviators preferred to dump them early in a fight, while they still had the luxury of flying straight and level toward the enemy.

"Fox one," someone called over the tactical frequency.

He was echoed a second later by someone else. "Fox one, fox one. Missile away." Then other voices joined in. It was the high-tech equivalent of volley fire, a throwback to the days when armies stood their soldiers shoulder to shoulder and fire en masse.

Batman's radar display rapidly became a tangle of blips as the sky filled with half-ton chunks of metal, hurtling north at Mach 4.

**0847 hours, 26 March**
**IAF Fulcrum 401**

Ramadutta's radar display was a blotchy, static-covered mess, partly from the sheer number of targets, partly from the American jamming that was turning out to be more effective than the New Delhi planners had anticipated. His tail threat receiver detected one target, however, with terrible clarity.

An air-to-air missile was coming in from behind.

"Enemy missile at one-eight-five!" he shouted, warning the other MiGs in his fight. "IR homing! Evasive!"

The formation of MiG-29s blossomed apart, breaking in four directions as the enemy Sidewinder raced in across the kilometers. Several seconds into a high-G turn, Ramadutta saw that the missile was not locked on him, but on Lieutenant Pahvi's MiG, number 404.

"Pahvi!" he snapped. "Use flares!"

Too late. Lieutenant Pahvi's MiG was angling straight into the sky, a dazzling trail of flares dropping away behind his ship as it rose, but the American missile was rising fast, ignoring the flares and centering on the center of the aircraft.

There was a flash. Ramadutta saw the orange ball of flame, smoke, and debris punch through the airplane squarely between the wings, rupturing the wing tanks. . . .

Pahvi's MiG was a mass of flame an instant later, still climbing into the sky atop a towering pillar of writhing black smoke.

On the radar, the American pilot was still coming, alone. Gritting his teeth against the G-force, Ramadutta completed his turn, bringing the nose of his Fulcrum around until it was aligned with the American, now five miles distant.

# CHAPTER 23

**0848 hours, 26 March**
**Tomcat 200**

Tombstone couldn't see the enemy plane yet, but he saw the symbol that marked it on his HUD shifting to the side as the other pilot positioned himself for the pass.

"Shit!" Hitman called from the backseat. "He's taking us head-to-head!"

"I'm going for Sidewinder," Tombstone said, aligning the HUD pipper and locking in. The AIM-9L Sidewinder was an all-aspect heat-seeker, meaning Tombstone did not have to hold his fire until he could give the missile a look at the target's white-hot exhaust. But Sidewinder head shots were still risky. When the closing speed between target and missile was in the vicinity of Mach 3 or 4, the enemy had a better chance of breaking the lock by maneuvering or launching flares.

"Take him, Stoney! Take him!"

"Fox two!"

**0848 hours, 26 March**
**IAF Fulcrum 401**

The American was launching as Munir Ramadutta pulled his nose up, climbing almost vertically as he popped flares. At ten thousand feet he pulled an Immelmann, dropping out of the climb inverted, again facing the oncoming enemy.

The range was now four miles. Still inverted, Ramadutta loosed an E-23 AAM.

The missile, called AA-7 "Apex" by the West, actually came in two flavors designated R-23R, a long-ranged SARH version, and E-23T, which used IR homing. Ramadutta carried two of the heat-seekers in his ordnance load. Apex could reach considerably farther than the four AA-8 Aphid missiles he also mounted.

As the missile slid off his wing, Ramadutta rolled his MiG, trading altitude for speed in a long plunge toward the sea.

**0848 hours, 26 March**
**Tomcat 200**

"Missed him!" Hitman warned. "We nailed a flare! He's launching!"

Tombstone held the F-14 steady for a torturously long four seconds. "Pop flares!"

As white-hot decoys spewed into the Tomcat's wake, Tombstone broke left, careful not to turn his exhaust in the direction of the approaching missile.

Scanning the horizon as it rolled past his cockpit, he caught sight of the other plane for the first time, a tiny speck angling toward the sea. In the dense, wet air close to the water, the MiG was dragging a contrail, a sharp white streak across the darker sea.

Something flashed past the cockpit, *feeling* close though it was at least a hundred yards away, then exploded astern. A lone fragment of shrapnel *pinged* off the canopy as Tombstone rolled toward the other plane.

"One Sidewinder left," he said. "Let's see if we can get on this bird's tail!"

**0848 hours, 26 March**
**Tomcat 216**

Explosions flashed and popped among the Indian aircraft. Streaks of black smoke scrawled from sky to sea as burning planes plummeted. Despite their bad rep, the Sparrows had struck, and struck hard.

Now the aircraft formations were penetrating one another,

swirling together in a colossal aerial dogfight that filled the sky with flashing planes and the long, white streaks of air-to-air missiles. The American Tomcats were heavily outnumbered, but the majority of their opponents were older, slower strike aircraft carrying bombs and missiles against the U.S. fleet: Canberras, Su-7 Fitters, and aging Hawker Hunters. Many of the more modern aircraft in the oncoming wave, Jaguars and swing-wing MiG-27 Flogger-Ds, were dedicated strike aircraft, slowed by the bombs and missiles slung from their ordnance hardpoints.

"Going for guns," Batman called automatically, snapping the selector switch on his stick as the F-14 slid gently onto the six of a Flogger.

"You'd better," Malibu replied. "That's all we got left!"

Batman let the HUD reticle drift across the other plane's fuselage, following as the Flogger began a slow break to the left. His Lead Computing Optical Sight drew a short line on his HUD, showing how much lead to give the MiG as it turned away.

His thumb came down on the firing switch, and the M61A12 Vulcan cannon thundered. White smoke trailed behind Batman's Tomcat in puffs as he pumped burst after burst into the fleeing MiG-27.

Chunks of metal sprayed from the Flogger's back and left wing. The Indian pilot tried to sharpen his break in a desperate attempt to throw himself clear of the deadly volleys but succeeded only in presenting his aircraft plan-view-on to his relentless pursuer. Twenty-millimeter cannon shells smashed through his fuselage. The MiG began coming apart.

The Flogger-D's hinged, squared-off canopy blew off. There was a flash, and Batman glimpsed the tiny figure of the pilot as his ejection seat rocketed him clear of the crumbling aircraft. Seconds later, there was another, far brighter flash . . . then another and another as the Flogger's load of half-ton bombs detonated.

"Splash one MiG," Batman called.

Around him, the dogfight swirled from just above the sea to over thirty thousand feet, dozens of aircraft circling one another in a melee across hundreds of square miles.

"We're turnin' and burnin' now, Batman!" Malibu called.

"Affirmative!" But the American defenses were already

leaking. Indian aircraft were falling from the sky one after another, but plenty of strike aircraft had already made it through, were holding a steady course for the southwest, for *Jefferson*.

There were just too many of them to stop.

Batman checked the readout on his HUD that registered the number of rounds he had remaining for his Vulcan cannon. The M61 was loaded with 675 rounds, but since it had a rate of fire that burned up seventy to one hundred rounds a second depending on the setting, the F-14's ammo store did not last for long.

The readout showed 206 rounds remaining. Three seconds' worth of fire at the 4000 RPM setting . . . perhaps four or five quick bursts.

And then he would have neither missiles nor guns.

Batman began searching for his next target.

**0850 hours, 26 March**
**Tomcat 200**

Tombstone pulled up hard as the MiG-29 in his sights cut in his afterburners and stood on his tail.

"Watch it, Stoney!" Hitman yelled. "He's goin' ballistic!"

"I'm on him!" Tombstone rammed his throttles forward to Zone Five to build up speed, then cut back to eighty-percent power, allowing the climbing MiG to drift into his line of fire. The angle was bad with a sharp deflection, but he squeezed off a long burst in hope of getting one or two hits that might, *might* puncture something vital.

The Fulcrum rolled sharply right, seeming to float just beyond the reach of the line of glowing tracers arcing past his wing.

"Damn," Tombstone muttered. "This guy can *fly!*"

The MiG-29 danced away, its pilot using his aircraft's superb maneuverability to best advantage. Tombstone cut back hard on his throttles as he tried to follow, putting the Tomcat into a hard, skidding turn to the right.

He could see before he was halfway into the turn that the MiG was outperforming him, circling *inside* the best turn radius he could manage. Unwilling to finish the maneuver on the other guy's terms, Tombstone punched in the throttles and pulled the stick hard left, slamming the F-14 into a split-S that carried him past the MiG's tail and off in the other direction.

"What's . . . he . . . doing . . . ?" He had to force each word out explosively through clenched teeth. The G-readout hit seven Gs. He felt his head growing fuzzy, saw blackness closing in at the periphery of his vision.

"Lost . . . *uh*! Lost him!" Hitman replied.

The compass reading swung around until Tombstone knew he was heading back toward where his opponent had vanished during the last pass. Damn it, were was he?

"On our six!" Hitman warned as Tombstone broke out of the turn. "Coming fast!"

Tombstone pulled up, twisting the F-14 into a short, fast-spinning Immelmann designed to bring him over the other plane and down on his tail. Looking "up" through his canopy as he went over the top, Tombstone caught a glimpse of the other plane between him and the ocean, already going into a break to counter the maneuver.

Another target loomed ahead as Tombstone righted the plane, a wingtip-to-wingtip pair of Jaguars, steady on course toward the southwest.

The Fulcrum pilot was one of the best Tombstone had ever gone up against. With so many bandits coming through the line, he was better off not wasting time jousting with the Fulcrum driver.

So he dropped on the Jaguars from behind and above, lining up the left-hand aircraft before he'd completed the rollout, squeezing off a burst from his cannon at a range of less than five hundred yards. It was a snap shot from a difficult angle, but he saw pieces flaking from the target plane as he dropped through its slipstream.

Then the Jaguars were behind him. More aircraft were scattered across the sky ahead and he dropped into position behind yet another strike plane, an ancient BAC Canberra. Lining up on the junction of the broad, almost triangular unswept wings, he opened fire from eight hundred yards and watched as his stream of tracer rounds drifted into the Indian bomber. The port engine began smoking, and the Canberra's wing dropped sharply. The aircraft slipped into a steeply falling turn, its engine ablaze. Three parachutes appeared in the falling bomber's wake.

"Hey! Just like fish in a barrel, Tombstone," Hitman said.

Tombstone didn't answer. Canberras had been hailed as a match for any fighter in the air when they'd first made their appearance with the RAF in 1951, but they were virtually helpless in a match with a modern F-14.

But there was no other way. The Indian attack planes were breaking through toward the American ships.

**0852 hours, 26 March**
**Tomcat 204**

Coyote had launched all four of his Sparrows within the first few minutes of the approach. Now he was switching to Sidewinders as a pair of Indian interceptors streaked toward him from the north. From two black specks in the sky, side by side, they grew with astonishing swiftness into sleek, delta-winged jets that flashed past his F-14 to port at a range of less than half a mile. In the instant's glimpse he had, he recognized them: Dassault-Breguet Mirage-2000Hs, a French design, though these particular aircraft were probably built in India under license. They were excellent aircraft, capable of bettering Mach 2 and mounting Magic AAMs for close-in fighting.

"Tally-ho!" he called over the tactical frequency. "Two Mirage two-triple-ohs. Two-oh-four is on them!"

"Roger, Two-oh-four," the Hawkeye controller said. "Stay on the strikers, over."

*Stay on the strikers.* The 2000H was an interceptor, a jet designed to kill jets. The people watching this fight from the bird farm would be concerned about strike aircraft, planes carrying anti-ship missiles and bombs. Obviously, it was better to shoot down a plane carrying several Exocets before it had a chance to release its payload . . . and complicate the electronic musings of *Jefferson*'s point defense system.

But it wouldn't pay to ignore the strike aircraft's fighter escorts, not when those escorts outnumbered the F-14s by at least three to one, and probably more.

He put his Tomcat into a hard left break, dumping speed

with flaps and spoilers in order to turn in the tightest possible radius. "Where are they?" he called to his RIO.

Radar Mendoza was one of *Jefferson*'s latest crop of replacements, a young j.g. with black eyes and mustache and a Hispanic's cocksure machismo.

"Tryin' to cut us out, Coyote," Mendoza replied. "Breakin' left, man. Comin' past our seven o'clock!"

"Hang onto your stomach."

Coyote slammed the Tomcat into a right-hand turn with a snapping half-twist, then brought the stick back as he cut in his afterburners. The Tomcat's nose came up . . . up . . . and over as he slid from a split-S into an Immelmann turn that left them flying inverted toward the two Mirages, now two miles to the south and still turning.

"Surprise, guys," Coyote said. The Mirages were presenting themselves in a perfect plan view as they crossed his line of sight from right to left. He let the Tomcat barrel-roll out of its inverted position and dropped the targeting pipper squarely across the lead Indian fighter. The target lock warble sounded in his headphones.

"Fox two!" he called, and a Sidewinder slid off his port wing. The Mirages, aware that they'd been outmaneuvered, split. The one he'd targeted changed his left turn into a split-S to the right, and the other one climbed sharply.

Coyote eased the stick back and started after the second Mirage. It had continued climbing, inserting itself into a twisting blur of aircraft dogfighting through a five-mile expanse of air thirty-five thousand feet above the sea.

The targeted Mirage continued holding its turn . . .

. . . then shattered as the Sidewinder rose to meet it. Flame boiled into the sky, and the delta-wing shape, its stabilizer missing now, began spinning in a wild, fiery plunge toward the sea.

"Bull's eye!" Mendoza yelled. "Splash one Mirage for Two-oh-four!"

"Where'd the other one get to, Radar?"

"Lost him. I think he—"

"He's on me! He's on me!" Coyote could hear the frantic cry of one of the American pilots. "This is Two-oh-eight. Bandit on my tail! I can't shake him!"

Coyote scanned the dogfight in front of him. Where . . .

*there!* The unmistakable profile of a Tomcat plunging toward the sea, wings folded back. A MiG-23 with Indian roundels on its camo-splotched wings followed.

Forgetting the second Mirage, Coyote nosed over, letting the Tomcat fall to pick up speed. "Two-oh-eight, this is Two-oh-four!" he called. "When I give the word, pull up!" When the F-14 pulled up, the MiG should follow. Coyote was positioning his Tomcat so that he could drop onto the MiG's tail as he tried to hold his position on 208's six.

"Two-oh-eight! Pull up!"

There was no response. What was the handle of 208's pilot? It was one of the replacements who'd flown out to the CBG on the COD from Masirah, he thought. Maverick, that was it. How could he forget the name Maverick?

"Pull up, Maverick! Pull up!"

An Apex missile whipped from the MiG on the tip of a streaming white contrail.

"Maverick! Pop flares and pull up!"

Flares arced from the Tomcat's tail, but the aircraft continued to plunge toward the sea. "Two-oh-four, this is Scout! Maverick's in trouble!"

Scout was Maverick's RIO. He must be launching the flares . . . but if the pilot had frozen at the stick . . .

"Maverick! Pull up!"

The Apex caught up with the Tomcat and plunged into its starboard engine. The explosion blew out part of the belly and skewed the aircraft into a flaming tumble.

"Eject! Scout, eject! Punch out!"

There was no answer, and the stricken Tomcat continued its plunge toward the sea. Coyote watched them fall, willing the canopy to blow, willing the chutes to appear.

Nothing. It happened, sometimes, the first time a man went into combat. Hours of simulators, of training, and men still lost it when they realized that this was real. Scout might have ejected the two of them after they were hit . . . but the explosion could easily have killed him or knocked him out.

A momentary paralysis gripped Coyote as he watched the other Tomcat vanish into the sea. *Experienced* pilots could become casualties too. He'd been shot down, over the Sea of Japan . . . and the memory of that experience, of holding his skull-crushed RIO in his arms in an icy sea, would be with him forever. Unexpectedly, the image of Coyote's wife flashed into his mind. She'd not wanted him to go back on active flight duty, and he'd come close to turning in his wings. No one would have blamed him. . . .

Then the MiG pulled its nose up. Julie's face was banished as training took over, and Coyote rolled onto the Indian fighter's tail just as he'd planned. He got the tone and triggered a Sidewinder. "Fox two!"

In the end, though, it was Julie who'd told him he *had* to come back. Not until this moment had he been certain she was right.

**0852 hours, 26 March**
**CIC, U.S.S. *Vicksburg***

Admiral Vaughn stood in the ship's CIC, watching the flood of information coming across the LSDs and ASTABs.

Once during his tenure at the Pentagon, he'd had a long conversation with the admiral who had commanded a battle group with the first Aegis cruiser, the U.S.S. *Ticonderoga,* off Beirut in the early 1980s. That man had preferred commanding from the *Tico* rather than from his carrier and claimed that the Aegis defenses had let him significantly reduce the group's CAP, despite the hazards of the operation.

Vaughn could understand that admiral's preference. From the *Vicksburg*'s CIC, he felt as though the entire battle zone was under his personal observation and control. Through the Aegis system, data from every one of the battle group's ships and aircraft was constantly relayed through the *Vicksburg*'s computers and displayed in her CIC. Through the Hawkeyes—if need be through a Navy comsat—he could talk to any of his ship captains, any aircraft . . . or to the Joint Chiefs themselves back in Washington.

Not that he was particularly eager to exercise *that* option. The Battle of the Arabian Sea was proving to be quite enough for him to handle. He would face the Battle of Washington later.

"Admiral," Captain Sharov said, standing stiffly at Vaughn's side. "Admiral Dmitriev reports that he has one squadron airborne as CAP. As there appears to be no immediate threat to

*Kreml,* he wishes to inform you that some of those aircraft can be made available to your command.''

Vaughn turned on the Russian Chief of Staff with a cold stare. ''Your commanding officer is so kind,'' he said. ''We would, of course, appreciate any help he condescends to make available!''

Sharov did not seem to hear the sarcasm . . . or perhaps he simply ignored it. ''Squadron leader is Kurasov. I will inform him of your need.''

Vaughn snorted with disgust as the Russian returned to the bank of communications gear that had been reserved for their use. He'd expected no more from the Russians . . . and perhaps he'd expected less.

At this point, he knew he'd be grateful for any help. On the LSD designated as the Primary Battle Board, the computer graphic symbols identifying the American Tomcats were becoming lost in the flood of Indian aircraft pouring south. They were holding their own individually—the reports coming through from both squadrons indicated large numbers of enemy planes already downed—but collectively there just weren't enough to stop the waves of Canberras, MiGs, and other planes descending on Turban Station. The range on the board had already been shifted from one hundred twenty-eight miles from the *Vicksburg* to sixty-four.

It was nearly time to bring the battle group's second line of defenses into play.

''Multiple bogies inbound,'' *Vicksburg*'s Tactical Officer reported formally from a console nearby. ''Range now three-five miles, bearing zero-zero-five to zero-four-zero.''

''Point defense on automatic!'' Cunningham snapped.

That was just a double check on Cunningham's part, Vaughn knew. Every Navy captain remembered the tragedy of *Stark,* and the Phalanx system that had been switched off at the beginning of the attack.

''Defenses activated, Captain. On automatic.''

''Lock on with VLS!''

''Tracking, Captain. Vertical Launch Systems locked.''

Cunningham looked at Admiral Vaughn. His eyes were bleak, but steady.

Vaughn nodded, and the ship's captain turned back to the TO. ''Fire!''

A closed-circuit television monitor displayed a view of *Vicksburg*'s forward deck. Between the bridge tower and the number-one five-inch turret, the twin arms of the ship's forward Mark 26 Mod 1 missile launcher slewed about and elevated, until the twin darts of the Standard missiles slung from its launch rails were pointed straight up.

At Cunningham's command, there was a burst of smoke and flame that engulfed the launcher and washed across the forward deck, blotting out the TV image. When the smoke cleared, the missile was gone, arrowing vertically into the sky. Almost immediately, the second Standard missile flashed skyward after its brother.

On the deck, the launcher swiveled again, realigning itself. Two hatches slid open automatically, one beneath each launch rail. Out of the deck, another pair of Standard SM-2(MR) missiles slid up the rails, reloading the empty launcher.

Seconds later these missiles followed the first two, shrieking into the wet morning air. Spray lashed across *Vicksburg*'s bow as the VLS reloaded once again.

*Vicksburg*'s weapon systems were so highly automated that it was theoretically possible for a single well-trained man to handle the ship in combat. Forward, she carried twenty-nine Standard SM-2(MR)s. Aft were sixty-one more, each with a range of thirty-five miles at Mach 2. When combined with her two Mark 15 Phalanx CIWS mounts, one port, one starboard—*Vicksburg*'s weaponry made her arguably the deadliest AAW vessel afloat, as well as one of the most complex.

As Vaughn watched the Indian aircraft approach the heart of the battle group, he wondered which would count for more in the coming fight, deadliness . . . or the complexity that more than once in the past had lead to errors, and disaster.

# CHAPTER 24

**0852 hours, 26 March**
**Sea Harrier 101**

Tahliani had been able to round up only five other Sea Harriers out of his flight. The others, evidently, had scattered or fled when two of their number had been downed by American Phoenix missiles earlier.

He checked his fuel gauge and winced. It would be a near thing making it back to *Viraat* now. His earlier maneuvers had spent far too much fuel.

Risking discovery, he brought the Harrier's nose up and climbed. At ten thousand feet his radar display showed his target, now less than eighty kilometers away but still well over the horizon from the Harrier formation that continued to hug the surface below. He did not chance using his own radar but remained in passive mode, recording the radar emissions of the target rather than sending out signals of his own.

The target plotted, he dropped to wave-top height once more. Carefully, they stalked their enemy, staying unseen below the horizon.

The American E-2Cs were the greatest danger, but those watched northward now, toward the heart of the vast, churning dogfight sprawling from Kathiawar to the fringes of the American fleet. The Harriers still had a chance to strike without being detected.

Tahliani had led his formation far to the south, circling past the *Jefferson*'s last-known position. At such a low altitude, and with nothing like the American Hawkeye to coordinate the battle, they had to rely on guesswork to find their prey.

"Target ahead," he said, breaking radio silence now for the first time since he'd decided to make this strike. "Range seventy-nine kilometers. Arm missiles!"

One by one the others reported their Sea Eagle ship-killers armed and ready for launch. The Sea Eagle had a range of one hundred kilometers. By narrowing that distance, they would shorten the enemy's reaction time once the missile had locked on.

If they got much closer, though, the enemy ship's radar would be certain to see them, if they hadn't been spotted already by the circling Hawkeyes.

"Blue King Leader to Blue King," Tahliani said. "Launch! Launch!"

His Sea Harrier leapt into the sky as the Sea Eagle dropped free and fired. He could see the reflection of the exhaust on the sea, a dazzling flare of orange and gold. One by one, the other Harriers dropped their deadly packages. In seconds, eleven missile contrails were speeding across the water toward their distant target.

"'If the slayer thinks he slays,'" Tahliani said, his voice a sonorous chant as he quoted from the *Katha Upanishad,* "'if the slain thinks he is slain, both these do not understand. He slays not, is not slain . . .'"

A suitable epitaph for the brave men who worked the ship that lay invisibly beyond the horizon. And perhaps it would serve as a plea for forgiveness as well.

It would take nearly five minutes for the Sea Eagles to reach their target. By then, the Harriers would be long gone. With a snap of his wrist he twisted his aircraft skyward, then around toward home.

**0855 hours, 26 March**
**CIC, U.S.S. *Vicksburg***

Vaughn looked away from the LSD he was studying as the Tactical Officer snapped a warning. "Missile launch!" the TO called. "Eleven new bogies, probable ASMs, bearing one-eight-five. Range seventy-five miles. Speed five-niner-four knots."

"Mach point eight-five," Cunningham said at Vaughn's

side. "Sea Eagles, just like the ones they smacked *Jefferson* with. Seventy-five miles, though. That's pretty far for Sea Eagles."

"Sir," Harkowicz, the TO, said. "We're not the target. It's . . . Sir, it's *Kreml!*"

Vaughn's eyes widened. "The *Kremlin?* You're sure?" He looked across the CIC suite toward the three Russian Officers at their communications center. "Where is she?"

Cunningham pointed to a graphic symbol on the LSD. "About seventy miles southwest of us, sir. Parallel course, west-northwest, eighteen knots."

"We'd better tell them, sir," Cunningham said, following the admiral's stare. "They're not tapped into our data network."

Vaughn's anger at the Russians, at the way they'd been dragging their feet earlier, surfaced again.

But no, Cunningham was right. They did have to be told.

He hurried across the room to tell them himself.

**0856 hours, 26 March**
**Flag bridge, Soviet aircraft carrier *Kreml***

"Urgent message from *Vicksburg,* Admiral," the aide said as he handed the message sheet to Dmitriev. "They report several antiship cruise missiles have been targeted on us from the southeast."

He took the message and scanned it. It had been signed by Sharov. Dmitriev knew his Chief of Staff was prone neither to exaggeration nor to sensationalism.

The Russian admiral checked his watch and the information on the sheet. According to the report, the missiles were a bit over twenty miles away . . . three minutes at eight tenths the speed of sound. "Is there anything on radar?"

The aide, already at attention, managed to convey a further crisp snap to his posture that came short of clicking his heels. "Negative, Admiral."

"Hmm." It *could* be an American ruse to hurry him in launching his aircraft, but he doubted that. Not that Vaughn wasn't capable of cheap theatrics, but . . .

"Point defenses on full alert," he ordered. "And notify

Kurasov to check in that direction. We will take no chances."

Admiral Dmitriev was painfully aware of the crowded state of *Kreml*'s flight deck, where bombs and incendiaries were still piled high as fueling and arming for the strike continued. He'd thought that the Russian squadron was well enough sheltered by the American task force. If it was not . . .

The lessons of the Battle of Midway were taught at Russian naval academies as well as at Annapolis, and Dmitriev was uncomfortably aware that he might well be about to be cast in the modern-day role of Nagumo.

He checked his watch again. Two minutes . . .

**0857 hours, 26 March**
**CIC, U.S.S. *Vicksburg***

The air battle was rolling south toward the *Vicksburg*. The Aegis cruiser had shifted course slightly in order to bring her closer to the *Jefferson*, now some twenty miles to the east, starboard of the cruiser and slightly astern, but her antiair umbrella extended well beyond the carrier, striking down incoming aircraft with almost clockwork precision and regularity.

Both Vertical Launch Systems were in operation almost continuously, with the Aegis controlling at times as many as a dozen Standard missiles in flight simultaneously. Both the DDG *Lawrence Kearny* and the destroyer *John A. Winslow* had pulled in closer to the core of the battle group and begun taking their directions from *Vicksburg*. Standard missiles fired from the U.S. destroyers were actually being guided to their targets by SARH from the Aegis cruiser, extending her range and deadliness.

And that deadliness was beginning to take its toll. Vaughn had long since lost track of how many Indian aircraft had been destroyed. Eight or ten in the dogfight with the American fighters, certainly, and at least twenty more had fallen victim to the implacable hunger of the Standard missiles as they stalked the radar reflections of their prey and hunted them down.

It was a close-run thing toward the end. Indian aircraft were actually coming in over the horizon, and the *Vicksburg*'s two five-inch turrets swung about and began slamming shells at the attackers. Vaughn watched the forward turret hammering away on the TV screen in CIC. In the distance, he could see the black specks that he knew were enemy planes, the black smears of triple-A and exploding aircraft, the smoky streak of a plane falling across the sky. A Jaguar howled past, long, black cigar shapes spilling from its belly as the carrier's point defenses swung to meet the new threat. Splashes rose off *Jefferson*'s port bow, thunderous avalanches of water. The Jaguar disintegrated in midair; the bombs missed.

In World War II, the face of war was changed forever when ships began striking at each other with carrier aircraft. Fleets maneuvered, came to grips, and sank one another . . . and the opposing ships never came within sight of each other directly.

Modern war, Vaughn had always been told, was to have taken that separation of the combatants another step. Ships would be struck and sunk by missiles launched by aircraft safely over the horizon. Enemy aircraft would never even appear in the skies over a naval squadron.

The Falklands campaign had proven the fallacy of that prediction, though the presence and terrain of those islands had shaped the battle to a large extent. Here in the Arabian Sea, it was the sheer numbers of the Indian attackers that carried them past the outer defenses and into range of the ship's guns.

Vaughn watched the struggle unfolding on the television monitor and thought of World War II. The scenes there looked like something out of a fifty-year-old newsreel.

**0859 hours, 26 March**
**Soviet aircraft carrier *Kreml***

Following the Western design philosophy in arming their first nuclear aircraft carrier, *Kreml* was not as heavily armed as the Kiev-class cruiser-carrier hybrids. The weapons mix did reflect Soviet concern about antiship missiles, however, for she carried a number of Gatling-type rapid-fire cannons designed to defeat incoming ASMs. Designed to operate much like the Phalanx, the 30-mm multi-barrel gun designated as AK-630 was housed in a squat, gray turret unlike the white silo of the American CIWS.

The six barrels were housed together in a single rotating tube. The weapon had a theoretical rate of fire of 3000 rounds per minute, but problems caused by overheating and the tendency of the ammunition to jam reduced this to short bursts of one or two hundred rounds apiece.

The missiles entered *Kreml*'s inner defensive zone, spread out now across a wide stretch of sea and skimming scant meters above the wave tops. Two of *Kreml*'s AK-630s began firing . . . then a third, and a fourth, all the point defense turrets that could bear on the tiny, elusive targets now spread across the horizon astern. Splashes on the sea, cascades of white spray, marked where the high-velocity rounds lashed out at the approaching ship-killers.

On the carrier's deck all was noise and confusion, as officers shouted orders and the CIWS Gatlings shrieked like chain saws. The heavy thumps of chaff launchers mingled with the chaos with a steady, rhythmic beat. Clouds of chaff surrounded the carrier as the Gatlings continued to track and fire, track and fire and fire and fire. . . .

The Sea Eagles were approaching *Kreml* from almost dead astern. In the last minute of the engagement, Captain Soni made one serious tactical mistake by deciding to maintain his course, rather than maneuvering to give either his port or starboard batteries a clearer field of fire. When the missiles first came within range, four separate CIWS turrets could bear on them, two to starboard, one aft, and one to port. By deciding to hold the carrier to its northwesterly course, he hoped to provide the CIWS turrets with a less complicated firing solution.

Unfortunately for the *Kreml,* when the missiles were within five hundred meters of the carrier's stern, the ship's hull itself blocked the line of fire for two of the guns.

Still, the fire was effective. At two miles' range, one Sea Eagle was struck simultaneously by twin streams of projectiles. Traveling at 1000 meters per second, the heavy rounds chewed through the missile like rocks through tissue, shredding electronics and control surfaces and scattering debris across the water. In the last instant, the remaining fuel on board ignited in an orange fireball.

A second missile exploded an instant later, followed by a third, twin detonations that momentarily flattened the surface of the water with dual shock waves.

The guns kept firing. One missile veered off, and then another. Either their guidance systems had malfunctioned or they'd been decoyed by chaff. Another missile, one fin blasted away by a grazing shot, fell into the sea like a leaping fish and vanished.

The guns of a pair of escorts came into play. The destroyers *Vliyatel'nyy* and *Moskovskiy Komsomolets* were cruising within sight of the *Kreml,* less than two miles away, and both turned their own CIWS on the missiles as they streaked in from the horizon. Without intership coordination such as that provided by Aegis, however, the help was too little and too late. One more missile exploded half a mile from the carrier. *Vliyatel'nyy* was tracking another speeding black-and-red missile when it vanished behind *Kreml*'s hull, and high-velocity 30-mm rounds slashed into the aircraft carrier's waterline.

Captain Soni's tactical error was most apparent for the last couple of seconds. Four missiles remained in the air, but for the last few tens of meters the ship's stern blocked three of the guns that had been firing at them. Only the AK-630 mounted on *Kreml*'s fantail could still bear.

It managed to knock down one of them.

Two missiles slammed into the *Kreml* from astern, one entering the fantail walkway close alongside the AK-630 mount and tunneling deep into the passageway leading into the bowels of the ship before exploding. The second missed the stern and passed along the ship's right side, too close to the hull for the starboard CIWS turrets to bear. It struck close to the waterline aft of *Kreml*'s island, but the angle was too oblique to cause detonation. The missile slammed off the steel plating and fell into the sea.

The blast from the first Sea Eagle engulfed the ship's stern, sending smoke and flame belching from the stern, the concussion warping two of *Kreml*'s propeller shafts. The carrier shuddered, sending men on her deck to their hands and knees. Fires began in a dozen places: the ship's machine shops, a paint locker, a jet engine service area. Choking smoke wreathed through the carrier's bowels as fire alarms shrieked warning.

Damage was bad, but not fatal, not yet. Soviet damage control parties, while not as well-trained or well-coordinated as their American counterparts, were able to seal off the damaged areas in short order and begin flooding the fires with water and foam.

The third missile, however, was far more deadly than the first. Following well behind the first two, it approached the carrier just as the blast wave erupted from the Soviet carrier's shattered fantail. Like a stone skipping on water, it was deflected high into the air and sent skimming above the *Kreml*'s ramp and across her crowded flight deck. The warhead smashed into parked Yak-38MP Forgers and navalized Su-27 Flankers in a close-spaced row along the ship's starboard side. One hundred fifty kilograms of high explosive detonated among closely spaced aircraft, all fueled and armed for the coming strike against the Indian supply lines ashore.

Hell descended on the *Kreml*'s flight line in flame and noise and hurtling death as the fireball writhed into the sky. The forward half of a Forger, furiously ablaze, cartwheeled across the deck and landed squarely on a Su-25 Frogfoot loaded with cluster bombs parked alongside the island. Fuel and ordnance went up together with a clattering roar like a Chinese New Year's celebration, blowing out windows on the carrier's bridge and Primary Flight Control. The blast sent deck crewmen skittering and tumbling across the deck as though swept away by a gigantic broom. R-60 air-to-air missiles, the AA-8 Aphids slung from Yak-38 wings, ignited, snapping across the deck on streamers of white flame. Explosion followed explosion followed explosion, a chain of interlocking blasts that rocked the carrier and sent a pall of greasy black smoke two miles into the sky.

A ship trembled on the edge of death.

**0903 hours, 26 March**
**CIC, U.S.S. *Vicksburg***

"Admiral! *Kremlin*'s been hit!"

"What? When? Just now?"

"They went off the air for a few minutes, sir. I thought it was a comm failure. Now they've started broadcasting an SOS. They must have gotten hit pretty bad."

Vaughn glanced toward the Russian liaison officers. Captain First Rank Sharov was already hurrying across the compartment, an expression of sharp concern etched into the lines of his face.

"Admiral . . ." he began.

"I heard, Sharov. I'm sorry."

"*Moskovskiy Komsomolets* and *Vliyatel'nyy* are alongside, Admiral," the Russian staff officer said. "But they need additional help, and quickly. The fire on the flight deck is out of control."

Vaughn looked up at one of the LSDs, a display set to show the dispositions of all of the vessels of the fleet. *Vicksburg, Jefferson, Kearny,* and *Winslow* were all steaming together in a fairly tight group forty miles across, with the destroyers serving as an antiair screen between the carrier and the coast. *Amarillo* and the *Peoria* followed a few miles astern of the *Jefferson. Kreml* and her two escorting destroyers lay seventy miles to the southwest. The Kresta-II cruiser *Marshal Timoshenko* was steaming sixty miles northwest of the Russian carrier, which put her nearly ninety miles due west of the *Vicksburg*. The other ships of the two squadrons, two American Perry-class frigates and a pair of Soviet ASW frigates, were part of an antisubmarine net thrown out along an arc from the southwest to the east. One of these, *Biddle,* was in pursuit of the Osas that had slipped through the American screen over an hour earlier.

"*Timoshenko* is closer than we are," Vaughn said.

"The *Marshal Timoshenko* is pursuing a sub contact, Admiral," Sharov said. "If they abandon the chase . . ." He left the warning unspoken. Submarines were a carrier's deadliest opponent, deadlier by far than any aircraft.

Vaughn pursed his lips. The strongest arm of the Indian navy was without doubt their submarine force: six German Type 1500s, four Russian Kilos, and eight . . . no, make that *seven* Foxtrots.

According to the latest satellite reconnaissance, *Chakra,* the nuclear sub on loan from the Russians, was still, as expected, conspicuously in port, but that still left the Indians with a fleet of seventeen conventional subs. At least ten or twelve of them would be off India's west coast and capable of striking at the joint task force.

Memories of his 1980 encounter with a Russian sub returned once more.

"I'm sorry, Captain Sharov," Vaughn said. "There's nothing we can do." He gestured toward the LSD that showed the swarm of radar contacts within thirty-two miles of the Aegis cruiser. "*Vicksburg* is coordinating the air defense for my entire battle group. It's just not possible."

Radio calls crackled back and forth across the comm net in the background, disembodied and distant.

"Get him! Get him!"

"Bring it around, Shooter, I'm on his six. Fox two!"

"This is One-oh-five. Looks like they're breaking through to the east. Somebody get over there and . . ."

"This is Two-two-oh! Two-two-oh! I'm hit! I'm hit! I'm—"

Sharov stared at Vaughn openly for a moment, then let out a breath. "Understood, Admiral. You can not sacrifice your battle group to save one ship."

"It'll come out right," Vaughn said, feeling the emptiness of his words. "You'll see."

On the television monitor behind him, *Vicksburg*'s five-inch gun continued to slam away at the approaching aircraft. Amidships, the cruiser's starboard CIWS Phalanx activated, pivoted, and fired.

The attackers were within two miles of the command ship now.

**0908 hours, 26 March**
**IAF Jaguar 102**

Colonel Singh held his Jaguar International at wave-top altitude. The sea was a gray blur beneath his plane as he raced toward the south.

The Illyushin-38 naval reconnaissance plane serving as coordinator for the strike had fed him the data he needed. The American target should be less than twenty-five kilometers ahead.

This time he was carrying only a single ASM, a bright-red, deadly-looking missile slung from his centerline stores rack. The AS.37 Martel had been developed in the early 1960s by France's SA Matra and England's British Aerospace Dynamics working together in one of the very first instances of European weapons collaboration. Weighing 550 kilos—over half a ton—and carrying a 150 kg warhead, the Martel had only recently been made available for export from France or Britain, and the missile had not been in production since the late seventies. India's recent and urgent arms buildup, however, had led to secret negotiations with France, and a limited number of AS.37s had been made available to India for "trials" with the HAL-production version of the SEPECAT Jaguar.

The name Martel was derived from Missile Anti-Radar Television. Where the AJ.168 version of the Martel used by Britain was guided by a television transmitter mounted in a blunt, glass nose, the French AS.37 was strictly radar-homing. As he approached the target, Singh dialed through a series of frequencies, searching for the particular band used by the American SPY-1 radar. When he heard the distinctive tone, he punched the buttons that locked the signal down in the missile's memory. Now, no matter how fast or frequently the hostile radar changed frequencies, so long as it remained within the same preset band, the Martel would track it.

Operating from a low-altitude launch, the Martel had a range of thirty kilometers, a little more than eighteen and a half miles. According to the data from the Il-38, Singh was now well within range. Obviously, the closer he could get before release, the more likely the possibility of a hit. He could hear the radio calls of the other Indian pilots in the sky around him as they attacked the American ships. Dozens of aircraft had been downed already, and missile after missile had been destroyed before they could strike their targets, shot down either by the American antiair missiles or, in the last seconds of their approach, by the deadly breath of their guardian CIWS Gatlings.

Somehow during the past hour, Jarnall Rajiv Singh had managed to acquire an almost passive fatalism about this mission, about his chances for success . . . and for survival. His initial terror had faded as his comrades on either side had fallen away, targeted by enemy missiles, shot down by enemy Tomcats.

Now, nothing remained beyond sea and sky, his aircraft and the load it carried. The enemy he had feared had been reduced by the miles and the continuing violence around him to an abstraction, *the target* . . . now twenty kilometers ahead.

With an icy calm he'd never realized he possessed, Singh readied the radar-homing ship-killer for launch.

# CHAPTER 25

**0908 hours, 26 March**
**Tomcat 216**

Batman closed to within fifty yards of the Sukhoi Su-7BM, close enough to see the Indian flag and tail numbers painted on the curiously bright orange tail. The rest of the aircraft was a dull blue-gray with camouflage dark olive blotches. A pair of 500-kilogram GP bombs was slung from the wings.

The Sukhoi Fitter was weaving back and forth, trying to lose its relentless pursuer. Batman held tight on the Fitter's six. The other plane broke left, trying to snap free of the Tomcat. Batman found himself looking into the Fitter's cockpit. He could see the other pilot, his helmet turned to watch Batman's approach.

Batman squeezed the trigger and the Tomcat shuddered. Tracer rounds snapped across the Fitter's nose, missing by feet, then walked back into the aircraft's blunt nose intake with its distinctive pointed shock cone. Holes appeared in the nose. . . .

And then Batman's cannon clicked empty. The ARM display on his HUD guns discrete was off, and the number of rounds left now showed 000.

He pulled back on the stick and cleared the slow-turning Su-7 by yards.

"He's still turning, Batman!" Malibu called. "Still turning. I think he's headed back to India!"

"Good thing," Batman replied. He dropped the Tomcat's right wing, banking to starboard and away from the Su-7. "We won't tell him our gun just went dry."

"Oh, shit."

"Yeah. I think we'd better start thinking about setting down and rearming."

"Yeah," Malibu said. "If we still have anyplace left to set down on."

"What's the word from the bird farm?"

"Under attack. The Indies are hitting the *Jeff* with everything they've got."

Batman swallowed the fear rising in his throat. They'd thrown everything at the Indians, and *still* they were coming!

Batman pulled the stick over, heading back toward the heart of the fleet. "Let's get back there and see what we can do, Mal," he said.

"What do you have in mind, dude?" Malibu said quietly. "Ramming them?"

"If we have to."

He held the F-14 in its starboard turn until it was again headed for the *Jefferson.*

**0908 hours, 26 March**
**IAF Jaguar 102**

The threat warning sounded in his helmet, and an orange light flashed urgently on his console. Colonel Singh's Jaguar had been targeted by an enemy missile. Death was on the way.

Singh searched the horizon ahead, then looked up in the sky. He'd been expecting his target to launch. The enemy's computers would be set to trigger SAM fire as soon as a target approached within certain parameters of speed and altitude. *There* . . . a white contrail, arcing sharply down from the zenith. That would be the missile intended for him.

Still calm, the Indian pilot waited, watching the missile's descent. At the last possible moment, he fired the Jaguar's chaff dispenser, then rammed the throttle into full afterburner. The Jaguar, already traveling at Mach .9, slammed through the sonic barrier, the shock wave raising spray in a straight line across the ocean's surface.

The American SAM fell. . . .

Decoyed by the expanding cloud of chaff, the missile smacked into the sea fifty meters behind Singh's aircraft. He neither felt nor heard the blast. At the Jaguar's maximum low-altitude speed of Mach 1.1, he flashed across the sea toward his target, a ship visible now as a tiny black silhouette on the horizon.

He'd studied that shape in recognition manuals often enough, the sharp-prowed hull, the twin, blunt towers housing the vessel's sophisticated radar and electronics. . . .

He pressed the missile release and felt the jolt as the Martel dropped from the Jaguar's belly. Unarmed now save for a Magic AAM mounted above each wingtip, Singh brought his aircraft up and banked toward the east.

**0909 hours, 26 March**
**Tomcat 216**

"Bandit! Bandit!" Malibu called. "Four o'clock, on the deck! He's launched!"

Batman saw the Jaguar, a tiny, toy-plane shape just above the *Vicksburg,* now some twelve miles to the south.

"What are gonna do?" Malibu asked.

"Call *Vicksburg!*" Batman snapped. He pushed the stick over and dropped the F-14's nose. "Warn them!"

"Oh my God, you *are* going to ram!"

Batman didn't answer. He couldn't answer as he tried to line up with the speeding missile. He could hear Malibu in the backseat, fiercely chanting a litany of warning. "*Vicksburg, Vicksburg,* this is Tomcat Two-one-six. Emergency! Missile launch! Launch!"

**0909 hours, 26 March**
**IAF Jaguar 102**

Singh banked right, angling toward the other Indian aircraft that were already beginning to straggle back toward the north and their home bases. As he glanced back over his shoulder in a reflexive check of the sky around him, though, he saw the distinctive nose-on silhouette of a Tomcat plunging toward him.

With no way of knowing that the American carried neither missiles nor ammunition, he turned left, toward the east.

To the east, however, lay the *Jefferson,* thirty kilometers from the *Vicksburg* and battling for her life against the Indian planes that continued to attack her at close quarters. Another ten kilometers to the northeast, the guided-missile destroyer *Lawrence Kearny* was adding her firepower to that of the *Jefferson,* swatting down Indian planes as quickly as her weapons and *Vicksburg*'s Aegis controllers could identify them.

Seconds after he was into the turn he saw that he was not going to make it. The silhouette of the *Jefferson,* looming huge on the horizon beneath the ghostly white traceries of Sea Sparrow contrails, was unmistakable. Singh held his turn, angling toward the northeast as he pushed for more altitude. At better than Mach 1, his turn radius was impossibly large. He passed the *Jefferson* less than a mile off her bow.

*Jefferson*'s starboard-side forward Sparrow launcher swung about and fired, and the RIM-7 Sea Sparrow slashed from its container in a shower of packaging fragments mingled with white smoke. The SARH-guided missile streaked skyward at Mach 3, slamming into the Jaguar's tail two seconds later. Ninety pounds of high explosives detonated in a searing flash, igniting the Jaguar's fuel in a blazing fireball.

A pair of Standard antiair missiles fired from the *Kearny* flashed into the expanding cloud of debris seconds later, adding their detonations to the fury. Very little recognizable as any part of an aircraft reached the water's surface.

**0909 hours, 26 March**
**Tomcat 216**

Batman knew almost at once that he was never going to catch the cruise missile. Drag had slowed it to subsonic velocity immediately after launch, but its solid fuel motor slammed it past the sound barrier as it homed on the Aegis cruiser's radar. The pursuing F-14 had been moving at barely 300 knots as it went into its dive, and the missile was now four miles ahead. Batman could no longer see it, save as a targeting square painted by his plane's AWG-9 radar on his HUD.

Malibu continued trying to raise the cruiser. "*Vicksburg!* We have a missile launch, bearing one-eight-three degrees, homing on your position. Do you copy?"

Batman watched the hollow square settle across the *Vicksburg*'s silhouette on the horizon, a raging frustration and helplessness burning in his throat and eyes.

**0910 hours, 26 March**
**U.S.S. *Vicksburg***

Since it gave off no radar emissions of its own, the Martel antiradar missile was not immediately spotted or recognized. *Vicksburg*'s communications department recorded Malibu's desperate warning, but seconds were lost because an inexperienced radio watchstander took Malibu's report bearing—183 degrees—and thought he meant a bearing of 183 degrees from the *ship*.

He alerted the men handling tactical to the wrong part of the horizon, south of the *Vicksburg* instead of north.

At the same moment, *Vicksburg*'s computer registered the target approaching the cruiser at Mach 1, but the warning was delayed several crucial seconds by higher levels of electronic alarms, a priority system established to deal with each target in the order of its perceived threat to the ship.

It failed because there were too many threats. Machines and humans alike were swamped at the moment with targets of every kind, in every part of the sky. By the time another human operator noted the alert-flagged blip racing in from the north, it was already too late. Even if everything and everyone aboard the Aegis cruiser had reacted perfectly, it would have been too late.

More seconds were lost when the human operator turned his attention to a second blip lagging miles behind the first. The Aegis system's computers had registered that target's IFF and recorded it as a friendly aircraft; for a fatigue-blurred moment, the sailor working the console thought that the blip it was chasing must be friendly too, a missile launched at some other target. The electronic displays in *Vicksburg*'s CIC were enough like video games that it was sometimes possible to lose track of what those moving points of light actually represented.

A *human* error . . .

The Martel struck *Vicksburg* close to the angle between her deck and the forward deckhouse tower, smashing through the deck plating and light armor on her starboard quarter. The warhead was triggered by a proximity fuze, but some minor fault delayed that triggering for the tenth of a second it took for the missile to literally tunnel into the ship's electronic entrails. Over three hundred pounds of high explosives detonated within a few yards of *Vicksburg*'s CIC.

Admiral Vaughn did not feel the blast. One moment he was standing in front of the primary battle board, watching, beginning to hope that possibly, just *possibly* the Indian aircraft were starting to turn away.

Then he was flying through air suddenly and unaccountably filled with whirling fragments of glass and plastic, bits of wire, pieces of bodies, whole sections of the overhead and bulkhead plating and insulation. He slammed into an instrument console, rolled across it, and dropped to the deck. The console gave way an instant later, smashing down on top of him.

Already unconscious, he was unaware of that final blow.

**0910 hours, 26 March**
**Tomcat 216**

"Oh . . . my . . . God . . ."

Batman watched the mushroom cloud of black smoke shot with flame rise above the stricken command cruiser. He banked left but kept his eyes on the ship as they passed her to starboard, still under way but slower now, wallowing in the heavy seas as flame broke from the smashed-in hole on her forward deckhouse.

"Batman . . ." Malibu's voice was subdued, almost stricken, over the ICS. "Batman, check your fuel."

He glanced at the fuel gauge. They had about fourteen hundred pounds. They'd burned a lot on a long patrol, most of it in fuel-burning ACM.

"Okay," he said. He felt drained . . . defeated. "Raise the boat, Mal. Tell 'em we're coming in. And . . ." He hesitated, watching the burning ship. Was Admiral Vaughn still alive? "Better tell them that *Vicksburg*'s been hit."

**0911 hours, 26 March**
**Tomcat 200**

Tombstone closed his finger over the red firing button on the stick. "Fox one, fox one!" His last missile, an AIM-7M Sparrow, ignited in a blast of white smoke and flame and streaked away from the Tomcat. At forty-five thousand feet, the air was diamond-clear, the sky an endless deep and crystal blue. The Sparrow's contrail stood out in sharp relief as it twisted to the north like a chalk line scrawled across a blackboard.

"He's turning, Tombstone," Hitman announced. Tombstone glanced down at his VDI. The target, a lumbering Il-38 reconnaissance aircraft thirty miles away, appeared to be banking away toward the north . . . and Kathiawar.

"They're running," Tombstone said, almost unable to believe what he was seeing. The wave of Indian aircraft had struck against the combined squadrons full-force . . . and broken.

He checked his fuel. It was low . . . down to thirty-five hundred pounds. They'd burned a hell of a lot on Zone Five.

"Hey, Tombstone?" Hitman said. "I'm getting a call . . . oh, God!"

Tombstone heard it over his headset as well. Batman was calling the *Jefferson,* reporting the *Vicksburg* hit by a missile. It was too early to tell how badly the Aegis cruiser was hit, but it didn't sound good.

"He's right," Hitman said a moment later. "Looks like the Aegis net is down. Shit, Tombstone, the squadron's *naked* now!"

With a stubborn determination, Tombstone held the Tomcat in level flight, continuing to paint the fleeing Illyushin with his Tomcat's radar. At Mach 4, the Sparrow traveled the thirty miles to the target in less than fifty seconds. The blips marking missile and target merged on Tombstone's VDI.

Hit!

He took a deep breath, watching the blips scattered across his VDI. It was clear that the Indian aircraft were in full retreat now. The Russian-American force had won.

But at what cost? *Kreml* was still burning at last report. And now *Vicksburg,* shattered by a missile that had knocked out the battle group's Aegis network.

The Tomcat squadrons had suffered as well, the two replacements, Maverick and Trapper and their RIOs, shot down during the aerial melee.

And Army and Dixie.

It took several minutes more for the Il-38 to die, falling from almost fifty thousand feet. By the time the radar trace fragmented and vanished, Tombstone and Hitman were already heading south and descending.

On the horizon, they could just make out the black speck that was the *Jefferson,* almost lost against the unending sea.

**0915 hours, 26 March**
**CIC, U.S.S. *Vicksburg***

Admiral Vaughn became aware first of the pain, a sharp-edged throbbing in his right arm that grated when he tried to move. The darkness was next, a stinking, pitch-black night that lay across his face, choking him with each breath.

He tried to call out but heard nothing, felt nothing but the pain in his arm and a searing rasp in his throat.

Hearing returned, gradually, beginning with a high-pitched ringing that slowly subsided, replaced by shouts and screams, by the crackle of an open flame and the hiss of a ruptured steam pipe, by the sobbing, agonized moaning of someone lying close by but out of his sight. The darkness was relieved now, he saw, by the orange tongues of flame dancing above a shattered radar console. *Vicksburg*'s CIC suite had been transformed into a black and twisted cavern, illuminated only by the acrid glare of burning wiring.

"*Syoodah!*" a raw voice beside him. "*Skaryehyeh! Pamageeteh!*"

Hands closed on his shoulders and Vaughn screamed, "My arm! It's broken!"

"Sorry, Admiral." English this time. Vaughn recognized Sharov's voice. "Lie still. Help is coming."

"My legs," he said. "Can't . . . feel them."

"*Skaryehyeh, pahzahloostah!*" Sharov yelled. "Hurry, please!"

The glare of flashlights danced and stabbed in the near-darkness. Vaughn heard other voices, speaking English, and the scrabble and clatter of men moving through the wreckage. The *shoosh-shoosh* of someone triggering a fire extinguisher cut above the babble.

"Admiral? Can you hear me?"

"Y-yeah. Cunningham?"

"No, Admiral. I'm Thurman. I'm a Corpsman."

Vaughn opened his eyes. In the dancing, smoke-wreathed light, he could make out a short-sleeved white shirt moving above him. On the right sleeve was the crow and caduceus of a Hospital Corpsman First Class.

"We're gonna get you out of there, Admiral."

"S'okay. Doc. I think I've had it. Can't move."

"You've got a console on your legs, sir. They're getting it off you now."

He still couldn't feel anything below his waist. There was a sharp jab as the Corpsman jabbed the needle of a morphine syrette in his arm.

"*Astarawjna!*" someone called. "*Gatovoh . . . t'ykep' yehr!*"

Vaughn managed to raise his head. In the uncertain light, he could see two of the Commonwealth liaison officers, Sharov and *Kreml*'s Tactical Officer, Besedin, straining together to lift the shattered console from his legs. Besedin wore a bandana torn from someone's white shirt, stained over his left eye with blood.

The console stirred, then lifted between the two straining men. "*Harohshee! Harohshee!*" They gave a concerted heave, and the wreckage crashed to the deck several feet away. Vaughn glanced down at his legs, half afraid of what he would see. They were still there, though the right leg was turned at an awkward angle.

But he could not feel them at all.

Turning away, he saw the bodies, blood-stained and crumpled by the force of the blast. One looked like the Russian Pokrovsky.

The other was Bersticer, his chest crushed and bloody.

Six men crowded around Vaughn, blocking the sight, the

horror. "Careful now," Thurman ordered. "Get that board under his back. Strap it tight . . . under his arms. His legs. Good. Okay, ready? Lift!"

Working together, they lifted him from the deck and lowered him into the wire embrace of a Stokes stretcher. Thurman began strapping him in.

"I think my back's broken," Vaughn said. Strange, he felt no emotion.

"Well, now," Thurman said. "We won't know until we get you back to the *Jeff* for some pictures, will we?"

"You can drop the bedside manner, Doc." He paused, listening to the shouts from outside the shattered CIC. "How bad is the ship?"

"I don't know, Admiral." Thurman reached down with a grease pencil and scrawled something across Vaughn's forehead. It would be the letter "M" for morphine and the time, he knew. "You'll have to talk to whoever's in command now."

*Whoever's in command.* Cunningham had been standing a few feet away before the explosion. Was he dead?

"We're evacuating casualties," Thurman continued as he pocketed the grease pencil. "We have helos working in relays, taking them across to the *Jefferson*. She's got the best sick bay facilities in the battle group."

Thurman started to turn away. Vaughn caught his arm. "Call . . . Captain Fitzgerald," he said. "Have him see me . . . when I get there."

Thurman smiled. "That shot I gave you might have you under by then, Admiral."

"Do . . . it! Must see . . . Fitzgerald." He could feel the muzzy-headed dopiness as the morphine took effect.

He had to fight it, to stay awake. He *had* to see Fitzgerald. . . .

**0920 hours, 29 March**
**Tomcat 200**

Tombstone eased his Tomcat into the slot astern of the *Jefferson* and cut back on his power. He checked his stores listing on his VDI and was startled to see that he'd expended all of his missiles and was down to his last eighty rounds for his

M61A1 Vulcan, and he wasn't even sure how many Indian aircraft he'd downed. The fight had been so confused, the sky so filled with planes and missiles. There was no way to sort it all out.

The fight had left him feeling so drained he didn't even feel the usual charge of adrenaline as he approached for his trap. He almost felt relaxed. "Tomcat Two-double-oh," he called. "Ball. Three point three."

"Roger ball," the LSO reported. "You're right in the groove. Check your hook."

Tombstone slapped the switch that lowered his tail hook. He'd been so relaxed he'd forgotten.

Somehow, the *Jefferson*'s flight deck had never looked so good from this vantage point, half a mile astern and coming in for a trap. He held the stick steady, making slight, second-by-second corrections.

The Tomcat swept in over the ramp, settling to the deck in a perfect approach. Tombstone rammed the throttles forward as the tail hook snagged on the number-three wire, and he felt the familiar wrench of deceleration as he hung by his harness straps for a second. He cut back on the power as the LSO called "Okay" over the radio.

"Let's clear the deck," the Air Boss said in Tombstone's headset as a yellow shirt started to direct him across the deck. "On the double. We have helos inbound."

*Okay.*

It was good to be home.

**0945 hours, 26 March**
**Flight deck, U.S.S. *Thomas Jefferson***

Captain Fitzgerald was waiting as several Corpsmen lowered the Stokes from the helo and eased Admiral Vaughn to the carrier's deck. The admiral found himself puzzling over an odd movement above his face, until he realized that he was lying on his back, looking up through the still-turning rotors of a Navy Sea King helicopter. Had he been asleep?

No matter. Fitzgerald's creased, anxious face bent low over his own. "Admiral? How are you?"

"Can't complain," Vaughn said, weakly. "Doesn't do any good."

"My people'll get you to sick bay, Admiral. They're good. They'll patch you up—"

"Listen, Captain," Vaughn interrupted. "You've got command of the battle group."

"They told me half an hour ago you were wounded, sir," he said, nodding. "As senior officer, I took command then."

"The . . . group?"

"We took a pasting. Can't deny that. *Kremlin* and *Vicksburg* are both hit pretty bad. But the Indian air force damn near busted a gut doing that much. We estimate they've lost fifty aircraft of all types. They turned tail and started running shortly after *Vicksburg* took that missile."

"Good. One . . . one more order, then."

"Of course, sir."

"Complete . . . the mission."

"Sir?"

"Carry out . . . mission." The pain in his arm was back, growing steadily worse despite the morphine. "We've got to follow through. If we don't . . . it's all been for nothing. Nothing . . ."

"Admiral, it may not be possible. We've got fifteen F-14s flying, period. And they're going to have to rearm and refuel. We have to guard the battle group. . . ."

"Use . . . Russians," Vaughn said.

"They haven't exactly been cooperative," Fitzgerald pointed out. "I don't—"

"Russians . . . have squadron up. Can't land. *Use* them. Somehow . . ." Suddenly, it seemed terribly important to Vaughn that their losses not be in vain. A waste.

Fitzgerald grinned suddenly. "Don't you worry, Admiral. They tell me the *Jeff*'ll have all four cats back on line in another hour, max. After that . . . well, like they say. Charlie Mike." *Continue mission.*

"Good . . ."

The blue sky behind Fitzgerald's head was darkening . . . darkening.

Admiral Vaughn slipped into oblivion.

**0947 hours, 26 March**
**Flight deck, U.S.S. *Thomas Jefferson***

Fitzgerald watched as they carried Vaughn off toward the island, then moved back out of the way as a deck officer waved for personnel to stand clear. The Sea King's pilot began gunning the helo's rotors. The deck officer lifted his hands in a final all-clear. With a roar, the helo lifted from the deck, then angled across the carrier's port side and out over the ocean.

On the horizon, he could see the smoky stain where *Vicksburg* was burning.

He checked his watch, then glanced toward the carrier's bow. He couldn't see the damage control parties, of course. They were all below, working on the steam lines that had been damaged by the Exocet hit.

They'd *better* have them ready in an hour.

Fitzgerald breathed a long, slightly unsteady sigh of relief. Before they'd flown the admiral back aboard, he'd already given the orders to continue readying the strike aircraft for the raid on India. Not that it would have made a lot of difference one way or the other at some later, formal board of inquiry or court-martial. It was just nice to know that he wasn't entirely alone in his decision.

The joint task force had been hit hard, but they could still carry out the mission. Hit the Indian supply columns. Force them to end their invasion of Pakistan.

*Charlie Mike.*

# CHAPTER 26

**1015 hours, 26 March**
**VF-95 Ready Room, U.S.S. *Thomas Jefferson***

CAG Marusko stood behind the lectern at the front of the Vipers' Ready Room, rocking back on his heels as he brought the squadron up to date. Tombstone sat with the others at the small metal desks with the folding wooden writing surfaces, like schoolboys being lectured by their teacher.

"We've hit them hard," Marusko said. "*Damned* hard."

Certainly, Tombstone thought, someone had decided to put the best possible face on things. CAG was running the briefing in the Ready Room in person rather than broadcasting it over closed-circuit TV. It was a way of maintaining contact with the men, for their morale . . . and probably for his own as well.

CAG continued the rundown, leaning against the lectern now.

The first phase of the Battle of the Arabian Sea seemed tragically one-sided to the men who'd participated in it. Two ships of the combined task force were badly damaged, a carrier and the all-important Aegis command cruiser, and the survival of both was in doubt. In the air, four Tomcats had been shot down—Army, Trapper, and Maverick from VF-95, and an aviator named Wildman Romanski in VF-97. So far, only two of the crews had been recovered from the choppy waters around the Battle Group.

And so far too, there'd been little to show for the blood and suffering of the past hour and a half.

There was another side to the numbers, though. CAG explained. A conservative estimate floating around the VF-95

Ready Room was that fifty Indian aircraft had been shot down, with as many more, possibly, damaged.

Fifty planes shot down, out of an estimated two hundred sent against the two F-14 squadrons. At least twenty of those had been accounted for by the Tomcats, for a kill ratio of five-for-one. Not the ten-for-one ratio of which Top Gun pilots were so justly proud . . . but then, the air battle had been confused beyond imagining, and one of the downed American planes had been hit before all of the aircraft could be launched.

Besides their air losses, the Indians had been hit on the surface and beneath it as well. The frigate *Biddle* had managed to cut off the four Osa-IIs as they fled back toward the Indian fleet. From a range of fifty miles she'd launched all four of her Harpoon antiship missiles, firing one after the other in rapid succession from the Mark 13 launcher on her forward deck. Three Osa missile boats had been sunk outright. The fourth was badly damaged and limping toward the east at reduced speed.

To the northwest, the *Marshal Timoshenko* had reported encountering an unidentified sub trying to work its way toward the heart of the task force. The Kresta II-class cruiser had fired a single SS-N-14 missile from one of the massive, awkward-looking quad launchers mounted on either side of the bridge. Called Silex by NATO, the missile carried an antisubmarine torpedo into the vicinity of the suspected sub and dropped it by parachute. At 0936 hours, the *Timoshenko* sonar operators had picked up the unmistakable crump of an undersea explosion.

There'd been no further submarine alerts since.

If all these reports were true, Tombstone thought, the Indians were probably feeling as badly used as the Americans were at the moment.

The question of the hour, however, was where they were going next. With *Vicksburg* badly damaged, it seemed all but certain that the battle group would be recalled, probably to either Masirah or Diego Garcia for temporary repairs, then up the Red Sea to the Med. The closest decent ship repair facilities were at Naples.

*Nimitz* and *Eisenhower* would arrive at Turban Station within the next few days. They would continue the fight. Tombstone studied the faces of the men around him and knew the same thought was in their minds. He read the anger there. They'd been hit hard and hurt. Now they wanted to hit *back.*

CAG paused in his narrative, watching the men closely. "Repairs to Cats One and Two have been completed," he said. "As of ten hundred hours, *Jefferson* is again fully operational. The deck crew is conducting a final FOD walkdown at this moment."

There was a stir among the listening aviators. With four cats on line, *Jefferson* could again launch and recover simultaneously. From CAG's tone, it sounded as though the battle wasn't over yet. The FOD—Foreign Object Damage—walkdown was designed to pick up any stray bits of debris or metal that might get sucked into a jet's air intakes. It was always conducted just before launch operations, a part of carrier routine.

Perhaps it was the routine that was carrying all of them forward now, despite exhaustion, despite their losses.

Routine and . . . determination.

CAG rocked forward on the podium, his hands clasped over the edge. He seemed to look at each of the men in the room. "I've just had the word from Captain Fitzgerald, acting CO for the battle group. Mongoose is going as planned."

There was an explosion of noise in the ready room, whistles, cheers, and shouts, men pounding the writing surfaces of their desks and stomping on the deck.

"*Jefferson* . . ." CAG started to say, then stopped until the noise subsided. "*Jefferson,*" he continued, "has a job to do. A mission. Captain Fitzgerald told me himself that we are not going *anywhere* until that mission is complete."

CAG turned his gaze on Tombstone, who thought he detected the faintest trace of a grin tugging at the man's mouth. "Tombstone? You feel up to leading your squadron?"

*My squadron.* The sense of belonging, of being *home,* returned, stronger than ever. "Yes, *sir*!"

"Good. We're making some minor changes. VF-95 will take the strike planes all the way in to the target. One Hornet squadron, VFA-173, will also be flying in the interdiction role, as planned. VF-97 will head for the rendezvous at Point Juliet and clear it until the strike assembles, then assist in the escort home. Yes . . . question?"

"What about CAP for the *Jeff,* CAG?" Coyote wanted to know. "We're leaving her kind of exposed, aren't we?"

"Well, the Intelligence boys all seem to think the Indies will have a lot more to worry about when they see the bunch of you coming after them than attacking our ships. Air defense over the land is expected to be heavy . . . but this soon after their heavy raid, they should be scattered and disorganized.'' CAG's grin became open, as though he was enjoying some humorous secret. ''Just to be on the safe side, though, we have some newbies coming in to help you out. Actually, they're up there now, have been for the last hour.''

Tombstone was tired, and couldn't understand at first what Marusko was getting at. Newbies? The only newbies aboard were the replacements who'd flown aboard on the COD aircraft two days ago.

From the reaction of the rest of the squadron, they didn't get it either.

''Don't worry about it,'' Marusko continued. ''We've got it covered. Yes, Wayne.''

''Is there any threat to the squadron from the Indian fleet?'' Batman wanted to know. ''It'd be kind of a shame to go all the way in, all the way back, and find you all on the bottom after tangling with half the Indian navy.''

A subdued chuckle ran through the room.

CAG nodded. ''Hey, the Captain thinks of everything. Don't worry, people, it's all in the bag.''

**1100 hours, 26 March**
**The Arabian Sea**

Beneath the waters of the Indian Ocean lay a canyon.

Called the Indus Canyon, it was a sheer-walled gouge through the rock of the continental shelf, a valley scoured out by the uncounted millions of tons of sand and sediment washed down over millennia from the Himalayas and carried by the river's current far to the south. For the first one hundred fifty miles beyond the mouths of the Indus, the canyon meandered through a plateau only a few hundred feet beneath the surface. Beyond that, however, the Indus currents broke from the channel in the continental shelf and plunged down . . . down into an eternal blackness nine thousand feet beneath the war and the sunlit waters of the surface.

At the edge of this blackness, a sea monster stirred, moving slowly from the valley's depths toward the light. Three hundred sixty feet long, thirty-three feet broad, and displacing nearly seven thousand tons submerged, the U.S.S. *Galveston* was one of the latest American Los Angeles-class attack submarines.

For the past twenty-four hours, *Galveston* had been listening, coasting slowly through the dark waters of the Indus Canyon, her sonar ears alert to any sound beyond the normal chirping, creaking, clacking cacophony of sea life around her. Twice, the far-off pings of sonobuoys had reached across miles and touched her, but too distant, too weak to reveal her location in the sheltering confines of the undersea valley. Once, her chief sonar operator had detected the chugging throb of propellers, a sound *Galveston*'s acoustic library had identified as a Gearing-class destroyer, undoubtedly one of the six World War II-era DDs sold to Pakistan in the late seventies.

Captain Gerald Hawkins's orders were both specific and vague. As part of the ASW screen for CBG-14, he was to precede the battle group toward the Indian-Pakistani border, remaining undetected by either side. All foreign submarines, whether Pakistani or Indian, were to be intercepted before they could approach the combined task force.

The vague aspect of his orders lay in what he was to do with the foreign subs once he'd caught them. A warning, transmitted through the water as a powerful chirp of sonar, might be sufficient to turn them away. But if necessary, he was to destroy potentially hostile subs before they could close with *Jefferson* or her escorts.

At prearranged times each day, *Galveston* was to rise to periscope depth. Additional orders and updates of the tactical situation could be passed on to the attack sub then. At 1100 hours on the morning of March 26, *Galveston*'s radar mast broke the surface one hundred twenty miles northwest of the U.S.S. *Jefferson.* The situation update, together with Captain Fitzgerald's new orders, were passed to the submarine via relay through a circling Hawkeye, and confirmed by satellite from Washington.

Minutes later, the radio mast vanished again, leaving scarcely a ripple to mark its passing.

At precisely 1125 hours, a series of round hatches set into the attack sub's hull forward of her sail slid open. At a word from her commanding officer, a twenty-foot-long cigar shape rose from one of the tubes, expelled by a high-pressure blast of water.

The Tomahawk was a cruise missile developed in two different models, the TLAM (Tomahawk Land Attack Missile) and the TASM (Tomahawk Anti-Ship Missile). Originally designed to be fired from a submarine's torpedo tubes, it was later discovered that each sub's torpedo-carrying capacity was severely restricted by including Tomahawks on board. Beginning with the U.S.S. *Providence,* SS-N-719, all Los Angeles-class subs had fifteen vertical launch tubes, designed especially for Tomahawks, mounted within the bow casing between the sub's inner and outer hulls, allowing them to carry full complements of both torpedoes and cruise missiles.

Triggered by a ten-foot lanyard connecting missile and launch tube, the solid-fuel rocket boost motor ignited in a cloud of gas bubbles and boiling water, driving the missile upward at a fifty-degree angle. The motor burned for seven seconds, long enough to punch through the surface and into the air. Then the booster fell away, wings deployed as the missile nosed over into horizontal flight only meters above the surface, and the missile's air-breathing gas turbine switched on.

Within seconds, another Tomahawk broke the surface, then another and another. At Mach .7, the cruise missiles arrowed southeast toward their target.

Three hundred miles away, another, much larger submarine was watching the approaches to Bombay. Four hundred seventy feet long and sixty feet through the beam, it was one of a special class of nuclear-powered attack subs known to the West as Oscar.

The Oscar had originally been conceived as a platform for anticarrier operations. Its primary mission was to stalk American aircraft carrier battle groups. In time of war, the Oscars would be directed to participate in long-range missile bombardment of the U.S. carriers, coordinating their strikes with missile launches from surface ships and long-range bombers. The Oscar's broad girth was made necessary by the cruise-missile launch tubes built into the hull on either side of the long, flat sail. Six square hatches on either side each covered two tubes. The sub carried a total of twenty-four SS-N-19 antiship missiles, high-speed, long-range weapons that could carry either conventional or nuclear warheads.

One after another, the sleek ship-killers burst from the waters above the submerged Oscar, discarded their empty boosters, and deployed the swept-back wings. Using information relayed to the Oscar from Soviet reconnaissance satellites orbiting overhead, the SS-N-19s began flying north, homing on the same targets as those already marked by the American Tomahawks.

**1148 hours, 26 March**
**INS *Viraat*, 160 miles west northwest of Bombay**

"Today, Lieutenant, you are a hero for all of India," Ramesh said. "Your triumph will be remembered always!"

Admiral Ramesh faced the young lieutenant. He was so young, so like Joshi, that for a moment he wanted to reach out and embrace the boy. But professional decorum, and Lieutenant Tahliani's obvious embarrassment, held him back.

"I did my duty, Admiral," the boy said. "We *all* only did our duty."

Admiral Ramesh shook his head. "You've done more than your duty, Lieutenant," he said softly. "You may well have won for us the victory we needed."

Tahliani's flight had been the stuff of legends, of the ancient Hindu epic legends. Decoying an American F-14 with one of his Sea Eagles, he'd then shot it down with a Magic AAM. He could have launched the rest of his antiship missiles then and fled, but the boy had known that the alerted American defenses would probably knock down the Sea Eagles long before they reached their targets.

Instead, he'd rounded up a few companions and set out on his long and fuel-costly detour around the American fleet, avoiding several U.S. pickets along the way. In a triumph of long-distance navigation and flying skill, he'd reached a point from which he and his men could launch their remaining missiles. Radio traffic between the Soviet and American vessels monitored from the shore indicated that the Russian carrier was now burning, incapacitated by at least one serious missile hit.

That strike, together with the damage done to an American command cruiser, had spelled victory for the Indian navy. Now there remained only one more task. The remaining carrier, the Americans' *Jefferson,* was launching aircraft. It seemed likely that they were a strike force, that their targets were the airstrips and military bases that had launched the attack on the combined squadron.

If this last, desperate thrust by the enemy could be blunted, the Americans would *have* to admit defeat. The old dream of an Indian Ocean free of outside influences and under New Delhi's firm political control would become reality at last.

A klaxon blared and Admiral Ramesh looked up. "Now hear this, now hear this," rasped from the loudspeaker. "Prepare for missile attack. Admiral Ramesh to the Flag Bridge, please. Admiral Ramesh . . ."

For Ramesh it was as though the pieces of a complex puzzle had suddenly snapped into place. He'd been expecting some form of retaliation by the Americans and Russians for the damage done to their forces. Still, when Tahliani had returned in triumph from his strike, when the news had come through from Naval Headquarters at Bombay that the land-based attack had overwhelmed the American defenses and hit their command ship, he'd allowed himself to believe that the enemy might cut their losses and retreat.

But that was not to be. This would not be a matter of raid and counterraid, but of two giants, battling to the death.

"Lieutenant," he snapped. Tahliani drew himself to attention. "Your aircraft are being fueled and rearmed. On my authority, you are to get as many aircraft off the deck as possible. I don't want the same thing happening to *Viraat* as happened to the *Kremlin*!"

"Yes, sir! Are we to fly the Sea Harriers ashore?"

Ramesh shook his head. "No, Lieutenant. I will have special instructions for you." He reached out and grasped the young man's arm. "But for now, go! While you still can!"

Then he turned and raced for *Viraat*'s island.

**1154 hours, 26 March**
**Blue King Leader, flight deck, INS *Viraat***

Lieutenant Tahliani adjusted his helmet strap as he performed a cursory run-through of the checklist strapped to his thigh. Fuel okay . . . power on . . . stick controls okay . . .

A deck officer was signaling. He saluted, glanced up at *Viraat*'s island, then adjusted the Sea Harrier's exhaust ports, vectoring them for a rolling takeoff. One of the Sea Harrier's many remarkable features was its short start-up time. He released the wheel brakes and was moving down the carrier's deck toward the ski jump ramp within five minutes of the alert.

The latest reports indicated that two separate groups of antiship missiles were approaching the Indian fleet, one from the northwest, one from the southeast. Almost certainly both missile flights had been launched from enemy submarines in the area, though the northwestern group could possibly have come from the surface ships of the enemy fleet. The nearest missile was still twenty kilometers out. There was time yet. . . .

The Sea Harrier vaulted from the ski jump and into the sky. Tahliani redirected the exhaust ports to full aft and climbed. Other Sea Harriers followed, gathering in an assembly area five kilometer southwest of the *Viraat.*

From the high perch of his cockpit, Tahliani had a splendid view of the Indian fleet, spread out from horizon beneath him. *Viraat* and the smaller carrier *Vikrant* were at the flotilla's heart. *Kalikata,* one of the Indian Navy's Kresta II cruisers newly purchased from the former Soviet Union, led the van ten kilometers ahead. And surrounding these three were, the destroyers, frigates, and corvettes that made up the body of the fleet, all steaming northwest at a steady twenty knots.

"Blue King Leader, this is *Viraat.*" He recognized the voice. Admiral Ramesh himself was calling.

"*Viraat,* this is Blue King Leader. Go ahead."

"Lieutenant . . . the battle may well be in your hands now." Tahliani heard the strain in Ramesh's voïce. "Execute Plan Three."

"Roger, *Viraat.* Plan Three."

American ECM eavesdroppers might well be listening in. The melodramatic-sounding Plan Three referred simply to a series of earlier briefings, covering possible contingencies in the event of an attack against the Indian naval squadron.

Plan Three called for Blue King to fly off the *Viraat* and head north for friendly airfields on Kathiawar. Along the way, they were to watch for targets of opportunity—American ships or aircraft that might be attacked with a minimum of risk for the Indian Sea Harriers.

Tahliani knew that Ramesh had been saying more but had not wanted to put it into words when he knew the Americans were listening in. The admiral was expecting some special effort from Tahliani's squadron, an attack that would make the Russian-American effort too costly for them to pursue.

A flicker caught Tahliani's eye. Looking down, he saw—*thought* he saw—a ghost of motion, something flashing low across the water at the very limit of vision. . . .

*Viraat* was firing her SAMs. He could see the contrails below him, like white threads against the dark water. The missiles were reaching toward the southeast. Seconds later, he saw a flash, like the popping of a strobe light, far off on the horizon. There was another . . . and another . . .

Something skimmed in from the northeast, streaking straight toward the Indian carrier. Tahliani saw it and wanted to scream warning, but it was too late. There was a soundless eruption of smoke and debris close alongside the Indian carrier, as the widening ring of the shock wave raced out from the vessel's hull on the water. The strike was so sudden that the surprise was like a physical blow.

*The carrier is hit!*

Surface-to-air missiles continued to rise, not only from the stricken *Viraat* but from the other ships in the fleet as well. The Indian navy had nothing like Aegis, however, to coordinate the defense, and the response was sluggish, befuddled possibly by the surprise and numbers of the attack, or by the fog of enemy ECM jamming on radars and fire control directors.

Another missile was hit short of the *Viraat,* but a companion skimmed past the fireball and planted itself in the carrier's side. Tahliani saw the cascade of debris spewing out of the hull opposite where the missile had struck, saw the mushrooming pillar of oily smoke shot through with flame rising from the carrier's deck. *Viraat* was burning now, her deck a sheet of flames fed by burst fuel lines and exploding munitions.

It took him several minutes to realize that *Viraat* had gone off the air, her radio dead. He wondered if Admiral Ramesh was still alive.

The sight of his carrier cloaked in rising smoke was so

shocking he scarcely noticed that other ships in the Indian fleet were hit. A pall of smoke was hanging above *Vikrant* where at least one missile had struck from the southeast, while the cruiser *Kalikata* was a blazing funeral pyre, dead in the water and listing hard to port.

There was no turning back now. Grimly, Lieutenant Tahliani gathered his squadron—eleven other Sea Harriers that had managed to launch before disaster struck—and turned toward the northwest.

The Sea Harriers, those that survived the next two hours, would be able to land in Kathiawar. But Lieutenant Tahliani was determined now that the American strike aircraft would have no place to land when they returned from their mission over India.

# CHAPTER 27

**1215 hours, 26 March**
**Tomcat 200**

Tombstone watched the brown-gray blur of the coast approaching. The water beneath him lightened, then flashed into barren, sun-parched hills as he led the Vipers across the beach and into India.

"This is Viper Lead," he said over the radio. "Feet dry."

"Eagle Lead," the voice of the War Eagles' CO added. "Feet dry."

One by one, the other strike elements called in, reporting that they were now crossing from sea to land. Desert quickly gave way to marshland as they passed over the Rann of Kutch. Smudges marred the eastern sky. The Hornets of Lucky Strike had already hit the airfields at Bhuj, Jamnagar, and Okha, misdirecting the Indians into thinking the strike's targets were their military bases near the coast.

A pillar of smoke to the west marked the remnants of an Indian coastal radar, victim of the VAQ-143 Sharks and the HARM missiles. Those High Speed Anti-Radiation ASMs were designed to home on coastal or SAM site radars and clear a path through India's electronic fences.

That too would help convince the Indians that the targets were air bases and coastal facilities.

"This is Gold Strike Leader," a voice called over the tactical net. "Passing Point Bravo."

Bravo was the code name for the Pakistani border, close to the Nara River. The Intruders of VA-89 would be spreading out now, preparing for their strike.

Tombstone thought about the squadron leader VA-89, Lieutenant Commander Isaac Greene. A big, bluff man called "Jolly Greene" by the other men in the air wing, he was one of several legends in Air Wing 20. During Operation Righteous Thunder, he'd led a strike against North Korean armor and been hit by ground fire from KorCom ZSU-23-4 antiaircraft vehicles.

Somehow, Jolly and his Bombardier-Navigator Chucker Vance had held their shattered Intruder together long enough to reach the sea and eject. A SAR helo had plucked them from the sea and returned them to *Jefferson*'s deck, half frozen but alive.

Tombstone thought of the other men he'd served with during the past nine months. Coyote, shot down over the Sea of Japan by a Korean MiG and captured.

Then there were Batman and Malibu, holding position now off his port wing. They'd been downed by a SAM over northern Thailand. Ejecting over the jungle, they'd somehow hiked back to civilization, bringing with them vital intelligence.

And there were so many others, men who'd given their *lives* in combat missions flown, ironically, to protect the peace.

He thought of Army and Dixie, shot down while trying to save the *Jefferson* from a cruise missile. Despite a search by SAR helos, they'd not been found in the choppy seas just a few miles from the carrier.

They'd not fought for any particular cause or label . . . though both were patriots in every sense of the word. Like all of the others, Tombstone thought, Army and Dixie had believed in what they were doing but had carried on not for the sake of the *mission* . . . but because they couldn't let down their friends, the other members of their squadrons, their shipmates.

Possibly, Tombstone reflected, that was what every soldier of every war fought for more than home or country: the men fighting with him at his side. They fought not to take the next hill or even to win the war, but because friends and comrades would suffer or die if they did not.

And after that . . . yeah, there was the mission. *Always* the mission.

"Viper Leader, Viper Two."

"Go ahead, Batman."

"Ho, Stoney. Looks like we're getting ready to rock and roll. We got bogies, bearing zero-niner-five."

"We see them," Tombstone replied, checking his VDI. The bandits were forming up, rising from airfields despite the damage done by the Hornet strikes. Well, that was expected. No strike was one hundred percent effective . . . especially when the opponent was as powerful and as well-dispersed as this one. "Okay, boys and girls. Stand by to break right on my signal. Weapons are free. Good luck!"

"Listen, guys," Batman added. "Drinks are on me when we get back to the bird farm!"

"If the bird farm's still there," Coyote said. "I'm not sure I like the idea of CAG's 'newbies'!"

"Only game in town, Coyote," Tombstone replied. "They'll hold the fort for as long as they can fly. Meanwhile, I think the locals are going to be way too interested in us to worry about aircraft carriers."

"Roger that."

Tombstone checked left and right once more. VF-95 consisted now of just six aircraft, a fraction of its usual strength: Tombstone and Batman, Coyote and Shooter, Nightmare and Ramrod. All were friends, all comrades in the sharp and bitter air engagements of the past nine months. The chances were good that not all of them would make it back to the carrier when this flight was over.

For perhaps the first time, Tombstone saw the odds and *accepted* them. He remembered his decision to leave the Navy, made during a string of accidents and near-misses . . . what? Was it only three days ago? He felt as though he'd lived a lifetime since then.

He was no longer certain about that decision.

*Let me get through this fight,* he thought. *Then I'll decide. But right now, I'm needed here.*

"Viper Leader to Vipers," he called. "On my command . . . break!"

The six Tomcats of VF-95 banked right in perfect unison, angling toward the Indian fighters rising to meet them.

**1218 hours, 26 March**
**Soviet Fulcrum 515, over the Arabian Sea**

Captain Kurasov saw the lumbering aircraft's approach and felt like crying with pent-up relief.

The bomber known to NATO as the Tu-16 Badger had been a mainstay of Soviet aviation for over three decades. Large, powered by a pair of massive turbojets slung close to the roots of swept-back wings, the Badger had a combat radius of nearly 2,000 miles. Nine major variants served a variety of roles with both the Russian strategic aviation forces and the Russian navy: anti-shipping, ELINT, ECM, conventional medium bomber, reconnaissance, and tanker.

This particular variant, a Badger-A fitted out for the tanker role, had taken off from the air base at Dushanbe among the mountains north of the Afghanistan border three hours earlier. Cruising southwest at its service ceiling of forty thousand feet, it had avoided Pakistan air space by violating Iran's hostile but poorly watched Baluchistan frontier until it was over the Gulf of Oman, before turning southeast on the final leg of its 2,000 mile journey.

The decision to send the Badger had been made with uncharacteristic haste by the officers of the small Russian naval aviation staff stationed at Dushanbe. Maintained by the Department of SNA to support Russian naval forces operating in the Indian Ocean, the facility had dispatched the tanker within minutes of learning that *Kreml*'s flight deck was burning, and that no fewer than twelve of the new navalized MiG-29 fighters were aloft at the time.

By loitering over the area and conserving fuel, the MiG-29s had hoped to stay airborne until the tanker reached them. They had the endurance . . . barely. They'd used lots of fuel during their launch, and they'd not begun flying conservatively until after the cruise missile hit *Kreml* at 0859. After more than three and a half hours aloft, the MiG squadron was running on fumes.

Captain Kurasov looked at the fuel gauge on his console. Things were desperate. His squadron was down to ten now. Uritski and Denisov had run dry minutes ago. The first to launch, they'd been the first to run out of fuel with no place to land, ejecting into the sea close by the American carrier. Both men had been rescued by one of *Jefferson*'s helicopters.

That would be the fate of the rest of the MiGs soon, if they could not get refueled in time. *Kreml*'s flight deck was still a ruin of twisted metal and debris, though the fires were out now, at last report. Attempting to land on the American carrier was out of the question. There were too many technical variables, too many differences in the technology. The aircraft did not have the Americans' ILS equipment for instrument landings and didn't know how to use American signaling and course-correction techniques—"calling the ball," as they referred to it.

As a good atheist, Kurasov could not call the appearance of the tanker a godsend. But he was damned glad to see it approach. "Red Soldier, this is Tower," he said, using the call sign and frequency given him by the new Soviet air control officer on board the *Marshal Timoshenko*.

"Tower, Red Soldier. We heard you boys were thirsty. Perhaps you would like a small drink, comrades?"

Kurasov grinned. The old communist honorific "comrade" had fallen into disfavor of late among the people of the Commonwealth. Somehow, it had managed to take on an entirely new meaning among those who served in Russia's armed forces. Comrade. *Brother*.

"Indeed we would, Red Soldier. Ten baby birds with mouths open wide!"

One by one, the MiGs approached the Russian tanker in order of their fuel needs. Each would take only five hundred liters, enough to remain airborne long enough for all of them to slake their thirst in turn. Then they would go through the list again, drinking their fill.

"Tower Leader, this is Tower Three," the pilot of one of the other MiGs said.

"Go ahead, Tower Three."

"Tower Leader, we have a message from the American radar plane."

"Read it." Tower Three, a young pilot named Lavrov, was the only one of the ten pilots still in the air who spoke passable English. He'd been designated as the go-between with American traffic control.

"They say, 'Estimated ten to twelve Indian aircraft approaching from one-six-zero degrees, range eight-five kilometers. Believed to be Sea Harriers from INS *Viraat*. Intercept and destroy.'"

"'Intercept and destroy,' eh?" He chuckled. "I never thought I would be flying air cover for an American aircraft carrier!"

"*Da,* Comrade Captain. But their defeat is ours as well."

That, at least, had been the reasoning used by Fitzgerald, the American carrier Captain. Fitzgerald had been unable to promise the MiGs a place to land if they ran out of fuel . . . but he had, rather eloquently, convinced the Russian aviators that to lose the *Jefferson* would doom their own ship. If the Indians broke through, they would find the scarred and battered *Kreml* a tempting target indeed.

It all would have been a moot point if the tanker had not arrived, of course. Sometimes, the fate of whole nations hung upon the unlikely, the incredible.

Like the decision by the SNA staff at Dushanbe to dispatch the Tupolev.

Or by a Russian squadron commander to defend an American nuclear carrier.

"Agreed, Lieutenant Lavrov. Reply: 'Will redeploy when fueling is complete.' They cannot expect us to attack Indian fighters when willpower alone keeps us aloft!"

Ahead, Tower Five began maneuvering toward the refueling boom suspended from the gigantic, swept-wing Tupolev. Kurasov's orders were to cover the American ships during the strike against India. In a sense, though, he was fighting less for the Americans than for the others of the squadron. If *Jefferson* was burning, there would be few helicopters to spare for fishing wet Russians from the sea!

He hoped that there would be time.

**0150 hours, EST (1220 hours, India time), 26 March**
**Situation Room, the White House**

For Admiral Magruder, the evening had dragged by with unmerciful deliberation. It had been four hours since the first report that *Jefferson* had been struck by a missile. An hour later the communications net had gone down, and for ten suspense-filled minutes, no one in the White House or the Pentagon had known what was going on half a globe away.

Then communications had been reestablished with *Jefferson*, and Washington learned that *Vicksburg* and *Kreml* had both been badly hit.

The President had come close to ordering Mongoose aborted. Magruder knew that, had seen it in the President's face. When Captain Fitzgerald had come on the line, however, *informing* the President and the Joint Chiefs that Mongoose was still on, the admiral had watched some measure of tension ease from the President's face. "I have this problem with my field commanders," he'd said, grinning at Magruder. "They always tell their Commander in Chief what to do."

"A piratical lot, Mr. President."

"Indeed." The President and picked up a mug filled with steaming coffee, a potent brew concocted in the Secret Service office outside for just such occasions as this. "What do you think, Tom? Can they pull it off?"

"There's a chance, sir. A good one."

That had been two hours ago. The Indian aircraft had been beaten off. The catapults on *Jefferson* had been repaired.

Now the strike force was over Highway 101, wreaking a special kind of hell on the Indian supply lines.

Members of the National Security Council had been coming and going all evening, most working in offices within the NSC complex in the White House basement. Victor Marlowe walked in, a folder in his hand. "Mr. President? These just came in from NPIC." He glanced uncertainly at Magruder. "I . . . thought you'd better see them."

"Do you want me to leave, Mr. President?"

"They're T-K clearance, sir," Marlowe said.

"That's okay, Tom," the President said. "Just excuse me a moment, will you?"

Magruder sat back, watching as the President leafed through what appeared to be a series of photographs. NPIC, Magruder knew, was the National Photographic Interpretation Center, the agency tasked with processing and producing photo intelligence from America's chain of reconnaissance satellites. T-K, short for "Talent-Keyhole," was the level of clearance necessary just to look at some of the photo imagery possible with the new breed of KH-12 satellites now in orbit. Magruder had heard the stories of reading newspapers over a man's shoulder from two hundred miles up. Ridiculous, of course.

And yet . . .

"Oh my God."

"Mr. President?"

The President looked up, his face ashen. He looked first at Magruder, then at Marlowe. "These were taken when?"

"Within the hour, sir. These are rushes. The tapes and the finished processing are on their way over now."

"Mr. President," Magruder said. "Perhaps I'd better wait outside while you—"

"He's got T-K clearance, Vic. Now. Damn it, I *need* him!"

"Of course, sir."

The President slid a photograph across the conference table to Magruder. He picked it up, careful not to touch the glossy finish.

It looked like a black-and-white photograph taken, perhaps, from the roof of a building. Several men in obviously military uniforms were gathered around a bulky, oblong something partly blocked by the wing of an aircraft.

Magruder squinted at the part of the plane he could see. "It looks like an Air Force Falcon," he said.

"Very good, Admiral," Marlowe said. "An F-16 Fighting Falcon. But it's not Air Force. Not *our* air force, at any rate."

Magruder looked at the photo again. "Pakistan."

"Bingo," Marlowe said. "The weapon being loaded onto that aircraft is a fair imitation of a B57 five- to ten-kiloton atomic bomb."

"My God in heaven."

"Why now?" Magruder asked. "In the middle of—"

"The battle has drawn Indian planes south." Marlowe said quickly. "Stripped their defenses. The Pakistanis probably see this as their one chance to get something in without having it be shot down."

The President gestured toward the picture. "Where is this?"

"That was taken at a PAF base outside of Bahawalpur from one hundred seventy-five miles up," Marlowe explained. "I have ground sources checking over there now, getting more data. I expect to hear more shortly."

"I want to hear it the second you do, Vic. The *second*."

"Yes, sir."

The President took the photo from Magruder and stared at it. "Damn them," he said. "*Damn* them!"

"I thought the Pakistanis promised to hold back on this," Magruder said.

"Promised?" The President's fist hit the desk. "You're damn right they promised! Assurances were given—"

"They are fighting for their survival," Marlowe said. He shrugged. "Or it may be a bluff. Another 'message.'"

"I'll give them a *message,*" the President said. "And her name is the *Thomas Jefferson.*" He looked at Magruder. "It seems, Admiral, that we must assume that the Pakistanis are loading an atomic device aboard one of their aircraft . . . and that they intend to use it."

"Yes, sir."

The President was quiet for a long moment. He rose from his chair, walked to the window, and stared for a time out across the Rose Garden, at the street lights of nighttime Washington. "Vic," he said at last. "I might have something we can try. Who do you have on tap at the American Embassy in New Delhi? Fast? I need to get a message passed on to the right person over there."

"I think I have the man, Mr. President."

The President turned to Magruder. "And I think now we're going to need your people more than ever now."

# CHAPTER 28

**1225 hours, 26 March**
**Intruder 500, west of Naya Chor**

Lieutenant Commander Greene held the stick steady as warm air currents above the desert set the A-6 Intruder to bumping and shuddering. They were traveling at 400 knots, less than 500 feet above the hot gravel of the Thar Desert.

"Gold Strike Five-double-oh," he called. "Coming up on Point Charlie. The clock is running."

"Copy, Gold Strike, Five-double-oh," the airborne controller on board the Hawkeye circling a hundred miles to the south replied. "Roger your Point Charlie. Good hunting, Jolly!"

"Roger, Victor Tango. Thanks. Five-double-nuts out."

Point Charlie was the village of Naya Chor itself, a collection of whitewashed walls and low buildings sprawled along the straight slash through the desert, marking the railroad and highway that crossed the Thar Desert from Jodhpur in India to Hyderabad on the banks of the Indus. Jolly banked the Intruder left, following the road that, in most places, was nothing more sophisticated than packed gravel.

Smoke curled into the sky from the wreckage of a vehicle close beside the railroad tracks. To Jolly's experienced eye, it looked like a ZSU with most of the broad, open turret peeled back like a steel-petaled flower. Nearby was the broken ruin of an SA-3 Goa launcher, the six-wheeled utility truck upended in the gravel and overturned by a near miss from an air-to-ground rocket. It was evident that Lucky Strike had passed through the area minutes before, smashing anything that looked like a SAM battery or antiaircraft vehicle.

Desert sped past on either side as the Intruder raced west.

"Gold Strike Five-zero-zero, this is Five-one-one." That was Coot Barswell, another member of VA-89.

"Copy, Coot. Go ahead."

"We're on your six, Jolly, range five miles. Save some of the good stuff for us, will ya?"

"Eat our dust, Coot!" He laughed. "No guarantees!" He switched to ICS, necessary for clarity even though his BN was sitting right beside him. "How we doin', Chucker?"

"Range to primary, twelve miles," Chucker replied. "I'm getting some ground radar now."

"The primary" had been spotted by recon satellite at dawn, an enormous ground convoy moving west along the highway toward Naya Chor. It had passed the village earlier that morning, and by now was well on the way to Hyderabad, where Indian and Pakistani forces were gearing up for a major battle. Much of the convoy had been hidden by clouds of dust, but the satellite's infrared scanners had suggested that the convoy included as many as thirty or forty large trucks: huge Maz-537 flatbed trailers with tanks and heavy equipment, smaller trucks with ammunition and troops, and the all-important tankers carrying fuel or water.

The threat light blinked on, and Jolly heard the warning tone of an enemy lock-on.

"SAM!" Chucker warned. "I see it! Two o'clock low!"

Jolly glanced right and saw it, a white streak rising from the desert. The Hornets could not possibly have suppressed *all* of the SAM sites and launchers.

He pressed the chaff button five times in rapid succession and eased the stick forward, letting the Intruder settle closer to the ground, but he kept the strike aircraft steadily on course. As the chaff clouds expanded above and behind the plane, the threat warning stopped its incessant chirping.

"I think we lost 'em." Jolly's mouth was dry, his heart hammering against his seat harness. He kept one eye on the missile as it rose past the starboard wing, traveling at Mach 3 a mile away.

His BN was leaning forward now, his face buried in the hood that shrouded his radar scope. "I've got a lock. Solid return . . . some serious heavy metal up there. Looks like the convoy. Come left a bit . . . more . . . there! Hold it!"

Chucker flipped a switch and Jolly's VDI screen shifted to Attack Mode. Graphic symbols drifted across the display, outlining possible targets illuminated by the Intruder's radar, showing position, drift angle, and steering corrections. Numbers flickered off the last few thousands of meters to the release point. Speed was 490 knots.

"Going up," Jolly reported. He nudged the Intruder back up to five hundred feet, the minimum distance required for arming a Mark 82 General Purpose bomb.

"Gettin' close," Chucker reported. "Your pickle is hot."

Jolly closed his thumb over the release switch, his eye on the targeting pipper on his VDI. The Intruder could be set to release its weapons load by computer, but in a case like this, when the target was strung out over a large area and of unknown composition, Jolly preferred to release manually. A surging, exultant excitement gripped him. Any second now . . .

Suddenly, the empty desert below was transformed into a nightmare out of the Los Angeles Freeway. Trucks, half-tracks, troop carriers, and tanks were crowded on the road or parked alongside. Ahead, the girders of a bridge stretched above the banks of the Nara River.

"Gold Strike Five-double-oh!" Jolly cried. "Bombs away!"

The A-6 Intruder could carry a maximum ordnance load of 15,000 pounds—in this case thirty 500-lb Mark 82 GP bombs. It never failed to amaze Jolly that, during World War II, the immortal B-17 had carried a maximum bomb load of only 17,600 pounds . . . and that was only for extremely short-range missions. *Typical* mission ordnance loads for the old Flying Fortress were only 4000 pounds, less than a third of what the Intruder carried.

And the A-6 Intruder could place its high-explosive eggs with far greater precision than the B-17 ever could, and from an altitude of only a few hundred feet.

Thirty quarter-ton bombs spilled away from the Intruder's hardpoints, a spray of deadly, finned cigars triggered to release in five groups of six along an elongated footprint across the center of the convoy. The retarder fins on each were designed to hold the bomb back just long enough to allow the A-6 to escape the fragments.

The bridge flashed below the A-6 as Jolly pulled back on the stick. There was heavy congestion on the bridge itself, probably brought on by a breakdown or a traffic accident that had held up the whole column. He almost imagined he could hear the honking of horns, the curses of the drivers. . . .

The detonations were like the flashes of a string of Chinese firecrackers, but silent . . . at least at first. Then the sound caught up with the speeding Intruder, an avalanche of raw, searing, booming noise, thunderclap upon thunderclap rolling across the desert on shock waves that rippled out from the blasts, driving walls of swirling sand before them. Jolly watched the display in his rearview mirror, thirty blasts in the space of less than two seconds. Black smoke, boiling orange fireballs rising like deadly trees, a pall of burning clouds spreading across the desert in a suffocating blanket.

And the explosions continued. White streamers curled out from the epicenter of destruction, flares like Roman candles. An ammunition truck had been hit . . . and the explosion added to the devastation that was hurling entire trucks, flaming and tumbling end for end, into the sky.

"My God," Jolly said, awe softening his voice. "My God . . ."

"Gold Strike Leader, this is Five-one-one. God, Jolly, what are you doing up there? Looks like you just trashed the whole Indian army."

"Uh . . . rog, Coot." He felt none of the earlier urge to banter. "Save your load for the bridge. It's . . . easy pickings."

"Copy that, Jolly. Thanks. Oh, God look at them *burn*!"

With the drag from the bomb load gone, the A-6 was racing now at almost 600 knots. Antiaircraft fire, scattered and ineffective, was reaching toward him from various sites among the marshes and canals that marked the western edge of the desert. A pair of ZSU-23s that had already crossed the river swung quad-mounted cannons toward the sky and stabbed at them as they hurtled past overhead.

"We're outa here, Chucker," he said. The elation he'd felt before was gone. "Job's over. Let's go home."

The Intruder banked left, heading south once more.

**1235 hours, 26 March**
**Tomcat 200**

Tombstone broke left, bleeding speed with his air brakes until his F-14's computer brought the swing wings forward. At less than two hundred fifty knots, he held the turn, left wing pointed at the blur of golden sand below, right wing pointed at the heavens.

"He's still coming!" Hitman called. "Stoney, he's still coming!"

Tombstone hadn't gotten close enough to see the MiG-29's number, but he had a strange feeling he was facing that same Indian pilot who had come close to killing him more than once already. It was a coincidence . . . but a small one. Good pilots survived longer than bad ones in the tangle of modern aerial combat . . . and good pilots tended to seek one another out in the closest thing the twentieth century had to a Medieval joust, knight against knight.

The insistent chirp of his radar threat warning sounded in his headset. "Tombstone! He's locked! He's going to take his shot!"

"Hang on, Hitman! Just a little further around . . ."

"Launch! Stoney! He's launched!"

"Chaff!"

"Chaff away!"

He'd deliberately gone into a hard, slow-speed turn directly across the Indian MiG's line of fire, hoping the other man would fire despite the difficult angle. Picturing the radar-homer's path in his mind, Tombstone waited another three beats . . . then rammed the stick back to the right, breaking into a hard split-S. His left hand hit the wing control override, folding the wings back to the sixty-eight degree combat sweep, then slammed the throttles forward to Zone Five burner. The roar of the twin engines kicked him in the spine like a sledgehammer, driving the breath from his lungs.

Tunnel vision closed in. His HUD readout showed seven Gs . . . eight . . . *nine* . . . !

His whole body hurt, and speech, even breathing, was impossible. He knew he was on the thin, ragged edge of blacking out, but he held the turn as his compass reading spun through the numbers . . . one-*ninety* . . . two *hundred* . . . two-*ten* . . .

The threat warning was off. The enemy missile had been decoyed by the chaff . . . or simply missed, unable to correct for Tombstone's wild maneuver.

And then the other plane was ahead, crossing from left to right with his belly facing Tombstone's F-14. The Indian MiG had held his own left turn a hair too long and was still in the break. Tombstone had snapped around in the unexpected maneuver and slid into position for a launch. It was a tough shot . . . as tough as the one the Indian flyer had tried a moment earlier.

Blinking against blurred vision, *willing* the pain in his throbbing head to subside, Tombstone dropped his targeting pipper across the MiG. No . . . too close, even for Sidewinders. He would have to go for guns.

The Indian was rolling toward him now . . . had seen him, less than a thousand yards away. Tombstone turned to keep with him, letting the target reticle lead the MiG.

Tombstone's sharp eyes picked out the hull number: 401.

He also spotted something else. There were no missiles slung beneath the MiG's wings. The radar-homer he'd just popped at Tombstone had been his last one. Possibly there'd not been time to rearm when he'd landed earlier. Or possibly he'd loosed five of his six AAMs earlier in the fight.

MiG and Tomcat closed with one another. At two hundred yards, Tombstone could see the other pilot, his helmet visor back. He was making no effort to escape but was watching Tombstone's approach with what could only be described as professional interest.

The guy knew Tombstone had him and was waiting to die.

Tombstone shook his head. What was it Army had always said. *Chivalry gets you dead.*

True enough, and the MiG pilot still had his cannon. Still, there came a time when there was simply no point in further slaughter. The Indian MiG pilot was an *opponent* now, not an enemy . . . and there was a sharp difference between the two. Tombstone waggled his wings in salute . . . then broke left, passing behind the other plane close enough to feel the shudder of his jet stream.

"Hey, Hitman? Hitman! Are you still with me?"

There was no response over the ICS. The nine-G turn had knocked his RIO out.

"Viper Leader, Viper Leader, this is Victor Tango One-one."

Tombstone jumped, wondering if the Hawkeye controller had spotted his rather unprofessional breach.

"Victor Tango, this is Viper Leader. Go ahead."

"Viper Leader, please give stores listing, over."

Stores? "Uh, roger, Victor Tango." He switched the VDI display to his stores listing and read them off, not trusting to memory in his current, somewhat battle-fogged state. "Two AIM-9Js, two AIM-54s. Six hundred seventy-five rounds."

He'd taken off with two Phoenix, one Sparrow, and four Sidewinder missiles. They'd already launched the Sparrow and two Sidewinders. What was Victor Tango One-one looking for?

"We copy you have two Phoenix missiles, Viper Leader. What about your squadron?"

Three of the other five Tomcats still had AIM-54 Phoenix missiles on board. Shooter and Ramrod had both already fired both of their Phoenix missiles, while Coyote still had his two and Nightmare and Batman each had one left.

"Viper Leader, we copy you have six missiles remaining in your squadron."

"That's a roger," Tombstone replied.

"Hey, Stoney?" Hitman said over the ICS circuit. "What the hell's goin' on?"

"Wish I knew, Hitman. Orders."

"Viper Leader, we have a new target for you. Ah . . . be advised that this is an extremely hazardous target . . . but it is also extremely important. *Extremely* important."

"Give us the vector."

"Roger. Come to new heading zero-four-zero at angels base plus thirty-nine. Make your speed five-five-zero knots. Do you copy that?"

"Copy. Zero-four-zero at five-five-zero knots, angels base plus three-niner."

"Hold that course and speed for fourteen, that's one-four minutes."

"Roger. Fourteen minutes."

"Endpoint is designated Point Lima. Your target will be at extreme Phoenix range at that time, bearing zero-zero-zero to zero-one-zero."

Tombstone was doing some fast calculations in his head. He reached down to the clipboard on his thigh and shuffled through the papers and checklists, exposing a map of northwest India.

Their current location was north of Highway 101, close to the Indian-Pakistan border and thirty miles from a border town called Gadra. He used the stub of a pencil to lightly sketch in lines. Point Lima, if he'd followed the instructions of the Hawkeye controller right, was deep within the Thar Desert, just south of the Rajasthan Canal. The closest settlement marked on the map was a village called Bikampur. He measured north one hundred nautical miles—the approximate range of a Phoenix missile. The end point was across the border into Pakistan, somewhere near a nondescript town called Fort Abbas.

"Okay, Victor Tango. I've got all that. Uh . . . we may have a problem, though." He was staring at his fuel gauge. "Fuel state eight point five."

They'd used a lot of JP-5 in the dogfighting over the border. Now the Hawkeye controller was telling them to fly another one hundred thirty miles inland. Then, from Point Lima, it would be almost four hundred *more* long desert miles before they were back over the Arabian Sea.

Well over five hundred miles before they could refuel, or even before they could eject with any hope of being picked up by friendly forces. They might just make it . . . but it would be damned tight.

"Copy your fuel state, Viper. I repeat, target is extremely important."

He sighed. "Roger, Victor Tango. How many missiles will target require, over?"

"Estimate four, Viper."

But he already knew he would have to take all six aircraft, just to make sure that at least four AIM-54s made it to Point Lima.

And God help their fuel state if they were forced to dogfight along the way. "Okay, Victor Tango One-one. That's roger. Viper Squadron is in." He swung the Tomcat onto its new heading, the other five F-14s matching the maneuver.

The dun and barren wastes of the Thar Desert flashed past beneath them as they accelerated, climbing toward fifty thousand feet.

# CHAPTER 29

**1235 hours, 26 March**
**Blue King Leader**

The Sea Harriers had been stalking their prey, traveling slowly and at low altitude in an attempt to lose themselves in the radar clutter at the surface of the ocean. The waves that had been so high and powerful earlier had dwindled, and the sea was relatively calm.

But Lieutenant Tahliani knew that death was near.

They'd first been challenged by an American frigate, one of the escorts that formed the picket line of ships around the American fleet, and had detoured far out of their way to evade it. Standard missiles had arced through the sky, locking onto the Harriers as they scattered, spewing chaff. One aircraft—Chani's—had been hit, the missile's warhead blasting it apart. A second—young Prakash Garbyal's—had flown into the sea while trying to evade the American missile that had locked onto him.

And now, like raptor birds circling above their prey, the Russian MiGs were stooping on the Sea Harriers from above.

The American carrier was less than sixty kilometers away . . . close enough! Admiral Ramesh might have vowed vengeance against the American and Russian forces . . . but the fight was over. *Over!* India had thrown everything she could muster at the invaders off her shores, and the result had only served to weaken her in the fight against the *real* enemy, Pakistan.

"Blue King Leader to Blue King," he radioed. "All aircraft . . . lock on primary target and launch missiles!"

He had already let his payload "see" the target and store it in its mindless memory. His thumb came down on the firing trigger.

"Blue King Leader! Launch! Launch! Enemy missiles . . ."

He saw the telltale blips of enemy missiles sprinkled across his own VDI. There wasn't much time left now.

He pressed the trigger and felt his Sea Harrier leap as the pair of Sea Eagle missiles dropped away, one following the other.

Within seconds, a spread of twenty missiles were racing toward the *Jefferson,* now thirty-six miles away.

**1241 hours, 26 March**
**Soviet Fulcrum 515, Over the Arabian Sea**

"They have launched antiship cruise missiles," Kurasov said. "Lavrov! Call the Americans. Warn them.

"*Da,* Captain."

He was already plunging through the sky toward the sea, adding power to his paired Tumansky R-33D turbofans as he brought his nose up, following the Indian missiles. The electronics of his cockpit suite were as sophisticated as any in the West. Course, range, and elevation flashed onto his HUD in precisely lettered Cyrillic characters. He locked on. . . .

Captain Kurasov carried six AA-10s slung beneath his wings. Code-named Alamo by NATO, the AA-10 had been designed for use with the MiG-29 but had not been part of the various arms packages sold to India. Kurasov's ordnance load consisted of all radar-seekers, with look-down/shoot-down lock-on capability that let him target the speeding Indian missile.

In his headset he heard the warble of target acquisition.

"*Strelyat!*" he yelled, calling to no one in particular. "Fire!"

His thumb closed on the firing switch, and an AA-10 speared from beneath his wing. He shifted his aim, locking onto a second missile.

"*Strelyat!*"

**1242 hours, 26 March**
**CIC, U.S.S. *Thomas Jefferson***

"We have missiles inbound, Captain," Commander Barnes announced. "The Hawkeyes have a good plot . . . at least twenty missiles, range thirty miles. Our Russian friends just alerted us."

Captain Fitzgerald nodded. "What do we have that can reach them?"

"*Kearny* is in a good position, sir. So's the *Winslow*. They'll take out some along the way with Standard missiles. We can begin launching Sea Sparrow in another . . ." He checked his watch. "About two minutes, sir."

"Very well. Defenses on automatic."

"Aye, sir."

Fitzgerald watched the battle board, the pattern of blips closing on *Jefferson*'s position. Strange . . . but he'd never gotten used to fighting a battle *this* way. In the cockpit of an F-4 Phantom, with SAMs lighting up the sky and MiGs turning and burning all around, yes . . . but this sterile, button-pushing war of nerve and waiting . . .

**1242 hours, 26 March**
**U.S.S. *Lawrence Kearny***

The *Kearny* was an Arleigh Burke-class guided missile destroyer (DDG). One of the newest ships in the U.S. inventory, she was equipped with the SPY-1 radar and was intended to supplement the Ticonderoga-class Aegis cruisers. Her primary weapons were two sets of Mark 41 Vertical Launch Systems set into her forward and after decks, loaded with Standard SM-2(MR) SAMs and Tomahawk cruise missiles.

Her SPY-1 had been tracking the missile flight for several minutes already, their course and speed fed into the ship's CIC computers.

Missiles broke from *Kearny*'s deck, fore and aft, in clouds of white smoke, and a shower of plastic shavings blasted from the protective covers of the Mark 41s. Guided by the Aegis computer system on board, the Standard SAMs accelerated into the sky, locked onto their targets, and descended.

**1243 hours, 26 March**
**Russian Fulcrum 515**

The last of his AA-10s left the launch rail on a trail of flame. ''*Strelyat!*'' He'd winnowed twenty cruise missiles down to sixteen and perhaps given the *Jefferson* a fighting chance.

But any closer and he would risk being downed himself by American point defenses. He pulled back on the Fulcrum's stick, arcing into the sky.

Across the water, a battle raged as Russian Fulcrums engaged Indian Sea Harriers. Magic missiles and AA-10s stabbed and twisted. A Harrier disintegrated as it banked too low, catching one wingtip in the sea.

Vectoring in high and behind an enemy Sea Harrier, Kurasov lined up the gun reticle on his HUD with the Indian aircraft's cockpit. At four hundred knots, he closed slowly, until the enemy plane filled his sights . . . an easy kill. His thumb closed on the firing button. . . .

The Indian plane was no longer there! Bewildered, the Soviet pilot pulled up, looking left and right as the MiG flashed past the spot where the Sea Harrier *should* have been. Too late, he caught the flash of wings in his rearview mirror. He'd forgotten that maneuver, that impossible maneuver that Harrier pilots called viffing. . . .

And now the Sea Harrier was squarely behind him, a Magic AAM sliding off its wingtip rail. . . .

The missile's detonation kicked the Fulcrum over, crumpling one wing and shredding the hull. The fireball lit up the sky three miles south of the *Kearny*. The sailors on the DDG's deck, not knowing the identity of the target, cheered wildly and tossed their white hats in the air.

*Jefferson*'s CIWS and short-ranged Sea Sparrows began marking down the remaining Sea Eagle missiles.

None hit the carrier, but the officers in CIC were subdued. They knew one of their own had fallen to hostile fire.

**1244 hours, 26 March**
**Ministry of Defense, New Delhi**

Defense Minister Kuldip Sundarji sat alone in his office, the latest stack of reports before him. The information was fragmentary. The Americans had an annoying habit of shooting down reconnaissance and communications aircraft as quickly as the Indians could put them up. Despite this, there was no question in his mind at all.

India was losing the battle.

The losses so far had been horrifying. Fifty-seven aircraft confirmed shot down, and as many more might never fly again. Reports of air losses were still coming in as the American strike force thundered over the western frontier. The last bold stroke by a Sea Harrier squadron had not achieved a single hit. The most recent report on his desk was from the young navy lieutenant, Tahliani. He and four other Sea Harriers were en route for Kathiawar. The others had been shot down in a dogfight with Russian MiGs.

*Russian* MiGs! He put his face in his hand. So much had depended on the inevitable friction between Russian and American commanders. Somehow, the enemy factions had managed to work together, something Sundarji had thought impossible.

The Bombay naval squadron had been stopped cold. *Kalikata* was sinking, and both *Viraat* and *Vikrant* were limping into port. Damage was so bad that they'd not yet been able to recover Admiral Ramesh's body. He thought of the dark, intense naval officer etched by the pain of his dead son, wondering if he'd found peace before he died.

So much suffering.

The telephone on his desk buzzed, and he stared at it. An earlier message had warned him to expect the call, and he'd been able to guess much when he learned who the caller would be. He had to will himself to pick up the receiver.

"Sundarji," he said.

He listened to the voice on the other end for a long while. "You're sure of your information?" he finally asked. "Yes, I suppose you would be. I . . . I agree. There is no other way."

He listened some more. "I cannot speak for my government," he said. "I will see what I can do with the Air Ministry. I have some small influence there." He allowed himself a smile. "Or at least, I did before this morning."

He hung up without ceremony, thought for several minutes, then picked up the phone again. "Get me the Air Ministry," he said. "Quickly. There is little time."

**1259 hours, 26 March**
**Tomcat 200**

They had reached the point on Tombstone's map, twenty-five miles southeast of Bikampur. The desert nine and a half miles below was barren and trackless, though sun flashed from the waters of the Rajasthan Canal far to the west.

Tombstone moved the stick experimentally. Fifty thousand feet was close to the Tomcat's service ceiling, and the controls had a tendency to mush somewhat at that altitude.

No problems so far. For the last five or ten minutes, they'd seen no Indian aircraft anywhere . . . a fact that Tombstone found strange. The F-14s must be registering on Indian ground radar. Where were the IAF interceptors?

There was nothing. They seemed to have the sky to themselves. The other F-14s in the squadron were spread across the sky, three groups of two traveling north at Mach .7. "Okay, Hitman. Whatcha got?"

"Not much, Tombstone," his RIO replied. "Pretty lonely out . . . hold it. Got them! Bearing three-five-nine, range . . . make it one hundred two nautical miles. Four targets, heading east at four hundred fifty knots."

"Rog. Feed it to me here."

His VDI showed the targets painted in the F-14's AWG-9 beam.

"Victor Tango One-one, this is Viper. We have reached Point Lima. We have four bogies, bearing now . . . zero-zero-zero. Due north. Range one-oh-two."

"Roger, Viper. That is your target. Take them down."

"Copy, Victor Tango. Wait one."

Time seemed suspended in the cold, thin air almost ten miles above the Thar Desert. Tombstone, Batman, and Coyote readied their Phoenix missiles for launch. Shooter, Ramrod, and Nightmare flew cover for the others. Tombstone and Coyote would loose four missiles. Batman would hold his single Phoenix in reserve.

What were those targets? Judging from their course, they were flying on a straight line from Bahawalpur, a Pakistani city located on the northern fringes of the Thar Desert about seventy miles from the border. He sketched a line across his map, extending their flight path. The four bogies were flying across fairly empty territory. There was very little of importance along their course. Villages, mostly: Fort Abbas, Mahajan, Rajgarh . . .

Tombstone's pencil stopped on a city and his blood turned cold. He thought now that he knew what those targets were, where they were going . . . and why.

"Vipers, Viper Leader," he said. "On my command, launch AIM-54s." He studied the VDI screen again. There were no other targets. The Indian air defenses must have been drawn to the south by *Jefferson*'s strike against the Jodhpur Road.

The Tomcats were far beyond the detection range of the aircraft they were stalking. Targets were already selected, locked in. . . .

"Fire!"

Two RIOs, Hitman and Radar, stabbed their fire control buttons, reset, then fired again. The heavy Phoenix missiles fell through cold, thin air, then ignited. One missile, for reasons unknown, failed to light, and Malibu loosed his remaining Phoenix from Tomcat 216.

At Mach 5, it took them less than two minutes to travel the 102 nautical miles to their targets, which were just crossing the border into India.

All hit.

**0745 hours EST (1815 hours, Indian time), 26 March**
**White House Press Room**

The reporters had been gathering in the Press Room since the wee hours of the morning, as word circulated through Washington news circles that a major break in the Indian Ocean crisis had occurred. As early as three a.m., word had gone out over the wire services that the President would hold a major press conference at eight o'clock, timed to coordinate with the various morning news shows.

Admiral Magruder searched for a particular face among the sea of reporters, cameramen, and assistants. White House technicians were still adjusting the lighting, and the room was a tumble of confusion and noise as journalists and reporters traded notes and guesses.

He saw her.

It took a moment to attract her attention, but perhaps she remembered where he'd been standing before and looked his way deliberately. Pamela Drake saw him, nodded, and began making her way across the room toward where he was standing.

"Good morning, Miss Drake."

"It's Pamela," she said. "Admiral, I should probably apologize—"

"Nonsense." He kept his voice low, unwilling to steal the President's thunder by giving anything away to other reporters who might be within earshot. "Listen, I just wanted to tell you. He's safe."

"Matt . . . ?"

Magruder nodded. "They're all back aboard *Jefferson.* The battle group left Turban Station about two hours ago."

Her eyes widened. "Then there *was* a raid! The rumors have been flying in this town all night—"

"I think I'd better let you get the details from the President," Magruder said. "But I wanted you to know that Matt is safe. Captain Fitzgerald called me personally to let me know."

She let out a pent-up breath. "Is it . . . over then? He won't be going back?"

Magruder relented somewhat. "India has requested a cease-fire," he whispered. "Pakistan has agreed to meet with them in Geneva. The battle group did take some heavy damage, so the President has ordered them to return. *Ike* and *Nimitz* will be taking *Jefferson*'s place in the Arabian Sea, just to make certain the cease-fire holds. But yes . . . it's over."

"Thank God."

"You'd better get back to your seat. We'll talk more later, if you like."

"Thank you, Admiral. I would."

He watched her make her way back across the room. There

was a lot the President would not be telling her and her peers within the press community. Like how close India and Pakistan had just come to nuclear war.

Or how close Tombstone and his squadron had been to running out of fuel high above the Thar Desert when they'd finally rendezvoused with a KA-6D tanker from the *Jefferson.* The way the admiral had heard it, Tombstone had waited until the other five aircraft refueled, one after the other, before taking his turn. If he'd missed spearing the fuel probe basket, he wouldn't have made it. It was *that* close.

But necessary.

He wondered if India's Minister of Defense shared the relief he felt now. It had been the President's idea to call the man directly, knowing that he held a unique liaison position between New Delhi's government and the military. It was the President who'd convinced him, first, that India could not possibly continue its war against Pakistan with their supply line savaged by the A-6 strike, and second, that a PAF flight was already en route to New Delhi with atomic bombs slung from their undercarriages.

There'd been no time to consult with the government. In another forty minutes, India's government would have ceased to exist. But he, and he alone, had been in a position to stop the war.

It was Sundarji who had ordered the IAF to stand down, to clear the skies for aircraft the U.S. already had in the skies above the Thar Desert. By shooting down the Pakistani planes, the President had proven America's determination to stop the conflict from going nuclear. By grounding his aircraft, Sundarji had shown his good faith. At that, it had been a risky gamble. Sundarji might have insisted on scrambling every interceptor he had in the New Delhi area. But *one* of those Falcons might have gotten through, and the Indian planes had nothing like Phoenix. They would have had to get close to make a kill, "knife-fighting distance" as Navy aviators liked to phrase it.

Sundarji had been convinced. Stay clear, and let the Tomcats shoot the bogies down. They had.

And with India's defeat in the Arabian Sea, suddenly there was no further reason to continue the war.

Magruder hoped Sundarji would survive the political turmoil that was certain to follow. A career at the Pentagon would seem peaceful by comparison. But Sundarji combined political professionalism and savvy with a realistic view of things as they were . . . an unusual and refreshing combination in government, from what Magruder had seen so far.

"Ladies and gentlemen, the President of the United States."

Magruder turned to watch his Commander in Chief walk onto the stage, as applause burst from the audience in a thunderous roar.

The President was about to announce the end to a war that had never officially begun.

# EPILOGUE

**0930 hours EST, 16 April**
**Chesapeake Bay, the approaches to Hampton Roads**

Tombstone leaned against the safety railing on Vulture's Row, high atop *Jefferson*'s island, unashamedly straining to see like any rubbernecking tourist. He was not alone. Every sailor and officer who could squeeze onto the narrow walkway beneath the carrier's billboard-sized radar antennae was there, and thousands more were on the flight deck below.

Ahead, the Hampton Roads Bridge stretched across the horizon, from Hampton on the right to Norfolk on the left. He could see the buildings of Virginia Beach to the south, beyond the gray shape and green wake of the *Lawrence Kearny.*

The water on every side of the carrier was crowded with small craft, sailboats, cabin cruisers, fireboats, vessels of every size and shape and description out on a glorious April day to welcome America's most famous nuclear aircraft carrier.

The decision had been made early on to send *Jefferson* home by the Atlantic route, sparing her jury-rigged hull repairs the uncertainties of a long Pacific crossing. They would be putting into Norfolk's shipyards for repairs, and the whole crew was looking forward to reunions with families ashore. The Navy had taken care of all of the arrangements for bringing families across the country from California, a logistical evolution as complex as anything in the Indian Ocean.

Of course, sailors with girlfriends or fiancées were out of luck, for the most part. The Navy recognized only legal dependents. But they too would be reunited soon enough. *Jefferson*'s Exec had already announced that leave and liberty policy would be fairly relaxed for the next few weeks. It would be a while before *Jefferson* went to sea again.

A siren sounded across the water, then another. Other sailors and officers on Vulture's Row on either side of Tombstone began cheering, waving their hats in response to the salutes from the water. The terror, the uncertainties of the Indian Ocean seemed forgotten.

Tombstone wondered if it had been worth it. So many were not coming back from the Arabian Sea. Army Garrison and Dixie. Over two hundred men aboard the *Kreml,* which had limped back to its Black Sea port two weeks after the battle. Thirty of *Vicksburg*'s men, including their Captain. Tombstone had attended the memorial services held for them in the Med. The *Vickie* was still at Naples, where she'd steamed slowly into port under her own power.

That Russian pilot, Captain Ivan Andreivich Kurasov, had been honored by a multinational service at sea. He'd died trying to save the American carrier, in what had to be one of the most ironic twists of the entire history of rivalry between the U.S. and Russian navies.

And Admiral Vaughn. Charles Lee Vaughn had died within an hour after arriving in *Jefferson*'s sick bay, that morning off the coast of Kathiawar. Tombstone still wasn't sure what he thought of the man. He'd made some undeniable blunders . . . but it looked like the Navy Department had already determined that he was the hero of the Arabian Sea, the strategist who single-handedly had fought superior Indian air and naval forces, and won.

Tombstone wondered how many of the established facts of history were like that, battles won through blunders and ignorance, and painted over later by the politicians and diplomats.

The paint job was still going on. The latest word from Geneva was that a formal peace was being hammered out between India and her neighbor. Tombstone didn't know how that was going to work out and, in fact, didn't really care. CBG-14 had done its part to bring them to the peace table, and that was enough. The word in VF-95's Ready Room was that the Indians had lost heavily in the raid at the Nara Bridge. While not irreplaceable, the supplies destroyed by the Intruders' bombs, the bridges knocked out by laser-guided missiles and special ordnance, had set back their timetable for an assault on Karachi by at least two weeks.

And after one particular incident in the skies above the Thar Desert, they knew that they did not have two weeks to spare.

Had those four aircraft, identified in satellite photos as Pakistani F-16s, been carrying nukes? The Indians weren't talking—they'd cordoned off the crash sites—and neither were the Pakistanis. Odds were they had been, and that Tombstone and the survivors of his squadron had saved a large percentage of the six million people living in New Delhi. It was estimated that a ten-kiloton nuclear warhead would have killed at least half a million people in the crowded Indian capital, and made millions homeless.

The whole story might never be known. The world's leaders were not eager to broadcast how close to tragedy the planet had come. It was interesting, though, that a U.S. Navy supercarrier, long seen in some quarters as a blatant symbol of American militarism, had in fact been responsible for preventing a nuclear war.

And that, of course, had been the understanding implicit in their design all along. With the decline of what had been the Soviet Union as a world power, the world was becoming more dangerous, not less. Iraq, North Korea, Thailand, and now India and Pakistan had all proven that. More and more countries that had been tribal states warring with their neighbors a generation ago were learning how to acquire or build nuclear weapons. Tombstone had heard that there were backroom talks underway now in both Washington and Moscow, talks that might lead to some kind of permanent multinational peacekeeping force organized along the lines of the joint Russian-American task force that had brought peace to the Indian Ocean.

Maybe the world needed a strong-armed policeman for the next decade or two . . . just until its more boisterous inhabitants grew up.

Whatever happened, Tombstone knew he'd found his place. He reached up to his jacket's breast pocket and touched the folded letter there that had been delivered by a COD Greyhound in the mid-Atlantic. *"My darling Matt! I can't wait to see you again. I'll be waiting for you on the dock in Norfolk when you come in. . . ."*

She was waiting for him.

And Tombstone *still* didn't know if he and Pamela had a future together. He'd deliberately not discussed his decision in his letters to her. Better to have it out face-to-face, when he saw her again. He hoped she would still have him . . . but Matthew Magruder knew now that he was a Navy aviator, that he had a *place* here . . . and that it was important.

His orders had already come through. He was being reassigned to Washington. And after that . . . well, there would be a chance at a CAG slot, maybe even aboard the *Jefferson* when Commander Marusko moved on to his own command. It was a bright future, a *good* future, and one that he was willing to fight for.

United Airlines seemed far less attractive now, now that he knew that he'd made a difference, he and Batman and Coyote and the other members of VF-95.

Tombstone hoped that she would understand.

He *belonged.*

## *SPECIAL PREVIEW!*

Introducing a brand new action series that takes you speeding across the nuclear-ravaged highways of America . . .

# STORMRIDER

Ride fast. Fight hard. Die free.

*Here is a special excerpt from this incredible adventure series—available from Jove Books . . .*

The clouds were white wisps, like the heads of wild wheat against the sun-bleached blue of the sky where Plains met Rockies, the day the Hardriders died.

They made their final stand on a low hill by the side of the road—not a Hard Road, just a dirt track through tan summer grassland, eroded into parallel gulleys by the rains since the legendary StarFall. On the track the convoy they had captured the day before burned, raising a black pillar against the white-streaked blue. The drivers—older men, and youths not quite old enough to be fledged as warriors—had torched the captured vehicles as a last gesture of defiance before withdrawing up the hill.

The smoke would be their sole memorial, unless their clan allies made up fanciful songs of their end, based on the City's dry yet boastful broadcasts of the fight. No one doubted that after seeing the dust plumes feathering out from beneath the tires of the cavalry company's light combat cars sweeping out east and west of them: the jaws of a trap already drawing shut. The heavy-laden cargo trucks had slowed the drivers to a pace hardly greater than a walking horse's, enabling the pursuers to half surround them before even the 'Riders' keen eyes could spot them.

Only true catastrophe could compel Wyatt Hardrider, *the* Hardrider of the Hardriders—the baddest, boldest biker on the Plains, who could outrace the prairie wind and strike like a thunderhead's lightning tongue—to accept a static defensive fight.

Mortar rounds were beginning to burst among the huddle of colorful ramshackle trucks and vans on the hilltop as the last

'Rider laid his bike down in the defensive circle around the hill's broad belly. The nomads' vehicles were spaced far enough apart that the low-powered, relatively cool explosions of their ethanol tanks wouldn't start a chain reaction.

The 'Riders began to return fire, with rifles and a few light machine guns. A recoilless rifle thumped three times from the rear of a pickup decorated all over with bits of bright plastic trash scavenged from ruins. An armored car blew apart in a yellow flare of diesel and sparkle of exploding ammunition. A burst from the quick-firing cannon in the turret of another found the recoilless gun, and the nomads had no more weapons that could both reach and breach the armored vehicles that now completely hemmed them in. A few teenagers huddled behind the perimeter, clutching buzz-bomb launchers that could crack heavier armor than any the City troops had brought. But these possessed short range, and would only serve when the enemy made his final assault.

But the cavalry captain was a man without honor. He had his men safe behind mobile walls of alloy plate. He had his mortars and his quick-firing cannon and the strange, terrible weapons the nomads called river guns, which poured out bullets in a torrent like the Platte in flood, so fast they made a whining noise instead of a crackle like honest gunfire.

He had all the ammo and all the time in Father Storm's wide world. And he preferred spending them to spending the lives of his men. He stood back and poured fire onto the hilltop until it looked like the gape of a newborn volcano.

Through it all he stood at the roll-bar–mounted gun of his own unarmored light-assault car and watched, a small, erect figure in a coal-scuttle helmet and spotless camo battle dress, his eyes invisible behind mirror shades glinting in the sun that looked down without favor or mercy.

When the bombardment had gone on an excruciatingly long time—when some of the green troops in the combat cars were beginning to be fearful of the protracted rippling thunder of their own guns, and their stomachs had rebelled against the smell of spent powder and explosives and hot lubricants—and the sick, thick smell of human meat roasting in the alcohol-fueled flames that crowned the hilltop—his troop commanders started to clamor in his headset for advance.

"Nothing could survive that bombardment," they said. "It's time to move."

He gave no order to move. The shelling continued. He was a young man, but the lines were deep at the corners of his mouth.

Finally from the hill came a snarl of engine, a whine thinly audible above the crackling and booming shells. A lone rider appeared from the smoke. He was a big man, made bulkier by a silver wolfskin vest. He had a sweeping mustachio and black hair tied in braids that flapped behind him like pennons. A single eagle feather bobbed at the nape of his neck. Tendrils of smoke streamed from his hair and shaggy vest.

Every weapon in sight of him opened up on him. He seemed to sense each bead as it was drawn. He whipped his gaunt chopped cycle this way and that, veering to avoid a line of shell-bursts from an auto-cannon, pivoting on a leather-clad leg around the dust-cloud of a mortar bomb, bounding his machine like a pronghorn over arroyos and hummocks.

The men of the City had never seen riding like that—not even among their own cycle scouts, their vaunted *corps d'élite*. They cried out in admiration even as they tried their damnedest to cut the wild rider down.

From a scabbard behind the low-slung seat the Hardrider whipped a box-fed light machine gun. He slapped it down between the upswept handlebars and triggered a burst. A light-assault car gunner down the line from the captain screamed and clutched at himself as the bullets clawed open his chest. Another burst and a vehicle commander slipped, noiselessly and bonelessly, down into the cupola of his armored car.

The firing redoubled as gunners single-mindedly hauled back on triggers or mashed firing studs. Already the Hardrider was too close for the mortars to be used. Automatic weapons began to fall silent as their barrels overheated or their feed-belts tangled.

A line of explosions from an automatic grenade launcher ripped open the tawny earth right in front of the bike's front wheel. The City soldiers held their breaths. Now the madman *had* to fall.

The bike merged from the smoke, airborne and mostly upright. It struck with a pelvis-crushing shock. A booted leg went down, steadied it, and it came on—the rider always firing, and always making for the erect captain in his car.

The captain spoke into the microphone that curved like an insect leg in front of his mouth: "Cease firing."

The command made no sense to the City officers and men. But they obeyed at once. Silence hit the prairie like a thunderclap.

In the sudden stillness the motorcycle's roar seemed harder to hear than in the midst of bombardment. The wild rider caught his machine gun under his right arm, punched the button to discharge a spent magazine, pulled a last mag from a pouch, and slammed it home in the well. Then he grasped the pistol-grip again, and uttering a hate-scream of fury fired the weapon at the command car, now less than a hundred yards away.

Moving without apparent haste the captain took hold of the pistol-grip of his own mounted machine gun and swung its barrel down to bear. His driver grunted softly and slumped behind the wheel as a pair of bullets struck him in the sternum with small slaps and puffs of dust.

The captain fired. The rider went over to his right, then down, into a rolling tumbling dust-spewing tangle. When momentum tore man and machine apart and sent them hurtling in diverging directions, it was as if one single body had been ripped in two.

The captain dismounted. Slowly he walked forward. The gray-brown dust matted out the mirror polish of his boots.

The rider lay on the ground thirty yards in front of the car. He had miraculously held onto his machine gun until the very end; now it lay ten feet away, and he was trying to drag himself to it, leaving a trail of brownish blood-mud behind him.

The captain stepped between him and the fallen weapon. Painfully the Hardrider raised his head to look at him. His mustache was soaked in blood, and blood poured in a constant stream down his chin. His right eye had either been shot out or swollen shut. His face was such a mask of blood and grime and soot that it was impossible to tell. The remaining eye was blue, and burned with hatred like a laser beam.

The nomad's left hand whipped to his belt, at the small of his back. As he yanked out a knife with a foot of gleaming saw-backed blade, the captain drew his sidearm from his shoulder holster and shot Wyatt Hardrider above his glaring blue eye.

The officer stood for a moment, gazing down at the body of his opponent. Then he holstered his handgun, ordered medics to tend to his driver, and ordered up another car so that he could lead the advance up the hill.

The hilltop was silent now, but for the sizzle of almost-invisible alcohol flames and the endless sighing of the Great Plains wind. The captain ordered his new driver to stop at the nomads' defensive perimeter. He ordered the infantry in the armored carriers to dismount and secure the hilltop on foot. Then he stepped to the ground next to the body of a blond-bearded giant who lay sprawled on his belly behind his bike, a lever-action rifle in his hands, his eyes staring at a neat blue hole in the center of his forehead. Bare-handed, the officer began to walk forward.

Behind him his aides rapped hasty orders. A squad of troopies with assault rifles double-timed up to escort him. He didn't acknowledge their presence.

He walked among the burning vehicles, ignoring the pale flames that reached for him and the stinking smoke of burning bodies. Once he paused, gazing down at a little blond girl in a dirty linen smock. Her left arm had been blown off. She had bled to death into the thirsty dust. Her remaining arm clutched a crude doll, a rag with a knot for a head and drawn-on eyes and idiot smile.

A muscle worked at the corner of the captain's jaw. He walked on, his escort discreetly behind.

A standard had been raised at the crest of a hill, a gleaming pair of handlebars swept like a wild bull's horns, fastened to the top of a metal pole along with a spray of hawk feathers and animal tails. A mortar burst had knocked it askew, but it still stood. A couple of the troopers snickered and spat about the absurdity of savage superstition.

At the base of the standard a woman lay. She was tall and rangy, and her unmarked face was beautiful, in a hard, drawn way. Her red-auburn hair was roached up in front in a defiant crest. Her right hand still clutched the grip of an unfired buzz bomb. A steel splinter from a mortar-casing stuck out of her neck, right behind an ear pierced with seven silver rings.

The captain stopped. From behind the dead woman a boy of

ten or eleven rose to a crouch. He wore buckskin pants stained with grease and blood, and his bare chest was a washboard beneath a tattered denim vest. An arrowhead chipped from obsidian hung from his neck by a rawhide thong. His hair was jet black and hung down his back in braids. His eyes were pale blue, and as wild and devoid of intelligence as the eyes of an animal in the jaws of a steel trap.

A soldier raised his assault rifle. The captain knocked the barrel up, and it stammered into the sky.

''What the hell do you think you're doing?'' the officer demanded.

The trooper looked hurt. ''But Captain Masefield, sir—nits make lice.''

''No one is to fire without my command. *No one.* Is that understood?''

Reluctantly, his escort nodded. The acknowledgments of his squad leaders chorused in his lightweight headset.

He turned back to the boy. The child rocked back on his heels and brought up his hands. They held an enormous single-action pistol. He aimed it at the center of the captain's chest and pulled the trigger.

The hammer snapped on a spent cartridge. It was the most forlorn sound in the world.

The boy stared at the weapon. It was as long as his skinny arm. He hauled back the hammer, pointed it, pulled the trigger again. Nothing.

Slowly the captain lowered the arm he had held up to prevent his men from firing. The boy snapped the hammer fruitlessly on every chamber, then started around the cylinder again. The officer reached forward, took the pistol by the barrel, and gently pulled it from his fingers.

The boy collapsed across the woman's body and clung, sobbing so violently it seemed his bones, connected by such little flesh, would shake themselves apart.

''Police up the weapons and blow them,'' the captain said. ''Finish any wounded. We pull out in fifteen minutes.''

He knelt and pulled the boy to his feet. ''Come on, son. This is your past. The City's your future now.''